BLUE SALVATION

BOOK THIRTEEN OF THE FALLEN WORLD

Benjamin Tyler Smith

Blood Moon Press
Virginia Beach, VA

Copyright © 2020 by Benjamin Tyler Smith.

All rights reserved. No part of this publication may be reproduced, distributed or transmitted in any form or by any means, including photocopying, recording, or other electronic or mechanical methods, without the prior written permission of the publisher, except in the case of brief quotations embodied in critical reviews and certain other noncommercial uses permitted by copyright law. For permission requests, write to the publisher, addressed "Attention: Permissions Coordinator," at the address below.

Chris Kennedy/Blood Moon Press
2052 Bierce Dr.
Virginia Beach, VA 23454
http://chriskennedypublishing.com/

Publisher's Note: This is a work of fiction. Names, characters, places, and incidents are a product of the author's imagination. Locales and public names are sometimes used for atmospheric purposes. Any resemblance to actual people, living or dead, or to businesses, companies, events, institutions, or locales is completely coincidental.

Cover Design by Elartwyne Estole.

Ordering Information:
Quantity sales. Special discounts are available on quantity purchases by corporations, associations, and others. For details, contact the "Special Sales Department" at the address above.

Blue Salvation/Benjamin Tyler Smith -- 1st ed.
ISBN: 978-1648552007

To my mother Glenda Gale Clolinger Smith, who taught me to love God, Jesus, the United States, and fantasy and science fiction! Without her, I wouldn't be here, in more than one sense of the word.

Also, to Lieutenant Thomas "Tommy" Paul Menton, Mobile Police Department. You will never be forgotten by the officers who served with you, and their families.

Acknowledgments

Man, 2020 has been an interesting year, hasn't it? Lockdowns, disease, civil unrest, economic downturns and recoveries, but through it all we've had two consistent things: God ruling from on high, and CKP putting out quality fiction, week after week! And I am very excited to have had two full-length novels—the first of mine to have been professionally published—included in the lineup!

I owe a lot of thanks to a lot of people for that. Christopher Woods and Chris Kennedy top that list, as they both were willing to take a chance on someone who had very few publishing credits to his name, not much of a social media presence (I'm working on it, y'all!) and, thus, not much of an active following. In a world where the biggest publishers are looking for established writers before they'll even consider publishing someone, it's really awesome to see a smaller press willing to take on a relative unknown like me. It's awesome, and humbling, and I am very grateful to you both for taking a chance on a guy.

And what a chance the two of them took! It was back in the spring of 2019 when I heard about an upcoming anthology for the Fallen World. I'd just finished listening to the first two books of the series (narrated by the great Mark Boyett) and had this idea I'd been kicking around about a unit of Mobile PD mounted officers driving up to New York City to help their brothers-in-blue deal with food riots in Manhattan. So, a couple dozen officers or so, and that's it. The nukes drop while they're on the way, Mobile and NYC are wiped out, and they're left to defend a small town somewhere in-between. After I shared the idea with them, I was given good news and bad news. The good news was they loved the idea, and thought it would be a great fit for the world.

The bad news: it wasn't going to be in the anthology. The idea was too big for a short story, but not quite big enough for a novel. It needed to be expanded, and together we came up with what became Blue Crucible, the first in this series about an international force of mounted police defending Columbia, Missouri.

After them, Beth Agejew is another warrior worthy of accolades! She is one of the best editors I've worked with, and she is able to take what I send her and whip it into shape! And before she receives it, my writer friends William Joseph Roberts and R.J. Ladon help me tear it apart, along with a couple of other readers that I'm close to but are willing to tell me I've written something dumb (Hi, Mom. Hi, Camille!) without worrying about my feelings.

For this particular book, I owe a lot to two retired officers I've become acquainted with over the last few months: Nicholas Ruggiero and Tamara Mickelson. Nick runs the Roll Call Room Podcast, a podcast with a focus on police mental health issues. There are some dark issues addressed in this book involving the stress our officer heroes face in a Fallen World, and I wanted Nick's take on it. Conversations with him, as well as a reading of his book Police Mental Barricade: A Survivor's Guide to Poor Law Enforcement Leadership really helped with those scenes. I cannot recommend his book and podcast enough.

And Tamara was a big help with a scene involving a little bit of CSI, and she makes a cameo in the story! Expect her character to appear in a bigger way in the third book of the series. She was gracious enough to interview me for her "The Real Life" podcast, and I look forward to future episodes with her! She also has a book detailing her experiences as a CSI officer from the perspective of the emotional toll the job took on her. Through My Eyes: CSI Memoirs That Haunt the Soul is an emotional read, but it's well worth it.

Last, but not least, I owe a big debt of gratitude to you, the one with a copy of this book. Whether you've read Blue Crucible, or this is the first of my books you've picked up, I hope you enjoy it! If you do, please leave a review on Amazon and feel free to reach out to me on Facebook or Twitter! And if you don't enjoy it, please leave a review and reach out to me! I would love your feedback. It is the only way for me to grow as a writer.

With all that said, on with the story. Strap on your armor, shoulder your weapon, and saddle up! It's going to be a wild ride through this Fallen World…

Benjamin Tyler Smith
November, 2020

Chapter One

The late-night air in downtown Columbia was quiet but for the sharp sound of booted and shoed hooves striking pavement. Calico Countess walked northeast along Paris Road at a steady pace, her natural night vision letting her see obstacles in the street I couldn't make out without a flashlight. I kept a loose hand on the reins and trusted my tri-colored American to get me where I needed to go—to the next intersection and then the next.

I rode at the head of a column of fifteen mounted officers, with my brother, Sergeant Danny Ward of the Mobile Alabama Police Department, on my left, and Sergeant Berengár Silva, of the Marajó military police, on my right. Each of us, human and animal, was decked out in bulletproof riot armor, which was a huge upgrade from the stuff previous generations of officers had worn. Well, an upgrade in protective qualities, anyway. Sweat trickled down my neck and soaked into my already drenched undershirt. Late July in Missouri wasn't nearly as hot and humid as late July back in Mobile, but that didn't mean it was enjoyable. And since armor didn't breathe too well…

"I'm glad there weren't ever any riots in Mobile," Danny said. He rode with the faceplate of his helmet raised, so he could periodically mop his face with a handkerchief. "Can you imagine wearing all this, day in and day out, in August?"

"I'd have died. No question about it." I glanced to my right. "Silva, how hot does it get in Brazil in the summer?"

The stout sergeant tilted his head up as he considered. "I can't speak for the mainland since I never spent much time outside Marajó. But on the island, the average temperature is around twenty-seven degrees Celsius. During the rainy season, it can go up to thirty-two."

I did the temperature conversion in my head. "That's between eighty and ninety degrees Fahrenheit."

Patrolman Jeremiah Jones whistled from somewhere behind us. Between his dark riot gear and his even darker skin, the six-foot-eight giant was practically invisible in the dim moonlight in an otherwise lightless city. It didn't help that his stallion, Rambo, was as black as Danny's aptly named Noir. He'd gotten beaten up pretty badly during the assault on the Country Hotel, but he'd recovered swiftly. "Damn, Sergeant Silva. I'd be happy to trade Mobile's weather for yours."

"Yeah, it's a lot hotter by us," I said. "Maybe it's why the fire ants like it so much."

"Isn't Mobile the port city that fire ants came in through?" Danny asked.

"Thanks for that!" Patrolman Lewis of the Atlanta PD said. "I hate those little bastards."

"Don't thank us!" I hiked my thumb in Silva's direction. "Take it up with him. They came from his neck of the woods."

"What is it you Americans like to say from time to time? 'Sharing is caring?'"

Everyone laughed. Well, most everyone. As I turned in my saddle, I noticed the only local riding with us tonight wasn't laughing. Lieutenant Kevin Hanson was the sole survivor of the St. Louis police department. He and his squad had ridden back to the neighboring city after the bombs dropped, but all they'd found was an irradiated wasteland. He and Patrolman Orson McGraw had been the only ones to make it back to Columbia, and both had been in bad shape. McGraw hadn't lived long enough for the responding medics to arrive, but Hanson had somehow made it to the hospital and pulled through, at least physically. "Kevin, is this kind of heat in the middle of the night normal for this area?"

Kevin had been idly stroking the dark mane of Watson, a red gelding our department had given him after his horse had to be put down due to radiation poisoning. He looked up at hearing his name, but I couldn't see his face in the shadows. "Been awhile since I was on night shift, but if the daytime's this hot, I don't see why the night would be much better."

His tone was that of someone who didn't care, and that worried me. Kevin was normally a jovial person, the kind who could put a smile on the sourest faces or calm the most violent criminals. He'd changed since the Fall. He was more withdrawn now—he only spoke when he was spoken to—and his eyes had a haunted quality about them. He had fallen into the habit of doing the absolute minimum when it came to personal care. His uniform was often wrinkled, his riot gear was dirty, and he had the unkempt beard he'd grown while in the hospital. It surprised me that Captain Graham and Sheriff Welliver had cleared him for duty, but maybe they thought getting back in the saddle would help snap him out of it.

I don't know that anyone could be "snapped out" of this situation. We'd all suffered in the Fall. Nearly every member of the unified mounted patrol that made up the core of Columbia's defensive garrison had lost their hometowns and families. Except for my two children and Danny, I'd lost every blood relative, and I was uniquely blessed in that regard. Or cursed, depending on your outlook. Many were glad their families hadn't survived the Fall, because they feared what was coming next. Compared to them, I had a lot more invested in keeping this city alive and functional, and it weighed on me daily.

Distant gunfire echoed through the moonless night, reminding us that the Fall had done more than change our demeanors. It had changed our entire way of life. "Imagine that," Jones said. "Gunfire in Columbia? Must be a Tuesday night!"

A bright ball of blue light suddenly lit up the eastern sky in the direction of the gunfire. The signal flare meant at least one of the parties involved in the firefight requested police protection. With telephones and most radios down, flares were the best way to notify us of trouble, which is why we distributed them to neighborhood leaders we could trust.

"Jones, I thought you said it was Tuesday." Danny pointed. "Signal flares are a Wednesday night thing."

"My bad, Sarge!"

I checked the nearby street sign to get my bearings. We were a little north of the university, and that flare had come from the east. There was only one neighborhood in that direction that I could remember giving flares to. "Gotta be Jay Dawson and his folks."

"That the guy you were having sweet tea with while I was getting shot at in a doughnut shop?" Danny asked.

"The very same. His wife brews a damn good pot."

He grinned. "Well, let's go get some then."

"My thoughts exactly." I squeezed Countess's sides with my knees, urging her into a trot, and then a canter. "Follow me!"

At a fast jog, a horse or buffalo can quickly eat up a lot of terrain, but situations like this reminded me how much slower animals were compared to vehicles. I chafed at the delay as the sounds of gunfire grew louder the closer to the scene we got. With so few vehicles working due to the EMP shockwave, the mounted police were often faster to respond than the Columbia PD. The CPD still had a few working police cars, but they had difficulty maneuvering them down narrow streets clogged with disabled vehicles. Horses, buffalos, and camels didn't have that problem.

"Why does it feel like we're never going fast enough?" Danny demanded.

I chuckled. "That's twice in one night you've read my mind." The staccato sound of automatic weapons fire stifled my levity. "It's the nature of the job. No matter how fast we go, it never seems like enough."

Jay's neighborhood was a relatively new development, built sometime in the last twenty to thirty years. After JalCom bought the city and knocked down and rebuilt huge swathes of it, many people had moved to what had once been farmland and put down roots there. They were close enough to the city to still be able to work there, but not so close that the Corporate hand was upon them. Trees surrounded the fenced-in subdivision on three sides, and the wrought-iron fence and gate facing the street had been fortified with sandbags, old furniture, scrap metal, and as much other debris as could be found. Some industrious individual had even hauled over a few broken-down trucks to add to the growing wall.

Shadowed figures stood in the beds of those trucks and fired across the road into a crop field that had been plowed back in early May, shortly after the bombs dropped. More shadowy figures crouched behind caged tomato plants or peeked between cornstalks to fire at the neighborhood entrance. I didn't need much deductive reasoning to figure out what was going on. Someone was rustling food someone else had gone to the trouble of growing, and that wasn't right.

I put my whistle to my lips and blew. The sharp trill pierced the night, rising over the gunfire and the distinct *clop-clop-clop* of our mounts' hooves. "It's the police!" one of the neighborhood defenders shouted.

"Kill 'em!" someone in the crop field yelled.

Rounds zipped past our heads or skimmed along the pavement. Countess snorted and danced away from an impact that showered us both with chips of asphalt. "Way to make the locals angry, Nate," Danny said as he pulled his Remington 870 pump-action shotgun from the scabbard connected to Noir's saddle. He put the weapon to his shoulder, lined up his ghost-ring sight on an enemy, and squeezed the trigger. I looked forward just in time to see the target dive for cover. Danny clicked his tongue. "Damn. Missed."

"At least his pants are ruined!" I drew my assault rifle, clicked it over to semi-auto, and stared down the glowing tritium sights at a bad guy crouched between two rows of caged tomatoes. I realized he was aiming at me, and we both froze. I recovered more quickly and squeezed the trigger once, twice, and again. The man's body shook with each bullet's impact, and he slumped to his knees, then fell face-first into the soft, tilled soil.

A round buzzed past my head, and I shifted to fire at a pair of men hiding in the cornstalks. I know I hit one, but both spun and disappeared into the corn. "Fall back!" someone shouted.

"Silva, take your squad around back on the right side! The rest of you, follow me!" I spurred Countess into a gallop. To the defenders of the neighborhood, I shouted, "Hold your fire!"

I led Danny, Jones, Kevin, and four other officers down the street, our horses' hooves thundering along the pavement. Countess and I raced past a pair of bodies lying on the hard-packed dirt shoulder. Both had died facing the crop field, so I wasn't sure which side they belonged to. One appeared to be a young boy. "Shit," someone muttered behind me. I knew how he felt. I'd seen a lot of corpses in my time as a cop and more than I had ever wanted to since the bombs dropped a couple months back, but the sight of dead kids never got any easier.

The day it did was the day I'd hand over my badge.

The tomato patch near the road turned into peppers, then summer squash, but the cornfield beyond them stretched for a good fifty yards or so, and there was no telling from here how deep it was. I had to hand it to the folks from Jay's neighborhood. They were hardworking.

As we neared the edge of the crop field, I turned Countess off the road and onto the grass. Row after row of leafy green cornstalks flashed past my peripheral vision in a blur as we galloped toward the far end of the field. Shouts and gunshots echoed from somewhere up ahead and to the right, along with Silva yelling, "Police! Drop your weapons!"

Movement in the corn up ahead caught my eye, and I reined Countess in. "Woah!" I called to the others.

A trio of figures burst from the cornstalks, each laden with sacks full of what I assumed had to be food. I flicked on the flashlight attached to my rifle and shined it in their faces. Even though it was directed away from me, the sudden intensity of the light brought tears to my eyes. "Freeze!"

The three men snapped their heads in my direction, their expressions like deer caught in the headlights of a speeding truck. If not for the seriousness of the situation, I'd have laughed. "Put down the sacks and get your hands in the air."

One of them had canted his body away from us slightly. My flashlight caught a glint of metal. I shifted my aim to him. "Drop the gun. Tomatoes and corn aren't worth dying over, man. I don't care how well-grown they are."

"Drop it, man!" one of his buddies hissed. "I don't wanna get shot!"

"Tch. Fine." The armed man tossed the rifle to the ground, then dropped the sack. He raised his hands over his head and glared at us, heedless of the light shining in his face. "Happy now, you pigs? You enjoy picking on hungry people?"

"Do you enjoy shooting it out with equally hungry people who are expending the effort to grow food?" Danny demanded.

"They're only in it for themselves! They're not helping us out."

"Mr. Dawson and his people regularly contribute vital supplies to the city." I kept the weapon's light focused on them, but I removed my finger from the trigger. "Supplies that get distributed every other day. Supplies you were stealing for yourself. Now, get about five feet apart from each other, turn your backs to us, and keep your hands in the air."

Kevin, Jones, and Lewis slid from their saddles and approached the trio. Jones and Lewis moved with purpose, but Kevin's slumped shoulders and downcast gaze didn't give me a good feeling. "Keep an eye on that one, Lieutenant Hanson," I said.

Kevin lifted his head, but only slightly.

Lewis reached his target first and pulled the man's arms down behind his back. The man let himself be cuffed without incident.

That wasn't the case for Kevin's suspect. When Kevin reached for the man's wrists, the man smashed an elbow into the side of Kevin's helmet. Kevin staggered and fell just as the suspect spun around and reached for something in his waistband.

I set my finger back on the trigger. "Put your hands in the air!" I prayed I wouldn't have to shoot over Kevin.

Jones appeared in my view and swung his fist into the man's face. The suspect's head snapped back, and he dropped like a sack of potatoes. Jones stood over him, his right arm extended, his left hooked around the man he'd cuffed. He'd dragged him along with him when he set out to neutralize the threat. Jones forced his charge down into a sitting position and put a finger in his face. "Don't go anywhere." Then he knelt next to the man he'd downed and started to cuff him with the set Kevin had dropped in the grass.

The man groaned as Jones roughly pulled his arms behind his back so he could cuff him. "Fuckin' pig."

Jones grinned. "Oink oink, baby."

Silva and his buffalo riders came around the corner. A few had dismounted to drag along a half-dozen cuffed thieves. Tonight, we'd had a good haul, it seemed.

* * *

"We appreciate the save, Lieutenant Ward." Jay Dawson looked down at us from the top of his wall of scrap and debris. He loosely held an old bolt-action rifle in his hands. "Mighty fine work ya did out there."

The older man slung the rifle over his shoulder, then clambered down and exited through the steel door that acted as the neighborhood's main gate. I slid from Countess's saddle so we could shake hands. He nodded toward the nine criminals we'd sat in a circle on the pavement in front of the subdivision. "You get 'em all?"

"If not all, then near enough." We'd captured nine and killed five, and there were another three dead that Jay's people had taken care of before we arrived. "We didn't see anyone else out there, but we also didn't want to comb the cornfield until the sun comes up. We've set up a perimeter, and we'll wait them out."

"Appreciate you not trampling too many of our crops." He tugged at the rifle sling to reposition it on his shoulder, then nodded toward Silva's men. "Weeks ago, ya brought camel jockeys with you. Now it's buffalo riders?"

"We've got quite a motley crew." I smiled. "Maybe next time we'll ride ostriches or some other kind of big bird over here."

Jay laughed. "I would pay to see that." His lined face grew somber as he looked over at the pair of bodies we'd ridden by in our pursuit of the thieves. Jones and Lewis were both certified in advanced trauma and first aid, and they'd gotten to work as soon as we secured the scene, but it was too late. Both the boy and the young man were dead, and they likely had been since before we arrived. "Thank you for trying to tend to Tim and Uriah," Jay said. "They were the first ones hit."

The neighborhood's gate flew open with a bang, and a woman ran out with two other women and a man in hot pursuit. The woman in the lead flung herself onto the body of the child and started wailing. "Uriah! My boy! Why?"

My eyes burned with tears that wanted to come, but I willed them back. "I wish we could've gotten here sooner."

"I wish you could've, too," Jay admitted, "but that's not how this works. Didn't work that way before the Fall, either. When seconds count—"

"The police are only minutes away, I know." I pointed at the slung rifle. "That's why good citizens need those, to stop things like this from being worse than they could be. All any of us can do is react to a bad situation. We can't completely stop them from happening…"

I trailed off. I knew I was preaching to the choir with Jay. He nodded. "It was a bad bit of luck tonight. We'd noticed crops were missing. A tomato here, an ear of corn there. At first, we thought it was animals but then more started to go missing. And things were a little too cleanly cut to be animals, unless there's a band of mutant raccoons running around with vegetable shears." He started to chuckle, but the chuckle died when the mother's wailing increased in volume. He shook his head. "Tim and Uriah didn't like the idea of people stealing our crops, so they were sneaking out each night to do their own 'patrols.' Silly kids. We tried stopping them, but…"

Now it was his turn to trail off. I put a hand on his shoulder and squeezed. "It wasn't your fault. Kids are willful, and they'll find a way. Best you can do is try and raise 'em right, but they'll still make their own decisions. I think about it with my kids all the time." Jason worried me because he was at that age where he had no fear and would plunge headlong into danger. Helen was old enough to know the world had changed, though she didn't yet know the full extent of the destruction, unless someone had told her, and she was hiding it from me. What worried me about her was her great sense of right and wrong. I loved that she had a strong sense of justice like me, but that had led me to this particular career path. Did I want her to follow in the same footsteps as me? Was this the kind of life I'd wish on her?

"How could you? How could you do this to him?"

The grieving mother had gotten to her feet. She pointed a shaking finger at the criminals, her eyes full of tears as she snarled, "What did he do to you? He was only *ten!*"

Jones stepped up to her. "Ma'am, I'm—"

"And *you!*" She whirled around and jabbed her finger into Jones's chest, again and again. "Where the hell were you? Why weren't you here in time?"

The big man stumbled back out of arm's reach. "Ma'am, I'm sorry."

I stepped forward. "Ma'am, these men are under my command. We got here as fast as we could when we saw the flare."

"It wasn't fast enough." The mother turned her baleful eyes on me, and my stomach twisted in knots.

"Kristen, that's enough," Jay snapped. He put himself between her and me. "They were the first ones shot. No one could've gotten to them in time, and you know it."

"Don't defend them, Uncle!" More tears spilled out of Kristen's eyes. "Look what happened to my boy! Look what happened to *your* nephew!"

"I know what happened to him," Jay growled. "I saw him go down." He unslung his rifle and held it out toward her, one hand clutching the action. "And I put a bullet through the eye of the bastard who pulled the trigger."

He paused and glanced at me. "I didn't just incriminate myself, did I?"

"My ears are ringing from all that shooting, sir." Danny pressed his hands against the sides of his riot helmet. "All I heard was a lot of mumbling."

The other officers shared similar statements. I hid my smile behind my hand. "In all seriousness, it sounds like legal self-defense to me. The DA seems to have her head screwed on straight, so I don't imagine it'll be a problem."

Jay slung his rifle again, then pointed at Kristen. "If you have to be mad at anyone, be mad at me. I wasn't quick enough. None of us on the wall were."

Kristen's face crumpled, and she ran forward and threw her arms around Jay's neck. She buried her head in his chest. "They took my boy, Uncle Jay! They took my boy!"

"I know." Jay kissed the top of her head and stroked her hair. "I know they did, girl. I'm sorry."

He and I shared a look, and a lump formed in my throat and stifled any words of condolence I wanted to offer. He nodded, as if he understood. I returned the nod, then walked back to Countess. We had a few hours left until daybreak, and we would remain on site long enough to ensure no one was hiding in the cornfield.

I climbed up into the saddle, then glared at the shadow-shrouded field, my anger directed at the coward—or cowards—who had to be hiding in there. Did Kristen's wails fill them with joy? Were they angry at us for taking down their buddies? Were they scared out of their minds, their pants wet with their own piss?

"Hey, you in the cornfield!" I cupped my hands around my mouth. "You have until dawn to get your asses out of there and surrender peacefully! If you don't, we'll come in looking for you. And if we have to do that, we'll turn you over to the good citizens of this neighborhood! They can decide what to do with you. We'll wash our hands of it."

"That's not right!" one of the cuffed thieves shouted. "You can't do that!"

Danny walked Noir up alongside the thief and nudged his head with the toe of his boot. "County jail's full of scum. I don't think Sheriff Welliver will care if a few child killers and murderers don't make it."

The man pulled his head away from Danny's boot. "That wasn't us! That was—"

"One of your buddies, but it could've been any of you." Danny leaned over in the saddle and glared down at the man. "Now, if I were you, I'd be encouraging your friends to come out. It won't just be them we hand over. It'll be all of you, too."

That got their attention, if the suddenly wide eyes were any indicator. I shook my head. This wasn't how things were supposed to be. What a difference a few months made between civilization and this Fallen World.

* * * * *

Chapter Two

Aster ran through the smoke-filled streets of downtown Columbia, her arms dripping blood. Gunfire, shouts, and screams echoed between the buildings, but she ignored them. The chatter crackling in her damaged earpiece was what mattered most. Agent Morris had made an appearance in the Country Hotel, and the police were hard-pressed to stop him. Several officers were already dead, including one of Nathan's men from Mobile, a Corporal Collins. Morris had escaped to the upper floors, with Nathan and the others in hot pursuit.

She had to get there before they cornered Morris, or it would be a bloodbath. She should've been there already, but Obsidian had brought down a building on her head. She'd eventually been pulled out, but so much time had been wasted, and so much blood spilled.

A gunshot cracked in front of her, and a form collapsed in the smoke. It was an officer from Columbia. A rifle round had punched through his soft armor, and blood was already pooling beneath him as his assailant, an Obsidian soldier, closed in for the kill.

The soldier never fired another shot. Aster pounced on him, her bloody fingers tearing through his throat as though his flesh were made of meringue. She snatched the rifle out of the dying soldier's hands and emptied the magazine into his squadmates before they could react. As the dead and dying soldiers tumbled to the ground, Aster reached into the trauma kit belted to her hip and administered first aid to the fallen officer. She didn't have time, but she couldn't leave a wounded man behind, especially one wearing a wedding ring. He had a wife to go home to and, maybe, children?

Several more Columbia officers arrived on scene as she finished patching the man up. All of them carried handguns, which were woefully inadequate as main battlefield weapons. She pointed at the dead Obsidian soldiers. "Take their weapons and get this man out of here."

One of the officers leveled his pistol at her. "Who're you? Get away from our—"

A gray-haired man wearing sergeant's stripes pushed the man's pistol down. "That's the Battle Flower, you idiot. Are you trying to get us all killed?"

The junior officer blanched and stammered an apology.

"Get this man out of here," Aster repeated, then she broke into a run again.

Buildings gave way to the trees and shrubs of the park that surrounded the Country Hotel, their bushy forms appearing as a green blur in her peripheral vision as she sped past them. In front of her, the hotel loomed large through the haze, like an imposing, wounded beast. A set of stairs led up to the lobby's main entrance, its bricks glittering from thousands of glass shards. At the top of the steps, the entrance smoldered, and the doors' bent and broken frames had been destroyed by one of her team's RPGs. Smoke rose from a blown-out window on one of the middle floors where a machine gun nest had been.

A deep roar rose over the cacophony in the streets, and a black armored personnel carrier smashed through the gate of the hotel's underground parking garage. The driver spun the wheeled vehicle to the left, and it sped down the street with a canvas-covered cargo truck following close behind. Mounted officers who were milling about in the street spun their animals around and gave chase, while fire from her Section Nine teammates rained down from the buildings above.

It looked as if one of Obsidian's directors was fleeing, or maybe all of them were. And if they were fleeing, Agent Morris would be with them. Agent Morris, the man who'd nearly killed six-year-old Jason Ward, a boy she considered a friend. She bared her teeth in a snarl and turned to join the hunt.

"Commander Ward, this is Lieutenant Ferguson," a voice said in her earpiece. "We hear a lot of gunfire above us. That you?"

"Yeah," Nathan answered. "We just breached the twelfth floor. Meeting heavy resistance."

Aster skidded to a halt so fast, she left a streak of sole rubber on the parking lot pavement.

"We were slowed at the tenth floor but haven't encountered anyone since. We're about to breach. We'll let—"

A shriek pierced the connection and then another officer screamed, *"Shit, he's behind us!"*

"Calm down!" Ferguson shouted. "He's just one man. He's just—Dear God in Heaven. Shoot him! Shoot him!"

Aster bounded up the steps toward the lobby entrance. Rather than go inside, she leaped onto the low roof directly over the entrance and ran toward the rough brick wall of the main building. She jumped about twenty feet into the air and grabbed the lip of a window, then she clambered up onto the narrow ledge, bunched her legs beneath her, and shot up to the next ledge. She did this until she reached the smoking hole where the machine gun nest had been.

With a grunt, she pulled herself into the wrecked room, her slender fingers chafed and bleeding from scrabbling along the bricks.

Chemically-treated water sprayed from the room's sprinkler systems, soaking the corpses of three Obsidian soldiers. Aster's boots squished in the soaked carpet as she made her way to the door. Smoke filled the hallway, so she held her breath as she ran to the nearest stairwell. Once inside, she paused long enough to take several deep breaths. Pockmarks in the concrete from bullets and fragmentation grenades told a violent story, and the soft moans of pain from higher up let her know that there were still living people up there.

She hopped onto the steel banister and leaped from landing to landing, kicking off the rails each time she did so. She scanned the flights of stairs for signs of life, and, as she reached the upper floors, she started to see the bodies of fallen officers and Obsidian soldiers. A few of the cops had been torn to pieces, proof that Agent Morris had come this way. She grimaced at the awful, bloody sight—more deaths she could've prevented—if she hadn't allowed herself to be incapacitated.

She found Ferguson, head of the St. Louis SWAT unit, sitting with his back pressed against the wall. The combat knife from another officer was lodged in his leg, and the other officer's hand was still attached to the knife hilt. He looked up at her approach, raised his pistol, and fired.

Aster dodged the first shot and landed right next to him. She gripped the pistol by the slide and pushed it back enough to knock it out-of-battery. Even if Ferguson pulled the trigger, nothing would happen. Not until she let go. "I'm a friend," she whispered.

Ferguson looked at her with wild eyes for a moment and then he blinked. "Specialist Aster? Oh, thank Christ. We thought we'd lost you."

"I thought I'd lost me." She touched her head and winced at the pain outside and inside. She was sure her skull had been fractured. Already, her nanites were working to repair everything, but it was the kind of injury that would take days to properly heal, and she didn't have days. She was glad she wasn't seeing double or suffering from vertigo. That had happened on more than one occasion when she had suffered a grievous head injury. "It'll take more than a building to take me out of the fight."

"Well, you're not a moment too soon," he said through gritted teeth. "That bastard traitor Morris is up on the top floor. Duffy, Ward, and Martinez are up there, too. They could use the help."

As if on cue, her damaged radio crackled. "*Ward, what's happening?*" Lieutenant Martinez of the LAPD barked.

"*It's Morris!*" Nathan called, his line filled with shouts and gunshots. "*Keep your men outside!*"

"Go!" Ferguson ordered. He tried to rise but grimaced in pain and sank back down. He clutched the knife in his leg. "Help's on the way for us, but you're the only one who can help them! *Go!*"

Aster put a hand on Ferguson's shoulder and squeezed it gently. Then she jumped onto the final landing and pushed through the doors onto the top floor. Gunfire that had been muffled by the insulated stairwell door suddenly sounded deafening to her enhanced ears. Up ahead, several cracks had formed in the sheetrock interior wall, as if something had been thrown against it. As she ran, she saw holes appear in the wall, which coincided with every gunshot she heard. That was where the fight was, and it was where she needed to be.

Without waiting, she slid to a halt in front of the broken sheetrock and then kicked off the opposite wall and launched herself into it. She burst through in a shower of gypsum dust and splintered wood. She entered a dimly lit room that looked like some kind of lounge, although the place was a mess with tables overturned, chairs broken, and lamps shattered.

Agent Morris stood in the center, his hands held high in triumph. He spun toward her, one hand closing into a fist he aimed at her face. The toe of Aster's boot crunched down on glass long enough for her to launch herself forward. She twisted in midair, dodged his attack, then slammed a shoulder into his broad chest. The blow staggered him, but he recovered and jabbed at her side. She dropped her arm to block the strike, but the impact pushed her several feet away.

Aster pushed off the wall and swept her leg out at his temple. He threw his head back to avoid the kick and reached for her leg, but she pulled back and launched another kick at his midsection. Her boot connected with a crack as loud as a gunshot. He grimaced and tried to grab her, but she danced back from his counterattack, her boots sliding against the slick floor. She didn't have to look down to know she was standing in someone's blood. The whole place reeked of it.

"You know, I actually felt that one, little lady." Morris touched his abdomen and chuckled. "I guess you're here to save the day, right? Well, you're too late!"

Aster blinked, and it was only then that she noticed all the bodies in the room. Patrolman Jones lay on his stomach near the hole she'd made, his head twisted around so he was staring up at the ceiling.

Mobile PD and Columbia SWAT officers had been torn to pieces, their bodies scattered throughout the room, cast aside like ragdolls in the hands of an angry child. The door to the lounge had been ripped from its hinges from the inside, and Lieutenant Martinez and her LAPD comrades lay dead just beyond, their bodies still twitching in their death throes. And Nathan…

She gasped. Nathan lay at Morris's feet, but he wasn't the only one there. Jason and Helen lay there as well, their tiny bodies on top of Nathan's, their eyes closed as if the family were merely sleeping. Jason was in the hospital, and Helen was with Brother Stephen back at the university! How—? Why—?

"Why didn't you stop me?" Mixed in with Morris's maniacal laughter came words filled with so much sorrow and pain, they made Aster take a step back. Her boot pressed into something soft, and she jumped like a cat whose tail had been stepped on. Beneath her boot was the body of another child, one she recognized despite the horrific burns covering it.

Tears ran down Morris's face as he pointed at her. "Why didn't you save them?" Blood mixed in with the tears, and she realized there was a hole in his forehead. Nathan had put that hole there at the end of the fight, when Jake Morris had taken control of his body long enough for them to put Agent Morris down. "Why didn't you save *us?*"

"Why didn't you save us?" a chorus of voices asked from all around her.

Nathan's, Jason's, and Helen's eyes had opened, and they stared at her. Jones twisted his broken neck once more so his lifeless gaze could fall on her. Out in the corridor, Martinez and her men looked at her, their mouths moving in unison as they all repeated the same phrase:

"Why didn't you save us?"

A hand gripped her ankle, and she yanked her foot out of its grasp. The burned child looked up at her with his one remaining blue eye.

"Why didn't you save me, sister?"

* * *

Aster's eyes snapped open, and her heart beat fast. She lay on a twin-sized bed in a dorm room that was nowhere near as spacious as her guest suite in Teledyne Tower had been. Early morning light filtered through the lone window, bathing the shelves with her dolls, figurines, and toys in a soft glow. Crimson-maned Red Sonja stood next to golden-haired Alice Zuberg on the top shelf, both ladies wielding swords against unseen foes.

She sat up and let the blanket slide off her body. A floor-to-ceiling mirror mounted on the door highlighted her features: long white hair ruffled from sleep, purple eyes that were alert and slightly dilated, alabaster skin that was smooth and unblemished, and a petite, yet shapely, frame clothed in Nintendo pajamas. One of her hands held a combat knife, and the other held her FN Five-seven semi-automatic pistol that had been taken from the sheath and holster hanging from the bedposts.

"The same dream," she murmured as she returned the weapons to their respective resting places. She'd been plagued by it for weeks, ever since she was put under anesthesia so the campus hospital's surgeons could mend her mangled right arm and tend to her fractured skull. The skull had healed quickly along with her other wounds, but her nanites had worked overtime to heal her arm. Agent Morris had nearly torn it off at the elbow, but a few stubborn threads of flesh, muscle, and tendon had held on. She clenched her right hand into a fist, relaxed, then clenched again. Even her body refused to yield to Obsidian's abuses. Not without a fight.

"*Why didn't you stop me?*" Agent Morris's—no, *Sergeant Jake Morris's*—accusation still echoed in her thoughts. Despite the maniacal laughter and despite the grin that was too wide for his face, those words had come from the man trapped inside the Agent's body, the real Jake Morris who had been childhood friends with Lieutenant Nathan Ward and who was an uncle to Nathan's kids, Jason and Helen. Jake had accused her of being too late to stop him.

But she *had* stopped him. Yes, he had seriously wounded Jason, but she had stopped him from killing the boy, and from killing Nathan, first in the hospital and then again in the hotel's penthouse lounge. Did he mean the other officers he had killed? When the Slipped Mask programming had activated, he had attacked several high-ranking officers. A few had been killed, and the rest were grievously injured. Sheriff Welliver of Boone County and Captain Phillips of the US Border Patrol were still recovering, and it would be months before any kind of replacement eye could be grown for Captain Andrew Graham of the Royal Canadian Mounted Police. Captain Ko Hsu of the Philadelphia PD had only come out of a coma a few weeks ago.

Her FN-P90 submachine gun lay atop the room's corner desk. The bullpup's black barrel gleamed from the fresh coat of oil she'd applied last night. She stood and ran her finger along the weapon's Picatinny rail. The dull serrations had always reminded her of the crenellations on a castle wall. Of all her weapons, this had been her first. And not just the first model she trained on. This P90 was the first weapon she had ever held when she officially entered Teledyne's service.

"Kid like you can't properly hold a full-length rifle," the armorer had told her as he sized up her tiny frame. He had turned away from the counter and walked back to one of several weapons racks that lined the long, brightly lit room. "Jesus, why do they keep sending me kids?" he muttered, rubbing his dark, bald head.

Aster had stood at parade rest, her hands clasped behind her back, her fingers clenched so tight her nails dug into her flesh. She tried to calm her hammering heart with the tactical breathing exercises her foster uncle had taught her, but with no luck.

The armorer leaned out from behind a storage locker. "What kind of work are they assigning you to?"

"B-bodyguard, sir!" Aster said, her voice much louder than she'd intended.

The armorer winced. "Kid, loosen up a little. You're wound tighter than a recoil spring in a short-barreled 1911."

Aster stared at him blankly.

"Sorry, gun guy talk. Get out of parade rest, all right? I'm not some general here to tear you a new one for that speck of dirt on your collar."

Her hand reached up for her collar, and he laughed. "Kidding! I'm kidding! Jesus, lighten up, please. Do it for my sake, all right?"

She let her arms fall to her side, but after a moment, she reached with her right hand across her body to grip her left arm at the elbow. She lowered her gaze and studied the countertop's polished surface.

"Can't say that's much better, but at least you're trying." The armorer walked back to the counter and set down the weapon he had chosen for her. "This is the FN-P90 which was designed for bodyguard work and personal protection in vehicles. It's the perfect size for, well, just about anyone, but especially those with a slighter frame. You take care of her, and she'll take care of you."

"Her?" Aster asked in a much softer tone than before.

"Sorry, old habit." The armorer cracked a smile. He ran his hand along the weapon's smooth surface. "It's a reminder to us ol' gun guys to treat our weapons like fine ladies. You treat a lady right, she's with you for life. You treat a gun right, she'll save your life, and those of your comrades. Understand?"

"No," Aster admitted, "but I want to." She stepped forward. "Please, show me."

"Woah, she speaks more than a couple words! First, I should introduce myself." He held out a calloused hand that was stained and glistening with gun oil. "Martin Duran. Everyone around here calls me Maître D' for some reason." He grinned. "I guess it's because I always take care of the people sent my way."

As she sat in the dorm room that had been her home for the last several weeks, Aster smiled to herself. Maître D' was a good man, one of the only commanders she had ever had who truly understood her motives and had been willing to work with her. Indeed, he had helped cultivate her personal code of honor—to fight against those she considered evil and guilty and to protect those she considered good and innocent. Now that she thought about it, he was an anomaly in the Corporations, and maybe an anomaly in the greater world.

She hoped he was still alive somewhere. He had been in Teledyne's headquarters in Portland when she and her Party of Nine were dispatched to Columbia as a potential check against any Obsidian incursions during the international mounted police convention both Corporations were sponsoring. He didn't spend much time at headquarters, though, so it was possible he had been sent elsewhere. Where, though? And would it make any difference? She had seen the missile tracking map. So few cities were left by the time the satellite connection cut out.

No, it was better to assume he was dead. And the only way to honor his memory was to keep doing what she felt was right.

* * *

Aster pulled her black tie into a full Windsor knot and nodded in satisfaction. Early on in her bodyguard days, one of the more particular Executives had demanded her servants and escorts wear real ties, despite the tactical disadvantages they presented. A regular necktie could easily be turned into a garrote during a fight, which is why most guards and cops wore clip-ons. But not if you protected this one lady. Aster had sworn she'd quit wearing them as soon as she could but, well, it became a habit. And since she now had the strength to rip through the silk like it was a wet piece of paper, she was no longer as concerned.

And it did look better, she had to admit.

Someone knocked at the common room's entrance. Aster quickly buttoned the collar flaps on her dark gray shirt, pulled her black leather shoulder holster on, then walked to the door. She briefly considered donning her suit jacket, then decided against it. She had an idea who was calling at this hour, and they wouldn't be surprised to see her armed.

"Aunt Aster!" Jason said as soon as she opened the door. The dark-haired five-year-old beamed up at her from his wheelchair. He held up a bag. "We brought cookies!"

A redheaded girl of about ten stood behind the wheelchair, her sunburned hands gripping the handles. Aster nodded to the blond-haired boy who waited in the grass a few feet away, his face shadowed by a straw hat. "Aunt Aster, have you met Billy? His parents run a horse farm!"

The boy removed his hat and squinted at her as the sun fell across his eyes. "Ma'am. It's an honor. You're a legend."

Aster didn't know how to respond. She was doing her job. There was nothing legendary about it.

After an awkward pause, Helen asked, "Aunt Aster, what do you prefer? Store-bought Oreos or homemade oatmeal raisin cookies?"

"Oreos!" Jason crowed.

"Quiet, you. Adults are talking."

"You're not an adult!"

"I'm more adult than you!"

Aster cocked her head to the side. "Aren't homemade chocolate chip cookies better than either?"

That brought the arguing children up short. They looked from her to each other and back to her again. "We didn't even think of that," Jason admitted.

"Speak for yourself." Helen snatched the bag from Jason and handed it to Aster before he could object. "Mrs. Brown made some especially for you. Would you like some for breakfast?"

As if on cue, Aster's stomach growled, loud and long. She put a hand on her abdomen. "I suppose I could eat."

"'Could?' You can eat Uncle Danny under the table!" Helen said. "And he can eat a lot!"

"Yeah! How come you're not fat?"

"Jason!" Helen raised her hand to smack him, then lightly tapped him on the forehead. "Don't talk to ladies about their weight! It's a sensitive topic!"

"Not to me." Aster opened the door wide and stepped out of the way so Helen could push Jason inside. "The augmentation I underwent doubled my bone density and muscle mass." She flexed her arm and muscle bulged beneath the dark, hand-tailored fabric. "I may not look it, but I weigh almost two hundred and fifty pounds."

Jason's jaw dropped. "Dad doesn't even weigh that much!"

"Jason!" Helen hissed, but she, too, studied Aster with wide eyes.

Billy shook his head. "That's amazing. I never would've guessed that."

Aster favored them with a small smile. "No, I suppose you wouldn't." She held up the bag of cookies and sniffed. Her heightened sense of smell detected at least four different types, including buttery shortbread and those chocolate chip cookies that were so soft, they practically dissolved on the tongue. Her smile widened. Mrs. Brown and her kitchen staff had outdone themselves again. "Tea or milk?"

"Milk!" Jason exclaimed just as Helen said, "Tea!"

She looked at Billy. "And you?"

"Milk's fine, ma'am."

"Please, call me Aster." She led them into the common room. "Make yourselves at home."

She walked over to the sink and poured water into a tea kettle. Helen poured the cookies onto the plate, then smacked Jason's hand as he tried to take one of the chocolate-dipped cookies that was like an Oreo, but bigger. "Work on your drawings," she commanded.

Jason grumbled for a moment, then he opened a folder that rested in his lap and set it on the table. He pulled out a well-used pencil and worked on a drawing of some kind of vehicle.

Helen hummed to herself as she grabbed four small plates and a set of napkins. "Is there anything I can do to help?" Billy asked.

"Just relax," Aster said. She set the tea kettle on one of the stove's electric elements and turned it on. "It won't be long before the tea's ready."

"Hey, where is everyone?" Helen looked around the common area. "Usually there are more people here."

"An emergency patrol was called late last night," Aster explained. "It was Lieutenant Paxton's turn on watch, so he mobilized his squad and went out with some of the mounted officers."

"They're with daddy, then!" Jason said.

"No. Lieutenant Ward was already responding to a different issue when they were sent out."

"Who?"

"That's our dad's name," Helen said.

"You mean his name isn't 'Daddy?'"

"Not to anyone but us. To everyone else, he's Nathan, or Nate, or Lieutenant Ward."

"What about Lieutenant Daddy? Or Daddy Ward?"

Helen rolled her eyes. "Boys."

Warmth flooded through Aster at the childish banter, and she fought to keep a straight face. She ignored Helen's last comment and said, "As for those resting overnight, Sergeant Aino and Corporal Elliott go for their morning PT—their morning exercise—around the time I usually wake up."

"They don't wait for you?"

"I have no need for exercise. The nanites keep me in peak physical condition. All I need to do is focus on weapons training and the like."

"Ooh, like with guns and stuff?" Billy asked. Then he remembered who he was talking to, and his face colored. "Er, ma'am."

"Yes. Guns, rockets, knives, martial arts, electronic warfare, vehicle combat. We train for everything."

When the teapot began to hiss, Aster removed it from the heat and poured the water into two mugs. She then dropped an Earl Grey teabag into each and looked at the clock. Three minutes, and it'd be ready. She opened the fridge and removed the pitcher of reconstituted powdered milk Elliott had mixed up the previous evening. She poured two glasses and set one next to Billy and the other next to Jason.

Billy murmured his thanks, but Jason didn't notice. He was too focused on his drawing. Aster leaned over his shoulder. "A tank?"

"It's an M87," Helen offered.

"It's an *M78*." Jason rolled his eyes. "Girls. Right, Billy?"

Billy wisely kept silent.

"The M87 and M78 have the same body, so it's easy to confuse them," Aster said. "One's newer than the other."

"Yeah, that's right!" Helen agreed.

Jason rolled his eyes again.

Aster leaned over the drawing. "Don't M78s have a bore evacuator on their barrels?" She ran her finger along the tank's slender barrel. "A bulge right around here. They also have a muzzle brake."

"Ooh, good catch, Aunt Aster!" Jason erased the section of barrel near Aster's finger, then drew it slightly bulged out.

"Why the interest in tanks?" Aster asked.

"Mr. Jones found a book in the university's library and picked it up for him," Helen explained. She swatted Jason's hand away from the cookies again.

Jason stuck his tongue out at Helen, then went back to his drawing. "Mr. Jones is nice! I'm glad he's doing better."

Patrolman Jeremiah Jones of the Mobile Police Department had been the last officer to fall to the berserk Agent Morris. The former football player had put up a good hand-to-hand fight, but no regular human was a match for someone who was augmented. Aster could beat him soundly if she had to, and she prayed that would never be necessary. As Jason had said, he was a nice man.

Aster pointed at the bottom of the tank. "What's going on down here?"

"That's the emergency escape hatch!" Jason retraced the lines of the open hatch for emphasis. "It's popped open while the tank's moving."

Wavy lines behind the tank hinted at movement from the left side of the page to the right. Aster frowned. "Why would they do that?" She'd fought alongside—and against—armor a number of times throughout her career, but she'd never seen an instance where the bottom hatch was left open during maneuvers.

"The M78 has a design slaw."

"You mean *flaw*."

"That's what I said! A design slaw that causes the hatch to sometimes unlock."

That surprised Aster. She'd never heard of such a thing. "Under what circumstances would this happen?"

"If it's going too fast for too long, and if it's shooting at the same time." He shrugged. "I don't know why."

Someone unlocked the common area's entrance door. Aster placed herself between it and the children, body tensed. Aino and Elliott weren't due back for another twenty minutes, at least.

But it was Corporal Elliott who opened the door. The short, well-muscled man was breathing hard, as if he'd just finished a sprint. "Boss, it's bad. One of the—" He noticed Helen, Jason, and Billy, and his jaw snapped shut with a click.

Aster stepped close to the man, and he whispered so low, she doubted he could hear his own words, but her enhanced hearing picked them up fine. "Something bad's happened in the Quadrangle." He glanced at the children. "Best they don't see it."

Elliott was one of the youngest members of Section Nine, but he wasn't given to emotional outbursts. What he'd seen must have shaken him. "A security threat?"

"No. The situation's under control. It's..." He left the thought unfinished.

She felt the children's eyes on her back. "Helen, Jason, Billy, I'll be back in a little while. Until then, feel free to have breakfast with Elliott." Her lips lifted in a faint smile. "He makes a mean stack of pancakes."

"Yay, pancakes!" Jason said. "Isn't that great, Helen?"

Helen didn't share the enthusiasm. She studied Aster, her expression unreadable.

Jason poked her. "Helen? Earth to Helen! Pancakes! You like pancakes, right, Billy?"

"Huh? Oh, yeah! Pancakes are great!"

"See, Helen? Billy wants them, too."

"Right," Helen said after a moment, "pancakes." Helen poked her brother back. "That'll be yummy! I can help mix the batter."

"That'd be great," Elliott said, stepping into his role as babysitter with barely a hiccup. "I'll man the skillet."

Aster returned to her room long enough to don her suit jacket. As she stepped back into the common area, her eyes met Helen's. The young girl's expression was blank, but her eyes looked haunted. She knew something was wrong, but she didn't want to say anything, likely for her brother's sake. It pained Aster to see it, but it also filled her with a sort of pride. Nathan had raised her right.

"I'll be back in a little while," Aster promised.

"Okay." Helen smiled, but it didn't quite reach her troubled eyes. "Be careful."

"Always." It was the only way to be in this Fallen World.

* * * * *

Chapter Three

Early morning light glinted off the windows of the buildings that lined either side of University Avenue. Mist rolled across the asphalt and swirled around our horses' hooves as we approached the weed-choked grass that marked the beginning of the Francis Quadrangle, a park in the center of the University of Missouri's campus. Already the temperature was starting to climb, promising another hot day. I wiped sweat from my forehead and said, "Well, that's enough excitement for one night."

"Enough excitement for only an hour or two, you mean," Danny countered. "We'll be back at it before the day is out, I'm sure."

"You're probably not wrong." I shrugged my shoulders and rolled my head around until my neck cracked, relieving a bit of my pain and tension. I stroked Countess's mane. "I hope you're holding up better than me, girl."

Countess snorted and quickened her step.

I wiped more sweat from my face and, for once, was thankful we'd drawn night patrol duty for the week. The week-to-week transition wasn't fun, but it was what we had to do until a more permanent shift schedule could be hammered out. If it could be hammered out. It seemed that just as things were starting to settle into some semblance of a routine, something came along and wrecked it. *I guess that's what living through a collapse is all about, right?* I didn't voice the thought. Too many of my subordinates were still within earshot, and none of them needed to hear that from their commander, even if that's what they were thinking.

Especially if that's what they were thinking.

I turned in my saddle, heedless of the aches and pains in my tired joints. "Who here's looking forward to a hot shower and a stack of Mrs. Brown's pancakes?"

That elicited a ragged cheer from the men, including Sergeant Silva's buffalo riders. "*Senhorita* Brown is a master in the kitchen," Silva agreed. "You wouldn't even know she mixes sawdust into her flour."

Jones threw back his head and laughed, then he paused. "Wait, does she really do that?"

"Not that she'll admit!" Patrolman Lewis said. "But it makes sense, considering how much she's able to feed us despite the shortages."

"Well...damn. I never would've guessed." Jones looked thoughtful. "I guess syrup covers a multitude of sins, right?"

Everyone laughed, except Kevin Hanson. The St. Louis PD officer rode in stoic silence, his face downcast. I needed to talk with him later, and maybe to Brother Stephen Pham, Mobile PD's chaplain. Stephen had taken personal charge of several officers who were struggling with depression, including Kevin and Lieutenant Wendy Alexander of the Miami PD. She had lost several members of her contingent in the hours before Obsidian was brought down, victims of Sergeant Jake Morris's initial rampage after his Agent programming had been activated.

My hand tightened on the reins. Director Gwendolyn Greenway had sworn up and down that it was her counterpart from St. Louis, Director Edgar Lloyd, who had brought the imprinter with him, and he was the one who had activated Jake. And when things weren't going his way, he'd escaped and left her and the others high and dry. He'd tried to take the imprinter with him, but an RPG fired by one of Aster's men had brought down the truck carrying it. Lloyd had gotten away in an APC, and he hadn't been seen since. I trusted

Greenway about as far as I could throw her well-endowed body, but Aster had confirmed that Lloyd was the likely mastermind behind everything, based on her knowledge of Obsidian's hierarchy. Part of me hoped we'd never have to deal with him again, that he and his cronies would drive into the wastes until they ran out of gas and then starve to death somewhere. Part of me hoped I'd get to bring him to justice so he could stand trial for his crimes.

And part of me worried we hadn't seen the last of him or his machinations.

The Quadrangle—or 'Quad' as the locals called it—had once been a peaceful place where students congregated, either for official gatherings or to hang out. It had been turned into a fortified rallying point for the officers and civilian defenders who now called Mizzou home. Sandbag barriers had been set up for riflemen to crouch behind, and snipers maintained positions on the rooftops and in the upper story windows of the old brick buildings that surrounded the park, along with spotters to keep an eye out for signal flares. Many of those defenders waved at us as we approached, while others pointed in the direction of Jesse Hall, which was south of our location.

I turned Countess left, and we rode across the grass in the indicated direction. On our right, a set of six towering pillars rose from the morning mist. These limestone columns were all that had survived the fire that claimed Academic Hall back in the 1800s. It had been a favorite place for us to gather after patrols since we first arrived, so in the days since the Fall, someone had pounded posts into the ground right in front of the columns. Stainless steel chain had been strung between the posts, and fifteen or so horses were tied to it. A couple of officers who were likely supposed to be on watch had their backs turned to us as they gawked at Jesse Hall.

It was an impressive building, to be fair: four stories of brick and concrete, with a domed roof that rose another five stories. The building's main entrance was protected from the elements by a balcony held up by square pillars of stone, which in turn was protected by an awning supported by a set of cylindrical columns. The roof dome lent Jesse Hall the same sense of majesty as the Capitol Building in Washington, DC, back before it had been sold off to Tong International in the earliest days of the Corporate Takeovers.

A crowd had gathered in front of the main entrance—a mix of students, staff, and civilian refugees who'd taken up residence. University police, mounted officers, and even a few off-duty cops stood in a semi-circle around the entrance, barring entry. For the most part, the crowd ignored them and craned their necks back so they could look up at something dangling from the domed roof.

No, not something. *Someone.*

A man in the dress uniform of a police officer swayed back and forth in the breeze, his limp body suspended by a noose around his neck. His head lolled, and his hands hung limp at his sides.

My heart sank at the sight. Danny cursed. "Who is it this time? One of ours?"

"They're all 'one of ours,'" I snapped.

Danny flinched at the rebuke. "You know what I mean, Nate."

I sighed. "I know. Sorry. But to answer your question, no, he's not one from Mobile. See the dress boots? They're a different style than ours."

Behind us, Silva swore. "*Vixe Maria*, how did he get up there?"

How did people wind up on the other side of suicide barriers for bridges and buildings? If there was a will, there was a way. And someone bound and determined to commit suicide wasn't going to be thwarted by a simple barrier. In this case, it didn't look like any of the windows could be opened, but looks could be deceiving, especially at more than a hundred and fifty feet. Maybe he broke one of the panes so he could get outside?

That question was answered a moment later, when two campus officers appeared from inside the window. One of them leaned out, grabbed hold of the rope, and started pulling. The dead officer's body twisted and turned as he was hauled up, his polished dress boots scraping against the side of the dome. They'd need to buff the scratches out of the leather for his burial. Who would do it? One of his buddies? Or would the boots be recycled and given to someone else?

And why did I care about the man's boots so much? I shook my head. The things we focus on during tragedies and crises....

One of the two men in the window shouted something I couldn't make out, and the one pulling the rope redoubled his efforts. The other officer dropped to a crouch and reached for the dead man's collar. The rope unraveled with a loud snapping sound, and the corpse plummeted. "No!" both men shouted, and the sentiment was echoed by several people with me below.

The dead officer struck the rounded lip of the dome that jutted out from beneath the windows. His body launched forward and crashed into the roof of the building with a meaty smack. He disappeared, until he rolled to a stop near the edge of the roof. He lay there, arms and head hanging over the edge at an awkward angle.

Nearby, someone snickered.

Anger flared inside me. Danny wheeled Noir in the direction of the sound, his usually pale face turning beet-red. He opened his mouth, but I gripped his arm and shook my head. He glared at me, then snapped his jaw shut with an audible click. Through gritted teeth he muttered, "Motherfucker."

Another collective gasp rose through the crowd, and I cringed. I didn't want to see the man as he tumbled the rest of the way down.

"Holy shit," Danny muttered. He'd twisted in his saddle to look back at the building. His mouth was agape.

I looked up. A small woman clad in a dark gray suit scrambled up the side of the building like Spider-Man. Her long white hair blew in the morning breeze, fanning out from her head like a banner. It was Aster, but what was she doing?

Within seconds, she'd reached the rooftop where the fallen officer lay in a tangled heap. She rolled him onto his back and picked him up. Even though the man was nearly twice her size, she cradled him against her body like she would a small child. She looked around the roof, as if considering something. After a long moment, she turned and walked off the edge of the roof.

Danny and I cursed aloud, but Aster was on the ground before we could do anything. Her powerful legs absorbed the impact with the soft grass. Her knees bent slightly, as if she'd stepped off a street curb. She set the fallen officer on the ground and started straightening his uniform. I urged Countess forward and pushed my way through the crowd. One of the officers in the picket noticed me and shouted, "Make a hole! *Make a hole!*"

The crowd parted, and Danny and I rode through. As we drew close, Aster gripped the noose that had been tight around the dead officer's throat. Her arm muscles bulged beneath her suit jacket as she strained, and then the noose came apart. Once she discarded the rope, she unbuttoned her jacket and used it to cover the man's face, but not before I identified him—Lieutenant Thomas Jackson from the Chicago PD.

I walked over to the body, my heart sinking further. "Thank you for doing that, Aster."

Aster looked up and cringed at the sight of Countess, and I backed my animal up with a muttered apology. It still shocked me that an augmented killer like Aster, who could scale buildings and leap across canyons, was afraid of a horse because of its size. I'd seen what Agent Morris had done to one of Sergeant Silva's water buffalos in the lobby of the Country Hotel, and I had no doubt Aster was capable of similar feats.

I handed Countess's reins to Danny, then slid from the saddle. I approached a much calmer Aster and knelt next to her. "Thank you," I told her again with a nod toward the jacket. "For that and for getting him down."

"Did you know him?" Aster gave Countess one last look, then her gaze dropped back to Jackson. She took his hands and clasped them together on his torso.

"He helped work Mardi Gras once, about five years ago. We didn't talk much then, but he was a good officer. Knew how to keep his men and horses calm under pressure." I'd gotten to know him better over the last few weeks. He'd been a great asset on patrols, so much so that Captain Graham had often sent him and his men into the worst of the unrest. I'd asked him if he needed a break. Hell, so had Sheriff Welliver now that he was attending briefings again. Jackson had just shaken his head and said he and his "boys and girls" would handle it.

And now he was dead. *Dear God, what must the rest of them be thinking?* I looked around, but it was difficult to see much from my vantage point. I hoped none of them were here, and I dreaded having to tell them in person.

Aster touched the wedding band on Jackson's ring finger. "Did he…have any children?"

I thought back to our past conversations. "Yes. Three. They're—" I shut my mouth, but I'd already said too much.

"I see." She stood and assumed a parade rest stance, feet spread shoulder-width apart, hands clasped behind her back. "I'll stay here until he can be taken away."

Before I could answer, the building's side door opened, and the two men who had tried pulling him up came outside. They were campus police officers, a corporal and a sergeant. The sergeant was middle-aged with a slender build and short-cropped hair gone mostly gray, while the corporal was a younger man with the body of a linebacker. They walked up to the jacket-shrouded body and removed their hats in respect. I stood and turned their way.

"Sorry, Lieutenant Ward," the sergeant said. He hiked a thumb at the corporal. "Jacobs and I tried our best, but that rope must've been old. We didn't notice it fraying until we started hauling him up, and by then, it was too late. A broken piece of windowpane sawed through it."

"No need to apologize, Sergeant Peterson. It could've happened to any of us."

Corporal Jacobs reached into his pocket and removed a note. "He left this behind, sir."

"I told you to leave that upstairs!" Peterson snapped. "CSI's going to go nuts over that. You know how particular they are."

"I didn't want it to get blown away in the wind." Jacobs gave the body a long, hard look. "And considering what else happened, I'd say taking the note is the least of our problems right now."

"Yes, but it's—" He sighed. "Never mind. Just show him the note, but please don't touch it, Lieutenant Ward. We don't need any more fingerprints on it."

I leaned in to look at the note in Jacobs' hand. A single line, scrawled in blue ink, read:

"I'm sorry for being so weak."

A lump formed in my throat. Dammit, Jackson. It didn't have to be this way.

A commotion at the back of the crowd alerted me to newcomers. Students and officers moved out of the way to let a pair of medics with a stretcher through. They jogged swiftly through the parting crowd, but they slowed when they saw Aster's jacket covering Jackson's face. Despite the obvious indicator that their patient was already dead, the pair dropped the stretcher and began examining the body, checking for any signs of life. It didn't take them long to conclude he was dead.

The crowd had started to close back up when someone shouted, "Make way!"

Four officers in the red uniforms of the Royal Canadian Mounted Police rode through the gap. The man at the head wore a black patch over his right eye. Captain Graham pulled his horse up alongside me, removed his black Stetson, and studied the body with his remaining eye. "Lieutenant Jackson?" he asked after a moment, turning his head toward me.

My throat was still constricted from the heartbreaking note, so I nodded.

"Jesus." Graham closed his eye and sighed. "I'll notify his department. Sergeant Zhao is next in command if I'm not mistaken."

I was impressed he remembered that much. Since taking over command of the unit while Sheriff Welliver recovered from his grievous injuries, Captain Graham had really stepped up to the plate. Other than the usual friendly rivalry between Americans and Canadians, there wasn't an officer who had a disrespectful thing to say about him or his Mounties. Undoubtedly, part of that was from the balls-out lancer charge he had led against some Obsidian foot soldiers in a bid to rescue Danny and his companions from what Welliver had called "the shootout at the DD Corral." They had taken out several Obsidian soldiers and the Corporation's gangbanger allies without suffering a single casualty.

The eye patch probably didn't hurt his reputation, either. What was more badass than that?

"Care to come with me, Lieutenant Ward?" Graham asked. "Sergeant Zhao is volunteering at city hall this morning. We can break the news to him, then attend the council meeting."

I'd seen George Zhao not too long ago as we made our way back from police headquarters after dropping off the prisoners. I really didn't want to ride back there, especially not for this. I knew Graham wouldn't force me to go if I told him as much. "Sure, let's go."

As I climbed up into Countess's saddle, Graham turned his attention to Aster. "Thank you for caring for one of my men, Specialist."

"It was the least I could do, Captain."

"Flare!" a female student called. She pointed to the west, where a streak of yellow smoke rose into the sky. A moment later, a second streak of blue smoke appeared.

"Trouble at the food distribution center," Aster said. She cocked her head to the side, and her long hair fell away from her ear, exposing the earpiece she wore. "Reinforcements requested to keep things from escalating."

I swore. If it wasn't one problem, it was another. "Sir, my men are ready to go."

"Your men just got back from a firefight if the radio chatter was any indicator. Let someone else handle it."

"Sir, we can—"

"Let someone else handle it, yes. I'm glad you agree." Graham leaned forward in the saddle. "I appreciate your eagerness, but I don't want a repeat of what happened here. Stand your men down, let them take a break. Lieutenant Saleh's and Sergeant Mosher's units are on duty now. Let them handle this."

As he spoke, movement on the other side of the Quad caught my eye. A half-dozen camel riders and nine horsemen rode west at a fast trot. All the camel riders and three of the horsemen were clad in green armor and wore red-and-white checkered *shemagh* that peaked out from under their riot helmets. The remaining six wore black armor emblazoned with the letters IDF in white.

"Saleh and Mosher together?" Danny asked. "I thought they hated each other."

"They requested it." Graham turned his horse around and started moving through the crowd. "Let's go, Lieutenant."

"I'll send the troops home." Danny glanced at Jackson's body. "Go deal with that."

* * *

Lieutenant Kevin Hanson had hung well behind the crowd as Nathan, Danny, and several of Silva's officers pushed through to the crowd's edge. The rest of the men pulled forward a bit, leaving him alone. It was an experience he had grown used to over the last couple months, and one that no longer cut as deeply as it once had. The less he interacted with his fellow officers, the better.

Not that that was a huge problem. Outside of Nathan Ward and a handful of deputies and Columbia PD officers, he didn't know any of the people who comprised the "blue cavalry" as they were starting to be known. And if any did know him, it was the officer who led six people to their doom in an irradiated St. Louis and then inadvertently led Obsidian reinforcements back here. That had caused a shitstorm of trouble in the city and had resulted in the deaths of even more officers. Yeah, who would want to befriend the fuck-up who accomplished all that?

He had watched with dispassion as the body of the dead officer fell, bounced, and rolled along Jesse Hall's roof. Some part of his withered soul raged at someone daring to *laugh* at what happened to a fellow human being who, only moments ago, had been living and breathing and *suffering*.

What had led the officer to do this? Kevin shook his head. The better question was, "What had kept him going?" Nearly every mounted officer, aside from the Boone County deputies, had come from out of state, and some of them from outside the country. Most of them knew their families were gone, lost in the same nuclear hellfire that had claimed their hometowns. It was possible a few towns had been spared like Columbia, but what did that matter? With a landscape tainted with radiation, how likely was it that anyone would survive a trek of thousands of miles on horseback? The idea of attempting it held a certain excitement for the cowboy inside every mounted cop, but practically speaking?

What good had a shorter trek to St. Louis done for Kevin's squad? They were dead, and it was his fault. If they'd stayed put, they could've still been here, making a difference along with Nathan and the others. *If only I'd listened to Orson.*

Several minutes later, Captain Graham had arrived on scene, and he and Nathan had ridden out shortly after. Danny had dismissed everyone, then he had joined Lieutenant Saleh and Sergeant Mosher as they responded to a mobilization flare. Kevin had briefly considered following along, but the drive wasn't there. Nor was it there to follow Sergeant Silva and the others back to the stables.

So, he waited. The crowd grew bigger as more students and staff filtered into the Quad, drawn to the commotion like flies to honey. The earliest arrivers started to leave a short while later, having had their fill of drama and death for the day. Through it all, Specialist Aster stood near the body in a silent vigil.

Brother Stephen Pham arrived before the medics could carry away the body. The tan-skinned man wore a navy blue polo shirt with Mobile PD's logo emblazoned on it, and he carried a bag that held his ever-present Bible. Kevin had seen more of that man and his

Bible in the last few weeks than anyone else, except for Nathan. He wasn't sure he was ready for him at the moment.

He listened more than he watched as Brother Stephen Pham began to pray loud enough for the crowd to hear. The prayer was pretty and full of sympathy for the pain that led to Lieutenant Thomas Jackson's terrible end and for the ripples of pain his death would cause in those who knew him best. He prayed that God would grant them peace in these tumultuous times, mercy for the afflicted, and healing for the land.

Kevin turned away. He couldn't bear to hear anymore. If God was listening, why didn't He stop the bombs from dropping in the first place? Why didn't He keep Jackson from killing himself? Why didn't He stop Kevin from making such a stupid, fatal decision? It wasn't that he didn't believe. He'd read his Bible every night before he came here. He'd accidentally left it on his nightstand and had the text message from Rebecca to prove it. She'd offered to bring it out to him that Sunday morning, the day the bombs dropped. She had wanted to bring the kids out so they could have a picnic together, then head home.

He'd told her not to trouble herself. Rebecca had a routine she stuck to, and he didn't want to disrupt that.

Kevin ground his teeth together. Why hadn't he listened to her? Why hadn't he listened to *anyone* that day?

He rode Watson west and then south at a slow walk, following the path that led around Jesse Hall. The red gelding was tired from being out all night, and Kevin was in no hurry to get to the stable. Students and staff walked past him, the "situation at Jesse" on all their tongues. He did his best to tune it out. Jackson was dead, and there was no point in dwelling on it further.

A couple of college students leaned against the stone wall of Townsend Hall, carrying on an animated conversation. Unlike everyone else in and around the Quad, these two appeared to be...jovial?

"Man, I can't believe the sound that cop made when he struck the roof. *Thwack!*" The one with short, dark hair raised a hand over his head and brought it down onto his other palm with a slap. "Just struck it and rag-dolled out."

The other college student, a man with blond bangs, chuckled. "It was really funny, like something in a video game. Couldn't help but laugh."

"Yeah, and did you see how that one cop glared at you? The ginger?"

"I swear his face was as red as his hair! You don't think he saw me, do you?"

"Naw. If he had, he'd have beaten you stupid. You know how these pigs are."

Kevin ground his teeth again. *These* were the people they were risking their lives for every day? He turned Watson toward them, his hand on his nightstick.

And then, just as quickly, his anger burned away, swallowed by a dark pit of apathy. What difference did it make? Beating them senseless would prove their point, and it wouldn't make him feel better. He knew he should say something, but he couldn't find the words.

"World would be better off without any of them here," the dark-haired one said. "Violence begets violence, and that's all cops and soldiers are good for, you know?"

A blur of motion caught Kevin's eye. Specialist Aster rushed the two students and slammed her fist into the wall right between their heads. The impact echoed like a gunshot and left a spiderweb of cracks in the stone. The students stood frozen in terror as they alternated between looking at her fist and looking at her face.

Aster's purple eyes blazed with quiet fury. "If violence begets violence," she said quietly, "does idiocy beget idiocy?"

Neither of the previously chatty students uttered a word.

She withdrew her hand from the wall and glanced at the blood welling up on her busted knuckles. "A good man is dead today, a man who lost everything, yet continued to do his best to keep this community safe. To keep *you* safe. He didn't owe you anything and yet he kept at it, until he couldn't bear it anymore."

She closed her bloody hand into a fist. "The wrong man was swinging from that rope this morning, and I'd hang you both myself if it meant he could come back to us. I'd hang *a thousand* of you for one of him."

Both students stared at her, mouths agape and eyes wide.

"Get out of my sight," she hissed.

The two ran as fast as their out-of-shape bodies could carry them.

Aster watched them go, then turned to face Kevin. Her eyes softened, and Kevin felt a wave of shame roll over him. She'd done what he should've done. She'd said what he should've said. He hadn't known the dead officer, but they'd shared a common cause. He'd owed it to him to defend his honor, but instead he'd left things in the hands of a young lady. He'd failed.

As he turned back toward the stables, Kevin realized failure was all he was good for in this Fallen World.

* * * * *

Chapter Four

Danny rode slightly separate from Mosher and Saleh's units, with them but out of the way. He'd sent his Mobile boys and girls back to bed, but Noir had been feeling frisky. He couldn't blame the filly. Even though he'd only gotten a few hours' sleep, the shootout in front of Jay Dawson's neighborhood had left him wide awake. If anything, there hadn't been enough action there to completely rid him of his adrenaline.

"How was your little outing?" Lieutenant Yousef Saleh asked. The Jordanian man sat astride a tall dromedary. Danny had to look up to make eye contact.

"Peachy," Danny replied. "Nothing like some night firing to make one feel alive."

"Especially with moving targets, right?" Saleh asked.

"Especially when they shoot back," Mosher added.

The three of them laughed, and some of the tension eased out of Danny's shoulders. "Well, hopefully we won't have to deal with any of that here."

"That would be a welcome relief."

"Indeed. I can't tell you how many times we've had to put down food riots." Saleh shook his head. "Even though order has to be maintained, it doesn't make fighting your own any easier."

"Amen to that," Danny muttered.

Columbia's city council had set up food distribution centers at different points throughout the city, so its citizens didn't have too far to walk to get the day's groceries. The University of Missouri maintained one in the southwest corner of the campus, at the old Tiger Pantry building. At one point, it had served as a local food bank, and now it was reprising that role. A second one was set up a few blocks south of Teledyne Tower, close enough for the Corporate thugs to provide security but not so close that they got itchy trigger fingers. A third had been established outside city hall, though it was only open once a week. It would've made more sense to set it up in a nearby park, but the former mayor had insisted, and Columbia PD's chief had backed him up. Doubtless, the politician wanted to get back into the public's good graces for when the council opted to have another mayoral election, whenever that was.

As such, he was usually there, shaking hands, kissing babies, and doing all the ass-kissing necessary to get elected. Danny had hated seeing that kind of pandering before the Fall, and it was ten times worse now. He was glad they weren't going there.

The fourth and final one had been set up in a three-way intersection in the New Downtown area, a part of Columbia Danny had become intimately familiar with not that many weeks ago, when he and the officers with him had been involved in a rolling gun battle with an Obsidian APC. As he examined the nearby buildings, he realized this was one of the intersections they had driven through in their mad dash to get away from the armored vehicle and its gun turret. The chase had ended not far from here, in a street too packed with disabled cars and trucks for him to maneuver past. The police SUV had been destroyed, leaving them holed up in a doughnut shop until help could arrive.

Now the intersection was filled with white tents and collapsible tables, surrounded on three sides by a double-layer of interlocked parade barricades. The sight of the steel barriers made Danny feel painfully nostalgic. How many miles of those had he and Noir marched past during Mardi Gras parades? He stroked Noir's black mane. *Never again, man. Never again.*

Columbia PD officers stood outside the barricades decked out in riot gear similar to his own. One of them looked up at their approach and raised a dark arm in greeting. "Sergeant Ward! Fancy meeting you in a dump like this!"

Danny smiled. "Reed, good to see you!" He'd been in Columbia for a couple months and still hadn't had much personal interaction with CPD officers. Most of the local cops had chosen to segregate themselves from the mounted units, a result of an earlier policy by Chief Ballantine that encouraged a softer touch on rioting and looting, at least until Sheriff Welliver came on scene and deputized anyone who wanted to fight the good fight. Corporal Chloe Reed had been one of those. She'd fought side-by-side with Danny and others in a few critical fights since then, including extracting Aster from a building's worth of rubble during the Country Hotel assault. Reed was an excellent shot, cool under fire even when she was pissed off, and she could rattle out insults as well as anyone else, if not better.

It didn't hurt that she was damn fine looking, too, at least in Danny's book.

Reed stepped out of the line of officers and said to her men, "Make a hole, all of you! Enough for—" She counted the number of mounted riders. "Five mounted cops in the center of each side of the barricade!"

"I hope our side doesn't get the camels!" one of the officers shouted from the other side of the barricades. "I can smell 'em from here!"

"If you can smell 'em from there, it doesn't make a difference where they are!" Reed snapped. "Just for that, you get the camels!"

That brought a round of laughter from the assembled men, including the one who objected. "Fortunately for everyone here," Saleh said, "we brought enough camels to go around! Two to each side. Maybe the stench will keep the crowds back."

That brought another round of laughter. Danny smiled. It was good to see that the officers still had a sense of humor, despite all the shit that was going on around them every day. Then he thought of Lieutenant Jackson hanging from the clock tower, and he lost his smile. Not everyone had that sense of humor, sadly.

More reason to try and keep things as light as possible. It could mean life and death on these mean streets.

"Speaking of crowds, where are they?" Mosher asked. "We thought we would be riding into a heated situation."

"Oh, it's about to get heated." Reed pointed to the roof of the building the distribution center had been set against. "Spotters noted a huge crowd forming, much bigger than the one two days ago, and that was bad enough."

True to his word, Saleh divided his men among the three sides, then took up a position at the north end. Mosher took command of the mounted cops to the east, leaving Danny with the cops on the south end, where they had approached from. He pulled Noir up next to Reed. "How've things been, Chloe?" he asked.

"Oh, same old, same old." Reed set her shield down against the barricade behind her and rested her nightstick on her shoulder. "Still not used to all this riot gear crap. Just got certified a couple weeks ago."

"Considering what's going on, I imagine everyone's been certified by now."

"Pretty much. We even got the ladies in dispatch and the office clerks to join in on the fun!"

"Probably not too much dispatching that needs doing, with most of the radios down for the count," Danny said.

"Oh, you'd be surprised. That smoke flare system you mounted cops came up with? We've got our dispatch team up on the roofs of city hall and the Tiger Hotel. Any time they see a flare, they call it in so officers can be sent in to help."

"It's a great system," Danny agreed. He looked around. "One you and I benefited from, right?"

She shivered. "Don't remind me. Just thinking about doughnuts gives me the shivers all over, and not the fun, sugar crash kind."

"Yeah, well, don't jinx it. We may end up in another doughnut shop shootout before too long."

"Lord, I hope not!"

* * *

"Well, that could've gone better," I growled as Graham and I rode along East Broadway away from city hall and its twice-damned Council.

"You should come to all the meetings," Graham said. "Those Corporate bosses are about as fun to be around as porcupines who love hugs."

Despite my anger, I laughed. "You have my condolences."

"And you have my condemnation. As I understand it, you're the reason those two are still around to look imperious and deliver edicts."

Back when we had stormed the Country Hotel, Aster and I had discovered Director Greenway of Obsidian and Manager Kazama of Teledyne hidden in a safe room beneath the top floor lounge where we'd fought and killed Agent Morris. The two of us had ended up in a Mexican standoff, outnumbered, but with our sidearms trained on Greenway and Kazama. We could've ended them both with a squeeze of the trigger, but then their bodyguards—what few were left at that point—would've made short work of us. Well, maybe just me. Even as wounded as she was, Aster would've won, through a combination of skill and augmentation.

"It's their lack of care that always gets to me," Graham said.

We lapsed into silence as we rode past the quaint little shops and restaurants that lined Columbia's main boulevard. Many of the businesses lay abandoned, although their glass fronts hadn't been smashed in due to the heavy police presence in the area. A few of the restaurants had even remained open, but they largely prepared and sold whatever they could find. Their traditional menus had long since been discarded in favor of perpetual "specials of the day" that frequently made use of shelf-stable items such as peanut butter, crackers, canned meat, and condiments like mustard and hot sauce—things that never really went bad if stored properly.

One such restaurant, Kim's Top Shelf, had a chalkboard set up in the window with the day's specials on it. At the top was a tuna melt, this time with real tuna! It didn't say whether the cheese portion of the tuna melt was real. Either way, my stomach grumbled. I hadn't had a tuna melt in a long time, not since leaving Mobile. Big Time

Diner off Cottage Hill Road had been my favorite. Since it was gone, maybe this one could claim that title?

Graham looked at me, then at the menu in the window. "Hmm. Tuna melts, rice omelets, and burritos of questionable authenticity...what were you thinking?"

"You want to stop and get lunch?" I asked.

"I don't see any food in my saddlebags." Graham made a show of looking. "Unless you count handfuls of oats and sugar cubes. You have any in yours?"

"Oh, plenty of oats and sugar cubes, but not much in the way of people food."

Graham turned his horse toward Kim's. "That settles it. Besides, you look like you could use some comfort food. What kind of superior officer would I be if I didn't look out for the wellbeing of my men?"

We tied our mounts to a lamppost outside the restaurant's entrance and went inside, but not before we slipped feedbags filled with the aforementioned oats and sugar cubes around the horses' faces. "We'll make sure you both get a real meal when we get home," I said, brushing Countess's nose with my fingers.

Countess snorted as she munched happily.

"Captain Graham, welcome back!" A young woman in the black trousers and white button-down shirt of a high-end barkeep waved to us from behind the bar. "I'm sorry we don't have the ingredients for your usual at the moment. Would you like one of our specials, instead?"

"The burrito of questionable authenticity, if you please, Kimberly," Graham said.

"And the tuna melt for me, ma'am," I added. "Oh, and sweet iced tea, if you have it."

"What kind of restaurant would we be without that?" Kimberly favored us with a pretty smile and turned toward the back. "Coming right up!" she called over her shoulder.

We both watched her go, but Graham *really* watched her go. "Looking out for the wellbeing of your men, eh, Mr. Superior Officer?" I asked after I figured she was out of earshot.

Graham had the decency to blush. "It's not like that," he muttered.

"Uh-huh."

"I'm a widower, and I don't mean since the Fall." He indicated a table where we could watch the street. Outside, Countess turned her head to follow my movements as I walked the length of the restaurant's storefront and sat down. We positioned ourselves so I could watch the street while Graham kept an eye on the kitchen door.

"I wasn't aware you were ever married," I said. "You have my condolences."

"It was years ago. Still hurts, admittedly, but present circumstances have put a damper on even that grief." Graham rubbed his ring finger, where a wedding band would have been. "Sometimes, though, it feels like yesterday."

Sadness crept across my soul. I grabbed my ring and twisted it on my finger, savoring the sensation as it rubbed against my skin. "I know that feeling."

"I figured you might."

Kimberly returned a moment later with a glass of sweet iced tea. "We may not be able to fix your usual meal, but we *can* fix your usual drink. Shall I get it?"

Graham glanced at me. "Yes, that would be fine. Cut it with a little extra ice and water. It's hot, and I have a long day ahead of me."

"Of course."

Kimberly went behind the bar and climbed onto a step stool so she could reach a bottle of what looked like Dad's Hat bourbon. I didn't know Pennsylvania brands were sold in Teledyne territory. "Are Mounties allowed to drink on duty?" I asked as she added ice and water to a glass, then topped it with the bourbon.

"It's frowned upon, generally speaking. I never used to drink on duty, but since we never seem to be off duty these days, I don't know when else I'd get the chance to indulge. And while I don't care to admit as much, it helps take the edge off."

He touched his eye patch as he said that. It had become a tell of his, a reminder that he was under a lot of stress and had lost more than some of the other officers, including me. I'd gotten banged up during my fights over the last few months, including the one with Agent Morris. Graham had lost an eye to Morris's IV needle.

"Besides, it's the only place around here I can find Dad's Hat. Developed a taste for the stuff when I was in Pennsylvania for an RCMP Music Ride at ICEF. The International Cultural Exchange Festival, in case you didn't know."

Kimberly brought him his drink. "Your orders will be up in a few minutes," she promised.

Graham raised his glass in salute. "To the Fallen."

"To the Fallen." We clinked glasses and drank. Graham gave a satisfied hiss after his first sip, and I sighed after the first swallow of the amber nectar known as sweet tea. It had just the right amount of sweetness. Not so much that it was syrup, but not so little that it didn't wash away the bitterness of black tea. "Almost as good as the professor's."

"Who?"

"Oh, you'll meet him at some point. This professor and his wife have one of the only working vehicles left in the city—a station wagon from last century."

"That's gotta be a sight."

"You should've seen it when they piled sandbags on its roof and put a machine gunner up on top."

Graham laughed in surprise. "An even better sight. Wait, I remember that. They brought back supplies from Boonville."

"Those are the ones."

"Good Lord, that wagon's roof was big enough to land a helicopter on." He paused, then he lowered his voice. "That reminds me, Nathan. Do you know what's become of that one weapon you brought back from there? The big one?"

"We handed it over to Dr. Schneider in the electrical engineering department." I shrugged. "Figured it was something he could play around with. I hear it sucks up a lot of juice."

"Yeah, it's probably not high on their priority list right now. They're busy trying to figure out the power source that's keeping a fifth of the city's lights on."

"I can respect that." It had been a surprise to learn that the backup generators hadn't been doing anything.

Movement in the street caught my eye. A black sedan pulled up to the curb, its window tint so dark I couldn't see the driver or any passengers. The front passenger door opened, and a bald man in a suit and sunglasses stepped out. He had Corporate bodyguard written all over him. The man opened the back door, and out came another bodyguard who might as well have been the first's twin.

They made room for another passenger to step onto the sidewalk—a voluptuous woman in a dress suit. The tea in my mouth soured. Director Gwendolyn Greenway, head of Obsidian's forces in Columbia, member of the city council, and an all-round pain in the ass. *What was she doing here?*

"Lord, what does she want?" Graham muttered, echoing my thoughts. We stood as one of the bodyguards opened the restaurant door, partly to be polite to Director Greenway, but also for tactical purposes. If it suddenly came down to a shooting match with her suited thugs, we wanted to be on our feet.

"My, if it isn't Captain Graham and Lieutenant Ward!" Greenway waltzed into the restaurant as if she owned the place. Considering how wealthy Corporate executives were, that was a possibility.

Graham clasped his hands behind his back and smiled. "Director Greenway, a pleasure. Care to join us for lunch?"

"Here?" Greenway looked around, her beautiful face marred by a slight sneer. "I've never eaten in such a…quaint establishment. Perhaps some other time."

"What can we do for you, ma'am?" I asked. In my experience, Greenway never went out of her way to socialize with anybody, not unless there was something to be gained from it.

Greenway's sneer turned into a frown. "I wanted to express my condolences on the loss of your officer. Sergeant Nixon, was it?"

"Lieutenant Jackson," Graham corrected before I could snap at her. "And thank you. Your concern is appreciated."

What concern? I didn't voice the thought, nor did I address my growing sense of anger. During the meeting, neither she nor Kazama had cared one bit about our report on Jackson's death, nor about the report on the increased mental strain the average officer was currently experiencing. Richard Cates of the Three Rivers Renaissance Fair had seemed genuinely disturbed and hurt by the situation, while President Oakford of Mizzou had been more concerned by the fact that it happened on his campus. Oakford was good people, but he could be a bit shortsighted at times.

Kazama and Greenway's focus had been on the raid against Jay Dawson's farm, and whether that would hurt their contribution to the city's food supply. The council had voted unanimously to increase patrols of police and volunteers to any farms that asked for it. Graham had the ability to veto any security issue, but he had agreed, despite our men being thinly stretched. I couldn't see that we had much choice in the matter. Was that what Greenway was here for? To reiterate how important it was that she and her fellow Corporate denizens of the Country Hotel get proper nutrition?

As she engaged Graham in pointless conversation, I turned my attention to her bodyguards. Both men had taken up positions on Greenway's flanks. Normally, I'd expect their bodies to be canted away from one another so they could better watch their sectors, but they'd angled their bodies so they could instantly turn toward each other. Stranger than that, they spent as much time watching each other as they did their surroundings. Looking at them made my body tense. What was going on?

Their heads suddenly snapped toward me. I couldn't see their eyes behind their dark shades, but I knew they were watching me. A chill ran down my spine. I don't scare easily, but the way they moved in unison was nothing short of creepy. I wondered if they were Agents, or if they were just specially trained. My cautionary side screamed it was the former, but I had to assume it was the latter. If they had more Agents than Jake Morris around, why not use them and make short work of us un-augmented humans?

"And how about you, Lieutenant Ward?"

I turned my attention to Greenway. "Sorry, ma'am. I didn't catch that."

"You soldier types are all the same." Greenway studied me with a steely gaze, a small smile on her full lips. "So busy assessing threats and tactics and means of escape that you lose sight of the good and pleasurable things in life." She lifted an eyebrow. "Things that could be right in front of you."

I felt my face grow hot. "Ma'am, in case you haven't noticed, there are threats everywhere. It pays to be vigilant."

"Yes, I suppose it does." She raised a hand and counted off with each painted fingernail. "Rioters, gang activity, food shortages, external invasion—" She closed her hand into a fist but extended her thumb so it pointed to her right as she added, "Internal treachery."

Kimberly chose that time to push through the kitchen door, a plate in either hand. "All right, gentlemen, here it…Oh, hello!" She smiled at Greenway. "Welcome to Top Shelf! Shall I get a table for the three of you?"

"Thank you, but we were just leaving." Greenway extended a hand to Graham, who took it in a gentle handshake. "Captain, I look forward to our next meeting." She then turned to me, hand still out. "You should come more often, Lieutenant Ward." She leaned in close enough for me to smell her perfume. "The conversation can be very stimulating."

I shook her hand. "As my duties permit. As you so eloquently put it, I have many threats to consider."

Her soft grip turned into hard iron, but her tone was airy as she said, "Yes. Yes, you do."

She turned and left without a word, her bodyguards scrambling to reach the door before she got there. Graham and I continued to stand as they piled into the sedan and drove away. Through the dark tint I could just make out Greenway's outline. Was it my imagination, or was she looking at us?

And then they were gone, and we returned to our seats. The tension in the room evaporated as quickly as it had arrived. What had that been about?

"Well, it's not every day Green Gwen herself graces my restaurant with her presence." Kimberly set the tuna melt down in front of me, then placed her now-free hand on her hip. Her expression was pouty as she added, "Shame she didn't stay to eat. I could've used that as a marketing gimmick."

The tuna melt smelled heavenly. "Well, she did at least enter the establishment, so it wouldn't be a lie if you said she visited."

Kimberly set down the burrito of questionable authenticity. It looked pretty good, despite being wrapped in pita bread instead of a tortilla. "Enjoy, you two! Oh, Lieutenant…" She glanced at my nameplate. "Lieutenant Ward, would you like more sweet tea?"

I blinked and looked down. My glass was empty, except for the ice at the bottom. "When did I do that?"

"Any time you weren't speaking," Graham said as he set his barely touched bourbon down and reached for his silverware. "And yes, he'll take more. A lot more, no doubt."

Kimberly laughed. "Understood. We'll slake your thirst, Lieutenant. Don't you worry." She took the glass, winked at me, then sauntered off. She had a very nice backside.

"Now who's staring?" Graham muttered as he dug into his burrito.

"Shut up."

As all good tuna melts should be, this one was far too messy to eat with my hands, at least not while in uniform. I cut into it with a knife and fork. I assumed the cheese was American, but when I took a bite, a mildly sharp note overrode the savory tuna. "It's cheddar!"

"Made in-house!" Kimberly called from the kitchen door. She set my refilled glass down next to me. "Aged three months, so it's a little older than, well, you know." The sparkle in her eyes dimmed for a moment before returning. "Isn't it wonderful?"

"It is, indeed, ma'am, and that is no exaggeration. Are you making more?"

"We are. We used up the last of our milk to make a batch a few days ago. If all goes well, it'll be ready in about two months. And if we're able to age it, it'll only get sharper."

Sharp would be better, but any kind of cheddar was a Godsend at this point. "Where do you get the milk?"

"My relatives own Clover Farm southwest of town." She grinned. "Best dairy cows in the whole region, and that's a fact."

"We patrol in that region fairly regularly," I said. "It's only a mile or so down the road from the Rock Bridge Ranch, where a number of our mounts are stabled."

"I'm out there once a month or so, and I've seen you mounted police hard at work, either training or patrolling." She tucked her hands behind her back and leaned forward so she was eye level with us. "And that's why your meals are on the house, now and any time you come back."

"What? No, that isn't right." The council hadn't figured out what would pass for currency yet, so for now, we were sticking with greenbacks or good ol' fashioned bartering. I reached for my wallet. "I've got—"

"You doing your duty is payment enough. I hope you know that a lot of us out here respect and support you, far more than don't." She smiled. "And that's a fact."

* * *

Rioters threw themselves at the Columbia PD shield wall, all of them screaming profanities as they tried to push through the distribution center's defenses. All around the makeshift facility, civilians armed with bats, bricks, and fists fought it out with the cops. And if that wasn't bad enough, the people already inside the barricades had joined in the mayhem.

"Push them back!" Danny shouted. He urged Noir forward, and the cluster of rioters in front of him stumbled and fell in their haste to get away from his horse. The mounted police on either side of him surged forward, the camels and horses more than enough to keep the crowd in retreat mode, at least for the moment.

Things had stayed peaceful at the distribution center for maybe a half hour and then it had all gone to hell in a heartbeat. Someone on the inside of the barricade had grown irate when he'd been told they were out of something he wanted, but all people had heard was, "What do you mean there isn't anymore?" People outside the barricade had taken up the cry, and a starvation-fueled panic had ensued. The crowd had charged forward, and the mayhem hadn't let up in the last five minutes.

A heavyset man in oil-stained overalls swung a pipe at a CPD officer. The officer tried to get his shield up in time, but the pipe connected with the side of his riot helmet. He staggered from the blow, and the man raised the pipe again.

Corporal Reed stepped in and cracked her nightstick across the man's head hard enough that he dropped the pipe. Another cop reached through the shield wall and dragged the pipe onto their side of the line. That was one less weapon in the hands of the rioters.

"Get back!" Reed shouted, her voice cracking like a whip. "All of you, get back!"

She slammed her shield into the chest of a man trying to push through to her. He crashed into the man behind him. The two staggered and collapsed to the ground. A third man attempted to jump over them to get to Reed, but she struck his shoulder hard enough to dislocate it. He stumbled over the two men beneath him and then his body wound up in the heap.

Danny urged Noir to continue her slow advance as he swung his nightstick down into the mass of bodies. "Get back!" he screamed. "Get the hell back!"

Something flew at his head. He raised his arm, and a bottle shattered against his armor. He smelled alcohol and looked down. The broken bottle lay on the ground, an unlit rag stuffed in its mouth. "Shit, they've got Molotovs!"

He stood in his saddle and looked out over the crowd. About twenty feet away, a man held up another bottle and put a lighter to the soaked rag hanging out of its mouth. It ignited immediately, and he cocked his arm back to throw it at the line of cops.

A gunshot rang out to Danny's right, and the man with the Molotov clutched his chest and dropped to the ground. The Molotov hit the pavement and shattered, sending a pool of burning alcohol across the asphalt. People screamed and slammed into each other to get away from the flames.

One of the Israeli cops, Corporal Perez, holstered her pistol. "Rubber bullets!" she yelled to Danny. "We brought more with us than we know what to do with."

"You'll find plenty of reason to use them at the moment," Danny called back. He tapped his pistol. "I've got nothing but hot rounds, so I'll save them."

Danny pushed forward with Reed and a few of the CPD officers. The crowd gave way, though they continued to hurl insults at the cops: "All we want to do is eat, you jackboots!" and "Only pigs would shoot an unarmed man!" and "What if you'd missed and hit a child?"

At the rate things are going, Danny thought, no one's going to eat. And how is someone with a burning bottle unarmed? And what if he'd missed with his throw, and instead of hitting us pigs, he hit some church group and set them ablaze? What, then? Danny ground his teeth together. If that happened, the crowd would be screaming at them for not stopping him in time. In situations like this, the cops couldn't win.

The fool with the Molotov had somehow managed not to set himself on fire, as the bottle had shattered several feet away from him. He lay curled up in the fetal position, moaning and clutching his chest. There was no blood pooling around him or staining his shirt, so Perez's statement about rubber bullets had been correct.

"Aw, poor baby," Chloe said as she handed her shield to another officer and slid her nightstick into her belt loop. "Why don't you tell

Mama Chloe where it hurts?" She roughly rolled the man over onto his stomach and forced his arms behind his back. "Maybe here?"

The man squirmed. "Get off me, you pig!"

"Oh, so that's where you got hurt! In your stupid, thick head!" Another officer knelt and pressed his hands against the man's shoulders, while another sat on his legs so he couldn't kick them. Chloe slipped her cuffs around his wrists and clicked them into place. "Now, stop squirming around like the little bitch you are, and we won't have to cuff your ankles together. You know what? To hell with it. Cuff his ankles, too. We'll drag him back like the prize piece he is."

She took a set of cuffs from one of the other two officers and cuffed the man's ankles, and together, the three of them hauled him back toward the parade barricades. Danny shook his head and laughed. One didn't mess with Corporal Reed, not unless they wanted to get trussed up like a pig ready for a roast. Ironic, considering what the man had called Reed.

There was a loud crack, and Reed suddenly dropped. Danny wheeled Noir around and scanned the crowd but saw no one with a gun. There was another crack, and a bullet zipped past his head. There, up in an open third-story window, a woman pointed what looked like an M16 at them. Danny drew his pistol, aimed, and fired.

The woman ducked down as his shots tore through the glass pane above her head. He cursed, adjusted his aim, and waited for her to peek back out. She didn't.

Around him, the crowd dispersed, many fleeing back the way they had come. A riot was all fun and games until people started getting shot or set on fire. Then the saner members usually wanted out.

Danny continued to watch the window. "Reed, you okay?" he called without looking back.

"My shoulder feels like it was broken into a million pieces and glued back together wrong," came the pained response. "And I might've pissed myself. Other than that, yeah. Doing peachy. How about you?"

Relieved, Danny laughed. "Better now that I know you can give me a nice helping of sass."

"Ha, ha, ha. Happy to oblige. Felix, help me up. Let's get this piece of shit back behind the barricade. Maybe he and whoever shot me were in on this. And if not, I may blame him anyway."

Perez rode up to Danny. "We'll ride around to the back of the building, see if we can't spot the shooter as she tries to flee."

"Good plan," Danny said. "I'll stay here and wait for CPD SWAT to clear the building." He hoped Reed's shooter hadn't gotten up on the roof and gone from building to building to get away.

Several gunshots rang out from the building where the shooter had been. Inside, a woman screamed until a final shot silenced her. Danny's chest constricted, and he had to force himself to breathe normally. What the hell had just happened?

A few moments later, the main door to the building opened slightly. Danny leveled his pistol. "Who's there, behind the door?"

"Teledyne security!"

That brought Danny up short. What were they doing out here? They ran their own food distribution center near Teledyne Tower. It was a way for them to engender some good will with the locals and, he figured, turn them against the rest of the city. He had no doubts both Corporations were still playing the dominance hierarchy game with each other, and they were using the police and citizenry to their own ends. "This is outside your jurisdiction. What're you doing here?"

"Private business. May we come out?"

Private business? Tying up some kind of loose end, he imagined. Stupid Corporate lingo. "How many are you?"

"Four, including me."

"Come out one at a time. You first. Nice and slow."

The door opened fully. A tall man in a black suit stepped outside, a bullpup rifle hanging from a single-point sling in front of him. He kept his hands raised as he looked across the street at Danny. "Quite a morning you're having, Sergeant Ward. First the Dawson situation, and now this?"

"How'd you know I was out on patrol earlier?" Danny demanded.

"Lucky guess. Name's Glover, by the way."

"Don't care who you are, by the way. Get the rest of your people out here."

The other three came out as slowly as their commander had. Unlike Glover, the others wore combat armor similar to that of Aster and her Section Nine crew. They were geared for war. The fourth and final man had two weapons slung on his shoulders, and one of them looked like the M16 the woman had used. "Where'd you get that weapon?" Danny asked.

"Oh, that? Teledyne property. Some of our weapons got stolen recently, and we've been trying to round them up."

Since when did Teledyne distribute M16s? M4-pattern rifles, maybe, but not the ol' A4 design favored by the US Military for decades. Hell, even the military had given most of those up, except for some Guard and Reserve units that made do with what they could get their hands on after the major cuts of the 2040s. State and federal laws required a certain number of Guard and Reserve units, but the laws didn't say how well equipped or trained they needed to be. They just needed to exist on paper.

"Give it here," Danny demanded. He urged Noir forward until he was a few feet away from the assembled men. He holstered his pistol and held out his hand. "That weapon was used in the commission of a crime against a CPD officer."

"The criminal is dead," Glover said. "You'll find her up in the stairwell. Bitch was trying to sneak out after she took some shots at your CPD friends."

"You killed her?"

"She resisted."

"Funny, the only guns I heard were yours."

"Since when does someone with a lethal weapon have to actually shoot it for it to be permissible to shoot them back? My men and I feared for our lives, so we did what we needed to do to protect ourselves." He shrugged. "Wouldn't you do the same thing in this situation?"

Danny couldn't argue. He continued to hold his hand out. "Still. That weapon is evidence."

Glover sighed. "Oh, very well. Hand it over."

The man pulled the M16 from his shoulder, reversed the grip, and held it up for Danny. Danny reached down and grabbed the weapon by the sling. He wanted to preserve the grip and trigger for fingerprints, but he somehow doubted these Teledyne thugs had left him much to work with.

"Are we free to go?" Glover asked. "Or would you like to search us?"

"I somehow doubt you're going to let us do that quietly," Danny said. "And as much as I'd love to have it out with you Teledyne pukes, I've got more important things to deal with right now. Thanks for dealing with the woman." *Provided you didn't put her up to that*, he thought.

"No problem. Consider it professional courtesy." Glover pulled a pack of cigarettes from his coat pocket and held them out. "Cigarette?"

"No, thanks. I don't smoke."

"Me, neither." He returned them to his pocket. "A lot of my charges do, though, so I try to keep them on hand for them. They never want to carry any, but they always want them."

"Is there a reason why you're still here?" Danny snapped. "Slink back to your Tower."

Glover's smile slid off his face. "Very well. Let's go."

Danny watched them until they disappeared down an alleyway. Then he called for a couple of CPD officers to guard the building's entrance until SWAT could arrive and clear the building. Glover might've been telling the truth about the woman being dead and the building empty, but he wasn't about to stake his life on the word of a Corporate soldier he didn't know.

He studied the M16 for a moment. What was Teledyne's angle in all this? Their real angle? If there was one thing he had learned, it was that the Corporations always had something else up their sleeve. It was one of many things that had led to the creation of this Fallen World.

* * * * *

Chapter Five

"Aunt Aster, how'd you get so good at fighting?" Helen asked.

"Yeah, you're so cool!" Jason added.

Helen pushed Jason's wheelchair down the sidewalk, and Aster walked alongside. The white-haired woman was in the same dark gray suit Helen first saw her in, back at the Renaissance Fair when she punched a police camel in the nose and knocked it out. Behind them, Corporal Elliott followed at a short distance. Both adults were constantly looking around, their heads "on a swivel" as Daddy liked to say. Always looking for trouble. The parents of some of her friends in school had found that weird, but she didn't mind. It made her feel safe when Daddy kept an eye out, and it made her feel safe when Aster and Elliott did, too.

"I was trained," Aster said. "First by the soldier who took me in and then by a Teledyne instructor."

"Not any instructor," Elliott added. "One of *the* instructors, a founder of Teledyne's special forces division."

"Woah." Jason tried to twist back in the chair to look at Elliott, but his face contorted into a pained grimace. "That sounds cool."

"It was tough." Aster tilted her head to study the top windows of a nearby building. "There were many times I wanted to quit."

"Why didn't you?" Helen asked.

"I owed it to my family."

"You wanted to protect them?"

Aster hesitated. "In a way."

"Just like Daddy!" Jason crowed. Then he paused. "Except Daddy can't knock out camels."

"How old were you when you first joined?" Helen asked.

"How old are you?"

"She's nine, and I'm six," Jason said.

"Nine and a *half*."

"You're not nine and a half! You're only nine!"

"I'll be ten in December!"

A twig snapped to the right, and Aster's head whipped in that direction. Her hand rose toward her coat, then dropped again as a bird flew out of a nearby maple tree. "I was eight when I started learning how to fight and ten when I joined Teledyne and received official training."

Helen's jaw dropped, and Jason uttered a soft, "Woah."

"Yeah, woah," Elliott agreed. "Teledyne wasn't squeamish about hiring child soldiers, but most of them were twelve or older and came from the third world. Our lovely Lady in Black came from the middle class, and she was the youngest ever brought in. It's one of the reasons why she's so good at what she does."

"You flatter me," Aster said flatly.

They approached a wide intersection. Aster held out her hand to stall Helen and Jason. She looked both ways, then motioned them to follow her. After a moment, she cocked her head to the side. "That probably wasn't necessary, was it?"

Elliott chuckled. "Considering ninety-nine percent of the city's vehicles are fried, I'd say that's accurate. Still a good habit, I suppose."

He didn't sound serious, and for some reason, that annoyed Helen. "Well, *I* think it's important. It's good to stay safe!"

"Yeah, me too!" Jason shouted.

Elliott's answering chuckle only annoyed Helen more.

They turned left once they crossed the intersection and followed the cross street toward the Brandon Hampton dormitory that peeked up over the thick canopies of the tall oaks which lined either side of the four lane roadway. Helen glanced at the street sign: "Mick Deaver Memorial Drive." It was the same road Aster had saved their lives on, when that mean Teledyne manager had threatened to kill them in front of their father and Uncle Danny. If Aster and Elliott and Paxton and the others hadn't been there, she and Jason wouldn't be alive.

A shiver ran down her spine at the thought, and it spurred her next question. "Aunt Aster, could you teach me to fight?"

That brought Aster up short. She turned her purple-eyed gaze on Helen. "I could, but why?"

Helen lowered her head and fixed her eyes on the back of Jason's head. "I keep thinking about the day Uncle…Uncle Jake got kidnapped by Obsidian." Tears came to her eyes. Thinking about Uncle Jake hurt so much. She still couldn't believe he was dead. It seemed like only yesterday he had been carrying them on his broad shoulders at a Mardi Gras parade, holding them up high so they could see Daddy and Uncle Danny and some of Uncle Jake's Philadelphia officers riding their horses down the street as part of the procession of fanciful floats and marching bands. And even if they made it back to Mobile, he wouldn't be there ever again. It hurt like it had hurt losing Mommy.

But she couldn't show her emotions in front of everyone, least of all Aster. She sniffled and blinked the tears away. "When I think about that, I wonder if there was something I could've done. Either then, or when Jason and I tried to run, and we got attacked. If you hadn't saved us then, Jason and I…"

Her throat constricted, and she fell silent. If Aster hadn't also saved them then, she and Jason would be dead. And if Aster hadn't been in the hospital when Daddy and Jason were attacked, they'd be dead, too. She owed Aster so much gratitude, but she also had a responsibility of her own, as the oldest child in the family. "I want to be able to protect myself and Jason and Daddy."

"I want to protect everyone, too!" Jason said.

"You're too young!" Helen snapped.

"Am not!"

She ignored Jason and looked back up at Aster. "Can you teach me, please?"

A ray of sunshine broke through the canopy and landed on Aster's head, causing her white hair to glow bright enough to make Helen squint. "I…will consider it. I need to talk to your father first."

Hope surged in Helen. "Thank you, Aunt Aster!" She pushed Jason's wheelchair with renewed vigor. "Let's go ask him now!"

"Wait, don't go so fast!" Aster called.

"Go faster!" Jason's laughter echoed up and down the empty street. "Go faster!"

"I didn't say I'd talk to Nathan right now!"

"Why not? He's right up ahead!"

Around the slight curve of the road, she had caught sight of a set of picnic benches that the officers and students who called the dormitory home liked to use whenever the weather was nice. The grass around the building was growing tall, but the green space where the benches were was cut short. Helen cast a disdainful eye over the tall grass. *If Grandpa weren't in Heaven, he'd be having fits about this.* Maybe they could let the horses graze there.

Daddy was sitting on one of those benches with three other people: Uncle Kevin, Aunt Wendy, and Brother Stephen. She opened her mouth to call out but then she saw that all four had their heads bowed and their eyes closed. Stephen's lips moved, though she couldn't hear what he was saying from this distance. That meant they were praying together. She lowered her arm. It'd be best to wait until they got closer.

"Daddy!" Jason shrieked happily. He waved his arms frantically. "Over here!"

Daddy looked in their direction, smiled, then put a finger to his lips before bowing his head once more. Uncle Kevin glanced their way, but Aunt Wendy and Brother Stephen continued as if nothing had interrupted them.

"Shh, Jason!" Helen clamped a hand over his mouth. "They're praying! Be quiet!"

Jason squirmed beneath her grip. He screamed at her, but the noise was muffled and nonsensical.

Aster stopped next to him, her eyes studying Daddy and the others. "What are they doing?"

That surprised Helen, and she let go of Jason, who sucked in a noisy breath, then sighed. "They're praying, Aunt Aster," he explained as if it were obvious.

"Haven't you seen people praying before?" Helen asked.

"Yes, at certain ceremonies and functions." She cocked her head to the side. "Never like this. I thought it was something people did at gatherings. What do they hope to accomplish?"

Helen and Jason shared a look. "Well, I can't hear them," Helen said, "but I imagine they're asking God for something. Like protection, or peace, or—"

"Toy trucks!"

"What kind of adult would ask for a toy truck?"

"They're cool!"

"Does praying for such things really work?" Aster asked.

"Daddy does it whenever he heads out to work," Helen said. "He always comes back, doesn't he?"

"Don't others do the same thing? What if they don't come back?"

Elliott cleared his throat. "Boss, I think that might be something you'd want to talk to Brother Stephen or Monsignor Owens about. Or maybe even Lieutenant Saleh. I hear he's acting as spiritual counsel for his Muslim brethren."

"Saleh hates Aster!" Jason said. "She punched one of his camels!"

Aster gave Jason a thin smile. "You love reminding me of that, don't you?"

"It was cool! But only because the camel didn't die," he added. "Camels are cool, too."

Elliott laughed. "I like this kid. We should make him Section Nine's commander of all things cool."

"Hmm, you make a good point," Aster said. "I'll talk with Brother Stephen at some point."

"Haven't you prayed for something before?" Helen asked Aster.

"If I have, it was so long ago, I don't remember."

They started forward again, and this time Jason kept quiet as they approached the picnic table. They came within Helen's earshot in time for Stephen to say "Amen."

"Amen," Daddy and Wendy replied.

Kevin nodded but remained silent as he opened his eyes.

"Aster, good morning." Daddy stood, a smile on his face. "Did my kids drag you away from something important?"

"No. Elliott and I were on our way back from an equipment inspection when we encountered your children, and we were headed this way anyway."

"Aster, you've met everyone here, correct?" Daddy quickly made introductions. "Brother Stephen Pham, Mobile PD chaplain. Lieutenant Wendy Alexander, Miami PD. And Lieutenant Kevin Hanson of the St. Louis PD."

"I *am* the St. Louis PD," Kevin muttered. "I'm all that's left."

Wendy's smile faltered as she nodded to Aster. "Ma'am, I can't thank you enough for what you and your men have done in the last several weeks. You've saved the lives of many officers and civilians with your actions."

"We were doing our duty, Lieutenant," Aster responded. "Section Nine may be a Corporate unit, but we pride ourselves on defending the innocent and minimizing collateral damage when possible."

"Says the woman who had a building dropped on her," Elliott muttered.

Aster looked sidelong at him. "That wasn't my fault." She turned to Kevin Hanson. "I saw you in the command bunker, back on—"

"The day this whole shitstorm began," Kevin finished. He glanced at Helen and Jason. "Sorry. Forgot there were kids around. Yes, that's when we met."

"I also saw you in the hospital," Aster said. "When I was visiting Jason."

"That was my home for nearly a month." He raised his thin arms. "I'm only now beginning to get meat back on my bones. The food was terrible, and the activity plan was even worse."

He smiled at the attempt at humor, but it didn't quite reach his eyes. To Helen, his eyes looked really sad. They reminded her of someone she'd known years ago, when she was closer to Jason's age.

Kevin stood. "Speaking of which, I need to get a jog in. Brother Stephen, thank you for your time and prayer. It's always appreciated. Nathan, Wendy." He smiled at Helen and Jason, and for a moment it seemed genuine, despite the growing pain in his eyes. "I'll see you both around. Don't give your father too much grief! I know what that's like."

Helen watched him go, with a growing sense of unease gnawing at her gut. Who did he remind her of?

Once he was out of earshot, Wendy let out a deep sigh. "He is one big bundle of nerves. And I thought I was bad."

"He's been through a lot," Daddy said quietly.

"I know that more than you," she snapped, then her expression softened. "Sorry, that was uncalled for. I was there when he came back from St. Louis. I saw how bad his condition was."

"His physical condition. I was there when he left for St. Louis." Daddy shook his head. "I should've made him stay. I tried to talk him out of it, but it wasn't enough. I should've gotten one of the captains involved."

"A captain from a different department wouldn't have made much difference." Wendy pushed off the table's surface as she stood. "You did the best you could. He oversaw his department's mounted unit. It was his call to make."

"And it was a bad call," Daddy said. "And people—" He stopped short and glanced in Helen and Jason's direction. "It was a bad call," he repeated.

Wendy checked her watch. "We can discuss this another time. We have a meeting to get to."

"Right; we do." Daddy smiled at Helen and Jason. "Kids, go with Brother Stephen." He looked at Aster. "Are you coming?"

Aster looked startled. "I wasn't aware I was invited to police briefings."

"Why not? You've been helping us out. It'd be great to include you in the discussion."

"Very well." She looked at Elliott. "Help the chaplain keep the children company."

Elliott snapped to attention and saluted. "Yes, ma'am!"

Jason giggled and saluted as well.

Aster smiled and turned to go. "Don't forget to ask Daddy!" Helen said.

"Ask me what?" Daddy asked without turning to look back.

Aster's quiet response was lost in a sudden gust of wind, but Daddy's reaction was unmistakable. He turned his head to look at Aster and then he looked over his shoulder at Helen, eyebrows raised. "I see."

Helen's cheeks grew hot, and she looked away. She really hoped Daddy would see reason. She was nine-and-a-half, after all! It was time she learned to take care of herself and those around her. Try as she might, she couldn't shake the feeling things were going to get a whole lot worse before they got better.

* * *

"The unrest is getting worse," Danny reported. I sat next to him and Aster in the auditorium Sheriff Welliver favored for meetings. With us were several officers, including Lieutenants Wendy Alexander, Cassandra Martinez, and Gregory Blackwood. Down in the center of the auditorium, Sheriff Welliver sat with Chief Ballantine, Captain Graham, and Captain Ko Hsu of the Philadelphia Police Department. Captain Phillips of the Border Patrol was still recovering from his wounds at the hands of Agent Morris, and he couldn't get away from his hospital bed. He would be briefed following the meeting.

"Even if we bring more food in, the mood of the city is sour, and that's putting it mildly," Danny continued. "Last week's situation in New Downtown was the worst it's been since I rotated back onto perimeter security from patrols. Weeks ago, people were worried, but friendly and willing to help one another out and be courteous. But yesterday?" He shook his head. "Yesterday, I thought we were going to have to start shooting people."

"Someone did get shot," Welliver said. The elderly officer held up a report in his left hand. His right arm hung in a sling that was tight against his chest. It had been torn off by Morris but had been reattached. It would be months before he fully recovered, but for a man nearly eighty years old, he was doing well. "Jessie Riggs, a punk with ties to the Ruby gang, if not a Ruby himself."

"Is that the guy Corporal Perez shot?" Mosher asked. "That was a rubber bullet."

"A bullet's a bullet in terms of how things get reported." Welliver idly scratched the sling. "I think our problem is the agitators. What are they really after? Are they looking for food for the hungry citizens like they claim, or is it something else?"

"Some psychos just want to watch the world burn, sir!" Blackwood said.

Welliver chuckled. "Sadly, you are not wrong."

"If one of the gangs is involved, then we already know the answer," Martinez said. She sat straight-backed on her bench a few tiers down from us, her dark-eyed gaze locked on Sheriff Welliver. "LAPD has dealt with its share of riots over the last several years—financial riots, food riots, political riots. In nearly every situation, the average citizen protested peacefully, at least at first. Then agitators would stir them up, break a few windows, set fire to a local business, and before you knew it, there was mayhem in the streets, and we could barely keep things under control, not without federal or Corporate help." She nodded toward Aster. "Our fair Specialist could tell you all about the troubles on Spring Street." She tapped her chest. "Her unit saved this brown pig's bacon on more than one occasion during that month-long campaign."

Aster stood. "My men and I were doing our duty. Our mission was to round up the local gang leaders and professional activists who were stirring up trouble in the streets and coordinating attacks against law enforcement and Corporate assets."

"Like I said, she saved our collective bacon. And our earlier thoughts proved true: professional agitators were at the heart of the unrest, working from the shadows at the behest of someone or something even deeper in those shadows. In that instance, Obsidian."

"Obsidian has wanted Los Angeles for a long time," Aster agreed.

Martinez chuckled, but there was no mirth in it. "Well, they have it now, after a fashion. It's gone."

She lapsed into momentary silence. A fresh wave of grief washed over me, and as I looked across the room, I knew I wasn't alone. Every mounted officer in there had come from a city that wasn't around any longer, gone in the blink of an eye and the flash of a nuclear detonation.

"Two people were shot in that incident yesterday," Chief Ballantine said. The older man ran a hand through his graying black hair. "The punk from the Ruby gang and the woman who took a crack at one of my officers."

"She wasn't shot by us," Danny said, "although I did shoot at her."

"Yes, your report says that. Glover of Teledyne took her out, then handed the rifle over for evidence."

"They reluctantly handed it over. Said it was Teledyne property, but I have my doubts."

"Well, we'll never know the full truth of it. The serial number, along with any manufacturer's stamps, have been scratched off the receiver. All we know is it is a military, Corporate, or LEO version of the M16, the A4 variant. It has two fire-settings: semi-auto and three-round burst. No fully automatic capability."

"If it really was a Teledyne weapon," Lieutenant Alexander said, "could it be that they've been handing them out as a way of stirring crap up? I know they'd love to be back in charge of this city, like they were a couple months back."

"If that were the case, why would they hand the weapon over?" Danny asked.

"To throw us off the scent? They had to leave the building at some point, right? Better to do it on good terms than deal with a breaching SWAT team."

"The only thing we know for sure about the woman is she was the cousin of Mr. Molotov," Chief Ballantine said. "She was probably shooting at Corporal Reed as a form of vengeance or maybe to help him escape."

Danny snorted. "Given that his feet and ankles were shackled, I don't think he was going anywhere."

"Not unless he was a champion potato sack racer back in high school," I added.

Aster cocked her head to the side. "Potato sack racer?"

"We'll have to put one together sometime. They're hilarious."

"For the viewers." Danny rubbed his jaw. "I lost a tooth the last time I had to hop around a track in one of those things."

"Well, before we get to that," Welliver said, "why don't we get back on task?"

"Good job," I whispered to Danny as the room quieted.

"You started it," he hissed back.

"So," Welliver continued, "we can assume there are two forces at work here: the first is legitimate fear and concern for the citizenry, and that should never be discounted. It's a scary time. Hell, I'm scared half the time, too, and that's not just because I had my arm sewn back on like I'm Frankenstein's monster. It's frightening out there, like we're in a never-ending disaster. Add onto that uncertainty a growing shortage of food, and it makes sense that people would be scared and desperate.

"However, that alone should not turn people to violence and mayhem. The average citizen desires law and order because it brings stability, and that's something we're sorely lacking. Something has to upset that desire for law and order, something has to act as the spark that leads us into chaos. And that's where the second force comes into play. Someone is pulling the strings. Someone is giving certain people ideas or weapons, or both, and then sitting back as what's left of society spirals into complete anarchy. Whoever is doing it will be the one who stands the most to gain. We have three choices."

He pushed himself up and walked over to the white board behind the table where a map of the city had been spread. He uncapped a marker with his left hand and wrote two words in poor handwriting. "Sorry for the messy handwriting. I'm still not used to writing with my off hand. Anyway, it's either the gangs or the Corporations. Or both, working together or against each other." He added that as a third option on the board, then looked at Aster. "Ma'am, do you have any idea if Teledyne could be behind this?"

"They certainly *could* be," Aster said after a moment's consideration. "As to whether they are, I don't think so. At least, not as official policy from the top. My contacts in Teledyne who still speak to me say they're worried about the growing unrest. There could be rogue elements in play, though—lower or middle management who want a chance at the top and are willing to do all sorts of unsavory things to get there."

She looked at me as she said the last part, and I was reminded of Manager Strohl and how he'd tried to use my kids to form an alliance between Teledyne and the cops against Obsidian. That would've benefited no one but Teledyne, so we'd refused. And Aster had dealt with Strohl, permanently. "Do you think it's Obsidian?" I asked.

Her eyes narrowed and her shoulders tensed, which was a common reaction of hers whenever Obsidian was mentioned. But she shook her head. "No. At least, not from the top. Director Greenway is an opportunist, but this isn't her style of leadership."

I remembered my conversation with Greenway after the council meeting a few days ago. She'd made it a point to mention internal treachery as a threat the city faced. Was she warning me that something was afoot inside her Obsidian force, something she wasn't fully in control of?

"Regardless, we know the Ruby gang is involved somehow, and they had ties to Obsidian during the fight for the city back in May." Welliver circled the organization's name on the board. "Gang members have been sighted or apprehended with weapons they shouldn't have had access to. The few we've been able to interrogate haven't had anything to say, other than their boss has quite the arsenal. If that's true, it's an arsenal we need to deal with, and the sooner the better."

Aster raised a hand. "Why not ask the leader of the Ruby gang about this?"

Welliver smiled. "Ma'am, if we knew where he was, we'd have done it already." His smile faded. "You don't happen to know where he is, do you?"

"I might." She tapped her earpiece. "Let me make a few calls. In the meantime, get your best men ready."

* * *

"Looks like the boys came through again," Porter said. The second-in-command of the Ruby Gang gestured to all the crates lining the underground storage chamber's wall. "Food, stolen directly from the bowels of Teledyne Tower." He pointed at another stack of crates. "Liquor taken from an Emerald hideout we neutralized last week." And again at another set of boxes. "We even found books and other forms of entertainment to keep people occupied, including some porn magazines. Real magazines, not digital!"

"With a full belly and an entertained mind, the masses are easily controlled." John Campos crossed his arms in front of his chest and rested them on his vastly diminished gut. Before the Fall, he had been known as a giant of a man, and not because he worked out. He was still pushing nearly three hundred pounds, but he was way down from his original weight. It was about the only good thing to come from this whole mess, something his wife enjoyed reminding him of. "Make sure the men know how grateful we are, but don't let them dive too deeply into the food and liquor."

"Good idea, sir." Porter grinned. "We'll need those supplies to weather what's coming next."

"And what would that be, exactly?" a soft voice whispered.

Both men jumped. Porter drew his pistol while John puffed out his chest and said, "Who the hell is that? Show yourself?"

One of the nearby crates moved. Porter fired his pistol several times. John flinched and covered his ears at the sudden noise as the bullets punched holes into the crate and shattered its contents. Red liquid dribbled from the bullet holes.

Shouts of alarm rose from the other gang members in the storage facility. Then more gunfire rang out, and those shouts turned into screams of pain. "It's the cops!" someone yelled.

"That's impossible!" John snapped. "How did the police find out about this location?" The facility they were in wasn't on any official map, and certainly not one that would've been in Teledyne or Obsidian's possession.

The crate next to the one Porter shot exploded into wood splinters. A petite woman with long, white hair and purple eyes flew out of the crate's remains and clamped an arm around John's neck. Before he could react, he felt the barrel of a pistol press against his temple hard enough to cause pain.

Porter spun to face them, his weapon raised and pointed dangerously close to John.

"Drop it," the woman whispered.

John struggled to break free of the much smaller woman's hold, but her grip was like iron. And the more he struggled, the tighter that grip became. His heart pounded in his ears as he felt the pressure of her arm against his neck increase. "Wai-wai-wait!" he stammered as his vision grew hazy. "Don't kill me!"

"That depends on what your lackey does next."

"Drop it, Porter!" John pleaded.

More of the gang members came running and joined Porter in pointing their weapons at John and the woman holding him hostage. She shifted her position so John's rotund body would act as a shield against the majority of the weapons aimed at them. He took that as a sign of fear and grinned. "Well, little girl, this was fun, but maybe you should consider surrendering now. I mean, you may kill me, but there's no way you'll survive against all of us."

"Oh? And what makes you so sure about that?"

The woman sounded amused! Well, anyone crazy enough to stuff themselves into a crate to infiltrate a hidden base couldn't very well be all that stable, now could they?

"Dear God," one of John's thugs said. The man's eyes were as wide as they could be. "It's her! It's the Battle Flower! It's Aster!"

A collective gasp rose from the assembled men, and as one, they stepped back. Some bumped into crates and sent them crashing to the floor.

Someone fired.

Suddenly, John was face down on the floor with the white-haired girl on top of him. Her arm was still clamped around his throat like a vice. Shit, she was heavy! A lot heavier than her delicate frame suggested. *Almost like—*

Fear seized his already quivering heart. As gunfire filled his ears, and the acrid tang of gunpowder prickled his nostrils, his brain numbly finished the thought: *Almost like an Agent or Specialist.*

He risked a glance up. Out of the corner of his eye, he could see Specialist Aster's extended arm and her FN Five-Seven pistol which was barking so fast, it sounded fully automatic. In less than a second, the slide locked back on an empty magazine. She ejected the magazine, and the gun disappeared for an instant before she brought it back up and kicked the slide forward on a full magazine. How had she reloaded so quickly, and one-handed, too?

A body crashed to the ground. It was Porter. His blood flowed from multiple gunshot wounds to his chest, neck, and face. Dear God, was anyone going to be left at the end?

Aster emptied another two magazines, and then the world fell silent, except for the ringing in John's ears. Bodies lay scattered around the floor, their blood running across the concrete in rivers. Some of it had even soaked into his pants. Or was that his own urine? Pain filled his chest, and his breath came in ragged gasps, made even more ragged by the woman's steely grip.

Rough hands bound his arms behind his back, then someone threw a black sack over his head, enclosing him in darkness. That same someone picked him up and slung him over a shoulder. "Wha-what are you going to do to me?" he demanded, the tremor in his voice ruining his act of bravado. "How'd you f-f-find this place?"

"We're going to ask you some questions," Aster said quietly, her voice almost lost in the gunfire echoing through the place. "And we expect them to be answered immediately."

"As for how we found you," a gruff male voice added, "here's a bit of advice: the next time you steal a crate of '45 Cabernet from Teledyne, make sure the crate isn't bugged. Director Ingersoll really hated when people took his favorite vintage without permission."

"Ingersoll? But he's dead!"

The man chuckled. "Yeah, hard to ask permission from someone who's dead. Doesn't change the fact that his prized crates had tracking devices on them."

"Concierge, this is Lady in Black," Aster said. "The turkey has been trussed."

Turkey? Was she referring to him? John's anger rose. No one talked about him like that! He opened his mouth to retort—

"Ask our guests if they would prefer it oven roasted or deep fried."

The words died on his tongue. He hoped that was code. Dear God, who were these people?

"Roger. Taking the turkey to the kitchen. Lady in Black, out."

* * *

"**N**ate, stop pacing," Welliver snapped. "Just watching you is making me nervous."

I turned to face the sheriff and planted both feet on the floor of his hospital room. "Sorry, sir. Old habit; hard to break."

"You mean your woman never—" He coughed. "Sorry. Another old habit that's hard to break. Making cracks about people's wives and husbands. I constantly have to remind myself that so many of you have lost your loved ones."

"That's all right, Terry. My wife died a few years ago, before this whole mess happened." I shrugged. "In some ways, it's a blessing. Had she still been alive, my children might've been home instead of with me."

"A positive way of looking at things. I like that." Welliver tried to spread his arms, but the sling prevented him from moving his right arm much. He grimaced. "What I don't like is this stupid thing. Can't I get out of it already? I want to go for a ride, damn it all."

"When did the doctors say you could ride again?"

"Not soon enough." Welliver laughed. "Truth be told, they told me I shouldn't ever get in the saddle again, regardless of the arm. 'If you took a tumble at your age...' Pah. What do they know? By and large, doctors are some of the worst at following medical advice. They drink too much, they eat all the wrong things, and they smoke like chimneys."

"Smoking's illegal now, though."

"And? Come on, Nate. You think because something's illegal, people are going to stop doing it?" He pointed at my badge with his left hand. "Then you might as well turn that in now. Once we announce that rioting, looting, and just plain being mean to one another is illegal, we'll be put to pasture, right?"

I chuckled. "All right, all right. I get it. Still, what'd they say about the progress of your arm?"

"That it's healing far better than it should for someone with my level of seasoning." He grinned, revealing a mouth full of perfect, straight teeth. "Must have good genes."

Someone knocked on the door. "Come on in!" Welliver called.

The door opened, and Lieutenant Paxton, Aster's second-in-command, stepped inside. He was a man in his early forties, with the square build of one who spent a lot of time lifting weights. "Sheriff Welliver, Lieutenant Ward, Lady in Black would like to speak with you."

I liked Paxton. From what I'd seen, he helped Aster run Section Nine—or the "Party of Nine" as they liked to refer to themselves in code—like a fine watch. Every member of the unit had a purpose, and it was his job to make sure they all worked in sync to carry out Aster's orders. If they ever officially joined the mounted unit, they'd make great officers.

At my insistence, Welliver reluctantly agreed to be taken downstairs in a wheelchair. He'd been out all day, speaking with the men, inspecting horses, and observing weapons training sessions, and it was clear he was fatigued, good genes or not. "Can't say I appreciate this kind of treatment," Welliver grumbled loudly. "No, not one little bit."

As his muttered rant continued, Paxton and I shared a look but said nothing.

Paxton led us to the elevators, and we waited until we had one to ourselves. Once inside, Paxton inserted a key into the control panel and pressed the button labeled B3. The doors closed immediately, and the elevator rocked as we began our descent. "Some super-secret lair beneath the hospital we don't know about?" I asked.

"No. At least, not with this." Paxton held up the key. "Maintenance gave it to me. It'll let us get onto the level where they store a lot of supplies."

A moment later, the elevator reached the bottom floor, and the doors opened with a ding. What greeted us was a dimly lit, unfinished corridor made of smooth concrete. We followed Paxton past several steel doors until he stopped at one and knocked. A voice from inside said, "Enter."

Paxton opened the door and waved us through. The smell of urine and feces assaulted my nostrils. My sense of smell isn't that great, so it had to have been bad in there.

"Jesus," Welliver muttered, confirming my suspicion.

Aster and a black-haired woman I didn't recognize stood on either side of a large man strapped to a chair. His head was covered in a black hood, and he slumped forward. Aster nodded in his direction. "We found the source of the Ruby gang's arsenal. Mr. Campos here told us quite an interesting story."

I tried to ignore the puddle of urine pooled beneath his chair. "Is he alive?"

Aster looked hurt by the question. "I have never lost someone during an interrogation."

"Has he been seen by a doctor?"

"Sergeant Louella Kirby is a combat surgeon." She indicated the woman next to her. "She has seen to his wounds and administered a sedative to put him to sleep."

I wrinkled my nose at the mixture of brine and copper that filled the room. "Get him cleaned up and in a hospital bed as soon as you can."

"That's not how we normally do things—" Aster began.

"I don't care how you normally do things," I snapped. "We police have protocols that must be followed, including caring for the health and wellbeing of suspects in our custody. Get him cleaned up and in a hospital bed, *now*."

Aster stared at me for a long moment. When she spoke, her voice was iron. "Very well. Paxton, Kirby."

I wheeled Sheriff Welliver out of the way so the two Section Nine soldiers could get John out of the room. "You sure do like to dance with fire," Welliver murmured to me. "I've seen what that girl's capable of. I wouldn't ever talk to her like that."

"Well, you just did," I said in a normal tone of voice. "She can hear every word."

Welliver glanced at Aster, who cocked her head to the side. "No offense intended, ma'am, but you understand."

"I am well aware of the fear people have for my abilities, yes," Aster said, her voice returning to its usual softness. "It is especially true for those who have experienced pain at the hands of a Specialist or Agent, such as yourself."

"So, about the source of the weapons," I prompted, both to change the subject and to get our conversation back on track. My anger at John Campos's treatment subsided as quickly as it had come, and it left me wondering why I felt that way at all. Aster was handling things the way a soldier did. It made sense that she would have a different way of doing things than a policeman. Different rules of engagement and all that. And for Aster, especially. She acted in a way she thought was right, with immediacy, with efficiency, and with deadly consequences.

And hadn't I been happy with that when she put a bullet through the throat of Manager Strohl to save my children? Hadn't I been happy when she'd stopped Morris from killing Jason, the rest of the leadership, and me? In both instances she'd acted without thought and without mercy. She did what she knew was right. Well, John was a man whose people terrorized the city through direct acts of violence and through theft of vital food and supplies. Left unchecked, his gang would destroy everything we had built up in the last several weeks.

And yet, there was still due process. If we wanted to be the kind of people who deserved to survive the Fall and to build something better from the ashes, we had to restore the justice system to what it was. That man was innocent until proven guilty, if not by a jury of his peers then at least by a police and military tribunal. I hoped the treatment he had already received at the hands of Aster didn't ruin that and let him walk. In the old days, it would have.

Aster led us to an adjacent room. Two of her men sat inside, one at a laptop, the other hovering over an open crate. They both stood and snapped to attention when they saw Aster, but she waved them back to their duties.

"Barry, show them what you've got," Aster said. She pointed to him. "Corporal Barry Ingram."

"Ma'am. Sirs." Ingram reached into the crate and removed what looked like a brand new M16. "We found twenty crates like this, each holding eight such rifles. With them was enough ammo to hold off an army or to invade your nearest, non-irradiated town or city."

"Where did they come from?" I asked. "The National Guard depot north of town?"

"A good guess, but no." Welliver shook his head. "The Guard unit was deployed down to Arkansas when this mess started. Their armory had been all but emptied. Maybe a few guns, but more than a hundred? And ammo for them? Impossible."

"Could one of the Corporations be supplying them?" Anger flashed through me at the thought. Were we being played by Greenway or Kazama? Both Corporations had worked with the two leading gangs in the city, the Rubies and the Emeralds, from the beginning.

"It wasn't us—" Ingram began, then stopped. "It wasn't Teledyne, sir."

"As much as I would love to blame my former employer," Aster said, "it's not them. At least, not openly. She indicated the soldier seated at the computer. "Sergeant Mandrell is analyzing the records we collected at the underground storehouse."

Mandrell nodded in our direction. "The Ruby gang is many things, but disorganized it is not." He turned the laptop around so we could see. "We found records of every kind of illicit activity they're involved with, from drugs to sex slave trafficking."

Maybe Aster hadn't been hard enough on that bastard Ruby leader. I let the dark thought slide and asked, "I assume you also found out where these guns came from?"

Mandrell reached around and clicked a couple of buttons until a map of the surrounding area appeared. Pins of differing colors littered the landscape, from inside the city all the way out to the edge of the map, which was nearly thirty miles outside the city if the scale was true. "From what I've been able to gather, these pins denote different drop-off and pick-up points for the gang's many operations. Drug houses, money laundering businesses, places for coyotes to drop off illegal immigrants, places for young women—well, you get the idea." Mandrell coughed. "Moving on, there's one drop-off point that's of particular note here."

He hovered the mouse pointer over an olive drab pin in an area southwest of the city on a road called West Route K. When he clicked on it, a note appeared that read: "NG drop-off point."

My stomach clenched at the implications. "The National Guard is supplying the Ruby gang? Directly?"

"If not, someone claiming to be the National Guard," Aster said. "John Campos was adamant that the one dealing with them was a Guard officer, a woman who wouldn't give her name."

Mandrell turned the laptop around long enough to punch in a few commands, then he turned it back. The monitor displayed a photograph taken with a night vision lens. A woman stood at parade rest in the center of the frame, dressed in a camouflaged army combat uniform. Two soldiers wearing full battle rattle and sporting NVGs flanked her, weapons held tight against their chests, ready to snap them up at a moment's notice. They stood in front of a Joint Light Tactical Vehicle with a cargo truck behind it and another JLTV behind that.

"Mr. Campos is a paranoid man, and he didn't like the idea of sending his boys in to meet with someone without surveillance. We're running an ID match now, but it'll be some time before we can confirm whether or not this woman is with the Missouri National Guard."

"Do you recognize her?" I asked Welliver.

"No, but that doesn't mean she's not Guard. The unit may be headquartered here, but that doesn't mean they all live in this area. If she's not from Columbia, she'd only be on base once a month, and that's if they weren't off somewhere else training. Still, I can circulate her photo, see if anyone in the department recognizes her."

"I will make it available," Aster said. She studied the image, her head cocked to the side again. "There's something about her that's familiar to me."

"Ever fight against any Guard units?" I asked as a joke.

"Not this state's, no."

Forget I asked, I thought. I really didn't want to know. I also didn't want to know how many cops her unit had killed throughout its storied career. What mattered was that they were on our side now and we needed them.

"Why would the National Guard supply a gang with weapons?" Welliver demanded. "It makes no sense."

"That's why we're not entirely convinced this is legitimate Guard activity," Mandrell said. "The 32nd MP Battalion hasn't been in contact with the home base since the Fall. Now, that could be due to communications blackouts that occurred as a result of the EMP strike, but it could also be because they were wiped out and someone is posing as them."

That Guard unit had been mobilized to deal with riots down in Arkansas. "Do we know what they deployed with?"

"They took nearly all their small arms and vehicles," Welliver said. "They're military police, so the biggest vehicle they had was a M1130 command vehicle, which was based on the old Stryker design. They had a few of those JLTVs plus some lightly armored Humvees."

"No tanks?"

"None attached to this unit. That doesn't mean they didn't link up with a unit in Arkansas that had some."

"What does this mean, though?" I asked. I pointed at the map. "Again, why is a National Guard unit—or another group posing as one—supplying criminals with weapons? All they're doing is destabilizing the city further."

"It's easier to take over a fractured city," Aster explained. "That's the only motive I can think of."

"Then whoever they are," Welliver growled, "we have to assume they're an enemy."

"I think that's a valid assumption," Aster agreed.

"I'll inform Graham and the other commanders," I said. "We need to be prepared for the possibility of an invasion."

"I'll get Teledyne and Obsidian on the horn," Welliver added. "They'll need to step up their game if they want to help us repulse whoever is coming."

Aster stiffened at the word "Obsidian" and asked, "Are you sure that's wise? What if Obsidian's behind this?"

"An elaborate scheme to point the finger elsewhere while Obsidian takes over from behind the scenes?" Welliver asked. "I agree there's a strong possibility, but if that's the case, they already know about this. Telling them won't hurt anything. In fact, hiding it from them might make things worse. There's no way we can hide the fact that the Ruby gang's been taken off the board, which means any information they have on this Guard-led insurrection will already be in our hands. If we try to sit on this information in the command channels, it'll tip off the enemy that we're suspicious of them. Better if they think we still trust them."

Aster considered that for a moment. "You…make sense, Sheriff. I agree."

Welliver hid it well, but I could see his shoulders relax ever so slightly at Aster's agreement. He really was shaken up by her power, and it was no wonder. The poor man had had his arm ripped clean off by Jake Morris moments after his Agent programming had activated and then he had seen Aster take that monster on in a hand-to-hand fight and run him off. I found her intimidating as well, but at the same time I felt…pity wasn't the right word, but something akin to sympathy for her. What I saw was a girl whose childhood had been stolen from her, who was shaped by circumstances beyond her control, and forged into a weapon of Corporate destruction. And what a weapon she was. If she set out to kill me, I knew she'd succeed with no problem. But I wasn't afraid of that.

Because Aster only targeted those she considered bad guys, and her judgment was pretty spot on. If she suddenly turned on me, then it meant I had died a long time ago, and all that was left was another villain who needed to be purged from this Fallen World.

* * * * *

Chapter Six

Kevin's breath came in ragged gasps as he knelt in the grass near the sidewalk, face toward the ground. Three weeks into his rehabilitation, and he still couldn't jog more than a few miles without being sapped of energy. Doctor Hollingsworth said he was doing very well, but he felt only frustration. Before this mess, he'd been able to jog for hours without much effort, even in the summer heat. How many months would it take him to get back to that?

What's the point in any of this?

He shook his head to clear it of dark thoughts, but they lingered, latching onto his mind like hitchhiker weeds on his socks and boots. What good would it do him to get back up to full physical strength? Would he be able to make any difference in a world like this one? Would it fix any of his past mistakes? Why was he still alive, when so many of his friends and loved ones were gone?

Kevin lifted his gaze. A field of wooden grave markers stood at eye level. A harsh chuckle escaped his throat. No matter where he intended to jog, he always wound up here, at the cemetery on the southern end of campus. He'd read somewhere that Hinkson Field had been intended for a new football stadium at some point in the future, but a portion of it had been repurposed in the days after the Fall as a place to bury dead students, staff, and officers. More than two hundred had been buried there since early May, and nearly seventy of those had come after the battle at the Country Hotel. Kevin had still been too sick to attend the funeral, but he'd heard the bagpipes from his hospital window.

Shame and bitterness flooded through him. Shame because he couldn't honor his fellow officers, and bitterness because of the waste it all represented. What had been gained from their sacrifice? By all reports, the city was tearing itself apart little by little. The so-called "safe zones" were shrinking by the week as gangs and anarchists pushed back the increasingly beleaguered police. How much longer would they be able to hold out?

A fresh mound of dirt lay before a cross-shaped marker. It was the grave of Lieutenant Thomas Jackson, the officer who had hanged himself a few days before. Kevin had been at that funeral, at least. Those in attendance had been stoic in their displays of grief, with downcast gazes and tears, if any, shed in respectful silence. Jackson's squad had been hit the hardest by it, and the rest of the officers had given them the space they needed. Kevin had stayed out of everyone's way, preferring to hang back as the funeral commenced. Monsignor Owens said a few words but could not preside over the funeral of a man who committed suicide, even if that man had been Catholic, or maybe because. Brother Stephen had conducted the service, closing with a prayer for the man's tortured soul and saying that God had forgiven him this final sin and welcomed him home.

Was suicide an unforgivable sin, an utterly selfish act from which there was no atonement? At one point, Kevin would have thought so, but now he could sympathize with Jackson and those like him. If he had to guess, Jackson must've felt like there was no other way out, from battling his own demons to the apocalyptic situation they all found themselves in. Maybe it was so he could be reunited with his family after they'd been taken from him.

Images of what he imagined had been his three boys' last moments flashed through Kevin's mind. They would've been at church: Cody, the oldest at ten, would've been fidgeting in the pew; Gabe, the middle one at eight, would've been riveted to Brother Walter's sermon, which was a strange but welcome sight; and James would've been nodding off like most four year olds after stuffing himself with cookies and juice at the end of Sunday School. They would've seen a bright flash through the clear windowpanes high up on the auditorium's walls. His wife, Rebecca, would've gasped aloud and placed a hand on her chest but then her instincts would've kicked in, and she'd have gathered their children to her. She'd have pulled them down behind the pew, pressed them flat to the floor, and then....

Kevin stood on legs made of jelly and wobbled through the cemetery, past Jackson's grave, and past many more who had died since May. The grave he was looking for was further in, one of the earliest ones dug: Patrolman Orson McGraw's, the last remaining member of his squad to make it back from the doomed journey to St. Louis. He knelt next to the man's grave marker and placed a hand on the grass-covered mound. "I should've listened to you," he said for what had to be the thousandth time. When Kevin had told the squad what had happened to St. Louis and what his plan was, McGraw had been the lone dissenter, the one who'd insisted they stay in Columbia where they could best make a difference. He and the others had shot him down, and Corporal Pierson had even accused him of cowardice.

Rather than get angry, McGraw had stood his ground, talking about the amount of good they could do here versus the amount of good it would do to make a dangerous trip back to an already doomed city. Even then, it had made logical sense to Kevin. But

McGraw didn't have any family in St. Louis. He hadn't understood the depth of Kevin's worry or the others' feelings, no matter what he had said. If his family had been that close, wouldn't he have gone?

In the end, McGraw had agreed to go along. "My place is with all of you," he'd said. "Even if we disagree, we all wear the same uniform. That's got to count for something."

"No," Kevin said in a hollow voice, his fingers digging into the loose, damp soil. "No, it didn't count for anything, Orson. Everyone's gone. I'm all that's left."

He turned his head toward Jackson's grave. "But maybe not for much longer."

* * *

The Country Hotel had taken a beating during the battle several weeks back, and the external damage was still clearly visible as Aster walked through the park that faced the front of the imposing structure. Windows had been blown out, and sections of brick and stone walls had either collapsed or been stained black from soot. Obsidian and Teledyne had fought hard to hold the place, but so had the police and Aster's teammates.

She, Corporal Elliott, and Sergeant Aino were escorting Doctor Ralph Schneider and a group of his research students from Mizzou's electrical engineering department. Someone in the sheriff's department had informed them they'd found something interesting on the top floor, and she'd volunteered her team for escort duty. She knew how important Schneider's efforts were to unlocking the mysteries of the city, and she wanted to do something other than sit around on garrison duty. Today, it was Paxton's turn to run reconnaissance, and she wouldn't undercut her second-in-command, no matter how much she wanted to be out there, searching for the theoretical invader.

The damage to the Country Hotel was present, but so were signs of repair. Huge, blue tarps had been spread across a gaping hole on one of the upper floors at the point where an Obsidian machine gun nest had been. The nest had been blown out with a rocket, and its crew killed. Aster had seen it when she scaled the outer wall to gain entrance to the building. The floor in that room had been flooded with chemically treated water from the fire suppression system, and it looked like someone didn't want it to get any worse.

"Watch your step, Dr. Schneider," Aster warned as her boots crunched on glass fragments scattered on and around the concrete steps that led up to the lobby entrance. "You should've worn better shoes for the occasion."

Schneider wore a lab coat and trousers, but his shoes were simple penny loafers with thin, rubber soles. Anything that might punch through Aster's boots would have to go through rubber, steel, and leather before it ever reached her flesh.

"I thought they would've swept the place clean already," Schneider admitted. He stepped around big pieces of glass as he navigated the steps.

"I think they have, sir," Elliott said. "There's a lot of it, is all."

The last time Aster had seen this place, there had been no barriers in place. The Obsidian commanders, in their arrogance, hadn't seen the need for external defenses other than what was on the upper floors and what they'd placed in the lobby. If she had to guess, it probably bothered Director Greenway's sense of aesthetics. Now, a chest-high wall of sandbags loomed over the steps, with a narrow opening in the center for people to enter and exit. Scaffolding had been erected over the makeshift guard post to help with repairing the front entrance's big glass doors and to provide shelter from the summer rains.

A pair of CPD officers waved them through. "They're expecting you upstairs, Specialist," one of them said. "We'll radio ahead."

Aster led her group into the lobby, and they saw a camp in the center of the vast chamber. Construction materials had been piled up by type: wooden beams, pallets of plaster and concrete, glass windows, and more. Tables laden with power tools in charging stations lined one side of the camp, while a set of tables covered in either food or maps lined the other. Several workers had gathered around the food tables while a group of foremen studied the maps, likely laying out the evening's labors.

The students with Schneider murmured their approval at the set-up. Some in the city wondered why so many resources were being expended to repair such a damaged building, but it made sense to those "in the know." The Country Hotel was one of the few buildings in the city that inexplicably still had electricity. If Aster had to guess, it was a secret Corporate backup system put in place by either Teledyne or JalCom. It was most likely JalCom since Teledyne seemed as much in the dark as everyone else. Before her time in Teledyne's paramilitary security force, she would've considered the idea of a secret base inside the city the fanciful imaginations of one of her friends from school, but she'd been in enough as either a visitor or a raider to know such a thing was possible and maybe even probable.

She led them around the far edge of the construction base camp, her boots leaving treaded prints in the sawdust that coated the lobby's marble tiles. Even beneath all that dust she could see that many of the tiles were scratched, cracked, or broken as a result of Nathan Ward's wild mounted charge through the lobby at the start of the final assault on the hotel. She could only imagine the noise of so many horses galloping through a chamber like this, accompanied by gunfire and screams. She couldn't stop a shiver that ran up her spine. She was glad she hadn't been there for that. Bad enough she had to be surrounded by horses while outside on the Quad or elsewhere, but to be stuck with them in a confined space?

The elevators were swamped with construction workers heading up to whatever floor they had been assigned to, but they made way for Aster and her team. She nodded her thanks, then ushered everyone into the wide service elevator. It was tight for twelve people, especially with the computer equipment and weapons they had brought with them. "Everyone suck in your guts," Elliott said as the door closed, and the elevator began to ascend.

The top floor was as Aster remembered it: a restaurant that looked like World War III had broken out in it. Tables were overturned and riddled with bullet holes, and fragments of shattered glass panes glittered in the light from several chandeliers that had miraculously survived the fight.

One of Sheriff Welliver's deputies greeted them at the door to the interior lounge, where she and Patrolman Jones and Nathan had fought Agent Morris. "Good evening, Specialist. Go on inside."

Aster started to step through the door but paused long enough to run her hand along its edge. It appeared to be made of wood but was actually solid steel. A quick glance at the hinges showed that it was meant to act as a security door, protecting the patrons inside the lounge from possible attack. It had likely been a recent addition in answer to the executive massacre in a Redmond hotel. She'd been sent in to clean that up. It hadn't been pretty.

Last month's gunfire had torn through the wooden facade on the wall next to the door, revealing chipped concrete beneath. It was a load-bearing wall, and it must've been made of steel-reinforced material. Another shiver passed through her. If all four of the room's walls had been made of this, she never would've gotten to Nathan and the others in time. No one would've been able to, not after the door locked behind them.

The room had been dimly lit, its dark wooden walls and floors adding to the dimness. But now, floodlights had been set up in the corners, bathing the entire space in a white light that was bright enough to make her squint until her eyes could adjust.

The bar had been cleared of glasses and bottles and was instead loaded down with computers, cameras, sample bags, and other evidence collection and analysis equipment. A tech who looked no older than twenty sat on one of the stools, her back to Aster, as she studied her laptop screen. The hole Aster had made in the wall had been covered with a clear piece of plastic. A deputy stood on the other side of the plastic, his back to her.

The top two rungs of a ladder poked up from the hole she and Nathan had fallen through with the body of Agent Morris. She hadn't realized she and Morris had spent the last moments of their fight right over the trapdoor that led to the plush speakeasy beneath the lounge. Brief flashes of that fight entered her mind: her busting through the wall, Morris spinning to meet her with his fist, her dodging and counterattacking. Then there was the moment he nearly ripped her arm off, followed by her last-ditch effort to pin him to the ground.

She looked down through the hole to make sure no one was coming up, then she hopped down and landed on the hardwood floor with barely a sound.

The room, which was part panic room and part private bar, was very well furnished. Sofas and armchairs surrounded coffee tables on one side, and a long dining table with twelve chairs occupied the other. And, to go with the speakeasy motif, there were even a couple of gaming tables: one set aside for cards, the other for roulette. For some, this would be the perfect place to sit and unwind from the day's labors or to hold clandestine meetings. For others, it would be a great spot to wait out a crisis. While the rest of the hotel dealt with terrorists or Corporate raiders, the occupants of this room could sit back in comfort.

A man and two women in the uniforms of the Boone County Sheriff's Department stood in a corner of the room on the far side of the roulette table. They had cleared a small side table and set their lunches out on it. Aster's stomach rumbled at the sight and smell of the peanut butter and jelly sandwiches: one with apple, one with grape, and one with apricot. Two of the open bottles on the table contained water, while the third held a brown liquid that smelled familiar.

"I'm tellin' ya, Sarge," the male deputy said, "no true Southerner goes around not drinking sweet tea. It just doesn't happen." He held up the container with the brown liquid. "Come on, try some."

The brunette with sergeant's stripes gagged and pushed the bottle away. "Pridgeon, get that away from me. I don't like any kind of tea, sweet or otherwise. And I'm not originally from the South. I'm from California."

Deputy Pridgeon looked askance at the other female deputy. "That explains everything."

The woman shrugged. "I'm not much of a fan, either, and I was born and raised in Mississippi."

"Et tu, Yates?" Pridgeon shook his head. "What is this world coming to?"

Aster cocked her head to the side. Was this guy serious? Didn't they have more important things to worry about than someone's drink preferences?

Up above, Schneider was making a racket as his computer case banged against the metal ladder. He cursed softly, then started to clamber down, followed by his student researchers.

"Oh, our guests have arrived!" The sergeant had turned to face Aster. "I didn't quite believe Joe when he said the Battle Flower was coming up, but here she is." She spread her hands. "Welcome to the scene of your crime, I guess?"

Aster glanced at the nameplate on her uniform. "Thank you, Sergeant Mickelson."

"Please, call me Tamara." She leaned in close. "My daughter is a huge fan of yours. It'd send her to the Moon if she heard we were on a first name basis."

"Very well, Tamara."

Tamara introduced deputies Pridgeon and Yates, then pointed to the hole in the ceiling. "I'm sure you met Gretchen upstairs. She's one of our computer analysts."

"I saw her." Aster indicated Schneider. "This is Doctor Schneider, from the university's electrical engineering department."

Schneider walked up to Tamara and held out a hand. "The pleasure is mine, Officer."

"Sergeant Tamara Mickelson, CSI." She hesitated, then took the man's hand. "We don't usually shake hands, professor, but I'll make an exception today. Sorry, it's a hazard of the profession."

"Oh. That makes sense," Schneider said, though it was clear to Aster he had no idea why shaking hands with a stranger could prove dangerous.

"You arrived just in time." Tamara turned toward a wall on the far side of the room, close to where she and her deputies had set up lunch. "We were about to head inside."

"Head inside?" Aster looked closer and saw a fine line running the length of the wooden wall.

Tamara pushed on the wall, and it swung open on well-oiled hinges. A darkened hallway greeted them, but after a moment, it lit up as motion-sensing lights in the ceiling came on. "Never, in all my years, did I think I'd come across a secret passage like this," she said, an excited gleam in her eyes. "We've gone as far as the stairwell, but then we turned back to call it in."

"I've requested that anyone inform me when they come across something out of the ordinary in any structures with electricity," Schneider explained. He studied the previously hidden corridor. "I meant things like power conduits that weren't on approved building plans, but secret chambers are pretty cool, too."

"Amen," Tamara said. She, Pridgeon, and Yates donned headsets with microphones and cameras attached. They pulled on nitrile gloves and slipped paper covers over their boots. Tamara looked at Aster and the growing number of research students climbing down into the room. "How many of you are coming inside with us for our initial walk-through?"

"Me, for sure," Schneider said.

Aster pointed at Elliott, Aino, then herself. "Where the doctor goes, we go."

"Okay, then. The rest of you will remain here," Tamara said to the student researchers. She held up a hand. "I know, it's no fun, but this may be an extension of a crime scene, and we can't have too many people dirtying it up. It's bad enough we're letting civilians tag along." She glanced at Aster and coughed. "Present company excepted, of course."

"We understand your meaning," Aster said. "What do we need to do?"

"Follow close behind us, and don't touch anything." Tamara handed Aster, Elliott, and Aino sets of gloves and booties. "And wear these."

Pridgeon walked several feet into the hallway, his head tilting up, down, left, and right as he took in everything with his camera. "Gretchen, you gettin' this?" he asked through his mic. After a moment's delay, he nodded. "Good. We're about to head deeper. No, you can't come. Stay in the lounge and work the computer."

It didn't take enhanced hearing for Aster to hear a frustrated groan echo from the room above. "But why not?" Gretchen called down the hole.

"Once we're done, I'll walk you through," Tamara said. "For now, you need to man your station."

Aster followed Tamara, Pridgeon, and Yates as they walked the length of the secret passageway. Schneider walked close behind her, with Aino and Elliott taking up the rear. The three deputies chatted as they walked, stopping from time to time to focus their cameras on a section of the wall or floor. "Very little dust," Yates noted.

"The hotel must've kept it clean," Elliott suggested, his voice echoing in the hallway.

"It doesn't show up on any of the hotel's schematics, though," Tamara said. "At least, that's what Gretch told me. The blueprints end at the speakeasy."

Aster thought about that a moment. "When was this hotel built?"

"It's designed to look like it's from the 1920s, but it's not that old." Tamara shined her light up at a vent in the ceiling. "I was a kid when they broke ground for this place, so sometime in the 2030s?"

The passageway ended at a stairwell that looked like the building's other stairwells, except for two things: the lack of any kind of numbering denoting what floor they were on and a small door barely big enough for a toddler to crawl through at the top of the stairs. The words "Cleaning Robot Access" had been etched into its metal surface. Yates pointed. "That explains why it's so clean in here."

It did, but it didn't explain why this was the only stairwell that had such a thing. Had Aster missed seeing it in the other stairwells? She hadn't exactly been looking for tiny access hatches the last time she ascended the building.

After a brief deliberation between Tamara and Gretchen back up in the lounge, Tamara waved them toward the stairs. They descended and their boots echoed in the otherwise silent shaft. Tiny LEDs running along the base of each landing lit up as Tamara approached. Pridgeon leaned over the banister and shined his light down into the depths. He whistled. "Climbing back up's gonna be a bitch."

"Poor baby," Yates said. "Should I break out my violin?"

The officers laughed, along with Elliott and Aino. Next to her, Schneider smiled but didn't turn his attention away from their surroundings. Even though they were in an otherwise plain-looking stairwell, he looked like he didn't want to be anywhere else. "It's amazing how long this secret passage went unnoticed!"

It wouldn't have been much of a secret passage if it could be easily found. Aster didn't bother to raise the point.

"I bet this kind of descent is nothing for you, Miss Aster," Tamara said with a look over her shoulder. "You and your crew probably run up and down stairwells a thousand times a day to stay in shape."

"I don't need to exercise to 'stay in shape,' but my men do need it, yes."

"Man, must be nice," Yates said. "How can I sign up to be a Specialist?"

Aster smiled, "I don't know that Teledyne is taking applications anymore, but you're welcome to ask. No matter the outcome, you wouldn't have to exercise again."

"What do you mean?"

"Well, if the nanites take to you, you'll end up like me. And if the nanites don't take, you'll die."

The three deputies shared a look. "And, uh, what are the odds of success for an operation like that?" Pridgeon asked.

"Things have improved quite a bit since I was augmented about five years ago. I'd say your odds of survival are around twenty-two percent."

Tamara stepped onto the next landing and turned her head to stare at Aster. "And what were the odds of survival when you underwent the treatment?"

"I'm not sure of the exact number because my handler did everything he could to dissuade me from undergoing the augmentation process, including exaggerating my low odds of survival. He told me less than one in twenty survived. I think it was closer to one in ten, but I can't confirm that."

"Five to ten percent," Tamara murmured after a moment. "Was it worth it?"

"Yes. I'm a much more effective soldier because of it." Her stomach growled. "The only downside is how much I have to eat to maintain the nanites, and it's worse if I get injured."

"She's not kidding about her caloric intake," Elliott said. "For her birthday party last year, we had to get two cakes: one for her and one for the rest of us."

"The boss likes her sweets," Aino agreed, speaking for the first time since they'd entered the hotel.

"Again, must be nice," Tamara murmured.

The stairwell continued uninterrupted for several moments until they suddenly hit the bottom. By Aster's estimation, they'd gone well below ground level and likely beyond the underground parking garage. She wouldn't have been surprised to find out they were even beneath the city's sewer system. Here they were greeted by another long corridor, its end lost in shadow. There was no door, save for a small hatch identical to the one above.

Tamara stepped off the lowest step, and the hatch opened with an audible hiss. A squat, round robot painted white with orange trim started to roll out of the hatch. One of its rubberized eyestalks turned in their direction, and it skidded to a halt and reversed course. Once back inside, the hatch slammed shut.

"Guess it's shy?" Pridgeon asked.

"Could be some kind of security protocol," Aino said. "To keep from getting damaged or stolen, it gets out of the way whenever humans are nearby."

At Aster's insistence, she and her men took the lead, while the deputies hung back with Doctor Schneider. Elliott and Aino used the flashlights on their rifles to scan the corridor as they walked its length. Aster walked behind them, her FN-P90 slung and her pistols holstered. She didn't sense any danger here. At least, nothing imminently dangerous.

The corridor turned to the left twice before ending at a huge metal door like those Aster had seen on bank vaults or Corporate fallout shelters. A nine-digit keypad had been built into the wall adjacent to the door. The keypad came online at their approach, and its glowing green screen demanded a password.

"What have we here?" Tamara stepped forward and pointed. "Did the hotel have some kind of secret storage down here?"

"Not unless the hotel was built by JalCom." Aster pointed at the words on the keypad.

They read, "Welcome to the Honeycomb, JalCom employee. Input password."

* * *

"And that's the long and short of what we found, sirs." Sergeant Mickelson handed a copy of her report to me, then set another copy in front of Sheriff Welliver. She stepped back until she was alongside Aster, who stood at parade rest in her charcoal gray three-piece suit.

"Thank you, Sergeant. Excellent work. Give Pridgeon and Yates my regards." He smiled. "How has Gretchen been working out for you?"

Mickelson smirked. "Are you asking as my boss or as a doting grandpa?"

Welliver pressed the report to his chest, his mouth agape in what I could only assume was faux outrage. "You wound me, Tamara! You think I would use my position to place my relatives in positions within the department?"

"You would, and you know it. But only if you thought they were qualified for the job." Mickelson's smirk softened into a genuine smile. "Gretchen's doing fine, for a rookie. Give her some time, and she'll be better at the job than me. Then I can retire." She made a show of checking a non-existent wristwatch. "Last I checked, I put in my twenty about two months ago."

"Yeah, well, permission to retire is denied. We're short-staffed and in the middle of chapter six of the Book of Revelation, in case you haven't noticed." Welliver shrugged. "Besides, it's not like you're going to be able to collect your pension and move to Tennessee like you wanted to anyway."

"It's not like I'm getting paid at all right now." Mickelson crossed her arms beneath her breasts. "I've got a daughter to raise. I'm all she's got. Lieutenant Ward, I hear you've got two kids of your own. You know what I'm going through."

I did, and it was something I was reminded of every time I had to head out for morning drills or when I rode out on an emergency patrol in the middle of the night. Each moment I was at my duties was another moment robbed from my children. And yet, if I didn't step up, if all of us didn't step up, wouldn't we be robbing our children of a future to spend time with them in the present? The city was in a tenuous position with the food shortages, the increased gang activity, and the fraying relations between law enforcement and the general public.

Before he could say anything, Sergeant Mickelson let out a long sigh. "I know, I know. We all have to come together, or there'll be nothing left to leave our kids, right? I get it. It's just...." She shook her head. "Obsidian and Teledyne really messed up the world good, didn't they? My daughter and I were going to take the rest of the summer and tour the country before her school year started in September. Now, I'm not even sure we'll have school."

"Oh, trust me," Welliver said, "there'll be school. My wife's already got plans for a homeschool setup for our grandkids, great-grandkids, and the kids of any officers who want to join in. That'll go for your daughter and your two kids as well, Nathan."

"Thank you, sir," I said and meant it. It had been increasingly weighing on my mind the closer we crept toward mid-August.

"So, what do we make of this vault door?" Welliver asked. "Specialist Aster?"

"It's for a JalCom facility known as 'The Honeycomb.' Section Nine is scouring the Teledyne records we still have access to, but we haven't found much. The occasional intelligence dispatch used the term in reference to something JalCom was up to, but no one knew the context." She shrugged. "We still don't know the context, other than that it's some kind of facility beneath the Country Hotel."

Welliver thumbed through his copy of the report. "I see Doctor Schneider thinks there are more doors like this one scattered throughout the city. Have any been found?"

"Not yet, but it's certainly possible. It's likely a facility of any real size would have multiple points of entry."

"Has Schneider's team been able to open the door?"

Aster shook her head. "The door has multiple security layers. There's a fifteen-digit passcode with an automatic lockout after three tries, followed by what looks like retina and fingerprint scans."

"Gretchen says the security system has quantum encryption," Tamara added. "She could hack the keypad and scanners, but she'd never make it past the encryption before the system realized what she was up to."

Welliver scratched the beard that had grown on his wrinkled cheeks since his hospital stay. "It's imperative we get into that facility, if only to find and secure our source of electricity."

"I'll talk to Gretchen about it," Tamara said. "Maybe she can work with someone in the university's computer science department."

"I'll ask Mandrell to assist," Aster offered. "I could also speak with my contacts at Teledyne."

I thought about that for a moment. "It's probably best if we keep both Corporations out of the loop on this. If they learn about a secret JalCom facility beneath Columbia, they'll tear the city apart trying to get to it."

"Good point," Welliver said. "See that it's done. Dismissed."

Tamara stayed behind to have a word with her boss, so I followed Aster out through the auditorium door and into the hallway. "Hey, got a minute?" I asked her.

She stopped and looked over her shoulder. "Yes?"

Her purple eyes drilled into mine. I scratched the back of my head and looked away. "So, I was thinking about what Helen asked the other day."

"About training her to fight?" She turned to fully face me. "What have you decided?"

"Actually, I was going to ask your opinion."

Aster studied me for a long moment. "I'm...hesitant. While I agree it makes tactical sense to train her and anyone else who wishes to learn, I fear she'll put herself in a position where she has to use those skills."

Sudden worry gnawed at my gut. "You think she'd go picking fights?"

"I think she wouldn't back down from one. She has a strong sense of justice."

"She does." I smiled. "It's a source of pride and anguish for me." The smile faded. "But, because she has that, sooner or later, she may put herself in a position where she needs to fight, regardless of whether she knows how. I hope and pray that won't be for some time, if ever, but...."

"But it's already happened." Aster nodded. "I'm happy to train her, but I'm not sure why you haven't done it."

"For the same reason I couldn't teach her how to ride, and I couldn't teach her how to drive a car." I put a hand on my aching stomach. "My body wouldn't be able to handle the stress."

Aster cocked her head. "Why is that?"

"It's an overprotective parent thing." I snapped my fingers. "Oh, that's right. Helen wanted to do this as an exchange. You train her, she'll train you."

"Train me? On what?"

I smiled. "Horseback riding."

Aster's alabaster skin somehow managed to pale even further. "I'm sorry, what?"

* * *

My name is Lieutenant Kevin Hanson, Shield # 227, St. Louis PD. This is—

The pen stopped, and he drew a line through the previous words.

To the men and women of the Combined Mounted Patrol, this is your brother, Kevin. I'm writing this so—

He crumpled up the page and grabbed a fresh one.

To my brothers and sisters in blue—

Kevin slammed his fist on the table. The impact knocked over his coffee mug, spilling the cold liquid onto the table's polished surface, where it pooled around the sheaf of notebook paper and flowed toward his sidearm. He picked up the pistol and watched as the coffee stained the pages a shade as dark as his mood. He'd wasted the whole damn morning at this table, sipping cold coffee and wasting ink and paper. And what did he have to show for it? Nothing.

Last night he'd turned down an early morning escort duty for a small wagon train headed to the neighboring town of Boonville. He'd done that so he'd have time to prepare everything, and it'd filled him with such a sense of peace that he'd slept like a rock. His first order of business had been to write a letter, and a good one at that. He'd seen too many that were rambling messes, and he didn't want to leave that kind of note behind. But now, the words wouldn't come.

He leaned back in his chair and balanced on the rear legs as he stared up at the textured ceiling of his dorm suite's kitchenette. Who would he write the letter to? His squad was gone. His family was dead. Most of the members of the JMP barely knew him, and a fair number considered him part of the reason why Obsidian had nearly won in its bid to take the city. Would any of them even care to read what he wrote? Would any of the commanders bother to read it publicly?

What about Nathan? His inner voice spoke as if it were addressing him independent of his own thoughts. *He's your friend. You could write it to him.*

He'd considered that, had even started one or two letters meant for his one remaining friend. But the words still wouldn't come. He knew that no matter what he wrote, no matter how much he tried to take the blame, Nathan would take it personally. Kevin could see it in his eyes any time they spoke. It was an expression that took them both back to that fateful evening on the first of May, when he'd tried to talk Kevin out of leaving.

You should've listened to him.

The hole Kevin felt his soul sliding into grew a little wider, a little deeper. His eyes stung, but he didn't have any tears left to shed. He should've listened to a lot of people, but he hadn't, and here he was. The least he could do was make it as easy as possible on the people who seemed to care about him. Brother Stephen, who would be there in a few minutes for their daily social time; Wendy Alexander, who was going through a rough time as well; Danny Ward, who managed to make Kevin laugh despite the dark pit of despair he found himself in; Nathan, with his two children—

Kevin sat up straight, an idea forming in the back of his mind. He took a moment to clean up the spilled coffee and throw out the ruined pages, then he walked into the small living room and sat on the sofa, next to a smaller stack of loose leaf paper. He took one of these pages, set it on the glass coffee table in front of the sofa, and started to write. *"Dear Helen and Jason..."*

By the time a knock came at the door a few minutes later, he was a few paragraphs in and feeling much better. He placed the rest of the notebook paper on top of the mostly full page and rose to answer the door. Brother Stephen stood there, his ever-present Bible case tucked under one arm. He smiled. "Good morning, Kevin. How are you this morning?"

For the first time since their counseling had begun, Kevin returned the smile. "Other than some spilled coffee, pretty well."

Stephen's cheerful expression slipped, and for a moment, Kevin wondered if Stephen was suspicious, if he knew something was up. Then he said, "Sorry to hear about the coffee! That's almost a sin these days. Should we head to the cafeteria and get you some more?"

Relief flooded through Kevin, and he chuckled. "Yes, that would be good. It's been one of those mornings. An extra cup or three wouldn't hurt."

Kevin followed Stephen out the door, toward the cafeteria on the other side of the dorm complex. He squinted at the brightness of the morning sun, but he didn't tear his gaze away from its burning light, not at first. He wanted to savor the sensation, to feel the heat of the sun on his skin. He'd spend as much time outside today as he could, then spend the evening making the last of his preparations.

Tomorrow would be a big day in this Fallen World.

* * * * *

Chapter Seven

I turned Countess off the narrow, paved road onto a driveway made of packed dirt. Acres of rolling grassland lay beyond a white fence, accessible through an open gate halfway up the drive. Two signs hung from the top of the gate: one bearing the name Rock Bridge Ranch, and the other one reading "Est. 2027." I pointed. "See that, Helen? This horse farm is even older than I am!"

Helen rode in front of me in the saddle. She looked up and squinted against the glare of the noontime sun. "No way, Daddy. You're much older than that."

"Than 2027?" I laughed and tapped her forehead. "I was born in 2036, dummy. That makes me nine years younger. This place is forty years old."

"If you say so, Daddy. You're old in my book."

"Wait until you're my age, and see if you say that."

If she makes it to your age.

I tried to squelch the dark thought, but it continued to linger in the back of my mind. I tightened my grip on her abdomen. *She'd make it to my age. To my age and beyond. She had to. She and Jason both had to.*

"Daddy, you're squeezing me!"

I eased up. "Sorry. Don't want you to fall."

Rock Bridge Ranch was situated south of Columbia, set in the middle of what used to be Rock Bridge Memorial Park. JalCom had leveled the entire park, all twenty-three hundred acres of it, and parceled it off as farmland, pastures, and woodland for timber harvesting. Most of the produce had been shuttled off to key JalCom strongholds throughout its territory. With JalCom gone and Teledyne out of the picture, it was imperative we keep these farms up and running, or Columbia would starve. And then there was winter to worry about....

We rode at the head of a small procession of officers, including Patrolman Jones and Corporal Stacey Ferris. Danny and the rest of the Mobile contingent had planned to come with us but then Welliver had called for an emergency supply run to the Combined Arms Conglomerate over in Boonville. Its owner, Elizabeth Erland, had given us many guns after we safely escorted her adult son, Harold, home. We'd distributed a good portion of those weapons among the various mounted units, civilian defenders, and even some of the outlying farms, but with the threat of an approaching army, we needed more.

They wouldn't be arriving empty-handed. Danny was escorting a convoy laden with crops taken from participating farms. These crops would bolster the food stores of both Boonville and our allies at the CAC. I still wasn't sure how that company had managed to stay independent despite the hostile Corporate takeovers of the last several decades. It was a miracle, and one that had helped save Columbia. If we hadn't gotten that first shipment of weapons, we wouldn't have stood a chance against the Corporations in the final battle for the city. Most of the mounted units, ours included, had come to Columbia with a limited number of guns and ammo. We had been there to train, not fight a war.

A white station wagon with fake woodgrain on the sides followed close behind us, its rear packed with guns and ammo. We'd distribute these to the farms around here in case they ran into trouble. Most of the farmers already had hunting rifles and shotguns, but the ones who wanted a bit more armament were welcome to them as thanks for providing the city with so much food, with more yet to come. We also wanted to help the owners of the Rock Bridge Ranch. They had been a sponsor of ours back when we were just visiting for an international mounted officer's convention, and now they continued volunteering their stables, their hay, and even the services of their full-time farrier. He was at the university now, hard at work shoeing horses whose boots were starting to fall apart.

The husband-wife professor team rode in the front of the station wagon, their Remington 870 shotgun and AR-15 rifle suspended between them in a vertical rack. Aster and Corporal Elliott of Section Nine rode in the backseat. Aster's eyes scanned the big farmhouse, the barn, and the stables. She then snapped her attention to the left, and I looked in that direction. Three riders galloped over a hill and raced toward the stables.

I shook my head. I still couldn't believe Helen and I had talked Aster into learning how to ride. Then again, I wasn't sure how the two of them had talked me into letting Helen learn how to fight. Not only in self-defense, but the way Aster fought. The thought of my daughter having to do some of the things I'd seen Aster do frightened me, but at the same time, I thought about the many times my children had nearly been killed. What if Aster hadn't been there for them? What if Helen and Jason had been on their own? No, it made sense. She needed to learn how to defend herself. And Jason did too, once he was a little older.

The world we lived in didn't afford anyone the illusion of safety anymore. If people couldn't protect themselves and the ones around them, they were sitting ducks.

Billy Vargas greeted us at the door to the farmhouse, along with his mother Harriet. I had to admit I liked the kid, even though the father in me wanted to strangle him for befriending my daughter. I didn't care that he was only eleven and she was nine. There was definitely something nefarious in that boy's mind, right? Well, no, probably not, but try convincing a dad of that and see how far you get.

"Mrs. Vargas," I said, "thank you for always taking care of my daughter."

"Oh, it's no trouble at all." Harriet ruffled Billy's hair until he jerked his head away from her. She laughed. "He needs friends close to his age. He even likes hanging out with Jason. It's rare that he finds someone who likes to draw too."

"I didn't know you were into drawing." I looked down at Billy. "What do you draw?"

"Horses, sir. And people, sometimes."

Another thing I liked about him: he was always respectful. He'd go far with that attitude. I slid from the saddle. "Well, what say you and Helen go help out Aster and Elliott while your parents and I discuss some business?"

Aster had gotten out of the car and started to walk toward us when Helen ran up, grabbed her hand, and pulled her toward the stable. "Come on, Aunt Aster! This way! You, too, Mr. Elliott! We'll get a horse picked out for you!"

Aster gave me a pleading look but ultimately let herself get dragged away. Elliott followed along, a bemused smile on his face.

I watched them for a moment, then turned to Harriet. "So, what kind of weapons would you and your husband like?"

"Why not ask him?" She pointed to the trio of horsemen reining in nearby. "Ray! Simon! Lieutenant Ward's here!"

"And he's brought some toys with him, it seems!" an old man called. He hopped off the back of his black-and-white Appaloosa and approached. "Simon Vargas. The strapping young lad over there is my son, Ray. And you've met my daughter-in-law. To what do we owe this sudden gift? Is Terry trying to bribe me so he can win reelection?"

I laughed. "I don't think Sheriff Welliver's the sort of man who cheats, but you're not wrong about it being his idea. See, there's a bit of a situation…."

* * *

Aster let Helen drag her toward the big, white stable to the right of the farmhouse. In her ten years in Teledyne, she'd fought her way into and out of buildings far more imposing than this one: Corporate offices with a sniper or machine gunner in every window, armored trains loaded with augmented soldiers, and secret bunkers filled with Geno-freaks, cyborgs, and the fruits of other hellish experiments. She'd survived all those ordeals, but for some reason this plain building filled her with apprehension. "H-how many horses are in there?"

"We have twenty stalls, though we usually let our horses stay in the pasture unless something's wrong with them or the weather's bad." Billy frowned. "Although we're considering keeping them in more often, with all the rumors of cattle thieves we keep hearing."

She swallowed hard. "And, uh, how are they secured?"

"The stalls are made of wood, and there's a gate."

She'd seen what a horse could do with its legs. Why in the world did these people think a wooden partition would be enough to keep them from escaping their confines?

Behind her, Elliott whistled tunelessly. She resisted the urge to turn around and glare at him. At least *someone* was having fun.

Actually, they all seemed to be having fun, except for her. Helen giggled as she pointed out different things about the building or their surroundings, but Aster wasn't really paying attention. She was too focused on the doom that awaited her in the building.

Why had she ever agreed to this?

At the entrance to the stable, she was assaulted by a combination of odors: the earthy tones of hay, the pungent musk of animals' body oils and saddle leather, the sweet scent of freshly brushed hair, and the stench of manure that hung over the whole place, despite what she assumed were the staff's best efforts to keep everything clean.

Helen tugged on her hand, and Aster realized she had stopped, her boots on the edge of the threshold of the wide set of double doors. "Come on, Aunt Aster. Let's step inside so you can see the horses!"

"Right. The horses." Aster looked down at her feet. She stood in the light, but one step would take her into the relative darkness of the stable. She'd be inside. With the horses. With the big, scary horses that snorted and whinnied and stamped around. She shivered.

Helen tugged again. "Come on!"

"What's the matter, Boss?" Elliott asked. He stepped past her into the stable, then turned around and flashed a cocky grin. "You scared?"

That set Aster's teeth on edge. "I am not!"

To prove herself, she let go of Helen's hand and strode forward into the stable. She turned her head and glared at Elliott as she did so, then turned around once she detected a wall in front of her. She spread her feet wide and crossed her arms beneath her breasts. "See? I'm not scared at all."

Something warm and fuzzy brushed against her cheek. She snapped her head to the side and found herself staring straight into the blue eye of a golden horse. Its jaw opened, revealing a set of flat, white teeth.

Aster sucked in a breath.

* * *

"What kind of weapons do you already have?" I asked Harriet, Ray, and Simon as we stood at the open tailgate of the station wagon. "What would you be comfortable with?"

A frightened shriek tore through the air. The professors ducked behind the left side of the wagon's hood, weapons in hand. I placed myself between the Vargas clan and the stable and reached for my holstered pistol as a white-haired blur shot from the stable and charged in our direction. My mouth fell open. "Aster?" I murmured.

She cleared the hundred or so yards between us and the stable in a few seconds, then leaped over the station wagon in a single bound and slid to a halt behind it. I ran round to where she was and found her on her knees, gasping for air. "Are you all right?" I asked.

From the stable, I heard calls of "Aunt Aster! Come back!" mixed with the laughter of a grown man and a boy.

I remembered how she had reacted when she was face-to-face with Countess outside the university stable, and I tried not to laugh. "What happened?"

"I was attacked," Aster said, her voice lacking its usual calm. She sounded ragged and breathless, like she'd run a marathon. Which, given her conditioning, she could do without so much as breaking a sweat. "By an animal!"

"Did Sunshine get you?" Harriet asked. She shook her head and covered her mouth to hide a smile. "She has a bad habit of playing pranks on people who get too close to her stall."

Aster put a hand on the back of her head. "She grabbed my hair. With her teeth. In her *mouth*."

"That's where teeth are usually stored," I agreed.

She glared at me. "She tried to eat my *hair*."

"It's her way of saying hello," old man Simon assured her. "She's done that with my suspenders, my sunglasses, and my hat. She really likes hats."

"And hair, it would seem," I said.

"Only certain people's hair." Harriet walked around and placed a hand on Aster's head. "Oh, wow, your hair is just the kind she likes. Bright and soft. What kind of conditioner do you use?"

"Whatever I can find," Aster said numbly. She pushed herself back to her feet. As she did, I saw that her usually pale face was flushed pink. She turned and stomped back toward the stable, her arms and back rigid.

"Yay, she's coming back! Aunt Aster, over here!" Helen called.

We watched her go. The professors shook their heads, though from their quiet conversation, it sounded like the wife agreed with Aster about how frightening horses could be while the husband thought it was silly. Harriet pushed a stray strand of hair from her face and said, "Oh, dear. That poor girl is so frightened."

"So frightened she broke a couple of world records getting to this side of the station wagon." Ray shook his head. "Damn, she can move!"

"She's a Specialist," I explained. "They're capable of a lot of things."

"Wait, she's *the* Aster?" Ray's eyes widened. "I've got to get her autograph. She's a legend among us Corporate war historians." He grinned. "I can't wait to tell the others that ol' Sunshine nearly scared the piss out of her."

Aster froze mid-step, and her shoulder muscles tensed.

"A word of advice," I murmured, leaning close. "She can hear you. Specialists have crazy good hearing and eyesight."

"Don't be rude, dear." Harriet gave her husband a playful shove that nearly sent him to the ground.

He laughed. "All right, all right." He cupped his hands together. "Specialist! I meant nothin' by it! But Sunshine doesn't mean any harm! She's the best horse we've got! I hope you and she take to one another!"

Aster didn't acknowledge his comments.

Ray lowered his hands and put them on his hips. "Man, I hope they take to each other. A legend with a legend."

"Legend? Who's Sunshine?"

"If you're the least bit into racing, you'd know her to see her. Her racing name is Golden Slipper."

My eyes widened. "Wait, Golden Slipper, the one who broke Secretariat's top speed? You have *that* horse?"

"Sunshine is the name she was given at birth, and the one she always preferred. She's a spirited animal, but kindhearted. Loves kids and loves those who are afraid of horses, like young Aster there. She likes to play pranks, but it's her way of breaking the ice, of getting them to loosen up a little bit. She also loves to run. If she gets Aster on her back, Aster's going to be in for the ride of her life."

"I'm not sure that's a good thing for the poor Specialist." Nanites could do wonderful things, but could they stop a heart attack? I hoped I wouldn't have to find out.

* * *

"Aren't we a little close?" Helen asked Aster. They stood about twenty feet from the wide berm the Vargas family used for sighting in deer rifles. Shadows cast by thick clouds rolled across the field, giving them relief from the late afternoon sun and its blistering heat. "Daddy's back a lot farther than this when he practices."

"He's been doing this a lot longer than you." Aster reached into her range bag and removed a pack of man-shaped silhouette targets, like the kind the police used. "I'm pretty sure he started this close or even closer when he first shot a pistol."

"She's probably right," Billy called. The boy approached from the direction of the house, with Corporal Elliott a step behind him. "I wasn't out much past ten yards when I first shot my dad's .30-30 lever gun."

"We're going to familiarize you with the gun first," Aster explained. "Let you shoot it a little and not worry about accuracy. Focus on grip, stance, trigger discipline, and not being afraid. That's the key here."

Helen smiled. "Oh, so it's like what you were doing with Sunshine today!"

Aster stiffened. "Yes. Yes, I suppose that's one way of looking at it."

"You did great out there, Miss Aster," Billy said.

"All I did was sit on top of Sunshine," Aster muttered. "You led her around by the lead rope while I did nothing but sit."

"Yeah, but by the end, you were not nearly as stiff in the saddle as you were at first, right? That's a good step."

"It's a *great* step!" Helen threw her arms around Aster's waist. "Thank you for doing it!"

"You heard the instructors, Boss." Elliott grinned. "They'll turn us into equestrians in no time."

"You did well for your first day, too," Billy said. "Next time, we'll let you take the reins yourselves."

Aster's body tensed beneath Helen's arms. "I'm…looking forward to it." She patted Helen's head. "But, for now, it's time for *your* training."

"Let me help you with those, Boss," Elliott said.

Helen and Billy stood back as Aster and Elliott walked up to the berm and stapled three targets to a set of metal frames Billy's family had set up. Once they were satisfied the targets were secure, they walked back to the range bag. "We'll use this bag as our firing line," Aster said as she crouched next to it. "No one steps past this line when we're shooting, all right?"

"Yes, Aunt Aster," Helen said.

"Good." Aster reached into the bag and removed a black pistol. She pulled back on the slide, showed Helen it was empty, then handed it to her. "How does that feel in your hands?"

"Kind of heavy," Helen admitted.

"Let me show you how to hold it." Aster walked her through the proper grip: dominant hand holding the pistol's grip, index finger outside the trigger guard; her left hand closed around her right from the opposite side, almost like they were clasped in prayer; her left thumb tucked up under her right as they both pressed against the left side of the weapon, close to what Aster called the "safety."

"Does that feel better?"

"Yeah, it does." Helen loosened her grip and looked at the writing on the barrel. "Five-Seven?"

"It's the model of the gun, as well as the caliber of rounds it shoots." Aster pulled a magazine from her pocket, popped one of the rounds inside it free, then held it up for Helen to see. "These are 5.7-millimeter cartridges. They're small, but they come out fast and can penetrate soft armor. I sometimes carry explosive tip rounds. They can go through any hard plate, from steel to ceramic."

Helen's eyes widened. "You mean they could penetrate Daddy's armor?"

"Potentially."

"But not likely," Elliott added hastily. "Right, Boss?"

"Oh, um, right. Anyway, I'll fire the first couple rounds so you can get used to the noise." Aster reached into the bag again and removed a few pairs of protective earmuffs. "Put these on."

Helen, Billy, and Elliott each put on a pair. Aster assumed a shooter's stance, weapon raised. "Shouldn't you put yours on too, Aunt Aster?"

"My hearing won't be damaged by this."

"Even so...."

Aster lowered her pistol and looked over her shoulder at Helen. "Well, it wouldn't hurt to do it, I suppose."

Helen smiled. "Safety first!"

Aster reached into the bag and pulled out another pair of earmuffs. She put them on one handed, then resumed her shooter's stance. "Clear to fire?" she asked.

"Clear to fire!" Elliott replied.

She squeezed off one shot. The small weapon let out a big *boom* that echoed across the open space. A hole appeared in the center of the leftmost target. She fired another shot, and a hole blossomed in the silhouette's head.

Aster clicked the safety back on and handed the gun to Helen. "Careful with this," she warned. "I'm sure your father taught you basic gun safety, right? Finger off the trigger until you're ready to fire. Don't point it at anything you don't intend to shoot. And be mindful of what's beyond your target." She pointed. "In our case, it's a dirt berm to catch the bullets as they fly through or past the targets. A bullet from some pistols can travel over a mile before it hits something, and a lot of people inside that mile could potentially be hurt or killed."

Helen nodded. "I've shot BB guns and .22s, but never a real weapon."

"A .22 in the right hands can be as deadly as anything else." Aster held up her hands as if she were holding a pistol. "Now, aim at the center target, click off the safety when you're ready, and squeeze the trigger."

Helen's heart pounded in her chest as she raised the pistol. She stared down the sight like her dad had taught her last year, then pushed the safety lever with her thumb until it clicked. She took a deep breath and willed her hands to stop shaking. When they did, she gently squeezed the trigger.

Boom!

The Five-Seven kicked back with so much force, she screamed and dropped the gun.

Aster was there in an instant, and she caught the pistol before it struck the ground. "Not bad for a first shot," she said. She clicked the safety back on and pointed with her free hand. "See? Look."

Helen's cheeks had grown hot with shame, but she looked. To her astonishment, there was a hole in the center of the silhouette's forehead. "That's right where I was aiming!"

"First, the shot was excellent, even if the follow-through was poor. Second, try not to aim for the head on your first shot." She put a hand on her chest. "Center-of-mass is where you should be aiming unless the head is your only viable target. While a brain shot is almost always a disabling shot, the head is much smaller than the torso. If you hit someone in the lungs, heart, or spine, they're not going to be in the fight for very long." She flicked the safety off and aimed. "Once you're more advanced, we'll have you doing these kinds of drills."

She fired twice into the chest of the leftmost target, paused, then fired once more through its head. "The goal is to neutralize the threat. If the first two rounds won't do it, odds are good he'll be stunned enough so you can aim for a solid head shot to finish him off." She clicked the safety back on and held the pistol out. "Care to try again?"

Helen's wrists ached from that one shot. How did Daddy and Aster and the others do this all the time? She took the Five-Seven and assumed her shooting stance again.

In the end, she emptied the rest of the weapon's twenty-round magazine into the center target. Half of her shots found the silhouette's torso, while the rest went wide. Of the wide shots, all but two stayed on the paper.

"How do you feel?" Aster asked as she took the empty pistol and set it aside to cool.

"Okay, I guess." Helen rubbed her wrists. The Five-Seven snapped so much in her tiny hands, and she wasn't sure if she liked it. "The recoil really hurts."

"You'll get used to it," Elliott assured her. He gave her a thumbs-up. "Nice shooting, kid!"

"Yeah, you did great!" Billy said. "Can I try it sometime?"

Aster smiled. "I brought plenty of ammo. Why don't you each shoot a few more magazines, then I'll show you how to fieldstrip a gun and clean it?"

"I'd like that." Billy hiked a thumb over his shoulder. "Want me to tell Mom and Dad you'll be staying for dinner?"

Aster's stomach growled, long and loud. Helen laughed. "I'd say that's a yes."

"I could eat," Aster admitted.

"When can you not eat, Boss?" Elliott asked. He shook his head. "Where do you store it all?"

A break formed in the cloud cover, and they were bathed in light from a sun venturing lower and lower in the sky. Helen squinted at the light and turned her attention to Aster as the woman reached into her range bag for a fresh magazine. She grinned as a wave of excitement washed over her. By the time Daddy got back, she'd know how to shoot!

She was taking her first steps in learning how to care for herself in this Fallen World.

*****

Chapter Eight

A hot wind blew across the pavement of I-70, carrying with it the clopping of horses' hooves and the creaking and clinking of iron-banded wagon wheels. Danny rode at the head of a small convoy of horse-drawn carts, heading east toward Columbia. With him were twenty-five mounted officers from three departments: Mobile, Miami, and New Orleans. Riding in the wagons were another twelve officers, three in each. The wagon warriors were from the Columbia PD, and each was armed with some kind of select-fire carbine or designated marksman rifle. It was their duty to defend the convoy in case the mounted officers had to ride out to engage a threat.

They had been accompanied by fifteen members of the Boonville Boogeymen, a militia unit that had formed in the absence of a police department after the corrupt sheriff of Cooper County had banished or killed his good officers in a bid to rule the town as some kind of petty lord. The Boogeymen, or B-Men as some people liked to call them, answered to Elizabeth Erland, owner and proprietor of the Combined Arms Conglomerate. Back in June, when Nathan, Danny, and the mounted cops had stirred up a hornet's nest trying to cross the river out of town, ol' Elizabeth had decided this was one fight she and her people couldn't sit out. She'd charged in to provide support, and their joint efforts had caused the citizens of Boonville to go from "Bend the knee and submit" to "Kneel, aim, and fire" in a matter of fast, lead-slinging moments. The sheriff and his so-called Posse hadn't stood much chance after that. Most of them had been rounded up, although the sheriff had vanished into the night like the coward he was. Danny hoped that would be the last they'd ever see of him, but he doubted it. In the old world, people had a habit of turning back up in one's life over and over again. And that had been in a world where people could move anywhere, provided they had the funds and Corporate permission to do so. Now, with so many cities destroyed and so many people killed? There'd be no escaping some people, and bad ones like the "King" of Boonville or Director Lloyd of Obsidian were the sorts to come back again and again.

They'd left the B-Men near the I-70 bridge on a hill that overlooked the bridge and the surrounding area. It was the spot where Nathan and Harold Erland had set up a sniper position and took out some bridge bandits who'd killed one of Sheriff Welliver's deputies in their ambush of the convoy. The B-Men would be up there for the next several days, keeping an eye out for the army Aster had warned everyone about. That was one of the reasons this convoy had been sent to Boonville. Allies didn't leave each other in the dark.

It wasn't the only reason, of course. They were returning loaded down with a lot of valuable goods: more guns and ammo for the police, as well as for some of the university's civilian defenders and the farming families who lived outside town. Everyone would be getting a share, with the bulk of the ammo going to the cops who needed replenishment after expending so much at the Battle of the Span and in the hotel assault.

And to think we were only supposed to be here for a couple of weeks of crowd control and parade training. Danny shook his head. *Hard to believe that was only a couple months ago. Feels like a lifetime.*

"Penny for your thoughts," Wendy Alexander said. The Miami lieutenant had pulled her black mare, Candace, up alongside Noir.

"We don't have pennies anymore. What decade are you from?"

"I'd hit you, but it's not fair for a superior officer to beat a subordinate."

"Who said anything about fair?" Danny spread his arms. "Has anything in the last couple months been the least bit fair?"

"Good point. I'll reserve the right to hit you at a time and place of my choosing, then."

Danny chuckled. "To answer the question that led to this violent turn of discussion, I was thinking about what we would've been up to if not for this mess we're in. All the plans we had, as departments, as families, and as individuals. All of it, gone." He snapped his fingers. "Just like that."

Noir's and Candace's ears flicked at the sound. He ruffled Noir's mane. "Sorry, girl."

"I'd have been at my brother's wedding," Wendy said. "Two weeks ago, in fact. He wanted to get married on a Wednesday, of all things. Can you believe it? A Wednesday."

"What's wrong with Wednesday? It's probably cheaper."

"Yeah, because no one wants it. Who's gonna go to a Wednesday wedding?"

"I don't see a downside." Danny counted off on his fingers. "You save money on fewer guests, you have more of the cake to yourself, and you can get to the main event a lot faster."

"On a belly filled with all that extra cake? Yeah, no thanks." She sighed. "So, yeah, the idiot somehow convinced his fiancée to get married on a Wednesday, and somehow convinced me to help her with the plans. The invitations, the flowers, the table settings, the cake, all of that was on her and me. He buried himself in his work. Said he didn't want to be involved in the planning, other than to make sure his priest did the ceremony."

"Lucky guy," Danny muttered. "Amy had me involved in everything. We spent an entire day looking at invitations, calligraphy pens, and envelopes. An entire day!"

"Yeah, but it worked out, didn't it? The one I received was beautiful."

A wave of melancholy rolled over Danny. "Yeah. Her handwriting was gorgeous." *Along with the rest of her.*

"As was Juniper's," she said. "I took calligraphy in high school, and I couldn't hold a candle to my brother's fiancée's writing." She looked off into the distance, studying the elm and pine trees that loomed large near the highway. "I miss them, Danny. I miss our whole way of life. I fear we're never going to get back to that."

Danny's hand touched the pocket where he kept his dead cell phone. It had been fried by the EMP that went off over Columbia just as the lights of the world went out. Before that happened, he'd received a call from his wife, Amy. He'd spoken with her earlier that morning, briefly, because he'd been out on patrol at the Renaissance fair. Then she'd tried calling again when the alerts went off, and he'd been too busy to answer. He never did find out if she'd left a voicemail because, by the time it would've registered, the missile had already exploded and done its damage.

If he'd known the earlier call would be his last, he'd have spent more time speaking with her.

He shook his head. Amy wouldn't want him to mope, as much as he wanted to. She'd expect him to soldier on, to help Nathan take care of the kids they both saw as their own. "We stand a good chance of turning things around now, Wendy. It won't ever be completely like it was before, but that might not be a bad thing. Not every part of the 'old world' was good, after all. Take Corporate tyranny for example."

"The Corporations are still around, though. They sit on the city council now."

"They always did, but now it's out in the open. And they only have one vote each. The other two belong to civilians who want no part of the Corporations."

"President Oakford's university must have received Corporate funds at some point. I can't imagine he's not beholden to them."

"If he was, I doubt we'd have been allowed to stay on campus as long as we have. I think he's good people." Danny paused. "I mean, as good as people in so-called 'higher education' can be."

Wendy laughed. "Spoken like a true college dropout."

"Why pay for an education when I can get a worldly education in the Corporate military and get paid to do it?"

"When you put it like that, it's so tempting." She shivered. "I don't know how you did it. My experiences with Corporate military types…Well, you know about my experiences."

He did. She'd told him all about the Miami riots of 2057 and how Obsidian had ultimately put them down when local cops hadn't been enough. They'd sent in Agents and a special unit of Geno-freaks known as the Evidence Shredders. The few Genos Danny had met in police life had been regular people, if you could call people who crossed their genes with animals "regular." The Evidence Shredders, though…Well, the rumors weren't good, and what Wendy had told him about the messes they left behind in Miami had verified most of those rumors. Now that he knew his childhood friend Jake had been an Agent, he wondered if Jake had ever been attached to that unit.

"Do you think he was part of that?" Wendy asked. "The Evidence Shredders?"

Danny chuckled. "Damn, girl, this is why you and I nearly got married. Always on the same wavelength."

"My ability to read minds is also what drove us apart. I know what you're thinking before you do, and I don't always like what I see. And I know what you're going to say next, and my response is 'Eyes on the road, Mister. Flattery will get you nowhere.'"

"Yes, ma'am." Danny looked ahead. I-70 stretched off into the distance, the air above the blacktop distorted by rising waves of heat. It wasn't as hot as Mobile could be in the summer, but damned if it wasn't close. At least the sun would set soon. He reached for his canteen. "I don't know if Jake was part of it, and he wouldn't have either, if what Aster told us is true."

"The Unknown Mask, was it?"

"Slipped Mask," Danny corrected. "I don't know much about the Agent program, but my basic understanding of it is that Obsidian takes its augmented soldiers, then uploads their personality into a database so their brain can be imprinted with the personality of another person for a time. In Jake's case, he had a personality imprinted over his own. He was still inside, but his personality was suppressed to make room for the Agent's persona." The thought of his friend being violated this way brought in a trainload of fresh anger and dumped it on the smoldering coals of rage he barely kept in check some days. "All those Corporate bastards need to die," he muttered.

"Even the ones who've been helping us out?" she asked. "I hear Director Greenway and her men have gone above and beyond in helping enforce peace and stability in the city."

"That's only because Obsidian's position is the weakest. Greenway's ally ran off and took a fair number of his troops with him. We killed a bunch of the rest. If we wanted to, we could cut Aster loose in the Country Hotel, and she'd wipe them out like she and her men did to the Ruby gang. Greenway's screwed if she doesn't play ball, and she knows it."

"A reluctant ally is still an ally, just one we'll want to keep an eye on."

Danny opened his mouth to reply, but movement in the distance along Highway 0, which ran perpendicular to I-70, distracted him. "Speaking of keeping an eye on things, what was that?" He removed his binoculars from his saddlebags and peered through them. Next to him, he heard Wendy doing the same thing.

A squat vehicle drove through the shimmering heat waves, its olive drab paint job blending in with the trees but standing out in stark contrast to the blacktop. The vehicle cut beneath I-70 and continued north along Highway 0. "You see that?"

"I think it was a JLTV, the kind the military still uses." Wendy lowered her binoculars. "The *American* military, that is."

A chill ran down Danny's spine. If that were true, this could be the opening moves of that National Guard assault the Ruby gang leader had warned them about. He pointed. "That was the route we were planning to take south. Wanna risk it or risk riding past Teledyne Tower?"

"As much as I dislike the idea of contending with the Tower and any rioters nearby, I dislike the idea of battling an armored vehicle even more. Even if it's only a recon vehicle, we don't have the firepower to bring it down, not easily."

"Agreed. We'll push straight into the city and hope we don't run into any trouble." He looked south in the direction the vehicle had come from. Nathan and Helen would've been in that area earlier today. He hoped nothing bad would happen, at least not until his brother and niece were clear of danger. He touched the pocket holding his phone again and silently prayed for their safety.

* * *

After leaving Aster and Corporal Elliott in the capable hands of Billy and Helen, we spent the rest of the afternoon visiting the neighboring farms to talk to the locals and drop off weapons with anyone who wanted them. No one had anything suspicious to report, other than there being more predatory animals about. A lot of the farmers had started bringing their animals in at night in case the coyotes and wolves figured out that most of the fences were no longer electrified.

Everyone was grateful for the weapons deliveries and the promise of increased patrols. My response to the gratitude was always the same: "Hey, we're grateful for you. Without your hard work, Columbia would starve."

Dinner was being served by the time we returned to the Vargas farm. It had been my intent to head back immediately, before the sun set, but Helen and Billy had been so insistent, and the hamburgers had smelled so good...My stomach growled at the memory, even though I was comfortably full. The food served in the cafeteria was a notch above what I was used to from such places, but nothing beat a home-cooked meal.

We started the return journey late in the evening. The professors led the way, their station wagon idling down the road with the high beams on. It had to pain them both to drive so slowly, but if they had any complaints, they kept quiet about them. From the laughter filtering out of the passenger compartment, it sounded as though Elliott was regaling them with funny military stories.

Helen rode in the saddle with me, just as she had on the way out. Only now, she was nodding off, forcing me to keep an arm hooked around her so she didn't slide off Countess's back. Corporal Ferris and Patrolman Jones rode on either side of me, and the rest of the squad rode slowly behind us.

Aster, against her better judgment it seemed, walked alongside Countess. She didn't do this by choice. She did it because Helen had requested that she help her up into my saddle. Once she had, Helen wouldn't let go of her hand. So, she walked beside me, her left hand raised so she could hold Helen's hand in her gloved fingers. She made a point of looking anywhere but at Countess, so I knew it was bothering her.

"You can always let go, you know," I said quietly. "Helen's asleep."

"I don't mind."

"All the same, you don't have to."

"Really, I don't mind." She glanced at me, then at Countess, then looked away again. "Well, mostly."

I chuckled. "How was your first time riding?"

"It could've gone worse."

"But it could've gone better?"

Aster thought about it for a moment, her eyes aglow in the darkness. "Training can always go better. It was a disaster the first time I tried shooting on a tactical level. Shooting and moving, fixing malfunctions on the fly, switching weapons, all of it had a steep learning curve." She shrugged. "But I managed. With patience, determination, and a good teacher, anything's possible."

"And how does Helen rank as a teacher?"

"Patient." The hint of a smile played on Aster's lips. "She has a lot of patience for one so young."

Says the young lady who's only about a decade older than her. Then again, I wasn't too much past a decade older than Aster, so what leg did I have to stand on? "It'll take some time, but I think you can get the hang of it, provided you can get over your fear of horses."

"I'm not afraid of them," she said in the tone of someone who was tired of the same, old argument.

"Right, right."

We settled into a companionable silence for a few moments. Aside from the clopping of our horses' boots against the pavement and the low rumble of the idling station wagon, the night air was alive with the sounds of buzzing insects, chirping crickets, and nocturnal creatures like owls and frogs. Growing up in cities and suburbs my whole life, I couldn't believe how loud the country could be, especially at night. It made me think of some fantasy novels I'd read, where the heroes would spend the night in a forest so quiet, they could hear a pin drop on the grass. Yeah, right. The only time the countryside would ever be that quiet was if it were winter or something bad was going on that made the animals and insects go to ground.

"How did Helen do with her shooting?" I asked.

"Better than some, worse than others," Aster said, with a glance at the girl to make sure she was asleep. "I want to run her through more pistol drills before we try her on anything more advanced."

"I appreciate that," I said. "And I appreciate your willingness to train her. I know it's good for her to learn how to fight, but I really don't want to be the one to train her." Target shooting for fun was one thing. Learning how to fight and kill?

"The dad in you?"

I chuckled. "Yeah. Hard to break that, you know?"

"My father was the same way." Aster's eyes grew distant. "Always wanted to make sure his kids were safe."

"Kids? You have siblings?"

"I had a younger brother."

My heart sank. "I'm sorry. I shouldn't have—"

"It was a long time ago." She paused. When she spoke again, her soft voice was barely audible. "It was a long time ago, yet I'm still haunted by it."

She looked so vulnerable, less like a trained killer and more like the young lady she could've been had circumstances been different. Of course, she would still be haunted by the deaths of her family members. I started to say as much.

Then I realized I didn't hear any insects or animals anymore.

Gunfire rattled in the distance, somewhere behind us. The noise jolted Helen awake. "What's going on?"

Aster turned. "I hear at least six guns, all around a mile from here." She pointed. "That way."

The only place in that direction was Rock Bridge Ranch. I rode Countess up to the stopped station wagon and helped Helen off the saddle. "Go with the professors," I instructed.

"But—"

"No buts! Get in so the professors can get you back to the university. It's too dangerous out here."

Helen obviously didn't like it, but she knew what to do when I switched on my "command" voice: obey, without question. She opened the passenger door and climbed inside.

Elliott started to get out, but Aster stepped up to his side of the wagon. They conferred quietly, and when Aster came back from the other side of the vehicle, she was carrying her FN-P90 and a magazine pouch that she slung over her shoulder. "He'll ride back with them. I'm coming with you."

"Makes sense to me." I leaned over and extended a hand. "Come on, up you go."

She stared at me. "What?"

"Climb up. You can ride behind me."

"I can run—"

"And be out of breath when we get there? Look, I know how fast Specialists can move, but even you need to catch your breath, right?"

She hesitated. Behind her, the professors' station wagon sped off into the night, the rear window rolled down so Elliott could poke his weapon barrel out as he scanned for threats on the left. Knowing the professor's wife, her AR-15 was hanging out the front passenger window, as well. I also had no doubt the professor had his hand on his 1911 in case he needed to shoot from the driver's seat. For a couple of civilians, they knew how to watch their sectors.

More shots rang out from the direction of the farm, and that seemed to wake Aster up. She grabbed my hand and then pulled herself into the saddle, using me as an anchor. I grunted. I still wasn't used to the weight of a Specialist.

She settled behind me. "Here, wrap an arm around me," I said.

"Why?"

"So you don't get thrown off."

"I'll be fine."

I shrugged. "Suit yourself." I nudged Countess forward at a walk. Countess, unused to the extra weight, started forward at a jolt. Behind me, Aster squeaked, and two arms snaked around my midsection and squeezed tight enough to make my ribs creak. "Aster, ease up a little," I whispered.

She loosened her grip so I could breathe again. "Okay, we're going to get up to a gallop. Hold on, but try not to squeeze my internal organs out, all right?"

"Sorry."

Jones shook his head. "Never thought I'd see the day when our very own Battle Flower was as scared as a little rabbit."

"I'm not scared!" Aster snapped. "Put me in front of an enemy, and I'll be fine."

Corporal Ferris laughed. "You heard the lady. Let's go!"

I got Countess up to a trot and then a canter. Each time, Aster's grip on me tightened but then loosened just in time for me to increase Countess's speed. By the time we reached a full gallop, Aster seemed to have calmed down as much as she was going to. I thought I heard her mumbling to herself, but with the wind I couldn't quite make it out. She was naturally quiet unless she was using her command voice. Add a whispering mumble, and she was practically inaudible, except maybe to dogs or Countess.

The sound of approaching hooves rose over the gunfire, and a herd of horses galloped around a bend in the road and raced past us, their frightened cries trumpeting through the night air. "Someone must've let them loose!" Ferris shouted.

Light blossomed ahead through the trees, and at first, I thought the Vargas clan had turned floodlights on so they could better engage targets out in the open fields around their home. It wasn't until we turned a bend in the road that I could see the real reason why: the farmhouse and stables were on fire.

Behind me, Aster tensed. "Who would do such a thing?" she growled. "Those are good people!"

I was just as angry, but right now, I needed to focus on the scene. "You've got the best eyes here," I said, raising my voice so my companions could hear me. "What do you see?"

Aster leaned forward until her head rested on my shoulder. At any other time, I might've been uncomfortably aware of how close her very attractive body was to mine, but we had a job to do. "Muzzle flashes in the field and woods behind the house. Someone is upstairs in the house as well, shooting down into the field to the west. There's a body on the front porch, and another in the yard. There's also someone right outside the stable. He looks too small to be an adult."

Damn. That was probably Billy. We'd last seen him heading into the stable to give Sunshine a brushing and feeding. I prayed he was alive, along with the others. "Lord, give me strength," I whispered.

"You even pray before a fight?"

She'd turned her head so she could look sidelong at me. "When is there a better time to pray than before a fight? When I need God most, I won't have time to pray. Better to do it now, while I've still got a clear head."

We galloped down the last stretch of road until we raced underneath the open gate. The flames from the manor house cast the sign in silhouette, so the words were no longer visible. I reined in close to the body Aster had sighted. It was Ray Vargas. Half his head was missing. His remaining eye stared up into night sky, but he had clearly gone on to the next world, and he had likely been ignorant of the sniper's round that had sent him there.

"Movement, LT!" Jones shouted. He pointed into the darkness beyond the burning house.

Rounds zipped past us. Countess danced sideways, and Aster once again tightened her grip on my midsection, but her tone held no fear as she said, "I see them." One of her arms pulled away, and suddenly I saw her FN-P90. "I'll take care of them."

"Let's do it together. H'yah!" I kicked Countess back into a gallop, and we raced along the same field Aster and Sunshine had ridden through earlier in the afternoon. I couldn't make out much of anything on the ground, so I trusted Countess's night vision to carry us along without stumbling into any pitfalls.

I spotted movement in front of us; it looked like a soldier in combat armor. He took a knee and aimed his rifle toward the manor house as more shots rang out behind us. Aster lined up her P90 and fired a short burst. The man clutched his ruined throat and collapsed.

More enemy soldiers appeared in the darkness. Aster shifted her aim and fired again and again. Jones, Ferris, and the others fired their shotguns and rifles as they raced along behind us. The enemy returned fire, but it was sporadic and poorly aimed. They hadn't been expecting reinforcements to show up so soon.

Aster continued to pour lead on the enemy soldiers, reloading twice in a matter of seconds. "Doesn't that barrel get overheated?" I shouted.

"Not for something this minor." She sprayed half a magazine into the distant tree line. "I've got a cooling pack for longer engagements."

I judged that we'd run in one direction long enough, so I wheeled Countess around and raced back toward the burning manor. Aster and my officers continued to exchange fire with more of the soldiers. "Can you identify them?" I yelled. "Are they Obsidian or Teledyne?"

"They're enemies." She fired her P90 until it ran dry again. "Reloading!"

A figure rose in the tall grass between the house and the stable and pointed his weapon our way. I tried to draw my pistol, but Jones fired his shotgun. The man staggered as a rifle slug struck him. Before he could recover, Aster finished reloading and brought him down with a short burst. He disappeared in the grass.

"They're retreating!" Ferris called.

"Affirmative but be careful." Aster twisted in the saddle, so she was aiming back toward the tree line. "They could be regrouping for another attack."

We rode back toward the gate and around to the front of the house. I saw movement in one of the upstairs windows. "That you, Nathan?" a voice called.

"Simon!" I cupped my hands around my mouth. "Are you all right, sir?"

"All right? These bastards murdered my family and butchered my horses! Do you think I'm all right?" There was a pause. "Did you kill them?"

"As many as we could. The rest ran off. Sir, we need to get you down from there!"

"The stairs are on fire! I can't get down."

"Then you'll have to climb out of a window. We can help!" I started to slide from the saddle.

"Movement in the stables!" Ferris shouted.

We turned toward the stables. A bulky silhouette appeared out of the inferno. Aster gasped. "It's Sunshine."

After a moment, the horse moved into the light cast by the manor house blaze. It *was* Sunshine, but she was walking backward. Her head was low to the ground, like she was dragging something. A bundle?

Aster dropped from the saddle and ran. I kicked Countess forward and rode over. Aster reached Sunshine before I did. The horse had suffered minor burns on her body, and the bundle she was dragging was Billy Vargas. The boy was pale and unmoving, and blood soaked the front of his shirt. Aster knelt and examined him. "He's been shot, but he's still breathing."

I reached into Countess's saddlebags and removed a first aid kit. I tossed it to her. "Get some QuikClot on that wound."

Aster got to work. Sunshine hovered over them, her face inches from Billy and Aster. If the Specialist was frightened by the horse's close proximity, she showed no outward sign. "Come on, Billy. Stay with me."

"What's going on over there?" Simon Vargas called. "Is it Billy?"

I spun Countess around and rode toward the house. "Simon, we're going to get you down from there!"

"Never mind me! Is Billy all right?"

"Aster's working on him! He's been shot, but he'll be fine if we get him to the hospital!"

"Then don't stick around here, trying to help an old man!" He made shooing motions with his hand. "Go! Get out of here!"

Shots rang out from the trees. Jones, Ferris, and the others returned fire. Simon picked up his rifle and ran around to the far side of the house. "Just go! I'll hold them off!"

The distinctive sound of his hunting rifle boomed again and again as the old man shot into the tree line. Rounds zipped past Aster, but she was so focused on treating Billy, she didn't notice. Even Sunshine didn't seem to care; she just flicked her ears in one direction or another as bullets landed next to her in the dirt.

Once she was finished, Aster picked up Billy and cradled him in her arms. Sunshine bumped her broad nose against the boy's face, then did the same to Aster. Aster retreated a step, then stepped forward long enough to touch her forehead to the horse's. "We'll get him help," she promised.

Sunshine snorted.

To me she said, "We'll go on ahead. You get Mr. Vargas—" Her eyes widened as she stared past us. "We need to go. We need to go now!"

That wasn't like her. I opened my mouth to ask why—

The top floor of the manor house exploded. Simon Vargas was flung into the yard, his body a broken, burning mess. Off in the distance, I heard the loud rumbling of an engine. "What the hell is that?" Jones shouted.

"It's a tank!" Aster turned and started running. "We need to go, now!"

I took one last look at the scene, including the bodies of Simon, Ray, and Harriet up on the front porch. Whoever was responsible would pay.

But not tonight. We couldn't do anything against a tank. I couldn't see it, but I didn't doubt Aster's eyesight. I kicked Countess into a gallop. "Follow me! To home!"

* * *

We were once again in the university auditorium that had been Sheriff Welliver's command and control center since the beginning of this whole mess. Danny, Cassandra Martinez, Wendy Alexander, Lieutenant Blackwood, Aster, and I sat or stood in the gallery while Graham, Welliver, and Captain Hsu sat at the table in the room's center, a map of the city and the surrounding area spread out before them. The map had been printed on material that allowed us to write on it with dry erase markers, and we had broken up the city into sections that fluctuated on a weekly or daily basis. Sections the city or mounted police controlled were outlined in green; sections the Corporations or private citizens like Jay Dawson held were outlined in blue; areas with a lot of unrest were outlined in yellow; and a few tiny no-go zones were outlined in red.

The map had been expanded, and a second table had been added, to show the territory beyond the city limits, from the farm country to the south and west to the suburban sprawl that had crept toward the north and east. Green army men and trucks taken from one of Welliver's grandkids rested on different points of the map, guarding major roadways and some back roads that flowed from the city limits.

Captain Hsu stood up, a remote control in his hand. He pointed to the projector screen above the map table. "This is the audio and video transmission that was broadcast on all public frequencies and a few encrypted ones."

He clicked the controller, and the image of a man in olive drab ACUs appeared on the screen. He was seated at a camp table, with his cap resting on its polished surface. He was flanked on either side by American flags in vertical stands. I found that surprising. Any time I'd seen an address by a political or military officer, a Teledyne or Obsidian flag had been present alongside the American flag. Which Corporate flag it was depended on which area of the country the broadcast was coming from.

"This is Colonel Eastman, formerly of the 32nd MP Battalion of the Missouri National Guard. Currently, I am commander of the Homeguard, which is comprised of brave patriots from Arkansas, Mississippi, and Missouri. Recently deployed to Fayetteville, Arkansas, we returned once we heard about the ongoing troubles in Columbia."

"Once Fayetteville was nuked, you mean," Martinez muttered.

I couldn't help but agree. I remembered the map in city hall's command bunker. Fayetteville had vanished only moments before our power was cut. It was likely the 32nd MPs had fused with whatever guard units had managed to escape the nukes, and they'd made tracks for Columbia. Maybe they'd been watching as the nukes fell and noticed we'd shot down a few before the EMP took us down. What would have delayed them from coming back, though? Fayetteville was a few hundred miles away, with Springfield between it and Columbia. It had been nuked hard, which could account for some of the delay.

"To all the good citizens of Columbia," Colonel Eastman continued, "I say this: the United States is here for you. We are here for you. We stand ready to throw off the shackles of Corporate rule and return things to the way they once were when the people ruled themselves. To that end, we demand all combatants within the city surrender. Obsidian and Teledyne have no place in the future as organizations, but as individuals you may be able to serve. That is only if you surrender to either the local authorities or to my unit. Continue to resist—as you did late last night—and you will be met with extreme prejudice."

Anger flashed through me. "Is he talking about us?"

"We are liberators, not invaders. Rescuers, not occupiers. We do not wish to enter the city and attack it, but neither will we continue to allow Corporate soldiers to run free to menace you or your neighbors in the outlying farming communities. We—"

Hsu paused the transmission. "And it just keeps going, on and on and on."

"Are all your military officers this long-winded?" Graham asked.

Welliver chuckled. "Depends on how much an officer fancies a life in politics."

"This was first broadcast around ten hours ago," Hsu said. "You can imagine how well-received it was by the good citizens of Columbia."

I grimaced. Given the current climate within the city, I could very well imagine.

"The good news is not many citizens have working radios or televisions, so not many of them heard it. The bad news is some did, and they're spreading the word. And Lord knows how fast rumors spread, even in bad times."

"Especially in bad times," Welliver corrected. He looked toward us. "Lieutenant Alexander, you and Sergeant Ward caught sight of one of their vehicles, correct?"

"We think so, sir." Alexander stood. "We can't say for sure because it was far off, but it looked like an old Joint Light Tactical Vehicle in olive drab."

"The 32nd MPs would've had a few of those," Welliver said. He frowned. "I can't say I remember a Colonel Eastman, though. Nor do I think a battalion would be commanded by a colonel."

"He looked rather young for someone of that rank," Graham said.

"Could've been a field promotion, sir," Danny offered. He looked at me and shrugged. "It's how I wound up with sergeant's stripes before my time in Obsidian's service ended."

Martinez raised her hand. " Do we know how many of them there are?"

Welliver stroked his beard with his good hand. "The 32nd would've left here with nearly four hundred MPs plus noncombatant staff. It wouldn't surprise me if they suffered casualties when the bombs fell, but it's better to assume they're at full strength."

Hsu swept a hand over the map. "These troop positions were taken from reports given to us by our patrols, concerned citizens, and Corporate allies like Specialist Aster and her team."

"We estimate their numbers are close to twelve hundred," Aster said, her quiet voice somehow carrying throughout the wide room. "They're also in possession of a small number of vehicles: transport trucks, fuel tankers, JLTVs, Humvees, a Stryker command vehicle, and one main battle tank."

Danny whistled into the silence that befell the room. "A tank? Sounds like what Obsidian St. Louis threw at us, but on steroids."

"Yeah, it wasn't much fun," I said. "And we weren't even the ones getting shot at, not directly."

"They've taken over key positions around the city." Hsu pointed at the locations of the toy trucks. "They pushed our officers out of the fuel depot east of town, and they've set up what we think is a headquarters smack in the center of the southern farmland."

That was close to where the Three Rivers Renaissance Fair was located. "What of Richard Cates and his people?"

"We've received word that they've relocated, but they haven't said where yet." Hsu pointed at a couple of forested areas close to where the fair had been. "Somewhere around here, we guess. By all reports, most of them made it to their hideout without any interference from the so-called Homeguard, although a few stragglers had their weapons confiscated before they were sent on their way."

While I couldn't agree with citizens being stripped of their arms, that they weren't imprisoned or killed spoke a lot about the force we were dealing with. Then I remembered what happened to the Vargas clan, and my anger returned. "What of our people? Have we had any further clashes with them?"

"Several." Hsu frowned. "Any attempts to run patrols out of town have been met with force, from simple warning shots to deadly attacks. So far, we haven't suffered any deaths, but a few of my officers from the Philadelphia PD were wounded by machine gun fire, and their animals had to be put down."

"Bastards," Martinez muttered.

"They're not advancing into the city, which is a blessing for the moment." Welliver swept his left arm around the map on the table. "They've taken up positions around the city and are waiting us out."

"A siege, then," Alexander murmured. "Just like in '57, only instead of us boxing in rioters, we're the ones getting boxed in."

"We'll have to plan our next steps carefully," Welliver said. "We are in a more defensible position, but that's only as long as the food holds out, which won't be long with the farms under their control."

"We need more information." Graham pointed at the map. "Firm numbers on their strength, where their people and vehicles are typically stationed, how much fuel they have access to, and anything else we can learn."

Aster stood. "My men and I will carry out reconnaissance. We'll also link up with the Three Rivers people if we can."

"Thank you, Specialist." Welliver looked around the room. "As for the rest of you, return to your posts, but be vigilant. I expect things in the city to heat up over the next several days, worse than they already have. And that's the last thing we need in this Fallen World."

* * * * *

Chapter Nine

"I'm sorry we couldn't see your friend, Helen," Brother Stephen said as the two of them walked out of the campus hospital's main entrance.

"It's okay." Helen pressed her straw hat against her blue blouse. She forced her fingers to relax so she didn't crush the hat. It had been a handmade gift from Billy's grandpa. "The doctors are still working on him, right?"

"They are. No visitors for patients in critical condition. Not even police chaplains, but that's a good sign. If they don't want a man of God, then it means they don't think it's Billy's time yet." He smiled faintly. "I don't think it's his time yet, either. I'm hopeful."

Helen bit her lip. She didn't feel very hopeful right now, not after what had happened to Billy and his family. Tears leaked from her eyes, and she sniffled to keep the snot in. Why had they been attacked like that? "They were good people, Brother Stephen."

He patted her head with a big, gentle hand. "They were, Helen. They were."

"Why did they have to die? Why didn't God protect them?"

Stephen's expression grew pained. "Bad things sometimes happen to good people. God protects the souls of His faithful, but not always their bodies. Sometimes…." He sighed. "Sometimes there are no easy answers."

Helen closed her eyes and stifled a sob. She'd cried herself to sleep last night, and she'd cried again after she and Stephen hadn't been allowed to visit Billy. She didn't feel like crying anymore, nor did she feel like going back to the dorm. Daddy was in another of his meetings, and Jason was with Aunt Wendy. If she went back, she'd be by herself, and she couldn't take that right now. She needed company. "Would you stay with me?" she asked. "At least until Daddy gets back?"

"I won't be able to stay for long." Stephen checked his watch. "I'm meeting Lieutenant Hanson for morning coffee in a little while."

Kevin Hanson was the officer who always looked so sad to Helen. She didn't know what was weighing him down but looking at him always made her worry. *Are my eyes like that now?* They had looked red and puffy in the mirror a few minutes ago, so maybe he was as sad as she, if not worse. She wouldn't wish this feeling on anyone, let alone someone she and Daddy cared about. "Can I come with you?" she asked.

Stephen hesitated. "Well, chaplains usually go on their own to these kinds of meetings. Sometimes the things we talk about with our officers are confidential."

"Just for a little while, then." Now that she'd decided, she was determined to go through with it. "I won't be a bother. I'll say hi, see how he's doing, then head back to the dorm if he doesn't want me around. Okay?"

"Oh, very well." Stephen smiled. "Let's see if we can't brighten up his morning with a cheerful face."

He started to pinch her cheek but tickled her neck instead. She giggled and pushed him away. "There we go!" he said. "That's better. Greet him with a smile, and you're sure to put him at ease."

Helen grinned. She still felt sad and a little hollow but focusing on someone else's pain helped put her own in perspective. She couldn't do anything to help Billy, other than pray for him. She might be able to help Kevin. "I'll do my best! Let's go get him some of Mrs. Brown's cookies!"

Stephen laughed. "An excellent idea."

* * *

Kevin placed the last letter on the coffee table. He'd managed to write three, all of them neatly folded so the "Dear" line was clearly visible. He'd finished his letter to Helen and Jason last night and then felt inspired to write a letter of apology to Stephen. He would most likely be the one to find him when the deed was done. The last letter was addressed to his children, and it contained only a single line: "I'll be with you soon, Lord willing."

As he thought about that, a wave of grief crashed into him. He really didn't know if he'd be with them soon. They were in Heaven with their mother. Would he have a place there?

He picked up his sidearm and turned to the bedroom. Had his weapon always been this heavy? He'd carried it for years and never noticed, but it really had some weight to it, like it wanted to drag him down to the floor. He set it on the nightstand and surveyed the bed. He'd stripped off the comforter and sheets and stuffed them in the closet. He'd then draped a plastic sheet over the bare mattress. A good mattress was going to be hard to reproduce the way things were, and he didn't want to ruin a perfectly good one with his blood.

His dress uniform hung from a hook in the closet. It'd be the first thing anyone saw when they opened the door. Pinned to it was a note requesting that it be given to someone it would fit. He'd heard from Nathan that they were considering training a class of recruits, so maybe it would go to a rookie. Until someone opened a tailor shop big enough for everyone, uniforms would be hard to come by. Same with medals and ribbons. He wanted those repurposed.

If he couldn't help the unit with his life, he could at least make sure his passing was as beneficial as possible. Besides, what difference did it make how he was dressed? It's not like there'd be an open viewing.

He checked his watch. It was almost time for Brother Stephen's arrival.

* * *

Helen and Brother Stephen walked along the paved pathway that led from the dorm complex's cafeteria to the building Uncle Kevin stayed in. Stephen carried a bag of Helen's favorite cookies, fresh from Mrs. Brown's oven. The bag was open so the cookies wouldn't get soggy from condensation, and the smell of baked dough and chocolate chips made her mouth water. She couldn't wait to dig into them, and she hoped Uncle Kevin would like them.

Her smiled faded. "Brother Stephen, is everything all right with Uncle Kevin?"

"Why do you ask?"

Helen squatted down next to a patch of yellow wildflowers growing in the increasingly weed-choked grass. She stroked the petals on the tallest flower. "He just seems…sad. Really sad."

"A lot of the officers are sad these days." Stephen knelt next to her, so they were eye-to-eye. "Lieutenant Hanson's a bit sadder than most right now. He's lost a lot."

"His family's gone, right?" Helen blinked back tears. "Just like Billy's?"

"Yes, his family and his squad." Brother Stephen hesitated, then added, "It would be like if your father lost you and Jason and your Uncle Danny and then lost everyone under his command, too."

"That's awful!"

"Yes. And that's why your father and I are trying to cheer him up as much as we can. He needs it. The rest of the officers need it, too, but his case is especially important. We don't want…Well, we want him to be happy."

Helen didn't like the way he hesitated with that last statement. He was hiding something from her, like the adults always did. She wanted to challenge him, but it wouldn't do any good. Instead, she put on her best smile and said, "I want that, too. Think these cookies will help?"

Stephen chuckled. "When have cookies not helped?"

Helen plucked one wildflower and then another. "Flowers will help as well, won't they?"

"They can't hurt, unless he's allergic."

"He won't be allergic to the sight of them. I can always give them to Daddy afterward."

"Isn't your father allergic?"

"Yeah, but he won't mind if I'm the one who gets him all sniffly."

"Ah, I see." Stephen set the bag of cookies on the sidewalk and checked his watch. "We have a few minutes, so let me help you. We'll make sure Lieutenant Hanson gets a big bunch of flowers."

Helen grinned. "Yeah!"

* * *

Kevin turned the pistol toward his face and looked down the barrel. The range officer in him screamed the rules of gun safety like a mantra, but he ignored the pleadings as his nostrils took in the earthy scent of gun oil and the strange fragrance of Hoppes #9 bore solution. He never could quite place the familiar smell, but Rebecca had clued in on it immediately the day she found him in the garage, cleaning his duty pistol and backup gun. She'd sniffed the air and wrinkled her freckled nose. "Why does it smell like banana liqueur in here? Are you trying to give me flashbacks to our honeymoon?"

He chuckled at the memory, even as tears stung his eyes. They'd gotten sick off banana daiquiris at the resort in Aruba to the point that Rebecca couldn't touch the stuff except once a year, on their anniversary. Then she'd have one "for old time's sake" and swear it off until the next time. They'd planned to go back to Aruba for their tenth anniversary, but finances had been too tight, so they'd agreed to hold off until their fifteenth. That would've been this year. This month.

The tears spilled down his cheeks as he opened his mouth and slid the pistol's barrel in. The weapon's front sight dug into the roof of his mouth, and his tongue tasted cold steel. He started to put his finger on the trigger, then jerked it back outside the guard. His breath came in ragged gasps, and he tried to calm his fluttering heart.

Images of his kids flashed through his mind. The boys, first as infants and then at their current—no, their *final* ages. James would've turned five August 28th, the day after his and Rebecca's anniversary. Gabe would've been nine November 19th, and Cody wouldn't have turned twelve until next year, on February 2nd. A little man, that one. Always the mature one, always taking care of his younger siblings, even when they drove him crazy.

He hoped James and Gabe weren't aggravating Cody too much on the other side.

Kevin's front teeth hurt, and he realized he was biting down on the gun. He relaxed his lower jaw and took a deep breath, held it, and let it out slowly. The breath was a shudder, and his body was wracked with silent sobs.

Memories of Rebecca rose in his mind next. Such a beautiful, caring woman. She was funny and charming, and she loved sports and sci-fi, a winning combination in his estimation. Her favorite series had been Kevin Steverson's *Salvage Title Universe*, although he guessed part of that was because he shared his first name with the author. Regardless, she had burned through his collection of Steverson's novels, and ripped through the spin-off series by Rath and Smith, and the *Smugglers'* stories by Roberts and Woods. She'd been just as excited as he was when they'd announced live-action and anime versions of the stories.

Why was he thinking about something so silly now, of all times?

Because that was his wife. Whatever she loved, she loved to the fullest. Books, TV shows, football, their sons, him. She'd deserved so much more than what he had provided for her in the time they were together, and it had been his intent to repay her several times over in the future.

And now he couldn't do that. He couldn't bury her, and he couldn't continue living as she would have wanted him to. Because he was weak.

The despair returned, washing away the warmth and love he'd been feeling. He was going to fail her again when he squeezed that trigger. But what choice did he have? What was left for him here?

Better to get this over with now before you lose your nerve completely.

He took a steadying breath. Yes, it needed to be now or not at all.

No sooner had he willed his finger to lift off the slide of the gun than the doorbell rang. He jumped, and his finger jerked harmlessly against the slide.

Do it now, the voice in his head urged. It's Brother Stephen. He'll be the first to find you, just like you wanted.

"Uncle Kevin!" a young voice called.

Kevin froze. *Helen*. Why was she out there?

"Uncle Kevin, it's Helen and Brother Stephen! We've come to visit you!"

He pulled the pistol from his mouth. It slid from suddenly numb fingers and struck the floor with a clatter. Shit, he couldn't do it now. Stephen would bust down the door, and he wouldn't be able to stop Helen. She'd come in and find him on the bed, his brain splattered on the wall behind him, his eyes staring sightlessly up at the ceiling. What would that do to a poor girl like her? Christ, she was about Gabe's age! How would he have reacted if he saw his dad like that?

The doorbell rang again. "Uncle Kevin!"

"Shh, Helen," Stephen warned. "Maybe he's sleeping."

Yes, that's right, he thought as a dark hope surged into him. *Go away so I can do this*. He'd wait fifteen minutes, and then—

"Nuh-uh! I heard him move around!" The bell rang again. "Come on, Uncle Kevin! Rise and shine!"

Get rid of her, the voice in his head snarled. *Chase her off*.

Suddenly angry, he picked up the pistol and dropped it on the bed, then stomped toward the door. He rubbed his eyes and said, "I'm coming!" in what he hoped was a cheerful voice.

He undid the latch and opened the door partway. Brother Stephen stood there in his chaplain's uniform, while Helen stood next to him in a blue blouse and a denim skirt. She wore a straw hat to protect her fair cheeks from the sun's rays. It was early morning, but heat already rose off the pavement of the circular driveway beyond the park. Several students and off-duty officers lounged on the picnic benches, enjoying breakfast outside.

"Lieutenant Hanson, I hope we didn't interrupt something important," Stephen said, although from the look of concern in his eyes, Kevin wasn't sure the good chaplain meant it.

"Uncle Kevin, are you all right?" Helen had initially greeted him with a grin that was bright, even in the shadow of her hat, but it had quickly faded to a slight frown. "You look like you've been crying."

He reflexively scrubbed his eyes. "What? No. I was up late and didn't get much sleep, that's all. That makes my eyes red."

"We were hoping you could have breakfast with us," Helen said. "And then maybe we can play!"

"She says breakfast, but it's actually just cookies." Stephen held up a paper bag, and a smile danced on his lips. "I mean, I'm not complaining, but if you want something more wholesome, we could go to the cafeteria."

Kevin's hands trembled. *Get rid of them, before you lose your nerve.* A numbness crept over him, washing away his anger and pushing down any other emotions. "That sounds great, but I'm really not hungry."

"Everyone's got room for cookies!" Helen snatched the bag from Stephen and opened it. "Mrs. Brown made them! Shortbread, chocolate chip, oatmeal raisin; what's your pick?"

"Really, I'm not hungry, Helen. Maybe later."

"You know what, I'm not hungry either." Helen tossed the bag back to Stephen, who struggled to catch it. She smiled. "Let's just play then! We can play hide and seek, or maybe walk over to the swing sets. Last time you were in Mobile, you pushed Jason and me so high, we thought we'd fly right off!"

Had he really done that? Christ, that was a lifetime ago. He gripped the doorknob. "Sorry, I'm really not in a playful mood right now."

"Then how about we just talk?" Helen took a step forward. There was something wrong with her smile, or maybe her eyes. She put a hand to her chest. "I can tell you about Aunt Aster's first ride yesterday, and how much it scared her. Jason really finds that funny, and who wouldn't? A woman as strong and tough as Aster scared by a horse? What in the world?"

Helen's incessant talking set his teeth on edge. "Maybe another time, Helen."

"Lieutenant Hanson, are you sure we can't get you outside for a bit?" Now Stephen was concerned. He knew something was wrong, and he was trying to prevent it from getting worse.

Kevin couldn't let that happen. "Maybe another time," he repeated. He started to close the door again.

"Don't close that door!"

Helen's piercing shriek startled Kevin. He let the door swing back open as he leaned against the doorframe, his mouth agape.

Tears ran down Helen's cheeks as she clutched the hem of her skirt with both hands. "If you close that door, you'll never open it again!"

Kevin's eyes widened. "What are you talking about?"

"Don't play dumb!" Helen sniffled. "It's just like with Lieutenant Menton! It's just like with Daddy's friend!"

Brother Stephen gasped. "Helen, how do you know about that?"

"Because Daddy told Mommy about it!" Helen let go of the hem of her skirt so she could rub her eyes. She glared at Stephen. "He said he went to see Lieutenant Menton because he was sad, but he wouldn't let Daddy inside the house. He told him, 'Maybe another time,' and closed the door in Daddy's face." Her face scrunched up, and fresh tears spilled out of her eyes. "A half hour later, *he was dead!*"

Stephen reached for her, but she shook him off. "I've never seen Daddy cry before, but he cried then. Right in Mommy's lap. He said, 'If only I'd stayed with him, he'd still be alive. If only I'd said something, he'd still be alive. If only I'd done something, *he'd still be alive.*'" Helen's lower lip trembled as she glared at Kevin. "I don't want Daddy to cry again, and that's what'll happen if you die!"

Kevin stared at her, his insides numb. This was exactly the kind of situation he'd wanted to avoid. That was why he wrote the letter. If she'd read it, she'd understand. She'd understand this was the only way.

But was it the only way? Hadn't he asked God for a sign, some way out that didn't involve him squeezing the trigger? Could Helen be that sign, that way out?

No, it isn't that simple. Life is never that simple.

The dark voice beckoned from the shadows of his soul, urging him to shut the door and get on with it. And for a moment, he was tempted. He grabbed the doorknob and tensed his arm to slam it shut.

And then Kevin remembered something Rebecca had told him a few months back, as they were planning their fifteenth anniversary trip back to the land of banana daiquiris. They'd put their boys to bed and had gone to the living room to catch an episode of a new spin-off in Kevin Steverson's *Salvage Title Universe*, a space cop show about two crime-fighting bombshells known as NightLight.

Just before the opening credits, she had turned to him and said, "What do you think about having a daughter?"

"We've had nothing but boys so far," Kevin had said with a laugh. "You really want to play those odds again?"

"I think God will give us a daughter if we really want one."

He'd pulled her into his arms. "Well, I'm never opposed to trying. What would you name her?"

Rebecca had smiled at him. "I've always been partial to Helen."

Kevin's knees buckled, and he sank to the floor. The cool tile felt strange against his warm legs. He shivered, and he wasn't sure if it was from the sensation of the tiles or the realization of how close he'd come to killing himself. Something inside Kevin cracked open, and warmth began to spread through him. Before he realized it, tears were streaming down his cheeks. He opened his mouth to say something, but only a strangled sob came out.

Helen ran forward and threw her arms around his neck. Their tears mingled as she pressed her cheek to his. "You're not alone," she whispered. "You're never alone."

Stephen knelt and pulled them both into an embrace. Tears glistened in his eyes, as well, but his voice was full of strength as he said, "Amen, Amen, and Amen."

Kevin cried like a baby in the open entryway of his dorm. People who had been sitting or standing in the park had looked their way when Helen started screaming, and a crowd had gathered. Normally, that would have embarrassed him, but he didn't care. All he cared about was the sense of relief, the feeling of the weights being lifted off his shoulders one by one.

He was still a mess on the inside, and he knew from experience with friends and family that he had a long way to go to fully recover, but he had finally glimpsed the path forward. A little girl had shone a light into his darkness and let him know he could come back from this. That it wasn't too late to have hope and purpose, even in this Fallen World.

* * * * *

Chapter Ten

Graham and I tied our horses to posts outside Laffere Hall on the west end of the Quad. It was home to the electrical engineering and computer science departments, and it was where we'd last seen a particular device. "You think Dr. Schneider will be home?" he asked.

"He's not at the Country Hotel," I said. "At least, he wasn't when I radioed over there. If he's not there, chances are he's here." I hoped that was the case. If not, tracking the professor down was going to be a difficult task. With so many phones and radios down, there weren't enough for everyone who could use one.

My stomach growled loud enough for Countess to notice. She lowered her head to the tall grass and started eating, her eyes rolling in my direction. I patted her on the head. "At least one of us isn't going hungry, right?" I murmured.

It'd been more than a week since the arrival of the Homeguard, and the city was feeling the effects of the siege. An already hungry populace was now on the verge of starvation, and that had led to an increase in desperate and violent acts by otherwise good people. Mounted patrols had been doubled in strength, and we found ourselves responding to calls day and night, mostly to help bolster the ranks of the Columbia PD, many of whom patrolled on foot. The rank-and-file were answering the call, but how much longer could they keep up this pace?

We'd tried to parlay with the Homeguard shortly after the radio broadcasts. Our transmissions were ignored, and when Graham and I rode out under a flag of truce, we'd been met with gunfire. After that failed attempt, several officers had been ambushed and killed on the outskirts of the city. To make matters worse, more farms had been burned to the ground, and the fates of the owners were unknown.

There had been some good news though. Lieutenant Kevin Hanson had admitted he was suicidal, and he was beginning to come around from that. His daily schedule was kept full, with counseling sessions with Brother Stephen and one of the psychiatrists from the hospital, with tending to Watson and the other mounts in the stables, and with keeping Helen and Jason occupied. He'd even started helping Helen with Aster's riding lessons. I hadn't had much chance to speak with Aster since she was busy either training or scouting with her team, but by all reports from both Kevin and Helen, she was doing well. Or as well as someone with a deep-seated phobia could manage.

Kevin still had a haunted look in his eyes, and I knew it would be many, many weeks and months before he was back to his old self, if he ever was. Still, it was good to see him on the mend. Something had happened between him and Stephen and Helen, but the three of them weren't talking, and it wasn't my place to pry. Certainly not with Stephen, as he had confidentiality rules to follow. And for some reason, I felt the same applied to Helen, at least in this instance.

She's starting to become a responsible young lady, Regina. I blinked away sudden tears and said, "I hope the good professor is able to help us out."

"We won't know until we ask," Graham replied.

He followed me into the building and down the main hallway. I scanned the nameplates next to each door. "He's had months to look at the thing. Surely, he's got some answers for us by now, right?"

A set of double-doors up ahead opened, and out came Dr. Schneider along with three other professors. A procession of students followed the four of them. "Ah, Lieutenant Ward!" Schneider called. "You're just in time to see it."

"See what?" I asked.

"We've found another JalCom door! We're headed out to see it now."

JalCom door? *Oh, right, the underground facility!* With everything going on, I'd forgotten about that. "Before you go, can we ask you something?"

Schneider stopped a few feet from us, and his entourage stumbled to a halt behind him. "What do you need?"

"It's about that device we brought back from Boonville." I wasn't sure how much the students knew, so I didn't want to name the weapon.

As it turns out, there was no need for caution. "Oh, the Big Beam! Yes, yes, let's have a look at it before we go."

Graham and I shared a look and a shrug. I guess it was one of those open secrets in the electrical engineering department. "That would be great, sir."

He led us downstairs to a large workshop filled with computer equipment and machinery, all of it buzzing with electricity. Student researchers manned different stations scattered throughout the room, and the students who had walked down with us went over to join them as Schneider ushered Graham, Danny, and me to a table near the center of the room. What greeted us was something much larger than the four-by-two plastic case I'd brought back from Boonville. The barrel alone had to be twelve feet long, and it was wide at its base and tapered off to a three-inch diameter at the muzzle. The barrel was connected to a silver box, which was connected to another box, this one sprouting cables out of all sides. "Lieutenant Ward, this is Teledyne's Big Beam," Schneider said, as if he were introducing a colleague. "Well, the barrel, optical resonator, and power pump. The battery array isn't set up, and we're still fabricating a base station for it. Our friends from Boonville didn't have everything we needed, but they gave us the guts."

"It's...not as impressive as I thought it would be," I admitted.

"Yeah." Alexander frowned. "It looks like a potato gun."

"Don't let appearances fool you." Schneider ran a hand along the barrel's smooth surface. "It was designed to annihilate enemy fortifications."

So Danny had told me. He'd never seen one in action. His squad had been sent in to help an Obsidian outpost in Iowa, but they had arrived too late to do anything other than evacuate the survivors. The outpost had been nailed by one or more Big Beams. The effects had been devastating.

"The problem with Teledyne's so-called 'Big Beam' is its huge power drain." Schneider pointed at the weapon's power supply. "In other words, she sucks up a lot of juice."

"How much juice are we talking about?" Graham asked.

"Remember *Back to the Future*? The amount of electricity needed to charge the flux capacitor? Well, think of it that way."

"So, we just hook it up to a lightning rod, and it's good to go?" I asked.

"Good man! You knew I was talking about the original trilogy, not the crappy reboot from a few years back." Schneider frowned. "I wish it were that easy. No, it needs a stable power source, or the battery array won't charge properly. And even with a connection to a stable source, it still needs time to build up the energy to fire. Remember, this was designed to be used against fortifications. It won't work against a maneuverable target."

"I guess that means we can't use it against the enemy tank," I said.

"Not unless you can find where they store the tank. And that's only assuming you can mount the cannon high enough to be used. Somewhere like Teledyne Tower. It's tall enough."

"That building's roof would be a great spot," Graham said. "I mean, if it wasn't controlled by Teledyne."

"And if the roof hadn't been blown up by Obsidian," I added.

Graham shuddered. "I'm glad Obsidian didn't aim that missile at the university. It would have made a complete mess of things."

"Tell me about it." I examined the paper map of the city. I missed the holographic projection they used at Teledyne Tower. "Yeah, I wonder if we should consider mounting the cannon on one of our buildings. Memorial Tower, or maybe Jesse Hall?"

"That's the other thing," Schneider said. "It can't be any building. It needs to have a direct connection with the JalCom facility beneath the city."

"Wouldn't that be any of the buildings with electricity?" I asked.

Schneider shook his head. "No. While yes, any building that currently has electricity has a connection to the JalCom facility's power source, they aren't all directly connected to it. For instance, all the buildings on Mizzou's campus are drawing power through the regular electrical grid. The wiring can't handle the amount of electricity needed for this weapon, not if we want to charge it quickly. The same goes for the Country Hotel, despite the presence of a facility access point."

"Does Teledyne Tower have a direct connection?"

"Yes, it does. That's why I suggested it."

"I don't think that's a good idea." Graham crossed his arms. "Giving them access to this kind of weapon is like making a deal with the devil."

"It's a last resort option, for sure." I looked back at Schneider. "Are there any other buildings?"

"Two that we know of for sure, though we're investigating others. The first is, oddly enough, the historic Central Dairy Building up on East Broadway. It's only two stories tall, so it wouldn't work unless the enemy is camped down the street. The second location is the Sharon Observatory on the east end of town. We can assume the municipal power plant also has a direct connection, but I wouldn't recommend firing an energy cannon from there. The weapon is volatile, and if it explodes…."

He left the thought unfinished, but I got the gist. Explosions and power plants didn't mix. "How fast can you set it up?"

"Assembling and testing it would take several hours. Close to twelve if we want to make sure it's done right." Schneider stroked his chin. "Once it's assembled, it will take forty to sixty minutes to charge it to full power. And I warn you, it'll probably drain the city's power source, so electricity will fail throughout Columbia. Some of the grid could be irreparably fried, too."

That brought me up short. "Are you sure?"

"No, but it's a possibility worth mentioning. The electrical grid is this city's lifeblood as much as food is. Without refrigeration and medical equipment, a lot of people will die of starvation or organ failure. You say giving this weapon to Teledyne is a last resort option, but I say using the weapon at all is a last resort option. If you can defeat this army without it, I urge you to do so. This cure could prove to be far worse than the disease, as it were."

Graham's radio squawked. He excused himself and walked over to the corner of the workshop. "Graham here," he said, his voice muffled by the hum of electricity.

I studied the Big Beam. *A cure worse than the disease.* Given the current situation, I wasn't sure I agreed, but I understood Schneider's concern. Food was the most pressing concern, but he was right. If we sacrificed the entire power grid to rid us of the Homeguard, we'd get our food back in the short term, but what would happen in the long run? This was a decision for Welliver and the council to consider.

Graham walked back over to us, his expression grim. "We need to go. There's a situation at city hall."

* * *

Columbia's city hall was a concave eight-story building. Its front was set back from the corner of East Broadway and North 8th Street, smack in the center of the Old Town District. The old building had been renovated and built upon over the decades, but not much had changed in the neighborhood. Banks, restaurants, and theaters surrounded city hall on all sides.

A decorative, keyhole-shaped arch stood in front of the entrance. Originally, police tape roped off the area between city hall and the keyhole so officers could funnel people in and out of the building through the arch. Now, a triple-deep array of interlocked steel barricades separated city hall from the street. A determined mob could still breach the barricades if they wanted to, but it would take time, and defenders could drive off anyone fool enough to attack the city's political and administrative heart. Columbia PD officers and Boone County deputies stood shoulder-to-shoulder with Teledyne and Obsidian troops, a public statement that all sides were working together.

As Graham, Danny, and I rode down East Broadway, we could see that a determined mob had shown up today. Hundreds of protesters crowded around the barricades, filling the intersection and shouting angrily at the politicians and administrators hidden inside city hall. While it looked like they weren't armed with anything more than signs and strong language, they still outnumbered the defenders by at least five to one.

The three of us rode at the head of a hundred officers. About half were from a mix of American departments, and the remainder wore the red riot armor of the Royal Canadian Mounted Police, Graham's unit. During the last several weeks, the Mounties had patrolled in groups of no more than sixteen, so seeing them all together was a real show of force. Word of the Mounties' lancer charge against Obsidian's forces in the New Downtown district had spread far and wide, so we knew the sight of the red and white pennants near the lances' pointed tips would do wonders for riot suppression.

I hoped they didn't need them, just as I hoped the rest of us didn't need our guns. This kind of situation could very easily turn into a bloodbath.

As we rode past Kim's Top Shelf, Kimberly and her staff peered out the front window. Her eyes were wide with fright, but she still managed to smile and wave at us. When she saw Graham, she started to step outside, but one of her waitresses laid a hand on her arm to keep her from coming out. Graham and I nodded toward her but offered no other greeting. Given the current climate, we didn't want anyone to know how much she supported us. And I think that's how her waitress felt too.

Someone in the crowd saw us coming and shouted a warning. Hundreds of eyes turned our way, and competing ripples moved through the protesters: some reflexively backed away from the sight of so many horses heading in their direction, while others surged forward, eager to confront us. There was a moment of confusion as the two sides battled each other in a mental and physical shoving match. Then the crowd coalesced again; half of them continued to face city hall, and the rest turned toward us.

"Would you look at that?" a woman shouted through a megaphone. Protesters cleared a path so she could step out and stand before us. Despite the sweltering heat, she wore an open sweater and a knit cap. Locks of red hair that were too bright to be natural peeked out from the cap. She studied us through her horn-rimmed glasses for a moment, then turned her back to address the crowd. "It looks like 'the man' has let his pigs loose to trample us and chew our bones, right as we're about to be liberated!"

Graham motioned for us to halt about thirty feet from her. "What's she talking about?" Danny asked.

"I know not all of you heard the broadcast," the woman continued, "but I did. Our liberation is at hand! No more Corporations! No more politicians! No more police!"

"Never mind that the Homeguard is commanded by a military policeman," I muttered.

Danny chuckled. "Yeah. She forgot that detail."

"Colonel Eastman said he would restore us to a government by the people and for the people! And that's what we want!" She raised her free hand and held it up in a fist. "Cops out, guard in! Cops out, guard in!"

The rest of the crowd took up the chant, shouting it over and over. The noise reverberated off the surrounding buildings. I couldn't believe what I was hearing. This so-called Homeguard had come in, murdered a well-known family, occupied several farms, had pressed their owners and workers into service, and now it was intent on starving the city into compliance. And the people were cheering for that?

"What the hell is wrong with these people?" Danny asked.

"They're scared," Graham said. "Scared people are easily whipped into frenzies by rabble-rousers like her."

The chant continued for a few more minutes, growing in intensity each time it was uttered. People were shouting themselves hoarse. Those closest to the barricades pushed on them, but the fences wouldn't budge. One man tried to pull the pins out of two interlocked barriers, but an officer hosed him down with pepper spray. Another tried to hurl a brick, but he was met with a beanbag round to the stomach.

The crowd recoiled at the sound of the shotgun going off, and their chant faltered. "See what the pigs are doing?" the rabble-rouser screamed. "They're resorting to violence! To protect their Corporate masters!"

"What the hell is going on here?" another woman shouted, her voice cracking like a whip over the heads of the protesters.

The redhead stumbled over her words and fell silent as all eyes turned toward city hall.

A CPD officer stepped through the keyhole arch and past the line of her fellow officers. She removed her riot helmet, revealing a head of cornrows I recognized from my first night in Columbia, post-Fall.

"What's she doing?" Danny hissed.

Corporal Chloe Reed tucked her helmet under her arm and strode through the crowd of protesters until she stood in front of the woman with the megaphone. "What the hell do you think you're doing?" she demanded, her voice loud enough to carry without the megaphone.

"We're trying to rid our city of invaders!" the woman replied.

"What invaders? The mounted cops? The ones who saved your sorry asses from the real invaders, like Obsidian and Teledyne?"

"We're grateful they rid us of the Corporations, but they're no better!" someone shouted.

"Yeah!" another in the crowd called. "They're starving us!"

"The only people doing any starving are those so-called, chicken shit Guardsmen who are laying siege to our city!" Reed snapped. "They're the ones raiding the farms and keeping us from getting any food!"

"You don't understand!" the woman with the megaphone shouted. "You're one of them!"

Even from here, I could see Reed bristle with fury. "What the hell is that supposed to mean?"

The girl raised her megaphone, but Chloe knocked it out of her hands. "Get that shit out of my face!"

"Hey, that's not right!" one of the protesters called.

"Police brutality, man!"

"Oh, come off it!" Chloe snapped. She pointed a finger at the bespectacled woman's face. "If by 'one of them' you mean cursed to deal with your bullshit, then yeah, I am one of them. I'm one of the people who risked her life to protect your sorry, ungrateful ass. And you know what? If these Guardsmen roll in here with their tanks and APCs and machine guns and shit, I'll be out there, doing it again. Saving your sorry ass, whether you like it or not."

Reed looked around the crowd. "How many of you have lost everything, like many of these officers have?" She pointed at us. "Most of their cities are gone. Most of their families are dead. Most of them have *no* reason to protect you or your families. But they do. Why do they do it? Because they're cops. They swore an oath to serve and protect the public, and that includes ungrateful pieces of fucking shit like you!" She put a hand on her chest. "I pray to Jesus Christ Himself that I never have to go through a tenth of what these men and women have gone through, that I never have to get up, strap on my vest, and go out and protect a city when I have *nothing* to return home to. When I don't even have a home.

"As for all of you." She leveled her finger at the crowd. "Scamper on home. If we can't rely on you to have our backs after all the times we've had yours, go huddle in your homes with your families and wait for us to do the heavy lifting. Wait for us to save this town. We don't need your thanks. Hell, after today, we don't want your thanks. Just stay the fuck out of our way."

Reed glared at them, then strode back toward the keyhole. Protesters shouted curses at her, but anyone within arm's reach backed away and gave her room. I don't know what kind of expression she had on her face, but I could feel the barely checked rage radiating off her from where I was. One didn't mess with Corporal Chloe Reed and get off lightly.

As she stepped through the keyhole, a cheer rose from her fellow CPD officers. One of the Teledyne soldiers gave her a high-five. She turned around and donned her helmet, a hint of a satisfied smile on her lips as she snapped the faceplate down.

"Man." Danny grinned widely. "What a woman."

I chuckled. "I know I wouldn't want to mess with her."

The rabble-rouser picked up her megaphone, dusted it off, and raised it to her lips. She stood there for a long moment, mouth open but no words coming out. Finally, she turned it off and walked back into the crowd.

"Orders from Welliver and Ballantine," Graham said, tapping the side of his helmet. "We're to disperse the protesters, as gently as we can."

"Well, it's a good thing we've got the Mounties to help, sir." Danny grinned. "Your boys are as polite as can be, with the sorries and thank yous."

Graham chuckled. "You have a point." He snapped down his helmet's faceplate and raised a hand. "Forward!"

As we started to slowly push the crowd out of the intersection, I couldn't help thinking about the ongoing siege. It couldn't continue like this. We had been forced into a defensive role, and all we had to show for it were hungry bellies, frayed tempers, and a city ready to explode. Something had to change. We had to go on the offense.

If we didn't, Columbia's bright light would be snuffed out of this Fallen World.

* * * * *

Chapter Eleven

Three nights later, I rode Countess up to the base of a hill covered in tall pine trees. Behind me, nearly fifty mounted officers reined in as quietly as they could. We'd moved off the roadways as soon as we left town, both to mask the noise of our mounts' shoes and boots, and to avoid enemy patrols. We'd ridden without the benefit of flashlights and instead relied on Aster's enhanced night vision to guide us.

I'd suggested she ride Sunshine, but she said it would be better if she scouted on foot. She had grown more comfortable riding the horse in the week and a half since Rock Ridge Ranch burned to the ground, but she still made any excuse she could to not ride her. I didn't press her.

"Movement up in the trees," Aster reported. She stood next to me. Her purple eyes glowed softly in the moonlight. "There's a guard, waving us in."

"Works for me," Danny grumbled. "I'd rather be up there than exposed down here."

"Ain't that the truth?" Patrolman Jones urged his black stallion, Rambo, forward.

Richard Cates greeted us as we entered the tree line. "Why do we always seem to meet at my place when something pivotal occurs?" He extended a gloved hand.

"The stars just line up that way, I guess." I shook his hand. "I love what you've done with the place."

Beyond him, campfires burned in holes dug in the ground. They didn't give off much light, but what little light there was illuminated the canvas tents surrounding them. At the old location, the tents had been in nice, even rows to facilitate foot traffic, but the many trees here didn't allow for that. Guards patrolled the tree labyrinth, their flashlights casting filtered red light on the ground.

I looked down at Richard. "Do you wear that all day? How do you survive the heat?"

Richard spread his arms and looked down at the long-sleeved tunic he was wearing. "Well, I can't say it's the airiest of clothing, but it's the only clean outfit I've got that's befitting of my station." He pointed. "Besides, it can't be worse than what you've got on. At least what I'm wearing isn't black."

"Touché." I put a hand to my mouth and feigned a cough to hide my smile. An outfit befitting his station? I knew Richard was a bit of a ham, but it sounded like he was really buying into his role as Prince of the Three Rivers. Then again, with the way things had collapsed, did it really matter what he called himself? A leader was a leader, and Richard was one of the good guys.

I hoped he didn't start demanding I call him "your highness" or "your grace."

"How have things been since you moved?"

"Oh, just dandy." Richard spun in a slow circle and extended his arm to point in every direction. "Surrounded on all sides by enemies, unable to move about in the daytime without getting shot at, having to bathe in cold water drawn from the well, although that last part isn't new. At least we've got access to running water."

"All the way out here?" Danny asked.

"This used to be a suburb, believe it or not. It got turned into a pine farm for power poles not too long after JalCom restructured the city. The suburb was bulldozed, more dirt was piled on, and the pines were planted." Richard grinned. "One of our more talented citizens gave us access to running water and sewage. No more latrines for us."

We spent a few minutes getting the men situated in a space set aside for us and our mounts. After that, Richard led Danny, Aster, the rest of the squad leaders, and me toward his pavilion. It was a large tent set up in the center of the hill. A guard held open the entrance flap. "Mind that you don't open the interior curtain until this one closes," Richard warned. "We're trying to maintain light discipline."

We entered the pavilion three at a time, with me, Richard, and Aster going first. The guard shut the tent flap behind us, cloaking us in darkness that would've been absolute except for Aster's glowing eyes. Richard pushed through the interior flap, and we were bathed in the soft glow of LED lanterns. The white light illuminated a wide chamber partitioned into two distinct areas separated by a thin bedsheet: a meeting area and a bed chamber. The meeting area contained a large, polished, wooden table, covered in maps and other documents.

We gathered around the table and waited until everyone came through the "airlock" before we took our seats. Lieutenants Blackwood, Alexander, Martinez, and Saleh and Sergeants Silva and Mosher were with us. Collectively, we commanded about seventy-five mounted officers from our respective departments. We'd also pulled volunteers from other departments, giving us a force of about ninety men and women. We represented a significant portion of our overall numbers, which highlighted how critical Welliver and Graham considered this mission.

Aster's Lieutenant Paxton and Corporal Elliott had also joined us. There wasn't enough room at the table, so they took up positions behind Aster's seat.

"Here's what we know about the so-called Homeguard," Richard said. He pointed to a position west of the Three Rivers camp location. "They've set up their main camp about three miles from here, at the Appleby farm. They must not have much in the way of construction materials, because it's all earthworks and felled trees—things they could either dig by hand or pull down with their JLTVs. There are no bunkers made of concrete, no prefab shelters, nothing like that."

"They wouldn't have been traveling with those kinds of resources," Alexander said. "Not for a riot control mission. At least, the units from Florida and Alabama that came to help quell the Miami riots didn't bring any of that stuff with them. Just riot gear, temporary barricades, and a lot of food, water, and medical supplies to distribute."

"That seems to be the case here, too. As such, their defenses aren't impregnable, but they are formidable." Richard pointed at three red X's drawn on the map. "Machine gun nests, in addition to whatever's on their JLTVs and Humvees. Some have empty turrets, and the others have either machine guns or grenade launchers."

"Any artillery?" Blackwood asked. "Howitzers, mortars?"

"None that we've seen. If they've got them, they're keeping them hidden."

"Maybe they're not as well-equipped as they would like us to believe," Paxton said.

"Except for the tank," Danny muttered. "Did we forget about the tank?"

Silva laughed. "How could I forget? My poor Donato still jumps at the slightest bit of heavy engine noise."

I winced in sympathy. In the opening days of the siege, Silva and Danny had ridden out to help a farm close to the university. While they'd driven off the convoy looting the farm, they hadn't expected the tank to intervene as quickly as it did. No one had been killed, thank God, but it had been a close one. "Well, at least you know what I went through with that Obsidian APC riding my tail."

"I didn't need to be reminded of that," Danny snapped. "Doughnut shop fight, remember?"

"Speaking of the tank," Richard said, "that's next on our list." He pointed to a red circle at the center of the camp. "They leave the tank parked here, night and day. There's natural cover to protect it from rocket attacks, and enough defenses dug around it so no one's getting close to it without their knowing about it." He looked at Aster. "Present company excepted, of course."

"No, I believe this would be difficult even for me." Aster studied the lines of trenches on the camp perimeter and near the tank's location. "If the trenches are fully staffed at all times, it would be very difficult to get past them."

"They are. They know the core of their strength is the tank. The threat of it is enough to pacify most people so they don't need to drive it around, except when needed.

"The good news is that they spend so much time guarding their weapon, they neglect their supply depot." Richard pointed at some buildings a few hundred yards behind the main camp. "They've set up in these barns, which are also owned by the Appleby family. I hope we can return their farm to them in one piece."

"We'll try our best," Aster promised.

"We're not exactly in the structural preservation business," Paxton warned.

Danny nudged me. "Neither are we," he whispered loud enough for everyone to hear. "Just ask the owners of the Country Hotel."

That brought a round of chuckles, though they were strained. None of us relished the idea of innocent people's property getting caught in the crossfire, but the truth was it already had. What happened from this point on was the fault of the invading "Homeguard," not ours. And as much as I wanted to preserve people's homes and return them in perfect condition, I'd much rather my people and Aster's return to the university unscathed. If the safest way to do that was to level a farmhouse or two, then so be it.

"An army runs on its stomach," Richard said. "My plan is to raid the supply depot for all we can take and destroy the rest."

"Well, they did it to us," Blackburn said. "Might be time for a bit of a turnabout."

Martinez drummed her fingers on the table. "How do you propose we get into the supply depot? Even if we're able to sneak in, it wouldn't take more than a few minutes for them to mobilize a counterstrike and get their tank up and running."

"That's where it gets tricky." Richard circled the tank with his finger. "We need to get rid of this thing."

"Didn't we already decide it's going to be impossible to destroy it where it is?" Saleh asked.

"I don't mean blow it up, although that would be nice." He touched the tank's symbol and then ran his finger along the map's surface until it was out in open farm country. "I mean get it and a good number of the infantry out of that base. Once they're gone, we can attack the supply depot."

"A diversion." Blackwood tapped the table repeatedly. "You're asking us to create a diversion for you."

"In a word, yes. Get the tank out of there, and we can deal with the rest."

"The only thing that got the tank to come out and play last time was a show of force, and that was dicey." He shook his head. "You're asking us to go on a suicide mission."

"Horses and buffalo aren't exactly effective against a tank," Silva agreed.

Saleh frowned. "Camels aren't going to be of much use against it, either."

"Don't you have RPGs?" Richard asked. "Did you use up all the ones you brought back from Boonville?"

It didn't surprise me that Richard knew about the RPGs. We'd tried to keep them hidden when we turned over a share, but Richard always seemed to know more than he should.

"The RPGs won't be effective," Aster said. "They were barely enough against Obsidian's APCs. They'll be all but useless against a main battle tank built in the last twenty years unless you score a lucky shot in the treads."

"And even then, it might not work," Danny added. "I saw this thing. It has an armored skirt. Very little of the tread is exposed."

"So, we're supposed to do what, exactly?" I asked. "Draw it out and distract it long enough for your men to do what needs to be done? Have it chase us around in circles until it either runs out of ammo or we run out of men?"

"Essentially, yes." Richard sighed. "I realize it's a tall order, but it's the only way I see this siege ending. If we can't starve the enemy army out of food and fuel, they're here to stay."

"It's a bloody shame we can't take out the tank," Blackwood said. "If we can't, it'll continue pressuring us."

"Who's to say we can't?" Aster asked quietly.

Everyone looked her way. "Begging your pardon, Specialist," Silva said, "but didn't you just say our rockets would have no effect on the tank's armor?"

"Yes, and I stand by that. I'm not talking about rockets or about defeating the tank's armor." Aster looked around. "What's the weakest point on a tank?"

"The treads?" Danny offered.

"The fuel tank, if it has one that's exposed?" Silva added.

I thought about it. "Openings in the armor? The hatch, the driver's viewport, and the like. Anything that would allow you to get to the crew."

"Close, but no. The weakest point on any armored creature is its soft organs. If you can attack the organs directly, the armor means nothing. In this case, the weak point on the tank is its soft, squishy crew." She placed a hand on her armored chest. "Get me onboard that tank, and I'll deal with the crew."

Danny leaned close to me. "Did she just compare a tank's crew to the guts of an animal?" he whispered.

"She can hear you and yes."

"If anyone can hurt the crew of a tank, it'd be her," Saleh grumbled.

Danny laughed. "Are you still hung up about your man's camel?"

"How would you feel if it was one of your horses that was nearly beaten to death?"

"She punched it once!"

I raised a hand. "Gentlemen, please." I asked Aster, "How do you propose getting onboard the tank? Aside from armor, its greatest strength is its speed. And its commander knows that because it's never in one spot for long."

"Bloody thing can shoot while moving, and accurately, too," Blackwood added.

"Could we sneak up on it with one of our vehicles?"

"The M7 and M8 series of main battle tanks that Obsidian produces—that Obsidian *produced*—are equipped with proximity sensors," Paxton said. "They'll detect anything larger than a human approaching it. Anything made of metal and plastic, anyway."

Aster squirmed in her seat. She murmured something inaudible.

"What was that?" I asked.

She repeated herself, but it came out as a mumble.

"Aster, we don't have your hearing. Speak up."

"I said, I'll use Sunshine!"

Her sudden outburst stunned us into silence. "Sun...shine?" Silva asked, confused.

"It's the name of a horse," I said.

"*The* horse." Blackwood smiled. "I thought she looked familiar. I remember when Golden Slipper won the Triple Crown. She's the fastest thing on four legs. That can be saddled and ridden, anyway."

"Agreed," Alexander said. "If anything can outpace that M87 at top speed, it's her. Get that tank on a clear patch of road or ground, and Sunshine'll get you there."

"Wait, I thought Aster was afraid of horses?" Danny asked.

"I'm not afraid of them," Aster snapped. "I just don't like being so high up."

Danny and I shared a look. "But, can't she jump—?"

I shook my head. "She and I've been through this before. Just roll with it."

"I'm not afraid," Aster muttered, her purple eyes aglow with murderous intent.

"So, what'll the rest of us be doing?" I asked Richard, more to take the sudden scrutiny off Aster than anything else. "What sort of distraction do you have planned?"

"The practical sort." Richard grabbed a toy truck and placed it on top of the army encampment. "They send patrols out to the local farms every day. They claim they're trying to protect the locals from the Corporations in the city, but they're really just supply raids." He moved the truck along the map as he spoke, first to one farm, then to another. "They'll do this for several hours—load up two or three trucks' worth of food and milk, then head back to base. Their Humvees then deliver supplies to the outposts they have around the city."

"Could we ambush the Humvees?" Martinez asked. "They'd be much easier targets for our RPGs."

"They vary the Humvees' routes too much. The supply raiders, though...." Richard dropped the truck back on the map with a loud clatter. "They're a bit more regimented about those. We've watched their routes over the last two weeks, and while they vary day-to-day, it's easy to predict which roads they'll take once they set out in a particular direction.

"And, if I'm right, they'll come through here sometime tomorrow morning." He tapped the map. "They should hit up this cluster of farms tomorrow. Their day to provide tribute and all that." He moved his finger. "And if that's where they go, these are the only two roads they can take. They'll take one going, and the other coming back."

"So, once we know which route they're taking, we'll wait for them to pass, then plan to ambush them on the return trip?" I asked.

"Precisely. If we attack that convoy, the tank will come out to play. I guarantee it."

* * *

Lieutenant DeSoto took a sip of hot coffee as he walked across the shadow-shrouded camp toward the array of bright lights that surrounded his tank. He squinted at the glare. "Thank God for blackout curtains," he muttered.

As an officer with a vital role, he was afforded one of the few rooms in the two farmhouses on the property. He hadn't known the family who owned this farm before they'd been run off, but they had good taste in mattresses. He shrugged one shoulder and then the other and was satisfied when each one popped. He hadn't had such a good night's rest in a long time, not since they'd had to flee Fayetteville with what was left of the National Guard units.

DeSoto was originally from Columbia but had moved to Mississippi years back for work. He'd transferred to a new National Guard post to match his move and wound up in an armored unit. Learning that Columbia hadn't suffered a direct hit was a welcome relief, but he'd been appalled to learn the Corporations had torn the place apart and taken over. He had no clue where these cavalry cops had come from, but he wished they'd go back. Or be part of the solution. They should be working together to take out the Corporate scum who occupied the city, but instead, they were trying to stop the Guard from doing its job. It made no sense to him. Not unless the officers were on the take. He'd heard a lot of police departments had been financed by the Corporations. Why would the Fall change that? They had to be beholden to their masters, like he was beholden to his commanders.

Well, at least his commanders knew who they fought for: the United States of America. And now that the Corporations had overplayed their hands and destroyed themselves, it was time for America to rise again.

Engines fired up on the other side of camp, their deep rumbles loud in the early morning quiet. That'd be the supply convoy, getting ready to head out. They'd maintain radio communication with the base, and if any trouble they couldn't handle came up, well, that's what he and his crew were here for.

Conquistadoris was a beast of a vehicle. She was larger than the M1 Abrams she was based on, she was faster, she had a higher profile to allow for emergency access through the bottom, and she carried a larger main gun. Her 130mm cannon was capable of firing multiple custom loads, including the infamous beehive round that chewed infantry to bloody shreds. They'd used up their share of those when their advance on Columbia stalled at the irradiated outskirts of Springfield. They'd also expended all their incendiary rounds during that nightmare. All they had left were high explosive rounds that would do a number on anything they hit directly, as well as deliver splash damage from the shockwave and fragmentation. There had long been rumors of low yield tactical nuke shells, but *Conquistadoris* had never been loaded with any. If she had, he'd have redone the turret art in glow-in-the-dark paint to commemorate the occasion.

"Yo, LT!" Corporal Ling called. He looked up from inspecting the right tread. "Think we'll get to see any action today?"

"Lord, I hope so," Sergeant Yoder said. He had field-stripped the turret's Ma Deuce and was busy cleaning it. "Last few days have been boring as hell. Why haven't we taken out that hilltop community yet?"

"Because the brass can't get good eyes on their defenses," DeSoto said. "Tree cover's too thick. Drones can't see much."

The JLTV at the head of the convoy blared its horn. DeSoto looked their way and raised his coffee cup in salute. Lieutenant Rogers waved through the bulletproof glass and then they headed down the dirt drive which led to a paved road. He'd sat in on the briefing the night before, when they discussed which farms they would hit up for supplies today, as well as the primary and secondary routes they would take back to base. He wished they would vary their plans a bit more, but the area only had so many roads, and the heavy cargo trucks weren't off-road capable, especially with the soft farm soil made softer by the rain. They would bring out *Conquistadoris* about midday—not to fight off any threats, but to haul those trucks out of mud pits.

He looked at the tank's namesake on the turret: Doris, a raven-haired beauty, wearing the conical helm and breastplate of a conquistador, and not much else, as she lay in the come-hither pose typical of a lot of pin-up girls. He imagined she'd look good covered in mud. It'd almost be a shame to wash her off afterward.

As he sipped his coffee, DeSoto wondered what the brass discussed after he and Rogers were excused. He slept in the farm's guest house, and the meetings were always held in the study of the main house. His room faced the study, and he could see the room's lamps burning well into the dark hours of the morning.

"That blacked-out APC came again last night," Ling muttered, as if to himself.

DeSoto cocked his head slightly. He put his coffee cup to his lips. "Mmm," he said, as if he were savoring the drink's flavor.

"Colonel Eastman and Major Patel got inside for a few minutes, then came out. Then Egghead and Anal went in, and the APC drove off. Haven't seen it or our computer specialists since."

DeSoto smirked. "Egghead" was the nickname for Lieutenant Egleton, who was the head of communications for the newly formed Homeguard. The man was a genius, an "egghead," which led to his name. After their comms were fried when the nukes hit Fayetteville, and most of their collective units were lost, he'd been able to get almost everything up and running again. He'd even tapped into an old comms satellite that wasn't as obsolete as everyone thought.

And Anal was his right-hand man, or woman, as it were. She was a computer analyst out of Quantico with no further details given, meaning she was either a Marine or a Fed. If Egghead was a genius, Anal—Lieutenant Alyssa Sullivan—was god-tier with cyber security. "There isn't a backdoor I can't find my way into," she had once said, leading to her nickname.

It didn't hurt that she never skipped leg day and had the ass to prove it.

He wondered about that APC. He'd seen it twice, though he knew it had been around more than that. The first time was when they arrived in Cassville along Highway 37. He'd seen it again two weeks ago, when they decided to make this farm their base of operations. He'd been in *Conquistadoris* that first night, and he had used the tank's thermal and night vision imaging to good effect. The only person he'd seen step out of the APC was a man in a dark suit, so he'd started calling him Mr. Suit. He figured he had to be a G-Man, someone who worked directly for the Pentagon or the CIA, or maybe even a close contact of the president. Rumor had it the president and most of his cabinet had survived the Fall and were already at work reestablishing contact with military units scattered across the land. If that was the case, they were part of a concerted effort to reestablish the United States the way it should be, without the influence of the Corporations. He could get behind that.

If the rumors were true, anyway.

DeSoto sipped his coffee. Whenever that APC appeared, their orders changed. At first, it had been their plan to get away from the irradiated areas around Fayetteville and regroup. They'd made camp in a Tel-Mart parking lot in Cassville and planned to stay there until they could reestablish contact with anyone up the chain of command but then Mr. Suit had arrived and ordered them to Columbia, citing intact infrastructure and a vulnerable citizenry in need of rescuing from Corporate tyranny.

Then several of their small arms had been requisitioned, along with a couple of JLTVs and a truck. Major Patel had led that mission. They'd driven off one afternoon and not returned until early the next morning. She wouldn't say where they'd gone or what they'd done, but the M16s were gone.

What did Mr. Suit's return last night mean? What did he need with Egghead and Anal? Maybe he was getting impatient with the way they were doing things, and he wanted them to assault the city. If so, DeSoto hoped Colonel Eastman talked him out of it. They were stretched too thin as it was, and they were not in any shape to engage in a street-by-street fight against the Corporations and their police lapdogs. The best they could hope for was to continue to starve them out, at least until the reinforcements Mr. Suit had promised arrived.

"What do you think it all means, Boss?" Ling asked.

DeSoto wished he knew. In the best of times, ignorance could get you killed. How much truer that was now that they were in this Fallen Word.

* * * * *

Chapter Twelve

I crouched in a stand of trees behind some bushes I hoped would keep me concealed from the road. My black riot armor wasn't exactly forest pattern. Most of the others waited about twenty feet behind me, with the horses.

Richard's scouts had alerted us the convoy was moving out. Just as the self-styled prince of the Three Rivers had predicted, the Homeguard raiders headed for the farms they hadn't hit in nearly a week. As we were in farm country, most of the roads ran through wide open fields, but there were a few areas of dense forest, similar to the wooded hill Richard had moved his community to. To hear some of the locals tell it, these areas had been tree farms prior to the timber market collapse of 2049.

We waited until the convoy passed along one of the two roads, then got to work on the other road, the one that would be the return route. We damaged several trees near the road, trimming off branches to make it look like the damage was from the rainstorm that had torn through the area shortly after we arrived at the Three Rivers camp. We scattered broken tree limbs across the shoulder and road, then felled a big pine close enough to the road that it fully blocked both lanes. We covered up the tree stump with as much foliage as we could find. It wouldn't pass close inspection, but I wasn't worried. If it came to that, it'd already be too late for the enemy.

I keyed my mic. "All units, status."

"Sergeant Ward, happy to have a mic, if only temporarily."

"Lieutenant Martinez, also happy to have a mic. More importantly, my men are ready. Give the word, and we'll hit them hard and fast."

"Sergeant Silva, ambivalent about the mic. My camaradas and I are eager for payback."

"Lieutenant Blackwood, waiting with Richard and his raiders."

"Lieutenant Saleh, ready to send the infidels straight to hell!"

I'll admit that didn't sit too well with me, but I understood the sentiment. "Try to avoid sending too many of the 'infidels' to hell. Even though they're on the wrong side at the moment, they're my countrymen."

"For your sake, I will try. But if it's Richard's or my men versus them, I will cut them down without mercy."

"Fair enough. That goes for everyone here. From what we understand, these are American soldiers, men and women who are serving their country but have somehow wound up on the wrong side. We can only assume it's through poor or corrupt leadership, or maybe Corporate manipulators. Consider that before committing an act you can't take back. But protect yourselves and the men and women next to you first and foremost. And may God judge us fair when all is said and done."

"Brother, I think you missed your calling as a statesman," Danny said. "Or maybe a preacher."

Quiet laughter echoed across the line. "Smartass," I muttered, which brought another round of laughter.

"LT, what's so funny?" Jones asked. The big man had somehow concealed himself better than I had, despite a much bigger profile. He leaned his RPG against a nearby tree. "You're grinnin' awful big."

I hadn't realized it. I shook my head. "Just happy to hear a bit of levity in everyone's tone this morning, that's all."

"Lord knows we need it."

"Amen to that." I keyed my mic again. "Lady in Black, status. We didn't hear from you, over."

Silence.

"Lady in Black? Aster, what's going on?"

"Corporal Elliott here, Lieutenant. Sorry, the boss is a little preoccupied, over."

"Preoccupied? What do you mean?"

"She's…well, you know how she is. She and I are having a difference of opinion right now. She'll be ready when it's show time, don't worry."

I was worried, especially after that last remark. I was going to say that, but the comms crackled with another voice. "This is Paxton. Enemy convoy is in sight. Three deuce-and-a-halfs, with a JLTV in the lead. Headed your way at approximately forty-two miles per hour."

That was oddly specific for an approximation, but I thanked him for it. "You heard the man. Get into position, everyone. Hold fire unless absolutely necessary. That goes for the RPGs, too."

To his credit, Jones didn't look too disappointed.

We settled down and waited. It was a tense few minutes. Jones crouched down and raised the RPG to his shoulder. Every few seconds he looked left, then slid back another couple inches until he was deeper in the bushes. I very much doubted anyone in the approaching convoy would be able to see us, but it was certainly possible, especially once their guard was up.

A soft snort behind me reminded me Countess was back there, her reins in the hands of Corporal Ferris, who sat astride her own horse and waited with the rest of the unit. I'd stay on the ground for the moment, so I could better direct fire, and then I'd climb in the saddle, and we'd head down to the road as fast as we could.

After a couple minutes, a low rumble filled the air. The rumbling increased in volume with each passing moment until we could distinguish it as engine noise from a few different vehicles. We'd chosen this stretch of road for the trees, but also for the blind turn. The convoy would see the downed limbs but wouldn't see the fallen tree until they were almost on it. Then they'd have to either back up or dismount to move the tree out of the way.

I pressed myself as low to the ground as I could while keeping eyes on the road. I took several deep breaths to steady my heart rate and to keep my anxiety at bay. Anticipating a fight was worse than the fight itself, at least for me. Once fists or lead started flying, there wasn't anything to do except fall back on training. Moments like now, though…Moments like now shortened my lifespan.

When the JLTV rounded the corner, the breath I let out was a small sigh of relief. Finally, the show could begin.

I expected the convoy to slow as they approached the forested area with downed limbs scattered across the roadway, but they sped up instead. They hit the turn doing at least fifty, and when the driver of the JLTV saw the fallen tree, he slammed on the brakes. The vehicle's wheels locked and screeched as rubber stuck to the pavement. The vehicle stopped in time to avoid the tree. The soldiers inside rolled down the windows and aimed their weapons into the tree lines on either side of the road. The man on the rotary grenade launcher spun his turret toward the side of the road opposite me, where Martinez and her people were.

All this transpired in the couple seconds it took the driver to slam on his brakes. National Guard or Corporate frauds, these people were good.

But no matter how good the drivers in this convoy were, gravity and mass still owned everyone's ass. The driver of the first deuce-and-a-half braked at nearly the same time as the JLTV, but he was too close, and his vehicle was way too heavy to stop on a dime. He crashed into the smaller JLTV. The crash shoved the JLTV up onto the tree, but its armored frame didn't appear to be damaged.

The man on the turret was startled, though. His finger must've been near the trigger because there was a loud *thump*, followed by an even louder explosion inside the tree line.

"Contact!" Martinez shouted. "Stoltz and McDonald are dead, and there are God only knows how many wounded! Make these fuckers pay!"

Gunshots rang out, and rounds pinged off the side of the JLTV. The Guardsmen shouted in alarm, and the one who'd initially fired swung his grenade launcher toward the muzzle flashes visible on the other side of the road.

"Light 'em up!" Danny yelled, and the men with him opened fire, too.

"No, wait—" I said, but it was too late.

The man in the turret dropped when a round hit him in the back. The infantry inside the JLTV fired through their narrow viewports. Soldiers spilled from the backs of the deuce-and-a-halfs and fired into the tree line. A bullet struck the tree next to me with a loud crack, and two more rounds zipped past. I pressed myself flat against the ground. Dammit, this wasn't how it was supposed to turn out!

Someone pulled the fallen grenadier inside the JLTV, and another soldier scrambled up to take his place. We couldn't let that grenade launcher reactivate. "Jones!"

"Already on it, LT!" Jones rested the RPG on his shoulder, and he stared down the optical sight. "Clear backblast!" he shouted.

"Clear!" someone called from behind.

"No more Mr. Nice Guy." Jones squeezed the trigger.

With a sharp hiss that turned into a roar, the rocket propelled grenade shot out. It flew in a straight arc out of the tree line, sailed across the street, and slammed into one of the JLTV's narrow side windows. The impact and resulting explosion blew the armored vehicle onto its side and sent burning shrapnel into the passenger cabin. Even from this distance, I could hear the men inside screaming as they tried to get out. My guts twisted. "It wasn't supposed to turn out this way," I muttered.

"What was that, LT?" Jones shouted to be heard over the din of the battle. He loaded another grenade into his RPG tube. "Should I fire another shot?"

Secondary explosions tore into the vehicle as the grenades in the turret's magazine ignited. "No. Save it for the tank. Who knows? You may get another lucky shot."

On the road, soldiers dropped one by one, hit by bullets or shrapnel from the explosions near the head of the convoy. We needed to end this, or there wouldn't be anyone left alive. "Mount up!" I shouted. "Let's see if we can take some prisoners!"

* * *

DeSoto's radio suddenly came alive with the sounds of gunfire and shouted orders. He set the bulky device on the ground and crawled under *Conquistadoris* to inspect her underside. He scrambled back out, his inspection only half-finished. He snatched up the radio as he heard one of the truck drivers call out, "Contact with the enemy! Rogers's vehicle is down! We're under attack!"

DeSoto clicked his radio to transmit. "Caravan One, Caravan One, this is *Conquistadoris*. Repeat your status and location."

More gunfire rattled across the line, followed by a pop that sounded like a tire losing its air. "We're under attack! It's the cops!"

Colonel Eastman came onto the line. "Conquistadoris, prepare to roll out. Caravan One is under attack and stalled at the following coordinates."

DeSoto didn't need to pull up the digital map to know where it was. He'd memorized all the roads and terrain around their base. "Roger that, Colonel! Caravan One, hold on! The cavalry is coming."

* * *

I surveyed the line of Guardsmen kneeling on the bullet-scarred asphalt, their hands behind their heads, their pistols and rifles confiscated. Beneath me, Countess shivered from nerves and dug at the pavement with her booted hoof. I stroked her mane. "Is this everyone?"

"Everyone except the wounded." Danny pointed to a shady spot on the shoulder, where several soldiers had been laid out. "Doc's treating them now."

Doctor Samuelson was one of the original sponsors of the mounted police convention. The older gentleman had spent his youth in the military, first as a combat medic and then as a surgeon. He now pulled double duty as a surgeon in the campus hospital and as a rapid response medic. He was one of only a few of the doctors and nurses who knew how to ride a horse. There was just one problem with having him out in the field: he didn't take orders very well.

"He's aware we're not going to be able to keep them here, right?" I asked. "The tank's going to be here any minute."

"He knew you'd object, and he doesn't care." Danny cracked a wry grin. "You know how he is. Mind of his own."

"Mind of his own," I agreed. Samuelson was as stubborn as a mule and would only follow orders if they didn't interfere with his Hippocratic Oath. If I hadn't known any better, I'd say that was probably why he wasn't in the military any longer.

If these were genuine National Guard soldiers, I doubted they'd do anything to the good doctor if they found him treating their wounded, but we couldn't risk losing him. "Give him two minutes to stabilize those he can, then get him back on his horse. Their cavalry's coming. They'll be able to treat these guys."

"I'll try." Danny wheeled Noir around and rode over to the Doctor Samuelson.

We loaded our wounded into the second truck in the convoy, after we turned it around. A couple of nurses who'd followed Doc from the hospital were inside with them. We also turned the third truck around, and that was where we put the bodies of officers Stoltz and McDonald. Other than the wounded and dead, the trucks were packed with crops and canisters of milk. We'd have to figure out a way to redistribute those to the farms they were taken from, but for now, we'd take them into custody.

I wished we could bring the first truck with us, but it had been too close when Jones' RPG struck the JLTV. Shrapnel from the RPG and the resulting grenade explosions had torn into the engine and radiator. The truck needed more than simple roadside repairs, so we slashed its tires and left it. It wouldn't be of any immediate use to the enemy. We now had two more trucks than they did, so I wasn't going to complain about the third one's loss.

To Corporal Ferris, I said, "Get these prisoners into the woods back there, then walk them to camp. We'll want to interrogate them and ascertain who they really are. If they're Guard, we need to tell them we're on the same side."

"I don't think Lieutenant Martinez feels that way." Ferris tilted her head in the Danny's direction.

Cassandra Martinez rode over to the aid station and dismounted so she could stand in front of Doc Samuelson. The doctor's greater height and bulk dwarfed the little woman, but in that instant, they looked like two titans about to square off. "Why the hell are you treating these dogs? I have wounded men back in the trees!"

"One of my nurses is up there treating them. These people need my help," Doc said.

"Ridiculous." She stomped her boot. "They fired on us first, the scum. We should let them bleed out on the pavement!"

I knew Martinez didn't mean it. At least, I hoped she didn't. To Ferris, I said, "This is why I'm asking you to escort the prisoners. Take six of our squad and get them back to base." I raised my voice loudly enough for the prisoners to hear. "If they try anything, shoot them. If they attempt to flee, shoot them."

More than one set of eyes widened, but I wasn't sure if it was from my words or from Martinez's ongoing tirade at the aid station.

Ferris winked at me. "I think we can manage, LT. All right, squad, gather round! Prisoners, you heard my boss. Up and at 'em. You'll be following me through the woods. It's not far back to camp, and we've got good food and hot showers." She grimaced. "Although, in this heat, I think we'd all prefer cold showers, right?"

"Don't give them anything of ours!" Martinez screamed at Ferris. "Put them in holes and be done with them!"

Ferris raised a hand without looking over her shoulder. "Good hunting, LT!"

Martinez spun away from the aid station and stomped back to her assembled men, tugging her horse by the reins. I rode over to her. "Nice act, Cassandra. I don't think they'll give Ferris any problems now."

"Wasn't much of an act." She smirked. "I'm pissed, but I'm professional enough to understand what happens in tense situations when guns are involved. Executing those prisoners won't bring back my men, and what's done is done. If these are actual Guardsmen, they need to know things are different around here."

"And if they're not?" I asked.

"If they're not, I get to kill them."

A low rumble interrupted my next thought. Our heads snapped toward the convoy. "Better get your men ready," I warned.

"On it. Good hunting! Stay alive, Nate."

"Everyone, mount up!" I said. "It's time for the chase to begin!"

* * *

"Boss, I think you need to come down from there," Corporal Elliott said.

"Why?" Aster looked down at her subordinate from a high branch of a pine tree close to the road. "I can jump down onto the tank just fine from here."

"You could, but isn't the plan to use Sunshine?" He pointed to the golden mare tied up close to his own horse.

"She might get hurt." Aster inspected her gear one last time. Grenades, flashbangs, her Five-Seven pistol, and a knife hung from the webbing of her green combat armor. Her FN-P90 rested tightly against her chest, held there by a sling she could easily loosen with one hand. "If I time it right, I can land on top of the tank as it passes over the fallen tree."

"What if you miss?"

"Then I'll switch to Plan B."

"Plan B?" Elliott shielded his eyes from a ray of sunlight shining through the thick canopy. "What's Plan B?"

"Riding Sunshine."

"I thought that was Plan A."

"It was before I thought of a better Plan A." Aster focused on a spot on the ground in front of the downed tree. An M87 could roll over an obstacle like that with little trouble, but it would have to slow down for a moment. That was when she'd jump. She tested the branch's resiliency. It creaked beneath her weight, but she didn't think it would give way.

Down on the road, the JLTV's passenger cabin smoldered. Even at this range, the stench of burning flesh was strong in Aster's nose. She hated that smell. It reminded her too much of the past. She hoped none of the men inside had families, but they'd left Nathan and his officers with no choice.

"It's time for the chase to begin!" she heard Nathan call over his radio. Her body tensed at the words, which caused the branch to creak. She

forced herself to relax. It was almost time. She couldn't let them down.

She turned her head to locate the vehicle and frowned. It wasn't anywhere in sight, even though the rumbling was so loud, it was practically all her enhanced hearing could detect. Her eyes narrowed. "I'm coming down. Time for Plan B."

"Wasn't riding the horse Plan A?"

"Not in my mind." She dropped off the branch, bounded off two others, and landed on the ground with a soft thud. She walked up to Sunshine, with knots in her stomach. She held up her hand, and Sunshine nuzzled it. The knots loosened a bit, but not by much.

"Are you ready, Boss?" Elliott asked. He had already mounted his horse, a bay-and-white named Cappuccino. "I'll be following close behind, but Cap here can't keep up with Sunshine."

"Stick as close as you can, and make sure Sunshine gets home," Aster said. Although she didn't like horses, there was something special about this one. A look in her blue eyes she kind of liked. She stroked Sunshine's face. "Are you ready?"

Sunshine snorted in what she thought was approval.

* * *

Less than a minute later, we were all mounted and riding hard back the way the convoy had come. The stolen trucks were in the lead with officers on the flanks and behind it. I hung back with the rear guard as we entered open countryside and raced toward the smoke rising in the distance. That was where we'd spring the next trap.

The rumbling continued to grow louder, but it was difficult to place its direction. Between the hills and the trees, the noise seemed to be coming from everywhere and nowhere at the same time. It was like being back in downtown Mobile late at night when someone with a hot rod or motorcycle went flat out down Government Street. The engine noise would bounce back and forth between the buildings, making it hard to determine the point of origin.

I looked over my shoulder. We had passed the bend in the road where we sprung the ambush, so the convoy was out of sight. Only the smoke plume from the JLTV was visible over the tree line. Any minute, I expected to see the M87 flying around the corner. As loud as it sounded, I was surprised it hadn't appeared yet.

A telephone pole suddenly vanished in an explosion that sent hot splinters and clods of dirt skittering across the pavement and raining down on our heads. Countess screamed and tried to bolt off the road. My heart hammered in my chest as I reined her in. "Stay on the road, girl!" I shouted, my voice muffled in my ringing ears.

"Contact!" cried Sergeant Silva. He twisted in his saddle and pointed behind us and to the right. "It's the tank!"

The M87 came down a connecting roadway that was little more than a hard-packed dirt road. Smoke rose from the barrel of its main gun as it tracked our position. The coaxial machine gun fired, and a dozen or more rounds zipped past us. Ahead of me, one of the horses screamed as it fell. Its rider was thrown from the saddle and rolled to a stop. He scrambled toward a ditch at the side of the road and threw himself in as more rounds impacted near his fallen horse. The bullets ripped into the shrieking animal's exposed underbelly, silencing it permanently.

I ducked low in the saddle and keyed my mic. "Aster, your dance partner is here! Don't be late!"

"The Lady in Black is never late, even if it's fashionable to be."

Normally, her quiet tone would be soothing, but there was a note of tension there, I didn't like. Or maybe it was my own tension.

"Well, it's certainly not fashionable now! Hurry up."

"On the way."

Another burst of gunfire raked the asphalt in front of me. Countess turned her head just enough to look at me through her helmet's faceplate. The look in her big eye said it all: *You take me to all the best places, you know?*

"Sorry, Countess! I promise you all the carrots and sugar cubes in the world once we're done here."

She snorted.

* * *

"Yeah, come get some!" Ling shouted as he fired *Conquistadoris'* coaxial gun.

"Careful with your ammo, Ling!" DeSoto said as he watched the rounds stitch across the landscape through the tank's forward cameras. In the distance, a horse and rider fell, but the others continued galloping. "We just need to drive them off. Our ammo's limited."

"Roger, LT." He fired a short burst, then cursed. "Damn, that calico horse is a slippery one."

"Calicos are supposed to be good luck!" Yoder said as he fired a burst from his turret machine gun. "Aw, damn, I missed 'im, too!"

"Does the good luck come from killing them or owning them?" DeSoto asked.

"Both?" Yoder and Ling asked at the same time.

"Reinforcements have arrived at the ambush site," Major Patel said. "JLTV destroyed, one deuce-and-a-half disabled, two missing."

DeSoto zoomed the forward camera until he could see a pair of trucks in the distance just ahead of the retreating riders. "Major Patel, this is Lieutenant DeSoto. *Conquistadoris* has eyes on the missing trucks. Looks like the cops made off with them. Shall we pursue, over?"

"Yes, but watch for an ambush. These cops got us good. Rogers is dead, along with two others."

DeSoto's face muscles tightened. "Roger that, Major. We'll get those trucks back."

"We've got more infantry on the way to assist you. Good hunting."

He switched off his mic and studied the feeds from *Conquistadoris'* forward cameras. Anger at what happened to Rogers gnawed at him. "On second thought, fuck these guys. Let's kill as many of 'em as we can."

"Hoo-ah!" Ling and Yoder shouted.

* * *

Bullets zipped through the air as we pushed our horses to the limit. I turned in my saddle and fired a smoke flare, as did a half-dozen other officers. The canisters sent trails of smoke through the air until they hit the ground, where they exploded into clouds of multi-colored gas. I had no doubt the tank had thermal optics that could see through smoke, but it was worth the attempt. It would at least blind the gunner on top of the tank.

At my order, the trucks pulled ahead of us, going much faster than the horses' top speeds. The Guard had seen the trucks, so they knew we had them. If all went as planned, they'd chase us to get the trucks back.

The trucks disappeared into the great cloud of gray smoke that spilled across the roadway, followed quickly by the first ranks of officers. As I entered the haze, the acrid stink of burning gasoline and rubber assaulted my nose and made my eyes water.

A sharp wind blew fresh air into my face, and some of the smoke dissipated, giving me a clearer view of the road ahead. More smoke poured from the tree line, coming from controlled fires set by some of the Three Rivers people and Silva's men. Judging by the stench, they must have used gasoline to ignite them. The good news was the fires would be easy to put out when it was time. That, and wet wood tended to produce more smoke than fire. A double win for our side.

I coughed. Provided we could make it through without losing consciousness. Damn, that stuff was hard to breathe. "Next time we set a distraction fire, let's bring our gas masks, people," I said.

A round of hacking laughter came back over the line.

"Lady in Black, how're you holding up?" I asked.

"...not..."

"What was that?" Martinez asked. "I couldn't make that out."

"—not scared. I'm not scared."

I blinked. Was that Aster?

The soft voice repeated itself in a quiet monotone. "I'm not scared. I'm not scared. I'm not scared. I'm not scared."

Danny laughed. "I never thought I'd see the day when a Specialist was afraid of anything."

More laughter rang out across the line as the commanders with headsets enjoyed a momentary reprieve from the insanity. I smiled. Aster would never live this one down; we'd all make sure of that.

I risked a glance back. The M87 was on the main road, and it was gaining speed as it raced toward us. If we didn't scatter, we'd be done for. But if we did, the tank would reach the trucks before they got back to camp. If that happened, we'd lose our chances at the tank and the destruction of the convoy.

Movement behind the tank caught my eye. It was a flash of white and gold in the sunlight, and then it was gone as a streamer of smoke blocked my view. Aster was there, and she was gaining ground. Relief surged in me until another blast of machine gun fire brought me back to reality. "Give 'em hell, Aster," I murmured.

I started to face forward, but something else caught my eye. Someone was coming up behind Aster.

* * *

Aster ignored the radio chatter as she stayed low in Sunshine's saddle and let the retired racehorse do her thing. Helen had told her the key wasn't to be an expert rider. She just needed to know enough to keep from interfering with the expert. Aster could respect that. She'd worked with several Corporate executives who knew next to nothing about tactics and combat, but they knew she was an expert who would keep them alive if they weren't idiots about it.

So, any time she felt her legs tense, she forced herself to relax them. Any time she wanted to wrap her arms around Sunshine's neck and squeeze, she resisted. She did everything she could to be nothing more than a two-hundred-and-fifty-pound backpack for the animal. *Stay out of the expert's way, Aster.*

"I'm not scared," she whispered as she forced herself to relax. "I'm not scared. I'm not scared."

"You're doing great, Boss!" Elliott called. He galloped along the road about a hundred yards behind her. He hadn't been kidding; his horse couldn't keep up with Sunshine.

And it wasn't only his horse. In the days since she'd started riding Sunshine, she hadn't found any horse capable of keeping pace with the golden mare. At first, she hadn't understood how special Sunshine was or why anyone paid her as much attention as they did. Now it made sense, especially as the speeding M87 grew closer by the second.

She made the mistake of looking down, and she saw just how quickly Sunshine's legs were eating up the pavement. If she fell, she'd suffer some scrapes and bruises and be fine. Anyone else would be grievously injured, if not killed outright. The thought didn't bring her much comfort as she forced her gaze straight ahead. "I'm not scared," she muttered. "I'm not scared."

Ahead of her, the M87 slowed slightly as it neared the wall of smoke. She knew the commander had thermal optics, but it still paid to be cautious. The periscope on top of the tank twisted left and right as he tried to find the source of the fire. The gunner who was working the Ma Deuce on top of the tank clambered inside and sealed the hatch, likely because he couldn't see anything.

While that would make things a little more difficult for Aster to achieve her objective, it would help her to get close to the tank.

"Support infantry sighted behind tank," Nathan said. "Silva, you and your boys are up."

Aster glanced back and saw what he was talking about. A deuce-and-a-half loaded with riflemen raced after her and Elliott. Elliott turned around in Cappuccino's saddle, saw the approaching truck, then reached into his saddlebags for a wireless Claymore. "Try not to kill them if you can avoid it," she warned as he dropped the mine on the pavement.

"Understood."

Elliott waited until the truck was almost on top of the mine before detonating it. The explosion cracked the windshield and shattered one of the headlights but didn't wound anyone. The driver panicked at the sudden blast and brought the truck to a skidding halt.

Sergeant Silva's buffalo riders charged the vehicle from a nearby farm. Tracer rounds sailed back and forth, and one of Silva's men tumbled from his buffalo's saddle. She briefly considered turning around to help, but she couldn't. "Help them, Elliott!" she called.

"*On it, Boss!*" Elliott waved at her, then wheeled around and put his rifle to his shoulder. How had he learned to ride so comfortably in only a week?

Aster leaned forward in the saddle, one hand on the reins, the other on Sunshine's mane. She didn't know much about horses, but she could tell the mare was laboring. "Just a little further, girl," she whispered. "Just a little further, and we'll win the race."

Sunshine snorted and added an extra burst of speed. Aster nearly lost her balance at the sudden jolt, but she righted herself. She took a deep breath to steady her nerves. "I'm not scared," she whispered. "I'm not scared."

As she and Sunshine pulled alongside the M87, Aster pushed herself up in the stirrups, then climbed onto the saddle. The fear she'd been feeling faded. She'd spent the last few, terrifying moments firmly in the world of the mounted police. Now, it was time to step back into her world, a world where she was fully in control.

The Battle Flower jumped.

* * *

A loud thump echoed through *Conquistadoris*. "What the hell was that?" DeSoto demanded.

"We run over something?" Yoder asked over a burst of machine gun fire.

"Possible!" Ling shifted the tank to the right, then back to the left to center it on the road. "It's hard to tell in all this smoke!"

DeSoto looked through the tank's array of cameras. The road immediately behind them was shrouded in a gray haze which obscured much of the pavement. If they'd run over something, it was long out of sight.

Movement attracted his eye to the right flank camera. The monitor showed a golden horse running after them through the smoke, although they were clearly outpacing it. There was something odd about it. He squinted and adjusted the brightness on the screen so he could see better. Then he found his answer: the horse was riderless.

His eyes widened, and he pulled up the turret's rear-facing camera and centered it on his monitor screen. A woman clad in dark green armor crouched on top of *Conquistadoris*, her white hair streaming in the wind. At first, he thought she was an old woman because of the hair color, but her skin was as smooth as his high school prom date's had been. She was just as hot, too.

She was also holding a satchel charge.

The mixture of surprise, admiration, and lust DeSoto felt for the woman burned to ash as he thought about what a satchel charge could do to his tank. "We've got company! Bank left!"

* * *

Aster pulled the satchel charge from her shoulder and primed it. It would explode in thirty seconds, tear through the M87's top armor, and ignite the fuel or the magazine. Either way, the tank would die, and not a moment too soon. Her earpiece was alive with the shouts and cries of the few officers who had radios, and she'd already heard of the deaths of several cops and their horses.

She stripped the protective plastic off the satchel charge's backside and exposed a thick layer of adhesive. She hoped the men inside this tank weren't family men, but even if they were, they had to be neutralized.

Suddenly, the tank turned hard to the left. Aster fell to the right and banged into the M87's comms array. Before she could recover, the tank swerved to the right. She rolled to the other side of the tank and crashed into a handrail used to climb up onto the body from the ground. The impact caused her hand to unclench, and the satchel charge fell out of her hands and struck the pavement.

Aster wasn't done yet. She reached for a grenade hanging from her webbing. If she timed it right, she could slip it behind the tank's armored skirt and blow out one or more of the tread gears. That'd bring it to a stop if nothing else.

The tank's top hatch opened with a bang, and a soldier peeked out, holding an MP5 in his hands.

Aster tried to grab her FN-P90, but the gun lay beneath her, and the was sling partly wrapped around her left arm. She instead drew the Five-Seven from her chest rig and pointed it at the soldier. Both opened fire at the same time. Aster's delicate finger stroked the Five-Seven's trigger so quickly, she seemed to be keeping pace with the

MP5's fully automatic fire. She rolled to the right as bullets sprayed the area she'd just occupied, though one clipped the side of her head. As a result of the sudden movement, most of her rounds went wide, but one struck the soldier. He dropped back inside, and a stream of pain-filled curses reached Aster's ears. Blood dripped from the glancing wound on the side of her head, but she ignored the stinging pain and got to her feet.

The tank resumed its side-to-side movements in an obvious attempt to dislodge her. Aster crouch-walked along the body of the tank to the turret. As she reached the hatch, a hand grabbed the locking wheel and pulled the hatch cover down. The exterior wheel spun as the crewman beneath the hatch sought to lock her out completely. She spread her legs to brace herself, then reached for the wheel.

* * *

DeSoto turned the hatch wheel clockwise with his left hand. His right hand hung at his side, dripping blood and burning with pain. *Shit, shit, shit.* The bitch had not only shot the MP5 out of his hand, but she'd also sent fragments of the ruined gun into his flesh. The weapon lay on the floor of the tank, its barrel and side completely blown out. He couldn't fire it in that state, or it would explode in his hand.

He suddenly felt resistance against the wheel, and it started to turn counterclockwise. "Shit, she's trying to get inside!" He grabbed the wheel with both hands, heedless of the pain and the blood falling into his eyes. He couldn't let her get in. If she did, it was over.

The wheel stopped turning for a moment, and he thought he had stopped her. Then it spun with so much force, it flew out of his hands. He banged his injured hand into the cupola's armored side, and ripples of pain shot down the length of his arm. He grunted. "Yoder, activate the ESD and the ADS! Hurry!"

"On it!" Yoder slipped from his position into the commander's seat. "This bitch is about to get lit up!" He looked up and noticed the blood all over DeSoto's hand. "Jesus, are you all right?"

"Don't worry about me!" DeSoto dropped down from the cupola and drew his 1911 with his good hand. He aimed it up at the hatch wheel that continued to spin. "Hurry up! She's almost inside!"

* * *

Aster continued to spin the hatch wheel. As soon as she opened the hatch, she would demand they surrender. If they didn't, she'd drop a frag grenade inside, and that would be the end of it. Or maybe she'd use one of the flashbangs. "This is Lady-in-Black," she said into her mic. "I'm onboard the M87. Preparing to breach—"

Paralyzing pain suddenly coursed through her body. The sensation was so intense, a scream escaped through her clenched teeth. Her body went rigid as electrical currents ran through her arms into the rest of her body. This tank had an Electric Shock Defense system? She thought Obsidian had phased those out of the M87s, citing too many complaints from crews of the older M78s, who'd been accidentally shocked more than once.

After what seemed like an eternity, but was only a few seconds, the electric discharge stopped, and her body went limp. She slid from the turret and crashed to the body of the tank. Her whole body ached, and she could only move her limbs with great difficulty. Those ESD systems were no joke. If she'd been a regular human, she'd be dead or unconscious.

Over the rumble of the tank's engine, she heard a pair of soft whines. She lifted her head and saw the machine gun on top of the tank slowly spinning toward her. The gun lowered and wiggled side to side, seemingly on its own. That was something else she wasn't expecting. Very few tanks had an Automated Defense System, which allowed the tank's machine guns to be AI-driven. She'd been wrong about this tank being an M87; it was an M78 with upgraded armament.

She willed her limbs to work and gathered as much strength as she could. If that barrel fully turned her way, she'd be dead. Her armor might be able to stop one .50 round, but a stream of them at six hundred rounds per second, at point-blank range? She'd be splattered all over the body of this M78. Then, where would Nathan and the others be?

Where would Helen and Jason be without their father?

She pulled her numb legs up until her boots rested flat on the M78's hull, with her knees pointed up. She dug her elbows into the cold metal and bunched her shoulder muscles. There was only one thing left to try.

The gun fired.

* * *

"My God, is she a machine?" DeSoto growled. He sat back in the commander's seat in front of the monitor screen. The rear-facing body cam was focused on the woman-shaped creature. She'd fallen off the turret after receiving several seconds' worth of enough current to power a house. She should've been dead or incapacitated, but she was still moving, and not in the twitchy way some people did after receiving near-lethal shocks. She was moving with purpose, albeit slowly.

The Ma Deuce appeared in the top-right corner of the camera's view and slowly tracked left as the woman pulled her legs up until her knees pointed straight at the sky. Was she trying to get up? God, how much fight was left in this bitch?

The gun's barrel stopped moving when it reached the center of the screen. It lowered slightly and paused. "Fire, you stupid AI!" DeSoto shouted.

As if it were listening, the Ma Deuce fired. The camera's view distorted as the weapon's recoil reverberated down the turret to the embedded camera lens. The view shook and filled with fire and smoke as Ma unloaded thirty rounds of whoop-ass on the wayward bitch of a daughter.

When the smoke cleared and the camera stopped shaking, the woman was no longer in sight. Had her body been blown off the tank? He expected to see a lot of blood, but there was only a small puddle. She'd been wearing high-tech combat armor like the Corporations loved to use, so it was possible the armor absorbed a lot of damage before her body was knocked clear off *Conquistadoris*.

He couldn't see anything in the haze behind them, and they were still going around forty-five miles an hour. She'd be long out of view in all the fog and smoke.

"Yo, LT, we get her?" Ling demanded.

"Yeah." DeSoto laughed. "Yeah, we did."

"Fuckin' A!" Yoder whooped.

DeSoto leaned back in his seat as the adrenaline leaked out of him. His hand throbbed, which was a reminder he needed to bandage it before he dirtied up *Conquistadoris* anymore than he already had. His blood stained the hatch, the cupola, and the floor, and it was soaking into his keyboard. That'd be a bitch to clean later. Those stupid little keys had to be pulled out one-by-one. At least the damn thing was waterproof.

The med kit, a white box with a red cross stamped on it, was down near the emergency escape hatch on the bottom of *Conquistadoris*. He climbed out of his seat and reached for the box.

The hatch's maglock indicator was green, which meant it had unlocked during their wild chase or when the ESD activated. Stupid damn thing. Whichever idiot engineer designed the M78 left that design flaw, even though it was a known issue. The argument was, "Well, it only happens at high speed. What difference does it make if the hatch unlocks at high speed, right?"

He supposed there was some truth to that, but it was still stupid. If there's a problem, fix it. Like the problem of his injured hand. He needed to bandage it. He returned to his seat. "Ling, are those mounted cops still in sight?"

"Yeah, LT. They seem to be gathering for a charge."

"Perfect." He needed to vent his frustration on someone or something. "Yoder, how much ammo we got left? We need to make these bastards pay—"

A loud hiss filled the inside of *Conquistadoris*. DeSoto spun around so fast, he banged his shoulder against the armored hull.

The emergency hatch opened, and the white-haired woman peered in. Her purple eyes were ablaze in the dim light.

"Holy shit!" Yoder shouted. He could see her perfectly from his position.

Holy shit, indeed. DeSoto threw the med kit at her head, then fumbled for his 1911 with his left hand.

* * *

Aster hung upside down beneath the tank's body. The pavement was less than a foot from her backside. If she let go of her handholds and fell, she had no doubt she'd survive, but it would be weeks before she'd recover, assuming they didn't wheel around and run over her broken body. *That* would kill her, and it didn't matter how augmented she was.

The emergency hatch on the M78 was magnetically locked and could be pulled open from either the inside or outside once the lock was disengaged. This allowed fast egress for the crew in the event of catastrophic failure, when they might only have seconds to escape before it exploded. Likewise, it allowed rescuers to quickly get in and out.

As she reached for the handle, she hoped Jason was correct about his favorite tank's "design slaw."

She yanked, and the hatch slid toward her, then rolled up under the armor plating she clung to. With the inside of the tank exposed, she could see the gunner in a seat suspended a few feet above her. The driver was in the forward-most position of the tank, and his helmet was barely visible beyond the autoloader for the main gun.

"Holy shit!" the gunner shouted. He stared down at her, eyes wide and mouth agape.

She drew her pistol and pulled herself in enough to aim. Movement caught her eye, and she ducked back outside the hatch. A med kit sailed through the space her head had occupied and struck the tank's far wall. Several gunshots echoed through the tank, and bullets impacted the lip of the open hatch or struck the pavement below.

She shoved the pistol up into the cabin and fired blindly. One of the crew cursed, then more gunfire rang out, and the rounds chewed into the pavement. At least two of them were shooting at her, the gunner and the commander.

The tank jerked to the side, and Aster holstered her pistol so she could hold on with both hands. Tall grass brushed against her head. She looked forward and saw they'd gone off-road. They rolled over the firm ground on the road's shoulder and headed for a wheat field. Thin, yellow-green stalks smacked into her face when they reached the edge of the field. The plants obscured her vision as they drove through it, casting her into darkness.

The tank's treads groaned as they kicked up loose, wet soil and churned it into mud. The vehicle slowed considerably, and it seemed to Aster they were starting to sink. The ground was much closer than it was, giving her very little room to maneuver.

Adrenaline surged through her. If they sank any further, she'd get buried. All they'd have to do was wait for her to quit breathing and then they could get themselves out of this mess.

"—can't get hold of Aster."

Aster's earpiece crackled with garbled sentences from a half-dozen different voices. She realized her radio must've been fried when she was electrocuted, but it had somehow come back, at least partially. "I'm here," she whispered into the comm.

"Something must've happened to her but look! The tank's getting bogged down in that field. Hurry, we can take it out!"

"Let's go!"

"Those cavalry cucks are headed this way!" the gunner shouted.

"Kill 'em!"

Anger burned within Aster. She couldn't let Nathan and the others get killed. Too many had fallen already! She reached for the only thing on her webbing she could prime one-handed. She thumbed the activator and threw the flashbang into the tank's cabin.

Before one of the crew could yell "Grenade!" she tossed two more in. The resulting detonations were deafening to her enhanced ears. The men screamed. Aster pulled herself inside as the tank slid completely into the mud. A puddle of the brown sludge followed her into the vehicle, filling the hole and rising inside a half-inch.

Aster pressed a knee into the mud, pulled her FN-P90 into her right hand, and drew her Five-Seven with her left. Before the gunner or the commander could aim their weapons at her, she shoved the barrels of her guns into their faces. She knelt there, and she didn't blink as she looked from one to the other.

"Drop it, bitch!" the driver shouted behind her. She risked a look. His eyes were red and filled with tears, but the pistol he pointed at her head didn't waver.

"Shoot me, and your two companions die." She narrowed her eyes. "Notice I said, 'shoot me' and not 'kill me.' You won't find that to be an easy task, not with a Teledyne Specialist."

The gunner gasped. "A Specialist?"

"Jesus Christ," the commander muttered.

"He's not here. Certainly not with the likes of you." She switched the FN-P90 to full-auto. The click was loud in the confines of the tank. She stared hard at the driver. "Your move, creep."

* * *

"It appears we've lost *Conquistadoris*," Lieutenant Egleton—Egghead—said. He looked up from the monitor. His glasses seemed to glow in the otherwise dim light of the command APC. "Along with a couple of trucks and a few dozen Guardsmen."

A flash of annoyance shot through Director Lloyd, but he quickly squashed it. "That was to be expected, unfortunately. I hoped the tank wouldn't have to be sacrificed until later, but it's served its purpose. Was it destroyed?"

"I don't know. The comms suddenly went dead, and we don't have any drones available to get a visual on it. It's possible the enemy captured it."

That could prove to be a good thing if Lloyd played his cards right. The tank was built by Obsidian, and Obsidian never sold weapons to third parties without certain failsafe measures in place, especially if the third party was the United States government. If the politicians had ever grown backbones to challenge the Corporations in the name of the people or their own petty greed, they would've found out how difficult it was with weapons that weren't really their own.

And if the cops tried to use that tank against him, they would pay just as dearly.

Lloyd turned to the hot little analyst he'd picked up from Colonel Eastman's unit. What had they jokingly called her? Anal? Well, he could get answers for that nickname later, in private. For now, he asked, "How are things on your end, Lieutenant Sullivan?"

"Lieutenant Egleton restored our connection to the satellite you indicated, but its security measures are more formidable than I expected an old satellite to have."

"It was part of a top-secret Obsidian project," Lloyd explained. "It's going to have some countermeasures to ensure its payload doesn't fall into the wrong hands."

"Payload?" Egghead frowned. "I was under the impression it was a spy satellite."

"Oh, it's that, too. You'll see. Sullivan, how many hours are we talking about?"

"Hours?" Anal looked over her shoulder and smiled. "Minutes, sir. No security measure's ever lasted more than a few minutes with me."

And not too many men, either, I'd wager. Lloyd savored the thought for a second, then pushed it away. Work before pleasure. That's how he got to be top dog in St. Louis, with prospects to climb even higher. Until this mess happened, but he was a resourceful man. He'd turn all these setbacks into payoffs. "Well, there's a first time for everything. Crack this code, and I'll have an even bigger challenge for you."

"Nothing's too big for me, sir."

"We'll see." *And you can take whatever meaning you want from that.* He shook his head to clear it. Focus, man.

Anal removed a hair tie from her shirt pocket and pulled her long brown hair into a ponytail. She cracked her knuckles and set her fingers to the keyboard. "All right, time to get serious!"

Silence filled the cabin, except for the clicking of keys. Anal's fingers danced so fast, they were a blur to Lloyd's eyes. Not that he was focused on her hands, not when there was so much else about her he liked the look of. She had the body and face of one of those pin-up girls bomber crews used to paint on the sides of their planes in World War II. He didn't remember much from his study of World War II history, other than the nose art and that it was capitalism that saved the Western world. Not even the greatest militaries could stand before the might of corporations in the black, nor could they be as ruthless as companies desperate to avoid going into the red.

Money, production capacity, and information ultimately won wars, if not all battles. And just because battles—or even a series of battles—were lost didn't mean the war was lost. The Allies were losing until their production capacity outpaced that of the Axis. The Union was losing until it outpaced the Confederacy in wartime production. The American Revolutionaries were losing until they dealt real damage to the Redcoats, damage they couldn't easily repair with reinforcements that were an ocean away, dealing with conflicts on the European continent.

And he would lose until he got his hands on the one thing that would turn this whole war around. Once he had that, this war would be over within a matter of days, if not hours. History would show him as the winner and the ruler of a new tomorrow, a tomorrow where Obsidian, and Obsidian alone, was the master, as the company was always meant to be.

Anal punched one last key command and then smiled. "We are in, sir."

Lloyd raised the lid on his laptop and saw something he hadn't seen in a long time. A menu appeared over a space-themed background, and the words "PROJECT TEZCA" filled the top of the screen. Beneath that, in smaller text, were the words "Satellite #103," which told him which satellite he was in direct communication with. "You can't gain access to the whole network?" he asked her.

"Negative, sir. The network is down. All we can do is access individual satellites."

He had known that, but he wanted to make sure he wasn't overlooking something only a hacker would notice. "It's possible too many of the company's cloud servers were destroyed, and the network has well and truly crashed."

"That's my assumption, sir." She shivered. "I saw a missile tracking map back in Fayetteville. It wasn't pretty."

"Try being in the middle of a nuke drop, then tell me how you feel." Lloyd ran his cursor over the menu buttons. "I was in St. Louis during the first strike. If my Agent hadn't gotten me to the emergency elevator in time, you wouldn't be blessed with my presence."

Her eyes widened. "How scary!"

"We had a fairly close call in Fayetteville, but nothing like that," Egghead added. "We're glad you made it out, sir."

"Not half as glad as I am." Lloyd frowned. "It was a shame about Agent Jacobs, though. He was a good man. I doubt he survived the blast. Even if he did, the building's collapse would've done him in."

"There's always hope, sir," Anal said. "Especially if he's an Agent."

Lloyd's frown deepened. There was something about Anal's cheerful attitude that bothered him, but he wouldn't mention it out loud as long as she continued to perform. A happy hacker wasn't a distracted hacker. She was a necessary part of his plan.

He accessed a map showing the satellite's current location and trajectory. It followed a repetitive path around Earth, revolving once every twelve hours and seven minutes. At that speed, it didn't spend much time over a target area before its camera or its payload was out of range. He activated the camera feed and put it up on the main monitor. Black clouds of smoke filled the screen, obscuring what was on the ground.

Anal gasped. "My God, is that a city? How is it still on fire after all this time?"

"It's certainly possible," Egghead explained. "Some materials can burn for weeks, like the rubber used to make vehicle tires. Set a few thousand cars and trucks on fire in a city and watch the smoke rise."

Lloyd hadn't thought about that. All he knew was that cars were useful for getting him from point A to point B, and that was only when a helicopter or plane wasn't available. He couldn't remember the last time he'd driven himself anywhere, much less messed with something so mundane as the vehicle's *tires*.

He turned the feed off. It was good to know the camera still worked. That would be useful when the satellite reached their area again. He would be able to get a better feel for how neighboring towns and cities were faring. Had they all been destroyed like he feared, or were there still a few out there, clinging to life after near-misses, like Columbia? If any such communities existed, they would be along this Midwest parallel, where neither Obsidian nor Teledyne had a particularly strong footing. This area had been one of JalCom's last holdouts.

And might still be a holdout if what he thought was beneath Columbia proved true.

Lloyd flipped over to the satellite's payload manifest. It was fully loaded and ready for deployment. The next time it would be over Columbia would be five hours and thirty-seven minutes from now. The approximate time for the payload to reach the target once launched was ten minutes.

Perfect. He smiled. Things were definitely going his way. In a few hours, the whole city would know who oversaw this Fallen World.

* * * * *

Chapter Thirteen

Countess and I galloped down the road, with Danny and twenty other officers right behind us. Jeremiah Jones rode on my right, with his RPG resting on his shoulder. Patrolman Lewis of the Atlanta PD rode on my left, holding an RPG in his hands. "Give the word, LT, and we'll light it up!"

"Wait until we know what's going on!" I said. "For all we know, Aster's inside and has neutralized them.

"That would explain why the tank suddenly went off-course like that!" Lewis said.

I rubbed Countess's neck. My hand came back covered in sweat. The poor animal had run all morning long, and it wouldn't be long before she was worn out. "Come on, girl, just a little more! We've got to see if Aster's all right!"

Countess snorted.

We got off the road where the tank had run off. Its tremendous weight had dug impressions into the soft shoulder. Those impressions grew into deep trenches the further into the wheat field the tank went. It had stopped, but even from our distance, I could hear the rumble of its engine.

I led the men up behind the tank out of view of its main gun and coaxial machine gun. An unmanned M2 faced the rear, its barrel pointed straight down at the tank's body.

The barrel suddenly inched upward until it lined up with me.

Oh, shit! I opened my mouth to scream at Jones and Lewis, but the tank's engine died, and the barrel of the gun suddenly dropped back down.

We fanned out around the rear of the tank and aimed our weapons at the top hatch. I raised my voice and shouted the words anyone who's seen any cop show has heard, "You in there, come out with your hands up!"

Jones snickered. "Been wanting to say that for a long time haven't you, LT?"

"It's why I wear the badge," I admitted.

A moment later, the hatch opened. "Don't shoot!" a voice called from deep inside. "We're coming out!"

I frowned. It wasn't Aster's voice, like I'd hoped. God, where was she? At last report, she was opening the hatch, then static filled the line for an instant before it went completely dead. "Keep your hands where we can see 'em!" I shouted.

"Yeah, we're a little pissed off right now," Danny added, looking down the barrel of his rifle. "It's hot, and we're itchin' to shoot someone."

A head peeked up over the lip of the hatch, followed by a pair of hands. One of them was covered in blood. "I'm Lieutenant DeSoto," he began.

"I don't care who you are," I snapped. "I care to know that you're unarmed. Are you?"

"Yes!"

"Good. You and I can be friends then. Now, get out of there nice and slow. How many are with you?"

"Two—no, three. Well, two plus one."

"What's he talking about?" Jones whispered loudly enough for the whole farm to hear.

"Is it two, or is it three?" I asked.

"Two of mine, and one of yours, I think."

"Aster?" I raised my voice. "Aster, you in there?"

"Yes!" came her answering call.

Relief flooded me for just a moment but then the tension returned. She was alive, but alone in a tank with two soldiers who—

I chuckled. This was *Aster* we were talking about. She'd be fine. I lowered my rifle. "Aster, keep those two occupied until we get DeSoto in handcuffs. Then, send the next one up and then the last one. We're going to do this nice and slow."

It took two of us to help DeSoto down from the tank. The man didn't want to make any sudden moves with so many rifles pointed at him, nor did he want to aggravate his wounded hand. Once we cuffed him, a squat man DeSoto said was Sergeant Yoder came out, followed by an Asian-American he called Corporal Ling.

When all three were seated on the grass, their hands cuffed behind their backs, Aster came out. Blood had soaked the white locks on the left of her face, and dried blood caked her cheek. Her armor was scratched and covered in clumps of wheat and mud, but otherwise, she looked fine. She hopped straight to the ground from the tank turret, and her boots sank a couple inches into the soft soil. She grimaced as she pulled herself free. "Well, that's one way to spend a morning, I suppose."

Jones laughed. "I'll say. Sweet Jesus, girl, that was some fine work!"

"He had my binoculars," I explained to Aster.

"My heart skipped a beat or three when you jumped from Sunshine onto the tank." Jones put a hand to his chest. "Then they started shooting at us again, and my heart returned to its usual rhythm."

"You really saved our necks out there," I said. "Good work, Aster."

She favored us with a small smile. "It's my job."

A *clop-clop-clop* made us turn toward the road. Sunshine approached at a trot, her golden hair glimmering with sweat. Upon seeing us, she increased her speed to a canter, but she stopped when she reached Aster. Before Aster could react, the horse bumped her shoulder with her nose. Aster laughed and petted Sunshine's nose. Foam dripped from the horse's mouth, and she was breathing hard, but she was clearly happy to see Aster. "It's good to see you, too, girl."

"Even though you were scared out of your wits?" Danny asked.

Aster's face reddened. "I was *not* scared."

"That's not what we heard over the comms," Jones said in a singsong tone.

Aster's face turned a brighter shade of red. "I wasn't scared," she muttered.

"Did you disable the tank?" I asked, changing the subject.

The look of gratitude Aster gave me almost made me laugh. She shook her head. "No, it's still operational."

That was better than we could have hoped for. "Well, then. Maybe we should get this thing back to base." I turned to the handcuffed crew. "Which one of you wants to drive us home?"

The crewmen shared a look. "Why should we help you?" DeSoto asked.

"Because we're the ones with the badges." Danny tapped the badge fixed to his plate carrier. "And if you don't, you might want to remember that we're the ones with the guns. Guns and a need for vengeance."

"Cop killers don't get much mercy 'round here," Lewis added.

DeSoto sighed. "You make a good point. Can we expect fair treatment if we do as you ask? Geneva Convention and all that?"

"I'm not sure what that is," I admitted.

"Right, sorry. That was superseded by the Five Corp Treaty of '29, wasn't it? Basically, don't treat us like crap. We're uniformed soldiers, as are you."

I recognized the Five Corp Treaty reference. "I have no problem with that." I pointed at the tank. "Provided you get us where we need to go. Only one of you, mind. Two of us will ride in the cab, with more on top."

"Very well. Ling, get back in there."

"I'll ride shotgun," Danny said. He slid from his saddle and handed Noir's reins to me.

"I will, too," Aster said. She climbed back onto the tank. "I think I've earned a seat."

I couldn't argue with her.

* * *

"Will wonders never cease?" Welliver shook his head. "Couple months back you rode in here with a wagon train full of weapons. Now you've brought a tank with you?"

"Not to mention two trucks full of food and a line of prisoners." Graham shook his head. His face was shaded by the black Stetson he wore when he wasn't gussied up in riot armor. "I'm afraid to ask how you intend to top this the next time you go out."

"Do I have to top it?" I asked. "I don't think my heart can take all these crazy missions. And I know Countess is getting tired of them."

Countess grunted as she munched on a few carrots I'd dropped on the ground in front of her.

We stood in the shade of a silver maple tree off Mick Deaver Memorial Drive, which was the same road we returned on with the aforementioned wagon train full of weapons. Back then, we were greeted by a mounted Welliver, a bunch of his deputies, and men like Saleh and Blackwood, who had been ready for a fight after the sound of gunfire echoed up their way. Their caution wasn't necessary, because the gunfire was Aster and her men dealing with Manager Strohl and his goons after they threatened my children.

I radioed our status and estimated arrival time to Captain Graham, and then I rode on ahead to greet him and the sheriff. We watched as the column of vehicles and horsemen approached and pulled off into the grass near the massive Mizzou Arena building. More officers waited, as did some student defenders who were on foot. Everyone was armed with a rifle; they were ready to fight if the prisoners suddenly tried something.

None did. The tank crew, under Aster's careful watch, didn't so much as twitch a finger out of turn, and the ones Corporal Ferris brought back seemed relaxed and talkative, as long as Cassandra Martinez wasn't looking their way. Silva brought back six prisoners and explained that the rest had either been killed or run off in a panic when he and his buffalo riders disabled the vehicle and trampled the first couple of soldiers who jumped out of the vehicle to try to fight them. The rest had given up pretty quickly, and they marched quietly between a knot of water buffalos.

"Losses?" Welliver asked, noting the wounded in the back of one of the trucks as it passed by.

My heart sank. This was a reason I hated these missions. "Five confirmed dead: Officers Stoltz and McDonald of the LAPD, Patrolman Bradley of New Orleans, Corporal White of Philadelphia, and Corporal Richardson of Raleigh. Twice as many wounded, and three missing. I saw their horses go down, but I didn't see what happened to them or who they were." Some officers had stayed behind in Three Rivers as backup in case the Homeguard decided to retaliate or chase Richard's Raiders home from the supply depot assault.

"Saleh reports a similar number of casualties from Richard's unit," Graham said. "Though none of his or Blackwood's men perished, thank God. Just a few wounded animals, including a camel that trampled the man who shot it. The camel survived. The man didn't."

All in all, it could've been worse. A lot worse. The odds were on our side, and maybe we received some divine favor, as well. I looked up at the sky and silently gave thanks.

Aster approached after the prisoners were marched off to the building where they would be housed. Welliver eyed her up and down. "Specialist, I hope you won't mind my saying this, but you look like you were taken for quite a ride."

"Two rides," she said. "First on Sunshine, then on *Conquistadoris*."

"And which was worse?"

She thought about it for a moment. "Well, the tank wasn't a horse, at least."

"Yeah, but it tried to kill you, first with electricity and then with guns."

"But it wasn't a horse."

I sighed. People don't normally get over deep-seated fears in a week, so why should Aster be any different? "You probably want to get all that mud and blood off your face." I reached into Countess's saddlebags and removed my canteen. I shook it, realized it was nearly empty, then put it back and removed a second one that was full. I tossed it to her.

She caught it, unscrewed the cap, and poured a bit on her face, then scrubbed furiously with her hands. Caked-on mud and blood turned back into liquid and dripped onto the ground. After a few more tries, her alabaster face was clean again. She shook her head like a dog shaking off water, and I tried not to laugh. I'd seen people do that as a joke, but she could move her head fast enough to make it work. And the way her white hair fluttered about as she did it was oddly attractive.

The sudden warmth in my chest made me uncomfortable, so I coughed and looked away.

After a moment, she screwed the cap back onto the canteen and handed it over. "Thank you. That'll hold me over until I can take a shower." She turned her head toward the line of prisoners being led away. "But first, I want to interrogate the tank crew."

Welliver and I shared a look. "Specialist, why don't you go ahead and freshen up? You might make more of an impact if you show up in that dark gray suit of yours."

"Or maybe the dress uniform you wore to the funerals," I added. "These are soldiers, after all. They'll respect you more if you're dressed like the high-ranking officer you are."

Aster looked down at her battered armor, at the mud caking it, and at the scratches where the green paint had been stripped away, revealing shiny metal beneath. "Hmm. I figured I'd be more intimidating like this, and that would get better results."

"I think you intimidated them plenty when you captured them," I said. "Now might be the time for a different tactic."

"I see." She thought about it a moment, then nodded. "You make a sound argument, Nathan. I'll do as you say."

"Perfect." Welliver hiked his left thumb over his shoulder. "We'll have them under guard in Jesse Hall. We'll let them stew for a bit, maybe soften 'em up for you, then let you deal with them."

"Understood, sir." Aster snapped a salute and walked away.

"And I'll make sure one of my men brushes down Sunshine for you," I called. "Make sure you visit her later!"

She paused and looked back over her shoulder. She surprised me with a small smile. "Thank you. I'm…glad she made it back safely."

Both of us waited until she was well out of earshot before heaving a collective sigh. "Good work," I whispered.

"Same to you. Now, let's go put the figurative screws to these guys before your young lady friend arrives with the literal screws."

* * *

"There you go, girl," Kevin murmured. He ran a brush along Countess's side. "I know I'm not Nathan, but he's a bit busy. You'll have to deal with me, instead."

Countess looked up from the hay she was munching on and bumped her face against Kevin's arm. He rubbed her nose, then stroked her mane as she returned to eating. "Good girl."

They stood outside one of the three campus stables positioned in a U-shape around a grassy yard. With them were several officers who'd returned from the morning's mission. They were all brushing down and feeding their tired mounts. Volunteers had stepped in to assist with the horses and buffalos whose riders weren't present. Some weren't present because they were busy with debriefings or interrogations. Others weren't there because they were wounded, and Doc Samuelson wouldn't let them. And a few weren't there because...because they would soon join Lieutenant Jackson, Patrolman McGraw, and the others in Hinkson Field.

That's where you'd be if you'd squeezed that trigger. Kevin's throat constricted. One finger twitch, and he wouldn't be standing there, helping brush down his friend's horse.

"Come on, Noir, stand still." Helen brushed Danny Ward's black filly and worked a particular area on the animal's shoulder. "There's a knot here I need to get out. Bear with me."

Despite the sadness that still threatened to overwhelm him, the mere sight of Helen brought a smile to Kevin's face. Nathan's nine-and-a-half-year-old daughter had somehow reached into his darkness and pulled him free of it. And any time he felt himself sinking back, all he needed was Helen's presence to give him the strength to push through another day. He'd always seen the children of friends as if they were nieces and nephews, and that feeling was compounded exponentially where Helen and, by extension, Jason were concerned. Even with so much death and destruction, children were a light that could not be snuffed out.

"It's good to see you smiling again."

Brother Stephen Pham stood nearby, brushing down a brown gelding that wore a bridle bearing the emblem of the New Orleans

PD. "I feared we'd never see you do so again," the pastor from Mobile said.

You almost didn't. Kevin shivered despite the heat. "I wasn't sure I would again, either."

"There!" Helen exclaimed as the knot of hair came loose. She went back to brushing Noir more gently. "I bet that feels loads better, doesn't it?"

Kevin watched her for a moment. "Kids have a way of bringing smiles to everyone nearby, you know? My boys—" His voice caught in his throat, but he pressed on. "I could be so furious at my boys one minute, then laughing so hard at them the next, my stomach hurt."

"My kids were the same." Stephen's eyes grew distant and pained. "Not a day goes by that I don't think about them, about what happened to them. I…"

Kevin's heart ached. He didn't know Stephen had children. The pastor spent so much time focused on the suffering of others that his own seemed nonexistent. "You pray it was quick, right?"

"Yeah." A tear rolled down Stephen's tan cheek, but he didn't wipe it away. "I know they're in Heaven and beyond all suffering and sadness now. I just pray they didn't suffer on their way there." He chuckled. "Although, knowing Marshall—he was my youngest—he'd have thought the missiles were the coolest thing ever."

"James would've been the same way." Kevin shook his head, a mixture of mirth and sorrow filling him. "Always loved the fireworks on the 4th of July and New Year's, or any other time of the year. If he heard someone shooting off bottle rockets, he'd be halfway down the street looking for them before Rebecca or I knew where he'd gone."

"That was Marshall." Stephen rubbed his eyes. "I bet our kids are giving their mothers a lot of grief up there right now."

"Oh, without a doubt!"

The two men laughed loudly enough to cause Helen to look over. "Hey, what's so funny?"

"We're just happy to be here," Kevin said, and he was surprised that he meant it. He walked around to Countess's other side and started brushing again, his back to Helen. "Happy that your father made it back safely, as did most of the officers. Happy the mission was successful."

"Daddy and the others did good. Maybe that means things will turn around for all of us soon."

"Maybe so."

"The Lord always provides," Stephen agreed.

Kevin suddenly felt arms encircle his waist, and a tiny form pressed against his back. "I'm glad you're here, too, Uncle Kevin," Helen said, her small arms squeezing for all they were worth.

"I won't be here long if you keep bear-hugging me like that," Kevin said, his words strained like he was being choked.

She let go and gave him a playful shove. "Oh, please. I'm not that strong."

Maybe not physically, but there was an iron will encased in that little body. Kevin could clearly see that. She'd be a formidable young lady in a few years, provided she lived that long.

No, she *would* live that long. That long and more. He shared a look with Brother Stephen, who nodded at him as if he'd been thinking the same thing.

As he returned to brushing Countess, Kevin made a promise to himself: he would keep Helen and Jason as safe as he could. His children may have perished, but that didn't mean Nathan's children had to. And as long as he was alive, they wouldn't.

* * *

"Your name is Hernando DeSoto?" I asked.

"You got a problem with that?" The captured tank commander glared at me as he rubbed his previously cuffed wrists. Someone had treated and bandaged his right hand.

Welliver, DeSoto, and I sat in an adjunct professor's office in the administration building. We were on one side of the desk, with DeSoto on the other. Patrolman Jones stood at the door. If DeSoto tried anything, he wasn't going to get anywhere.

"No problem at all, other than it piques my interest in history," I said. "Hernando DeSoto was the name of the conquistador who explored the area around west Florida and southern Alabama. He conquered and scattered the Mauvillan tribe of American Indians my hometown's named after."

"The same!" DeSoto grinned. "My family supposedly traces our lineage back to him. He may not have been a nice guy, but he got results."

"Kind of like you, I suppose," Welliver said.

His grin faded. "What do you mean?"

"You and your boys came to Columbia for the express purpose of stirring shit up. You didn't care who got hurt in the process, so long as the mission was accomplished, right?" Welliver rose from his chair and pressed his left fist against the desk's polished surface. "You killed a lot of good men out there today, and that's not counting what you and your so-called Homeguard did to the Vargas horse ranch."

"You're not scaring me, old man, so you can cut the good cop, bad cop routine." DeSoto leaned back in his chair. "As for the ranch...I don't know what you mean."

"Rock Bridge Ranch?" I prompted. "Burned to the ground a week and a half ago? Everyone but one young boy was killed. They were shot by *your* people. I know because I was there."

"That ranch was on fire when we arrived! We sent in soldiers to help, but we started getting shot at, so we returned fire. Then your people arrived and started shooting at us, too." His eyes narrowed. "We assumed you set the fire."

I was too puzzled to be angry at the accusation. Welliver and I shared a look, and then he said, "I am—*was*—good friends with Simon Vargas, that household's patriarch. He and I go way back. We were schoolyard buddies, then we served together at Fort Bragg before it was turned into an Obsidian boot camp. I'd never order him, and his family, hurt." He gestured toward Nathan. "Nor would any of my commanders. The Vargas household has been friendly to the visiting mounted units since before this mess began."

"Visiting?" For the first time, DeSoto looked at our uniforms. "Wait, you're from Mobile? The Colonel's from there. Or he went to school there, at least."

I couldn't help the excitement that shot through me, followed by the sudden melancholy that threatened to pull me into depression. Another Mobilian, even a transplant, so far from home after all that had happened? I didn't believe in coincidence, so maybe this was some sort of sign. "We're from all over the place. Alabama, Florida, Pennsylvania, California, pretty much every state. We've also got

Canadians, Brazilians, Japanese, Jordanians, Israelis, Britons, and Nepalis, to name a few of our international brothers and sisters in uniform."

"No shit?" DeSoto crossed his arms. "We assumed you had cobbled a bunch of uniforms together to build your tyrant army."

I laughed. "Well, I guess I can see how it could look that way, but no. We're all sworn officers. Admittedly, we're outside our jurisdiction, and we lack a bit in the monetary compensation department—"

"Don't we all?" DeSoto and Welliver muttered in unison.

"But we've all been deputized by the good sheriff, and we're doing our best to hold together what might be one of the last cities the United States has left. One that hasn't been turned into a smoking crater in any event."

"It's that bad?" DeSoto asked, leaning forward. "We were just outside Fayetteville when it disappeared in a flash. Lost a bunch of men who were inside the city. We hoped it was a localized event, but long-range comms were down for days, and then we linked up with Anal—analysts from a different Guard unit who gave us more of the story. And then there was Springfield…" He shivered.

I looked at Welliver, who nodded. "It's nationwide, or possibly worldwide," I said. Anger rose in me as I added, "Obsidian and Teledyne really did a number everywhere, including Mobile."

"And Tucson? That's where I'm from originally."

"I don't remember, but we have records at city hall, as well as a memorial board set up in the student union building."

"Lot of out-of-staters here for final exams the day it all went to shit," Welliver added.

DeSoto was quiet for a long moment. Finally, he muttered, "Shit. Things get better and better, don't they?" He looked up at us. "So, why are you working with the Corporations?"

"It's less about us working with them," Welliver said, "and more about them working with us. Both Corporations joined forces a couple of months back to try and take us off the board. It backfired, and what you see of either Teledyne or Obsidian is what's left after the attempt."

"The Obsidian force in the city was always small," I added, "before reinforcements arrived from St. Louis. They're a small force again, led by a real witch of a woman named Gwendolyn Greenway."

"And you trust them?"

"About as far as we can throw them." I crossed my arms. "Though, in truth, neither Manager Kazama nor Director Greenway has been all that bad to work with. They're arrogant and out of touch as you'd expect any Corporate executive to be, but they keep their districts under control without too heavy a hand."

DeSoto fell silent again. After a moment, he said, "It's…possible we have bad intel."

"Bad intel? With the military?" Welliver chuckled. "Say it ain't so, Hernando."

DeSoto cracked a smile. "Yeah, hard to believe, right? You figure the G-Men would get their shit together, especially now of all times."

"G-Men?" I asked.

"Suits. Feds. Government agents."

"I get the term. What G-Men are you talking about?"

"One in particular: this guy who only meets with Colonel Eastman. Showed up about a month ago in a black APC, while we were headed up Highway 37. He was headed south, so we crossed paths.

The APC looked like it'd been in quite a firefight at some point. We rolled out ahead of our column to confront it and had a bit of a Mexican standoff until the radio crackled, and someone called Colonel Eastman by name. The G-Man stepped out long enough to greet the colonel and then the two of them disappeared inside to talk privately." He shrugged. "It's been that way ever since. The APC disappears for days, then it comes back so the G-Man can brief the colonel or invite a few of our intelligence officers in for discussions."

A black APC? The back of my neck started to itch, as it always did when there was trouble. "Did you get a good look at this G-Man?"

"A brief glimpse through *Conquistadoris'* NVG setup, yeah."

Welliver reached into his briefcase and removed a manila envelope which he handed to me. I opened and held it as he reached inside and removed a dossier with a set of photographs clipped to the front. They were all of the same man: Director Lloyd of Obsidian. Welliver removed one of the photos and set it in front of DeSoto. "Is this your guy?"

"Holy shit, yeah." DeSoto picked up the photo and looked at it closely. "This is him."

"You're sure?"

"Sure as the stench of a bloated corpse."

"That's a thought I could do without." I took back the photo and set it on the table.

"Who is he? I'm guessing he's no G-Man."

"More like an O-Man." Welliver spun the dossier around and pushed it over to DeSoto so he could view it right-side up. DeSoto skimmed the first few lines of Lloyd's biography and cursed. "Obsidian? Bastard swore up and down to the colonel he was with the Pentagon. Had all the proper clearances to back it up, too."

"Is that what your commanding officer told you?" Welliver asked.

"It is. And before you say anything, I trust Colonel Eastman. He's no Corporate lackey. He hates the bastards almost as much as I do."

"You can both join the club," I muttered.

"So, there you have it," Welliver said. "It looks like it's your side that's working for the Corporations, or at least one of them. Lloyd was the Director of Obsidian's St. Louis office. He brought reinforcements for Director Greenway and an imprinter so he could turn one of ours into an Agent."

My chest tightened and fresh anger welled up inside. "Lloyd's actions resulted in the deaths of a lot of good men, including one of my best friends." My trigger finger twitched as I remembered that fatal shot. Jake had deserved so much better than that.

"And you think he's using us to take over the city for his own gain?"

"That's practically a given." Welliver scratched his beard. "That man wants this city at any cost. And it wouldn't surprise me if you're a pawn in his greater scheme."

"It would explain the hostile actions we can't reconcile," I added. "The attack on Rock Bridge Ranch. The burning of the farms by those we assumed were your men."

"We assumed that was your boys, along with the murders of some of our scouts. Well, shit." DeSoto placed his elbows on the table and rested his chin on interlaced fingers. His eyes slid left to right as he considered the situation, then he chuckled. "I'm reminded of an old internet meme I saw when I was a kid, 'That look you have when you realize you're actually the villain.'"

"It's not as simple as that," I said. "Things have become so murky since the Fall, it's hard to tell where heroism ends, and villainy begins." I thought about Danny's extreme measures against the home-invading degenerates in Boonville weeks back and how Saleh and some of the other commanders dealt with murderers in the streets of Columbia. With the jails already full and the courts overwhelmed and nonfunctional, what was left to do besides enforce harsh measures when actual crimes—heinous crimes, at that—were being committed?

"What my friend from Alabama means to say," Welliver explained, "is that it's not too late to come back from this. We're willing to work with the Corporations if they play ball. We'll extend the same courtesy to your Guard unit. Blood's been shed on both sides, but it doesn't have to be that way forever. We can join forces to protect this city, its surroundings, and our way of life."

"For all we know, this is the last city on Earth," I said. "And I want a place where my kids can grow up in relative peace."

"It's the dream, isn't it?" DeSoto asked. "I'll need to talk to my crew, but I can't imagine they'll want to continue fighting for the Corporations, not when they can fight against them."

Welliver and I stood. "We'd be happy to have you and your men join us," I said. "And the same goes for your whole unit."

Before DeSoto could respond, there was a knock at the door. When it opened, Aster stepped in, wearing her black military dress uniform, complete with skirt and peaked officer's cap. "Sheriff, Lieutenant, my men and I are ready for the interro…gation." She looked from Welliver and me to DeSoto, her head cocked to the side. "Why do I get the feeling that won't be necessary?"

I looked at DeSoto. "You made the right call, Lieutenant."

DeSoto had frozen at the sight of Aster. "Yeah…I can't say that you're wrong on that one, Lieutenant Ward."

He stood and held out a shaky hand. I shook it. "Glad to have you onboard. We can use all the help we can get in this Fallen World."

* * * * *

Chapter Fourteen

Helen had just finished cleaning the cookie crumbs out of Jason's wheelchair when there was a knock at the door. "Coming!" she called.

Jason looked up from what had to be his hundredth tank drawing. "Maybe it's Dad!"

"Nuh-uh. He's way too busy to be back this early in the day."

"But he was gone *all* night!"

"Yeah, and he'll be gone *all* day, too, I bet."

"Man…" Jason dropped his pencil on the table and rested his chin on his fist, the pose he always took when he was pouting.

Helen rolled her eyes as she walked to the door. *So immature. He needs to control his emotions better.*

She opened the door and found Aster in an olive-drab uniform. "Aunt Aster, you're back!" Helen ran through the open doorway and threw her arms around the petite woman. "How was your ride with Sunshine?"

Aster rubbed Helen's back. "She ran like the wind, like you said she would."

"I know, right?" Helen pulled herself free of Aster's embrace. "Wasn't that so much fun?"

"Fun…is a relative term." Aster looked uncomfortable, but the smile she gave Helen seemed genuine.

"Aunt Aster!" Jason hurried over and held his arms out for a hug.

Aster knelt and pulled him into a gentle embrace. "I'm glad to see you up and about without the wheelchair."

"I can do it as long as we're around the gorm," he said.

"*Dorm*," Helen corrected.

"That's what I said. Gorm." He tugged on Aster. "Come in. We've got cookies!"

"We *had* cookies. You ate them all."

"Oh. Sorry. We *had* cookies. Do you wanna see my newest tank drawing?"

Aster let herself be pulled to the table. "I'd love to. Oh, is this a T803?"

"Uh-huh!" Jason's lips split open into a gap-toothed grin. "How could you tell?"

"Its armored skirt has a unique design. You drew it very well." She ruffled Jason's hair. "Your eye for detail saved my life out there. If you hadn't told me about that loose emergency hatch, I wouldn't have been able to capture the enemy's M78."

"Woah, you caught a tank?"

"The term is *captured*," Helen explained. "You catch fish. You capture tanks."

"How'd you do it?"

Aster explained to them exactly how she'd done it, from the race along the highway with Sunshine, to the fight on top of the tank, to the final showdown inside the tank as she fought against mud and men. Helen's respect and awe for Aster grew with each new detail she shared. Even Jason was left speechless at the end, save for a final, "Woah."

"Shouldn't you get some rest?" Helen asked after Aster finished the tale. "From the sound of it, you've been up since last night."

"I've been up for the last three nights." Aster shrugged. "I don't need much sleep. I also…" She shook her head as if to clear it. "I don't need much sleep."

"Do you have bad dreams?" Helen asked.

Aster blinked. "What makes you say that?"

"Daddy has them from time to time." Helen's mood turned somber. "There are some nights he talks in his sleep, and other nights when he's not in his bed. He's on the balcony, or outside, or out in the living room. He used to do that at home, but now it's worse."

"A lot of officers are going through that," Aster said. "At least, according to Brother Stephen."

"It's true," a voice called from outside.

Brother Stephen stood in the open doorway. He pointed to the bag Aster left on the ground. "Range time?"

"Yes. How'd you know?"

Stephen chuckled. "Lord knows I've seen enough range bags to know one. You don't minister to cops without the obligatory 'Hey, Padre, why don't you come shooting with us?' invitation getting thrown at you every other shift." He patted the holstered sidearm on his hip. "And it finally paid off, I guess. Department policy doesn't allow me to carry, but, well, we're not exactly within the department's jurisdiction anymore, are we?"

"It *does* look like Daddy's range bag," Helen said as she studied the sack's canvas material. Excitement surged through her. "Wait, are you going now? Is that why you—"

"Came here?" Aster smiled. "Yes. I promised you I'd teach you how to shoot, right?" She stepped back through the door and picked up the bag. "One lesson isn't going to cut it. You need more range time, and where we're headed, there'll be plenty of room."

Helen wanted to jump for joy, but she forced her feet to stay on the floor. She'd had so much fun when she shot Aster's pistol. She and Billy—

The excitement she was feeling evaporated, leaving her hollow. Billy had pulled through, but he was still comatose. The doctors were confident it was only a matter of time before he woke up. Until then, she'd keep going to see him as often as she could, with Brother Stephen or Kevin or whoever wanted to go with her. What happened to him and his family served as another reminder for why Helen wanted to learn how to fight.

"Can I come, too?" Jason asked. "Pretty please?"

Aster shook her head. "Sorry, but we don't have any way to transport your wheelchair. The men already took the APC out there, and it was loaded with equipment. We'll get you out another time, okay?"

"You can hang out with me," Stephen promised. "We'll head over to the pond. There should be a lot of frogs there after all that rain."

"Frogs? Yay! I'll get my boots!"

Jason hurried off to the bedroom. Stephen looked at Helen and Aster and made shooing gestures. "Better get while the gettin's good."

Aster led Helen outside, then down the stairs to the ground level. They walked around the side of the building toward Brandon Hampton dormitory's circular drive. The black APC she and her people used sat there, its idling engine audible even at this distance. "I thought you said your men already took the APC?"

"They did. They're inside it. There really isn't room for his wheelchair, and we wouldn't have time to push him all the way to the Sharon Observatory."

Helen's eyes widened. "We're going to an observatory? With the big telescope and everything?"

"You'll see."

The front passenger door opened, and Helen was surprised at how thick it was. Aster must've noticed because she explained. "That's armor, to better protect the driver and navigator." She tapped the glass. "This is bulletproof, too."

One of Aster's men, a giant named Sergeant William Grumbine, peered out from the driver's seat. "Well, looks like we've got a guest! Is she riding shotgun?"

Helen giggled. "Daddy says that a lot."

Grumbine's bushy beard split into a grin. "I bet he does. Does that mean you're his riding partner pretty often?"

"Yep! I'm the oldest."

"So you are! Well, hop on in. You can hold onto the boss's range bag for her."

"Okay!"

Aster helped Helen into the front seat, then handed her the range bag. Helen grunted at the heft, but she managed to pull it up into her lap. Her feet didn't quite touch the passenger cabin's steel floor, so she kicked her feet as she looked around.

"Watch your hands," Aster warned, then slammed the door shut with a loud boom. She then clambered up onto the side of the door and planted her feet firmly on the steel running board. She looked around, then banged the side of the APC.

Helen grimaced at the sudden noise. "Why'd she do that?"

"That means we're clear to go." Grumbine threw the vehicle into drive and started forward. He drove around the circular drive, then turned onto the road that would take them south out of the university. He keyed his mic. "Point Chiffon, this is Little Bill. We are en route, with Lady in Black and—" He glanced at Helen and covered his mic. "What's your call sign?"

Helen shrugged. "I don't think I have one."

"With Lady in Black and Miss Ward, She-Without-a-Call-Sign, over." He winked at her. "We'll come up with something for you before too long, little lady. If it's one thing we're good at, it's giving each other nicknames."

"Like Lady in Black? Where'd that come from?"

"Dammit, why can't they get this crap out of the way?" Grumbine maneuvered the APC around a disabled van. "All the rest of the nearby roads have been cleared, so why not this one?"

Grumbine kept an eye on the van as they rolled past. Helen noticed Aster doing the same thing. "You know what the boss's name means, right?"

"Aster? It's a flower."

"Right. Well, Lady in Black is a type of aster. Kind of like how there are different colored roses or different kinds of apples." He gunned the engine as they approached an intersection and sped right through it. "Intersections are prime ambush points," he told her. "Best not to slow down if you can avoid it.

"Anyway, our unit commander—over even the boss lady herself—called her that after he saw her in action for the first time. She came back from a night mission inside an Obsidian radar station decked out all in black, except for her white hair and a red splotch across her chest. Blood from some Obsidian punk, I guess. Colonel

Tazi took one look at her, then told her Lady in Black was her call sign from then on." He laughed. "And then there was this other time…"

Grumbine regaled Helen with stories of Aster's early days in the unit the rest of the way to the observatory. They rolled past a couple of suburban neighborhoods, past stands of trees, then finally through open farmland before they arrived. Helen didn't know exactly what to expect when she first heard of a nearby observatory, but what she saw exceeded her expectations and disappointed her at the same time, if that was possible. She'd expected a gigantic stone building on a high cliff, with a bulbous dome that had a massive telescope, taller than the observatory, jutting up out of it. Like something out of an old fantasy game art book that was her grandpa's. What game had that been? One of the original Final Fantasy ones, she thought.

Instead, what she got was a quaint brick building surrounded by a freshly paved parking lot on one side and tall hedges on the other. The observatory's main entrance faced open farmland, while the city rose behind it, with dense woodland between. It still had a big dome on top, but she didn't see a giant telescope peeking out of it.

The parking lot was surrounded by a low fence made of fieldstones, similar to the perimeters around some of the farms she'd seen on the short trip here. She could climb over it if she needed to, but it looked pretty and kept small animals from getting run over in the parking lot. Unless they slipped through the iron gate. Or, she realized as they turned toward it, they could just go around the back. The stone fence ended at a marsh.

That gate was open, and a dark-haired woman who looked familiar stood outside it. An AR-15 similar to Aunt Amy's was slung from her shoulder. She waved, and Grumbine returned the gesture as they pulled through the gate. The parking lot was empty save for a few seemingly disabled vehicles and the white station wagon with fake wood paneling she'd ridden in from Billy's farm. A group of students milled around the car as a man about Daddy's age opened the tailgate and started unloading spools of cabling and other materials she couldn't identify.

"The two profs have been busy all day, it seems," Grumbine said. "That's gotta be their third or fourth trip out this way so far. They offered to help get things set up, and we've been alternating transporting people and equipment."

"They've helped Daddy several times now." She pointed at one of the big spools of cable. "What're you working on?"

"That's a bit of a secret, doll." He pulled into all three handicapped spaces against the building. As he turned the engine off, he stroked his beard. "Hmm. Doll. Something with doll. Yeah, that could work."

He opened the door and reached for the giant scoped rifle in the vehicle's vertical gun rack. He carefully pulled it free and slung it over his shoulder once he climbed out. Aster opened Helen's door from the outside and helped her get down.

The back door of the observatory opened, and out came Sergeant Louella Kirby, the unit medic. A lollipop stick hung out of her mouth, and she raised a hand in lazy salute. "Yo, Lady! And little Miss Ward, too!" She placed her hands on her knees and bent over so she was at eye level with Helen. "What're you doing here?"

"Aster's gonna teach me how to shoot!"

"Is she now?" Kirby reached in her pocket and pulled out a watermelon lollipop. "How about I give you one of these if you do well?"

Helen grinned. "I like the sound of that."

Kirby ruffled her hair. "I bet you do. All right, Boss, we won't keep you. The eggheads want us to help 'em with their toy."

"What kind of perimeter security do we have?" Aster asked. "I saw Paxton and Aino up on the second floor."

"There're a couple of large classrooms that look out to the east and south. Paxton's making sure Aino has more ammo belts for his M240 than he knows what to do with. We're considering having the students fill some sandbags to make a barrier up there and on the roof, similar to what we've got in the parking lot here."

Kirby pointed. Beyond the station wagon, Helen could see the makings of a sandbag barrier, like the kind she'd seen on the news during hurricanes, before the power went out, and all they had left was the radio. She frowned. Were they expecting a flood?

"We'll have the Ma Deuce set up there within the hour." Corporal Barry Crick hiked a thumb over his shoulder. "We wanted to put her up on the roof, but there's no good vantage point for the western approach from up there. That's why we wanted a bit of extra firepower on this side. Terrain is too poor for the APC to do much good behind the complex, and we don't want it sitting in the gated parking lot for obvious reasons."

It wasn't obvious to Helen, but she didn't want to interrupt the adults when they were talking.

"Good," Aster said after a moment. "I'll walk through it all later, but now, we need to do some target practice. Is there a safe direction for us?"

"Across the way, there's a good-sized berm the local farmer uses for sighting in deer rifles." Grumbine pointed toward the farmhouse directly across from the observatory's main entrance. "He and his wife brought over all kinds of cheeses and baked goods earlier today. Thanked us for helping out and said we could use anything they have, including the berm." Grumbine grinned. "I think he saw my rifle and wanted to have a competition."

Aster climbed into the back of the APC for a few minutes. When she hopped back down, she held four different weapons, one on each shoulder and one in each hand. She jerked her head toward the farm. "Let's go, Helen."

Helen swallowed. Nervousness suddenly washed over her. Kirby must've noticed because she ruffled her hair again. "It'll be all right, Helen. You'll see!"

* * *

Aster and Helen set up in the farmer's field across from the observatory at a berm made of piled dirt. Aster had her shoot her Five-Seven pistol again, and Helen worked her way through several magazines. Rather than simple target practice, Aster made her wear a holster and train in drawing, aiming, shooting, holstering, then drawing again. "The repetition is what helps you learn," she explained.

After a half hour, Aster set down the Five-Seven and took a bigger gun from her range bag. She held it up. "This is the FN-P90. It fires the same cartridge as the Five-Seven pistol, but it can go fully automatic. Would you like to try it out?"

Helen's eyes widened. "That's the gun you saved Jason and me with!"

"It is." Aster brushed the weapon's barrel. "I've had this my entire career. It's saved my life countless times. Maître D'—my trainer—picked it out for me because of my small stature when I was ten. I was shorter than you at the time."

"No way."

"It's true. You'll be taller than me before you know it." She held out the P90. "The safety's on. Keep your finger away from the trigger guard and let me know how it feels."

The gun was a lot lighter than Helen imagined. It might have been lighter than Aunt Amy's AR-15. And it was a lot shorter, too. She could see the weapon tucked away in a vehicle or in someone's violin case, like Tommy guns in the old gangster movies she sometimes caught Daddy and Uncle Danny watching on the weekends.

"Aim down the sight with it," Aster said, "but don't touch the trigger."

Helen did as instructed. She shouldered the weapon. Her right thumb slipped through the hole in the weapon's grip while her left hand held the foregrip. The fit and feel was similar to the .22 rifle Daddy had. She looked down the sight and was surprised to see a red dot staring back at her.

"That's an optical sight," Aster explained. "It should help you sight in better. Although, at this range, you really won't need that. When you're ready, push the safety forward until it clicks once. That'll put it in semi-auto mode."

Helen lined up on the target, switched off the safety, and squeezed the trigger. The weapon kicked back into her shoulder, but the recoil felt much lighter than it had with the handgun. When she brought the barrel back down in line with the target, she saw a hole in the center of the silhouette's chest.

"Nice shot!" Aster said with a smile.

Helen grinned and aimed again. She clicked the safety and started to squeeze the trigger.

"Stop!" Aster snapped.

Helen reflexively clenched her finger, and the gun came alive in her hands. An earsplitting roar filled the air as the weapon went fully automatic. Round after round shot out of the barrel, and the stock hammered into her shoulder again and again. The recoil caused her arms to rise until she was shooting well above the berm, and the rounds were flying off somewhere into the sky.

A steadying hand pressed against her back, while another grabbed her left hand and pulled the weapon back down on target. The remaining rounds in the gun's magazine emptied into the paper target, shredding it into barely recognizable pieces.

When the bolt at last locked back on an empty magazine, Helen's knees gave out. She would've sunk to the ground, but Aster's reassuring grip held her in place. With her other hand, Aster took the P90 from Helen's trembling fingers. "Sorry, that was my fault," Aster said. "I taught you to turn the safety off every time you shoot, and you went ahead and did it this time. Only you changed it from semi-auto to full-auto."

"No, it was my fault," Helen said. "I wasn't careful." She tucked her legs against her body and wrapped her arms around her knees. "Maybe I shouldn't be doing this."

"You did well with the handgun," Aster said. "And you would've done fine with the P90, too." She put a hand to her chin as she studied the other guns she'd brought. One was a shotgun, and the other was a long-barreled rifle with a scope. Both freaked Helen out, and she hoped she wouldn't have to shoot them.

Finally, Aster said, "I have an idea. Would you like to shoot one more gun? It's big, but I think it'll be a lot more manageable."

Helen felt a fresh jolt of fear at the word "big," but she nodded. "Okay. If you think it'll be fine."

"It's what I trained with back when I had a similar accident." Aster keyed her mic. "Little Bill, would you mind bringing the Ma Deuce out here? I think she could use a little bit of crew-served weapons familiarization."

Aster gathered up their gear and moved them back a hundred feet. "It won't be fair for the targets if we are too close," she told Helen.

That made sense, Helen guessed.

Grumbine arrived in the APC a few minutes later. He and Aster hefted a big machine gun out of the back. The size of it instantly set Helen's teeth on edge, but she'd agreed, so she was going to be a good girl and suck it up. Besides, Aster said it would work for her, right?

"This is the M2 Browning machine gun," Aster explained as Grumbine set the weapon on a tripod. "Otherwise known as the Ma Deuce."

"Why Ma Deuce?" Helen asked.

"It's a military thing," Grumbine explained. "We often abbreviate terms so they're faster to say. So, we say Ma Deuce instead of… Hmm." He looked at Aster. "Wait, why do we call it that instead of M2? It's the same number of syllables."

Aster shrugged. "Regardless, it's either the M2 or the Ma Deuce. A .50 caliber machine gun. It's a crew-served weapon, meaning two or more individuals work it together to make sure it stays up and running. One person can operate it as both the loader and gunner, but it's faster with two people."

Grumbine sized Helen up, then spent a moment adjusting the tripod. He stopped when the Ma Deuce was level with Helen's shoulders. He then motioned toward a green ammo can like the one Daddy stored his shotgun shells in. "Try picking this up, doll. Careful, it's heavy."

Helen leaned over, grabbed the metal handle with both hands, and lifted. She grunted at the sudden strain on her shoulders, but she managed to keep the can off the ground.

"Good! Now bring it over here." He slapped a flat spot on the left side of the gun. "Near the action, see?"

Helen lugged the ammo can over and set it down in the designated spot. Grumbine popped the lid on the can, then spun it around so it locked in place. Inside the can was a belt of shiny cartridges. Big cartridges. Her eyes widened. "I've never seen a bullet that big! It's like a cannon shell!"

"Of a sort," Grumbine said with a laugh. "They make a crazy amount of noise, and their bite is a lot worse than their bark. You would not want to get hit with one of these things, that's for sure."

He pushed a tab, and the top cover of the machine gun lifted. "Now, once you lift his cover, it exposes the action. You take the end of the belt and feed it in like this. See?"

Grumbine had Helen repeat the drill several times, until she could easily fit the belt into the gun without any hiccups. "Perfect work, doll! We'll make a gunner out of you yet. Now, take hold of this wooden handle—it's called the charging handle—and pull back on it twice."

She did as instructed.

"Excellent. Now the weapon is in what we call Condition One. It's ready to fire. So, for aiming, it's like any other gun you've shot. There's an iron sight on either end, and you line them up until they're on the target you hate so much, you want to annihilate it." Grumbine chuckled. "After this baby's done with something, not even God can put it back together."

"I don't think that's true," Helen said. "God can put anything back together."

"It's a figure of speech, doll." Grumbine ruffled her hair. "Anyway, this thing does a ton of damage, but it's surprisingly manageable for the gunner. It's heavy, and the tripod helps. The trick is to fire in short bursts, so the recoil doesn't get away from you." He gripped the pair of vertical handles on the rear of the gun and pantomimed depressing the butterfly-shaped trigger with his thumbs. "Press, hold for one or two seconds, then let go." He straightened his thumbs, then bent them again. "Press, hold for one to two seconds, then let go."

Helen repeated the exercise, mouthing the instructions as she did.

"Excellent. Would you like to destroy some targets?"

"Would you fire it first?" Helen asked.

"Hmm, I would, but I'm afraid it would scare you. It's really noisy."

"What if I'm already scared to fire it?"

"That's just anticipation. You'll be fine once you see that it's not all that bad." He grinned. "And better than bad, it's *fun*."

Helen looked at Aster, who nodded. "You'll be fine. I felt the same way at first."

"Yeah, and now, she's able to carry this thing around and fire it from the hip if she has to!" Grumbine laughed. "Remember that time in Lexington? Damn, but that was some fine work, Boss. You saved our bacon."

"It was stupid and could've backfired horribly."

"But it didn't, did it?"

Aster smiled. "Ever the optimist. No, it didn't."

Helen couldn't believe Aster had walked around with this gun and shot it! It looked so heavy! Then again, Aster was super strong. She guessed anything was possible for her. But, hadn't she said there was a time when she had been as small and weak as Helen? She'd been able to shoot this gun then, and that meant Helen could do it, too. She nodded. "All right, I'm ready."

"Excellent!" Grumbine slid over so she could sit behind the gun. He placed a hand on her back. "Remember three things: one, the boss and I are here to keep you safe. That's the most important thing to remember. You will be fine as long as we're here."

Helen felt butterflies in her stomach, but she nodded. "Okay."

"Two, remember to depress the trigger in very short bursts. No more than a second or two, then let go. That's the most important thing to remember."

"Okay."

"Uh," Aster began.

"Three, and this is the most important thing to remember: have fun!" He gave her a gentle slap on the back. "That's what target shooting's all about!"

Helen grinned. "Okay!"

"You just said all three things were the most important," Aster objected.

"I couldn't decide which one was most important," Grumbine said, "so they're all most important. Right, Helen?"

Helen giggled. "Right!"

"You're not nervous anymore, are you?" Grumbine asked.

Helen thought about it and was surprised to find she wasn't. "No. I'm not."

Grumbine's beard split into his familiar grin. "Then that's the fourth most important thing. Don't be scared and stay in control of your emotions and your weapon. Are you in control, doll?"

Helen nodded. "Yes."

"Excellent. Then take aim and send some letters to God."

She gripped the M2's handles and lifted them to drop the barrel and line it up with the paper target fixed to the berm. "We're gonna have to rebuild this farmer's berm," Grumbine muttered to Aster.

"Shh," Aster said.

Helen stared down the sight until she was sure it was lined up on the center of the target, then she placed her thumb over the trigger button. "Press, hold, release. Press, hold, release."

She pressed.

The M2 roared, firing a burst of hot lead in a deafening cacophony. Helen immediately released the button and grabbed her earmuffs. "Wow, that's loud!" she shouted.

Grumbine laughed. "It is indeed. But how was the recoil?"

She thought about it. "Not that bad. Nowhere near as bad as the P90's."

"The P90's not bad, either, but you weren't prepared for it," Grumbine said. "Now, put your hands back on the grips and try again. You barely fired three rounds. Give it a two-second burst and watch the mess it makes of the targets. And this time, when the recoil starts pushing the gun up, push up on the handles. It'll dip the barrel back down and help you stay on target. Kind of like a seesaw."

She looked down the sight again. Aster had replaced the targets with fresh ones. There was a big hole in the middle one, and holes that looked like three small craters in the berm behind it.

This time she held the trigger down for a full two seconds. The gun kicked in her hands with each deafening blast from the barrel, but it didn't ride up as much as the P90 had. She did as instructed and pushed up on the handles to drive the barrel back down.

When she let go of the trigger, she forgot to stop pushing up on the handles, and the barrel dipped toward the ground before she righted it again. A thin stream of smoke rose from the muzzle, but it didn't obscure her view of the center target, or what was left of it. A narrow strip of paper was all that remained against the berm. The rest had been chewed into scraps that fluttered away in the wind. And the berm behind the gun had even more craters in it.

Grumbine whistled. "Excellent, doll. Excellent." The hand that had been resting on her back lifted, then came back down in a stinging slap. "Well done! How was that?"

Helen coughed and rubbed her back. "It was fun!"

"Want to finish up with the targets?" Aster pointed at the berm. "There are two left. Fire a few bursts at each and then we'll pack it in."

A few moments and fifty rounds later, the other targets went to join their companion in Silhouette Heaven. The flow of smoke streaming from the gun's muzzle was greater now. Grumbine pointed. "See all those holes in the barrel? They keep the weapon from overheating. It's air-cooled. Without those, it'd overheat in no time."

"You'd have to shoot it a lot more than she did to get it to overheat," Aster commented.

Grumbine leaned in close to Helen and put his hand between himself and Aster. "She speaks from experience," he whispered loud enough for the farmer to hear in his house. "One time, she adjusted the timing on a Ma Deuce so it was practically spitting out a solid line of lead, and she shot it so much, she melted the barrel."

"I took out the target, didn't I?" Aster crossed her arms beneath her breasts. "It wasn't that big of a deal."

"It was a big deal! You know how much these guns cost? And some of them are super old! They've been around since the 1920s! They're practically heirlooms! Historical artifacts!"

Aster rolled her eyes. "I somehow doubt Teledyne is using weapons from the 1920's. They're probably newly manufactured."

"Still! You think it'll be easy to replace these, with everything that's happened? Going to be hard to get the factories up and running at a time like this, you know?" He looked at Helen. "Now, do me a favor and police this brass while the boss and I get this gun broken down and loaded up."

Helen picked the big brass casings up out of the grass and dirt while Grumbine and Aster broke down the gun. Grumbine unloaded it, packed away what was left of the ammo belt, then unsnapped the base of the M2 from its tripod. Aster then picked up the weapon in one hand and grabbed the tripod in the other and walked back to the APC. "Show-off," Grumbine muttered as he walked along behind her.

"Did you say something?"

"No, ma'am!"

He returned a moment later with an empty ammo can and helped Helen pick up the remaining brass. "What will you do with all of these?" she asked. "Recycle them?"

"After a fashion. Our armorer will reload them when he can. Or we'll take them to Boonville and have them done professionally."

Helen cocked her head to the side. She didn't know what any of that meant. She held up an empty casing. "You mean they can put another bullet in here?"

"It's a bit more than that, but yes. That's what it means to reload a cartridge."

She studied the casing for a moment. "That's...really helpful, I would imagine. Especially nowadays." She paused. "But can they do it without electricity?"

A bright flash of light appeared on the far side of the city, followed by the booming of thunder several seconds later. Helen clapped her hands to her ears, her frightened squeak lost in the sudden noise.

"The fuck was that?" Grumbine demanded. He glanced at Helen. "Sorry, doll. Slip of the tongue."

Aster put a hand up to shield her eyes from the sun. Her expression turned grim. "Teledyne Tower's been attacked."

* * *

"Holy shit," Danny muttered as he hopped off the rear bumper of the deuce-and-a-half truck he'd ridden in across town. He stepped out of the way so the next man could jump down and fixed his gaze on the inferno in front of him.

The enemy had hit Teledyne Tower with a weapon that was powerful enough to wipe out the top half of it. Concrete, steel, glass, sheetrock, and burning insulation rained down, setting fires in the smaller structures in Teledyne's industrial park on the northwest end of Columbia. Those fires were now under control, but parts of Teledyne Tower burned freely. Its fire suppression system seemed to be overwhelmed. Huge piles of smoldering rubble surrounded the building, making it difficult for vehicles to approach. A couple of city fire trucks that had somehow survived the EMP pulled up as close to the building as they could. Their ladders were fully extended, and firemen who were strapped to the top rungs worked their hoses back and forth, sending torrents of water into the surviving upper floors. "Thank God, the water's still running," one of the officers muttered.

"For now, anyway," another said.

"Well, as I live and breathe," a familiar voice called. "Sergeant Daniel Ward, we keep meeting in the most exciting places, don't we?"

Corporal Chloe Reed walked over, flanked by a pair of her fellow CPD officers. Her normally immaculate uniform was stained with soot and mud, and her left sleeve bore a few scorch marks. A dirty respirator hung around her neck, and a damp beanie covered her cornrows to protect them from the heat. "To what do we owe the pleasure?"

Danny spread his arms to indicate the officers and students with him. "We're here to help with perimeter security or to form a bucket brigade. Whatever's needed." He looked around. "And, between you and me, I kind of wanted to see the destruction up close and personal."

Reed's smile faded, then turned into a scowl. "You getting some kicks out of this? Seeing Teledyne take one up the ass?"

"Well, more like down the mouth—" Danny began.

"Don't start with me." She hiked a thumb over her shoulder toward the building. "Not everyone in there is a bad guy, and you know it. So, don't start with me about how Teledyne nuked your hometown and all that. I get it, or I get it as much as I can."

Danny was taken aback by the vehemence in Reed's words. Just the other day, she had stood in front of the angry crowd at city hall and defended the mounted officers' right to be in this city. She'd said the citizens owed them a great deal when they protected the city from Obsidian's and Teledyne's plans to tear up Columbia. Now, she seemed to have turned that anger on Danny. "All right, Chloe, I get it."

"And another thing—Oh. All right, then." She nodded. "So long as we understand each other."

"We do, and I'm sorry." He pointed. "Any idea how half the building seems to have survived relatively unscathed?"

Reed smirked. "Oh, you mean other than the huge ball of fire that is the 20th floor?" She turned to look at the building. "No. We're not sure, and Teledyne's not telling us. But whatever they got hit with tore through the building from the top down and only stopped when it reached the 20th floor. I guess the bomb or missile or whatever it was could only go so far. Did a lot of damage on the way down, though, so I guess it did its job."

Danny whistled. "Man, this building can't catch any breaks, can it? First it gets hit by an Obsidian missile, and now this."

"You're telling me. Anyway, we could use the help. If your boys and girls will maintain the perimeter, it'll free up more of us to go inside and help with rescue efforts. The fire suppression systems are working on the lower floors, and the fire department says they can get the 20th floor under control, but they want us to evacuate everyone in case the building decides to give up the ghost."

"We can definitely help with that."

"Much appreciated!" Reed turned to walk away.

Danny stared up at the blaze. He shivered. Cops and firemen had their friendly rivalries, but he didn't envy them one bit. There was something particularly nasty about fire, so his hat was off to anyone who willingly ran into burning buildings. Danny waved at the volunteers with him and opened his mouth to speak.

"Oh, and Sergeant Ward?" Reed smiled over her shoulder at him. "I'm glad you made it back from your fight with the National Guard. I was praying for you and your squad."

Danny felt his cheeks flush. "Thank you, Chloe."

He tried to keep his focus on the blazing building, but his eyes kept dropping back to watch Chloe Reed's retreating figure. There was something about her he couldn't quite place, but that was all right. If they survived the coming weeks and months, maybe there'd be time to explore what that "something" was. And maybe things would be just a little brighter in this Fallen World.

*****

Chapter Fifteen

"Well, I'd say that was as successful a deployment as we could hope for," Lloyd said. He leaned back in the commander's chair and crossed his arms over his chest. He tried to lean back like he would if he were in his office, but the seat wasn't that flexible. "Any word on Teledyne's casualties, Egleton?"

"Nothing that's confirmed." Egghead leaned over his computer screen. "There was a disturbance in the district south of Teledyne Tower, so several of their security forces were deployed there when the rod struck. It's probably safe to assume twenty percent casualties, maybe thirty."

"What I'd like to know is how any of the building survived." Anal stretched her lithe body until something cracked. "Ah, that's better. Um, sorry, sir."

Lloyd waved off the apology. "Sometimes you gotta stretch. I can respect that. As to how Teledyne Tower is still standing, who can say?"

He had his suspicions. That tower had originally been JalCom property. Teledyne had added onto it when they gained control of the city. Could the part that survived be the original building? If so, it was made of very tough stuff. He didn't voice the thought aloud, though. There were things he needed to keep close to the vest, even with subordinates who were vital to his plans. Egghead had been an Obsidian plant in the American military since before this whole debacle began, and Anal had happily changed colors when a new challenge presented itself, but he could only trust them so far.

"Any word from Colonel Eastman?" Lloyd asked Egghead.

"The Colonel's pissed, sir. Eager to take the fight to the enemy, but he knows he doesn't have the manpower for it. Not on his own."

"He may not have to do anything if we play our cards right." Now that the city was aware of the satellite weapon, he could have Eastman claim credit for the strike and use it as leverage to force a surrender. Although, there was something to be said for pushing an opponent into the worst position possible before allowing them to throw in the towel. An intact police force or Teledyne security team could lay the groundwork for a rebellion down the line, and that was a wrinkle he didn't need.

There was also the matter of the Obsidian reinforcements he'd called in. They would be arriving in the city in the hours prior to the satellite weapon once again being in position. If he ordered them to attack, then pulled them out just before the tungsten rain began, the combination attack would break what little resistance was left in the city. Besides, he doubted if he'd be able to keep this unit from getting involved, not until it tasted blood.

"On second thought, get Eastman on the horn," Lloyd said. "Ask him if he and his men are ready for a night mission."

* * *

"Project Tezca," Director Gwendolyn Greenwood said. She pointed at the holographic image of a satellite high over the planet. The satellite's body was oval, with several solar arrays extending from its top. A telescope protruded from the bottom on the right of a set of bay doors.

"That's what they hit us with. Or, more precisely, they hit us with a portion of its payload."

In the aftermath of the attack, we gathered in the command bunker beneath city hall in the auditorium reserved for council meetings. I sat up in the gallery with Aster and Sheriff Welliver, along with a few officers from different departments. Most of us were there to give reports on the growing unrest in the city, as well as the current movements of the Homeguard. We'd seen movement north of the city, so a force of officers was sent to investigate, including Lieutenant Wendy Alexander, Lieutenant Blackwood, and Sergeant Mosher. They were due back soon.

I tapped my earpiece. There was a crackle of static and then silence. I grimaced. We'd been using Teledyne Tower's communications system since Aster's Section Nine joined our ranks, but the array was destroyed along with half the tower. Section Nine's analyst and some of the faculty and students at the university were working on a solution, but it would be hours before we had anything. The headsets Aster's team used had a backup system that allowed very short wireless transmissions, but nothing beyond a typical city block.

Every member of the council was seated around the table, except for Kazama. The Teledyne executive was busy battling the fires raging in and around Teledyne Tower. Former Mayor Reynolds was out there as well, commanding every regular and volunteer fireman the city could spare, as well as any civilians brave enough to help. It was a miracle the tower was still standing after the hit it took, and it seemed as though there was more to it than met the eye.

A young woman named Patricia Long sat in Kazama's place. I didn't know her, but she looked good in a dress suit. "She was Director Ingersoll's personal secretary," Aster whispered.

"How come she's not in charge, then?" I asked.

"Kazama's people moved faster."

I shook my head. Corporate politics sounded about as bad as regular politics.

"An operational Tezca satellite is a nightmare scenario for us." Greenway manipulated the console, and the 3D representation's bay doors opened, revealing a series of metal cylinders tucked safely inside. A pair of robot arms grabbed one of the cylinders and pulled it out. "This is a rod of solid tungsten, which is one of the densest metals currently known. On Earth, a thirty-foot rod would weigh around three tons. If deployed from orbit, it'll hit with the force of a low-yield tactical nuke. Kinetic bombardment: all the force without the radioactive mess that comes along with it."

Welliver whistled. "The Corporations had everything, didn't they?"

I raised my hand. "Miss Greenway, which Corporation owns this satellite?"

Greenway hesitated, and her eyes darted around. Finally, she said, "Both Corporations—as well as the American, Russian, and Chinese governments—own their own versions of these satellites, but this particular one is operated by Obsidian."

Aster hissed loud enough for the whole room to hear. Greenway flinched, and one of her two bodyguards stepped forward. She waved him off, and he returned to stand next to the man who looked like his twin.

"It makes sense that Obsidian owns Project Tezca," Oakford said. "Tezcatlipoca was often represented by obsidian. He was the Aztec god of lightning."

"Fitting name," I muttered.

"Can you swear up and down that Obsidian had nothing to do with this?" Graham asked, his tone flat.

"I resent the insinuation," Greenway said in an equally flat tone, "but I can't blame you for it. I can't say that someone in Obsidian didn't order the satellite to fire, but I can say it wasn't me or any of the men and women loyal to me." She glanced back at her bodyguards. "I don't have that kind of access."

"Not even emergency access?" President Oakford asked. The president of Missouri University removed his glasses and ran a cloth over the lenses. "Like the way different people take over for a national leader if he's ever incapacitated or killed?"

"There is a chain of command in Obsidian, but I'm not part of it." Greenway bared her teeth. "And even if I were, how would I receive access codes when the home office was destroyed? Everything would come from there."

"Who was in this chain of command?" Graham asked.

"Anyone on the top floor of Charlotte's headquarters." Greenway counted off with her manicured fingers. "The chiefs, the vice presidents, even a few of the executive secretaries would be in there somewhere. After them, it would go to the branch office directors and their seconds-in-command. Beyond that..." She lifted a hand in an elegant shrug. "I have no idea. Even as high up as I was, I could only pierce the Corporate veil so far. What I did fell outside the scope of what one would call 'command and control.'"

Just then, a thought occurred to me. The shock of Teledyne Tower's destruction had pushed my conversation with DeSoto away, but Greenway's words brought it all back. "Would Director Lloyd have had access to them?"

Greenway's eyes widened, then narrowed as she stared at me. "He would be in the chain of command, yes. But I don't think he does. At least, he didn't have it while he was here. Maybe that's changed. If he communicated with the home office somehow...." She left the thought unfinished. "Why do you ask?"

I didn't think she was lying, not about this. I still didn't trust her, as she was a Corporate creature through and through. But I couldn't hide this kind of information, not from the Council. "The captured National Guard tank commander positively ID'd Director Lloyd as the man giving Colonel Eastman his marching orders. He's been posing as someone from the Pentagon and is the reason why the National Guard thought Columbia was under enemy occupation."

"Some of us would argue that it is," Patricia Long muttered.

Richard and Graham glared at her until she fell silent.

Patricia's outburst may have distracted the others, but I'd kept my eyes on Greenway as I shared the news. Her eyes didn't widen nearly as much as they had when I brought Lloyd's name up. What I'd said was news to her, but I couldn't quite tell if she was surprised by what Lloyd was up to or surprised I'd figured it out.

"Is there a way to stop this satellite?" President Oakford asked. "Some backdoor means of shutting it down?"

"I'm sure there is, but without the proper access codes or some kind of wizard-class hacker, it's not going to happen. And last I checked, we don't have any hackers of that caliber around here."

Graham looked at Patricia. "What about your people?"

Patricia shook her head. "Our cyber warfare lab was on the twenty-seventh floor. The so-called Tezca Bolt penetrated all the way to the reinforced blast shield on the twentieth floor. Everything above there was completely annihilated."

"Is that true?" I asked Aster.

"Hey!" Patricia objected.

"That is where the cyber warfare lab was, yes." Aster winced. "I had friends up there."

I squeezed her arm. As heinous as the Corporations could be, they still had good people working for them.

"Sounds like they wanted to hamstring us from the get-go," Welliver said.

Now, I understood why the enemy attacked Teledyne Tower rather than city hall or even the university. Wipe out the group most likely to bring you down. It was a sensible approach. "How come it hasn't struck again?"

"It's out of range." Greenway zoomed the display away from the satellite until its orbital pathway around the globe was completely visible. She used a laser-pointer to trace the pathway. "This satellite is in an intermediate circular orbit, meaning it's not geostationary like a lot of communications satellites are." She smiled a bit sheepishly. "I'm a bit rusty on orbital mechanics—"

"Along with most of us!" Martinez said.

That brought a round of laughter. Greenway beamed at Martinez and continued. "Basically, it orbits the earth once every twelve hours. It'll be overhead again early tomorrow morning, while it's still dark."

"So, we can expect lots of fireworks," Richard said. "Is there any way we can stop it?"

"Short of capturing Lloyd and forcing him to stop it, no. Once it's overhead, we'll be at its mercy. If it has a full payload, it'll be enough to level most of Columbia."

"We'll have to abandon the city," one of the officers in attendance said.

"We can't do that!" another officer hissed.

"How can we fight against something like that?"

I rested my clenched hands on the desk and squeezed so hard it hurt. What were we supposed to do against a threat like this? Sure, the possibility existed that they only fired once because they only had one rod left. Or maybe the targeting system failed. Or maybe Lloyd wanted to see if the damn thing would work. Well, it worked. And tonight could bring more of the same. Much more of the same. What were they going to do?

For the second time in the meeting, an idea occurred to me. I raised my hand. "What about shooting it down?"

Greenway and Richard looked as if they wanted to laugh, while Graham and President Oakford looked thoughtful. Patricia said, "The only weapons capable of doing that would be surface-to-orbit missiles or energy weapons." She spread her hands, and a smirk formed on her face. "We don't have either of those in the Tower, but maybe your local departmental budget allows for such things? If that's the case, Obsidian was a lot more generous with you badge-wearers than Teledyne could afford to be."

I smiled, but not at the poor attempt at snide humor. "What if I told you we have our hands on a Big Beam, Miss Teledyne?"

The look Patricia gave me made me laugh out loud. Her pretty face flushed deep red, but she kept her voice level as she said, "That...could very well change the game, but how do you intend to deal with the massive power needs?"

Thinking about how close we came to moving the Big Beam to Teledyne Tower made me shiver. We'd come very close to losing our only means of fighting back. The location we chose for it wouldn't be ideal for fighting against a ground-based enemy anywhere other than the eastern side of the city, but it was in the perfect spot to take out a satellite. "I don't have any idea how we'll deal with the power constraints, but I know someone who does." I looked at a Columbia PD officer standing guard at the door. "Could you get Dr. Schneider in here, please?"

Before the officer could react, the auditorium's doors flew open and Lieutenant Alexander rushed in, her chest heaving as if she'd run a marathon. She bent over, with her hands on her knees as she caught her breath. Lieutenant Blackburn stepped in a moment later. His helmet was tucked under one arm, and his face dripping with sweat. "We've got a bit of trouble up on the north end of town," he explained. "Obsidian reinforcements."

"More…than…that." Alexander gasped for air between words. Her face was pale, and her eyes were wide with fright. "Evidence Shredders."

* * *

"Into the shelters!" I cupped my hands around my mouth. "Everyone not critical to the university's defense, please get into the shelters!"

"There's room for everyone!" Danny shouted. "It'll be tight, but it's only for a few hours!"

I sat astride Countess, close to the entrance to Jesse Hall. All the interior and exterior lamps were on, bathing this section of the Francis Quadrangle in a mix of harsh white and soft yellow light. The sun hadn't fully set, but it would within minutes. Campus police and volunteer defenders waited at the entrance, directing the flow of human traffic entering the old building.

During the height of the Cold War between Communism and Capitalism, universities, city governments, and wealthy private citizens had built bomb shelters everywhere. Some were little more than windowless basements, while other, more elaborate ones, were dug deep into the ground, with ventilation systems, backup generators, food supplies, and—in the case of Cheyenne Mountain—gigantic shock systems to absorb and distribute the force of a direct impact.

Many of the shelters had fallen into disrepair after the Berlin Wall fell, but when the Corporate Cold War started up, fallout shelters became all the rage once again, and the University of Missouri hadn't missed out. They'd built a series of shelters beneath the dormitories and Jesse Hall that were connected by maintenance tunnels that weren't open to the general student body. We had no idea whether this underground labyrinth could withstand a direct hit from a tungsten rod at terminal velocity, but it was better than nothing.

It was here that we directed everyone who wasn't critical to the university's defense. Students, faculty, refugees from destroyed neighborhoods, and children marched into the depths of the shelter. Down there they would find food, battery-powered lights, and more books and board games than someone could shake a stick at. Everything from Four Horsemen books and comics to the entire Baen library, both in digital and paperback. There was even a theater to keep people entertained as the world ended overhead.

"This is gonna be fun!" a boy no older than Helen shouted.

"Yeah!" another called. "Let's play hide-and-seek!"

More kids joined in, and I fought back a smile. They thought it was a fun overnight trip in a cool place, and I couldn't blame them. At any other time, this would've reminded me of overnight trips on the USS *Alabama* back in Mobile Bay. The few nights I got to spend there with the Boy Scouts created some of my best memories.

Of course, those memories were now tainted with the thought of the *Alabama* in what I had to assume was its post-Fall state: capsized by a nuclear blast and rusting at the bottom of the bay. Had Danny's wife Amy been there when it happened? She had been part of the team working on restoring it. Specifically, she'd been working on restoring the ship's complement of Vought OS2U Kingfisher seaplanes, along with the aircraft catapults that launched them.

Danny rubbed the pocket on his cargo pants where he kept his dead phone. He noticed me looking at him and grimaced. "Thinking about old times."

"That first night on the *Alabama?*" I grinned. "When we snuck Amy in with our Cub Scout Troop?"

A smile cracked through his severe expression. "We made her wear a baseball cap to hide her long hair. It didn't work too well, and I think Scout Master Peterson knew what was up, but he didn't have the heart to send her home. Who would? She was so enamored with everything, more so than the rest of us."

"Started her on the path to becoming a pilot," I said.

"Don't I know it."

"Nathan!" a male voice called.

Kevin rode toward us on Watson, with Welliver alongside. The sheriff had removed his sling so he could clutch the reins of his blue dun, Patches. His left hand rested on the square handle of his 1911. "Sheriff, what are you doing out of your sling?" I asked.

Danny pointed. "More importantly, where'd you get a left-handed holster on such short notice?"

"I have my ways." Welliver smiled. "To answer your question, Nate, do you think I'm going to sit this one out? If what Alexander and Blackwood said was true, we need every man we can get on the proverbial wall, children and old men included."

"With respect, sir—"

"Save it." Welliver patted Patches on the head. "Do you know what a bitch it was to get into the saddle with only one good arm? The only way I'm getting down is if I fall off."

"Let's try to avoid that," Danny said.

"Do you have a radio, sir?" I patted the one on my belt. Teledyne's comms were still spotty at best, but Columbia PD had scrounged up a few more radios for a select few mounted commanders. As soon as they got Teledyne's comms up and running again, they would tie them into the CPD radio system, much as they had during the assault on the Country Hotel. Until then, it was back to the old-fashioned way of doing things.

"No, but Graham is supposed to be bringing more from CPD headquarters." Welliver pointed to a two-story house on the other side of the Quad. "We'll be meeting up there when he gets back, which should be soon."

"Speaking of getting back soon," I said, "what's keeping Brother Stephen? He was supposed to gather the civilians staying at Brandon Hampton and bring them here, along with my kids." As the newest dormitory, it was one of the few that didn't have access to the underground bunker system.

"Maybe he's having trouble rounding them up?" Danny asked.

"Who, the civilians or the kids?"

"Well, considering how your kids can be…both?"

It was intended as a joke, but given the current state of things, it did little to ease my nervousness. "Sheriff, with your permission, I'd like to go get them."

"I can go," Kevin said. "You've got command responsibilities, Nathan. I'm just another officer who won't be missed."

I flinched. "Kevin, that's not true—"

He held up a hand. "I don't mean it that way." His lips twitched into the ghost of a smile. "A couple weeks ago, yes, I would've meant it that way. Not now. I have a purpose again, and I owe it to your daughter and to Brother Stephen. Let me repay them. Let me repay you. Focus on the fight ahead. I'll see to your kids."

I hesitated. Part of me wanted to go and get my kids, but Kevin was right. I had duties to see to, whereas Kevin was currently outside the chain of command and had no other responsibilities beyond that of a volunteer defender. He loved my kids like he was their uncle. "It would mean a lot to me, Kevin."

"It means a lot to me, too." He wheeled Watson around. "I'll see that they're safe!"

We watched him ride off into the gloom. Danny shook his head. "What a difference a couple of weeks makes, right?"

"The same could be said for all of us," I said. At the beginning of this mess, I'd been ready to crack. There were times when I still felt that way, and no wonder. We were barely three months into what many sci-fi writers and readers would call the post-apocalypse. We'd lost many of our brothers and sisters in blue already to enemy action, to accidents, and to suicide. By his own admission, Kevin had come as close to the brink as he could without going over. He'd almost become another Lieutenant Jackson, or Sergeant Kowalski, or Patrolman Hang. He hadn't, though. He'd won. It was a small victory in the cosmic scheme of things, but a victory, nonetheless.

Now it was up to us to secure an even greater victory for this city, so the sacrifices made wouldn't be in vain.

* * *

"Helen, I wanna see the observatory!" Jason whined. He looked up at her from his wheelchair, his eyes sad like a puppy's. "It's not fair you got to see it!"

"I knew I shouldn't have told you about it." Helen pushed him through the gloom toward the Francis Quadrangle near the northern end of campus. "All you keep talking about is the observatory. It's driving me nuts!"

"Then take me there!" He reached over his shoulder to clutch her sleeve.

She shook him off. "We *drove* there, dummy! I can't take you there, not unless Aunt Aster or Corporal Elliott is going."

"Then ask them!"

"And *how* am I supposed to do that?" She stopped pushing the wheelchair and walked around it so she could face Jason. Her hands were on her hips. "Just close my eyes, raise my voice, and yell, 'Aunt Aster! Mr. Elliott! Please take us to the observatory!'"

"Hey, stop yelling!" a deep voice called. "I'm not deaf!"

Corporal Elliott stepped out of a neighboring building. He was holding a giant, plastic case. He grinned. "What are you doing out here? Shouldn't you be in the underground shelter?"

"Are you headed to the observatory?"

"Well, yeah, but—"

"I wanna look through the telescope!" Jason yelled.

Elliott frowned. "The telescope's…under maintenance right now. You won't be able to see much out of it, unfortunately."

"Aw…" Jason lowered his head and sniffled.

Helen did *not* want to hear him start bawling again. "Would it be all right if we ride over there with you? We promise we won't be in the way."

Elliott shook his head. "I really don't think it's a good idea."

"Pretty please?" Jason begged. He clasped his hands together and turned his puppy dog look on, full-blast.

"Well…" Elliott looked uncomfortable. "Tell you what: I think there are a couple of smaller telescopes at the observatory. Why don't we we take a quick look through one of them and then I'll get you back to your dad?"

"Yay!" Jason jumped out of his wheelchair and threw his arms around Elliott's waist. "Thank you!"

"Woah, don't knock me over!" Elliott laughed. "Look, we're not really supposed to do this, but I can't leave you alone out here, and I need to deliver these ASAP." He nodded toward the case in his hands.

"A sap? What's that?"

"It means 'as soon as possible.' As in, we shouldn't be dawdling here, so follow me. The APC's around the corner."

Helen and Jason shared a grin. Jason climbed back into the wheelchair, and Helen pushed for all she was worth. They quickly outpaced the burdened Elliott as they plunged ahead.

"Hey, wait up!" Elliott called.

* * *

"Everything's hooked up, Lieutenant Paxton," Schneider reported.

Paxton's eyes swept around the observatory's vast, domed room. The giant telescope that had previously taken up the center of the room had been carefully disassembled and placed against the rounded walls, where it would be out of the way. Teledyne's Big Beam and its bigger bank of batteries replaced it. The long weapon's silver barrel extended out through the slit in the dome roof. Wires of varying colors and thicknesses descended from various points on the weapon's barrel and body and connected to the battery bank. Cables as thick as Paxton's wrist snaked out of the bank and disappeared into new holes in the floor.

Schneider followed Paxton's gaze and pointed at the holes. "Those cables descend directly into the sublevel, to a direct connection to JalCom's fusion plant. As soon as we boot up the Big Beam, it'll begin charging."

"How long will that take?"

"If we want to fire the weapon at full power—"

"We do," Paxton interrupted. "The satellite is built for war. We have to assume it has some kind of armor. Only a direct hit at full power will be enough to bring it down."

"It seems like overkill to me," Schneider said, "but I am not in charge, so I will defer."

"Please do."

"It will take approximately eighty-three minutes to charge to full power."

"And where does that put us on the timetable for the satellite's arrival?"

"The satellite will be within range in ninety-five minutes." He checked his watch. "And twenty-two seconds."

"That doesn't leave us a lot of wiggle room. Get it powered up."

Paxton stepped out of the room and started to walk down the spiral staircase that led to the observatory's lower levels. He paused at a narrow, open window about midway down. For some reason, the building had no rear windows other than this one. With most of the roof taken up by the telescope dome, this was one of the only real vantage points that looked out over the parking lot. Grumbine stood there with his Barrett M107 rifle leaning against the wall. "Sir, how's it shakin' up there?"

"The shaking's done. Now it's time to bake."

They'd finished work on the Ma Deuce gun nest a few hours before. They'd piled sandbags in front and pushed a few disabled vehicles over to cover the sides, after draining their fuel tanks. Elliott was manning that position now, along with…two kids? The three of them were fiddling with a telescope near the machine gun nest.

Paxton leaned out of the window to get a closer look. "What're the Ward kids doing here?"

"Stargazing, by the looks of it, sir."

"I can see that. Why are they here?"

"Elliott found 'em when he was on his way back with equipment for the Big Beam and brought 'em here for safekeeping. He was going to take them back in the APC, but Crick took it for some recon at the boss lady's request."

Paxton frowned. He remembered the recon request, but he had been so focused on keeping Dr. Schneider from wandering off task that he hadn't paid much attention.

A staccato burst of distant gunfire tore through the night air, followed by a cascade of answering shots. Down in the parking lot, Helen and Jason looked up, but Elliott directed their attention back to the telescope. "It's probably just the usual crime sprees we see at night," he said.

"Where's Aunt Aster?" Jason asked.

"She'll be along shortly, as will your ride back to your dad."

The volume of gunfire increased, but it was still far away. It was difficult to place it, but Paxton assumed it was coming from the north side of town, where the Obsidian reinforcements were supposed to be. "Which way did Crick go?"

Paxton's radio, borrowed from the CPD, crackled. "Lady in Black, this is Creaky Crick. Our green guests are on the way to the party, coming along the southerly routes, over."

The Homeguard was on the move, too, it seemed.

"Understood," Aster responded. "Maintain observation but keep your distance."

"Roger."

Aster was meeting with the police commanders, which meant Lieutenant Ward was with her. He needed to know his children were here. He keyed his radio. "Lady in Black, this is Paxton."

* * *

"Roger, Lieutenant Paxton. Lady in Black, out." Aster set the police radio down on the table. She looked at me, the hint of a smile on her lips. "Your children know how to get around."

I chuckled, and some of the tension eased out of my gut. "They're troublemakers, through and through."

We sat at a round table in some administrator's private conference room, along with Danny, Graham, Blackwood, Martinez, Silva, and Alexander. Someone had set an LED lantern next to a map of the university and the surrounding streets. It covered the area from city hall to the northwest, to the Country Hotel to the north, to the observatory to the east, to the outskirts of the city to the south.

True to his word, Welliver didn't bother to dismount, choosing instead to wait on the grass next to an open window. He leaned over in the saddle and stared into the room. "Children, troublemakers? Say it ain't so."

That brought a round of laughter from everyone. I'd need to let Kevin and Brother Stephen know where the kids were as soon as we were done with the meeting. Stephen was completely distraught when he returned from the dorm with the rest of the civilians and children. "They weren't in your room! A few people saw Helen pushing Jason up the road toward the Quad, but no one's seen them since."

Kevin and a few volunteers were scouring the underground shelter for signs of them. I heaved another sigh of relief. Thank God they were all right.

Aster stood. "I better get back to the observatory." She held out the radio for me.

"You should hold onto this."

"Paxton has one." She tapped her earpiece. "If I'm near the observatory, I'll be able to communicate with him, and he can communicate with you."

I closed her fingers around the radio. "Hold onto it. What if Paxton loses his? Two is one—"

"And one is none," Aster finished. She hooked the radio to her belt. "Very well. I'll hold onto it." She looked down at me. "My men and I will keep your children safe. I promise."

She'd already done that more times than I could count. Of all of them, she was the one I trusted the most. "Keep yourself safe, too. We need you, and so do the kids."

And so do I.

The thought came unbidden, but I dared not utter it aloud. I wasn't sure what it meant. Not yet.

Aster nodded, then hurried from the room.

"Oh ho ho." Danny grinned. "I always figured you liked what you saw in the back of that van on May Day."

"Wait, what did he see?" Blackwood demanded as the others laughed.

I felt my cheeks flush. "It's not like that," I said, which brought a fresh round of laughter.

"You sure you don't want to go with her?" Graham asked after a moment. "These are your kids we're talking about."

"We can hold our own here," Danny said.

I was seriously tempted, but I shook my head. "At the observatory, I'd just be one more gun. Here is where I can make the most difference: leading men against the forces assaulting our city." Aster's job was important, but so was ours. If we destroyed the satellite, but lost the city in the process, we'd have a hell of a time retaking it.

A long burst of machine gun fire erupted in the distance, followed by an answering cascade. The noise was growing closer.

Graham pointed at the map. "The campus police and volunteer defenders are positioned in the windows of these three buildings." Graham indicated them on the map with the beam of his flashlight.

"They've traded potshots with Obsidian scouts, but that's it. I don't expect that to last, and I'm worried about the enemy trying to flank us."

"Is CPD coming to help?" I asked.

"Not this time. They've got their own problems to deal with." Graham indicated the area around city hall on the map. "Chief Ballantine's reported several soldiers pushing their defenses, likely to get to the command bunker beneath city hall. Teledyne's moving in to help secure the site, but that means we're on our own for the moment."

"And Director Greenway?"

"Still in the Country Hotel." Graham frowned. "She reported that several of her people have deserted, presumably to fight with the Obsidian invaders. The rest, the ones loyal to her, remain inside."

"They don't want to fight their buddies?" The thought irritated me, but I could understand the feeling. I don't know how I'd feel if I suddenly got into a shootout with Graham or Welliver or another good cop.

"I think it's less to do with that and more to do with not wanting to get caught in the crossfire." Graham smiled faintly. "It'd be confusing if we had to ask every Obsidian soldier in the street, 'Excuse me, sir or madam, are you good Obsidian or bad Obsidian?'"

Martinez chuckled. "You make a good point."

"They said they'll defend the Country Hotel and the streets immediately surrounding it. Of course, I've also got officers positioned on the roofs of nearby buildings. If she suddenly makes a move, we'll know about it."

"Hey!" Welliver turned on his flashlight and shined it into the night. "What're you doing with him? Why is he out of his room?"

I sprang to my feet alongside Danny and Martinez, our hands on our pistols. "What's going on?" I asked.

"Sheriff Welliver!" a familiar voice called. "I need to talk with you!"

"Sorry, Sheriff," another voice said. "The prisoner overheard some of the radio chatter and learned that the Homeguard is on the way. He insisted on talking to you and wouldn't take no for an answer."

"I didn't think I was a prisoner anymore," the first voice said. "I thought we were on the same page!"

"We are, but that doesn't mean you're totally in the clear," Welliver snapped. "Well, DeSoto? Talk. What do you want?"

"Get him in here," Graham said, raising his voice to be heard through the window.

A minute later, Lieutenant DeSoto stood at parade rest on the side of the table opposite the window, so he could look at all of us. "Let me talk to Colonel Eastman. He needs to know he's fighting on the wrong side."

"How do you propose to do that?" Danny asked. "Call him up on the radio, talk about old times, then tell him he's a Corporate stooge?"

DeSoto smirked. "While that would be funny, no. Eastman's the kind of man who won't take a transmission at face value, not in these circumstances. Someone could be holding a gun to my head, my voice could be faked, there are any number of possibilities."

"You want to meet with him in person?" Alexander crossed her arms. "Well, this is getting better by the minute."

"I can go with him," Danny said. "If it'll get the Homeguard on our side, it's worth a shot. Send me with a squad of volunteers."

"We'd still have the problem of Colonel Eastman thinking he's doing this under duress," Graham said. "If he shows up with an escort of officers, won't they think he's still a prisoner?"

"Send him in with his tank," I suggested.

Everyone looked at me, eyes wide. Even DeSoto, who laughed. "That would certainly get Colonel Eastman's attention."

"Are you sure that's a wise idea?" Welliver demanded. "After all the trouble we went through to capture that tank?"

"It's the best idea I've got." I spread my hands. "We're under the gun. If we can get the Homeguard to change sides quickly, they can help us push Obsidian out of the city."

"Again, let me go with him," Danny said. "We'll take a few officers in the tank with his crew and make sure everything's on the up and up."

"Gonna be a tight fit," DeSoto muttered. "*Conquistadoris* is a tank, not a limousine."

"I'm sure your boys can manage."

"I'll go with them, too," Alexander said. She shivered. "If we can get the Homeguard to help us fight the Evidence Shredders, all the better."

No one had seen any sign of Obsidian's infamous riot-annihilation unit since Alexander and Blackwood's initial report. The unit was filled with Geno-freaks trained in everything from small squad tactics to brutal hand-to-hand fighting, and they never backed down from a fight or a massacre. Director Lloyd, and whoever else was with him, were probably holding them in reserve, waiting for the right opportunity to send in the shock troops.

Graham looked around the table. "Objections?"

"Donato won't like it very much," Silva grumbled, "but he's a buffalo. He doesn't get a vote."

"The more allies, the better," Blackwood said.

Martinez jabbed a finger at DeSoto. "Your people have a lot of blue blood to answer for when this is all over."

"Mistakes happen in war," DeSoto replied. "Your side killed a number of ours, too, remember?"

Martinez glared across the table at him for a long moment. "I've no objections, but if he stabs us in the back, I get to kill him."

DeSoto started to chuckle, but her unblinking gaze caused the noise to die in his throat.

"Let's get this show on the road, then!" Welliver said. "No time like the present in this Fallen World."

* * * * *

Chapter Sixteen

"That confirms it," Egghead said. He pulled his headset off. "Something is going on at the observatory."

"Hmm." Lloyd stroked his chin. It was one of the buildings his team in St. Louis had selected as a possible entrance into the JalCom facility. It'd been built around the same time as the Country Hotel, Teledyne Tower, and a few other places scattered throughout the city. "I wonder what they're up to."

"I don't know, but if a Specialist and her team are there, it's got to be something big."

Lloyd frowned. He wished his informant inside Director Greenway's inner circle hadn't been silenced mid-transmission. All he'd had time to mention was the observatory's name and then there'd been a gunshot, followed by silence. Greenway had finally realized the soldiers he'd left behind in St. Louis weren't exactly loyal to her. She probably already knew that, the wily little vixen. He hoped some of the people who'd left the Country Hotel to join Manager Bianchi's assault force would know more.

Egghead had once again proven his worth by tapping into the CPD's radio system. He'd spent the last half hour sifting through police chatter and military code to get a better idea of the disposition of the city's defenders. Teledyne's security force was the largest in the city until their tower was hit. Even as diminished as they were, they still had enough men to defend their territory, plus send reinforcements to city hall. That suited Lloyd just fine. The more cops and soldiers at city hall when they dropped a few Tezca Bolts on it, the better. Destroy it and a couple of university buildings, and it'd be all over.

Anal sat in the far corner of the APC, close to the door that led to the driver's compartment. She was bent over her laptop screen, typing furiously. Discarded energy bar wrappers and empty cans of coffee lay in a heap next to her. She hadn't left that spot in hours, except to relieve herself and work the knots and kinks out of her body. The young hacker was like a bloodhound chasing after a scent. Once she was on the hunt, she wouldn't quit until she got what she wanted. Lloyd had no idea how close she was to breaking through JalCom's security barrier, but from her occasional mutterings, it sounded like she'd run into a wall of quantum-level encryption. If anyone could crack it, it'd be her. She'd come highly recommended, after all. Anal needed a flash of inspiration, or a lucky break, and then she'd be in.

That just left the problem of Specialist Aster. Teledyne's Battle Flower was a huge thorn in their side, especially with no Agent of their own to match against her. She and her men needed to be bottled up until this was over. "Who do we have near the observatory?" Lloyd asked.

Egghead had put his headset back on, so Lloyd brought up the digital map on his armrest's console. He centered it over the observatory and smiled. "Well, they should be able to do the job." He pulled his phone from his pocket, dialed a number, then said, "Bianchi? I've got a job for the Shredders...."

* * *

"Are you sure this is a good idea?" Danny had to shout to be heard over the rumble of the tank's engine and the clank of its treads rolling along the asphalt.

"No, but it's the best I could come up with!" DeSoto rode high in the turret of *Conquistadoris*, with a white flag held up in the universal sign of truce and ceasefire. Its fabric was illuminated by a vehicle light twisted around to shine straight up. Danny, Jeremiah Jones, and a half dozen volunteers from different departments rode on either side of the tank as they headed down the road toward the approaching Homeguard force. "I don't think they'll shoot at us, not when my crew could operate the tank fine without me."

"What about us?" Danny asked.

"Oh, they'd shoot you without any concerns. And they might."

"You really know how to make a man feel better about his circumstances. You know that, right?"

"It's a spiritual gift!"

Despite himself, Danny laughed. There was something about this DeSoto guy that he liked. Even though he and his crew had been responsible for the deaths of several officers, he couldn't help thinking they were good people fooled into taking the wrong side. The situation could've just as easily been reversed had events turned out differently.

Richard Cates's people had informed them of the approaching Guard army and had pulled back into their forest camp like Robin Hood's Merry Men. He couldn't blame them. The Three Rivers folk had some guns, but nowhere near what the police or the Corporations had. And if they were going up against hundreds of soldiers, they wouldn't stand much chance. Then again, neither would Danny and his small number of horsemen if DeSoto turned out to be a traitor. Danny rested his hand on his sidearm. If nothing else, he'd make sure DeSoto died before he went down.

They stopped about a half mile from the main line of soldiers, who also stopped. To Danny's relief, none of the soldiers fired, though a fair number did point weapons at them. The space between his eyebrows itched as he thought about more than one set of sniper rifles aimed his way. Would he even feel the round that took him out if it was a headshot? He'd always wondered how that would work. Would the brain have time to react and feel the fatal shot, or would his soul be ejected from his dying body, sparing him the final bit of pain that sent him to the next world? He hoped he didn't have to find out today, or ever.

After what seemed like an eternity, a vehicle that looked like a Jeep from *Band of Brothers* rolled toward them. When it stopped, three soldiers and a man with the silver eagle of a full-bird colonel stepped out of it and approached *Conquistadoris*. "DeSoto?" Colonel Eastman asked. "That you up there, son?"

"What? You don't see my handsome face for a day, and you've already forgotten me?"

"I've been trying to forget your ugly mug ever since you first rolled into my unit." Eastman looked at Danny. "Interesting company you're keeping these days. May I ask what's going on?"

"This is Sergeant Daniel Ward of the Mobile Police Department."

"Mobile? As in Alabama?" He scrutinized Danny, especially the badge pinned to his chest rig. "I spent a couple years in Mobile, working on my military history degree at Spring Hill College. You know where that is?"

"Right off Old Shell, sir."

"Is the coffee shop still there? The Latte Dah?"

"You mean the Carpe Diem? It is. And it's still full of hipster students talking about Marxism as if it's the new hotness."

Colonel Eastman laughed. "Well, that describes most coffee shops in the country, but you got the name right. That verifies you've been in Mobile at some point in your life. Now, what in the world is a Mobile cop doing all the way out here?"

Jones and Danny shared a look. "It's a long story, sir," they said in unison.

Eastman tucked his hands behind his back. "I've got nowhere to go other than to liberate this town, although now I'm starting to wonder from whom. We were told Corporate thugs dressed up as cops, but that doesn't seem to be the case. Maybe your story can enlighten me."

* * *

"Well, well, well, look who finally showed up!" Corporal Elliott waved. "Welcome to Point Chiffon, Boss. Have a hard time finding the place?"

Aster approached the machine gun nest at a jog. The western approach to the observatory was a narrow one through a grassy field, with swampy marsh to the right of it and a drop of about thirty feet to the left. One gun on a swivel point would be more than enough to deal with any threats unless they brought vehicles. And at last report, the assaulting Obsidian force had no vehicles, at least none that anyone had seen.

That didn't mean they were out of the woods, though. If Danny and DeSoto couldn't convince Colonel Eastman to assist them, they'd have the Homeguard's remaining Humvees and JLTVs to worry about. And if that wasn't enough, the enemy could still have anti-tank weapons, and those could prove to be a problem for both the nest and the Big Beam.

The weapon peeked out of the slit on the domed roof of the observatory behind Elliott's position. Light shone from the observatory's windows and through the roof slit, and it grew brighter as she approached the site. Most of the city's lights were out as electricity was siphoned away to fuel the Big Beam and prepare it for the one shot they would get. Aster hoped it would be charged in time for the main event in—she checked her watch—forty-seven minutes.

She leaped over the sandbag barrier and landed inside the machine gun nest. She was surprised to see Helen and Jason sitting there. Helen was wearing Elliott's headset, and Jason held a handful of .50 cartridges. The two kids stared at her for a moment, then they threw their arms around her. "Aunt Aster!"

Aster rubbed their backs. "There, there. There, there." To Elliott, she said, "I thought you'd have them both inside already."

"They wanted to wait for you."

"Why?"

Elliott shrugged. "You have that effect on kids, I guess."

"Did you see Daddy?" Helen asked. Her eyes were red, and her cheeks were wet. "Is he okay?"

"We heard loud booms!" Jason sobbed.

Aster smiled. "Your father's fine. I told him I would keep you both safe."

Jason rubbed snot from his nose. "Why isn't he here?"

"He's…got a job to do." Aster wasn't sure how much to tell the kids. "He'll be along after he's finished with it."

"When will that be?"

"I don't know, but I do know he can't do his job if he's worried about you. Come on, let's get you into the observatory."

"There's an old bomb shelter in the basement," Elliott said. "Doc Samuelson's got an aid station set up down there. It'll be a good place for them."

"How did he end up with us?"

"He's friends with Dr. Schneider, so he agreed to come along to help with the Big Beam. Once he was finished, he decided to stick around and help Kirby with medical duties."

"Any wounded so far?"

"None of ours, but a few locals were wounded in a skirmish, the brave idiots." Elliott shook his head. "They may not have the training we have, but they've got guts. I'll give 'em that."

She had seen a lot of people like that in the past few weeks. Columbia had no shortage of these so-called "brave idiots," but the city was better off for their presence. Elliott hadn't thought much of them, but they gave Aster hope for the future. It wasn't a feeling she was used to.

Aster looked around. "Why aren't there more people out there?" She'd expected at least two or three men besides Elliott to man this position.

"Little Bill Grumbine's got overwatch." Elliott nodded toward the narrow window up on the cylindrical, tower-like portion of the observatory, where the spiral staircase was. "The skirmish happened on the north side of the compound. Obsidian scouts we quickly drove off."

"Glad to have you back, Boss!" Grumbine's voice came in through her earpiece.

Aster smiled. "Glad to be back in comms range, Little Bill." To the kids, she said, "Come on, then, let's get you both to the bomb shelter. If I know Dr. Samuelson, he'll have some candy for you."

"Candy?" Jason's sobs subsided into hiccups. He looked at her. "What kind of candy?"

"You'll have to ask the doctor."

"Will he give you some, too?"

"I don't see why not."

"Yay!" Jason grabbed Aster's hand and pulled her along. "Come on, let's go!"

Helen grabbed Elliott's hand. "Will you come with us?"

"I'm really not supposed to leave this position—" Elliott gave Aster a resigned look.

"I guess you have that effect on kids, Corporal."

Elliott sighed. "Well, if it'll get you inside quicker, fine. Let's hurry."

The four of them moved at a fast walk toward the observatory's rear doors. Aster and Jason took the lead, with Helen and Elliott in the rear. "How are the others situated?" Aster asked.

"We're spread pretty thin. Paxton, Aino, and a couple others are up in the second-floor classrooms, looking east and south. Ortiz and Epcar are keeping an eye on the north from the top floor. You've got Grumbine and me watching the west, and—"

A shot rang out, and something struck the pavement with a wet smack. Aster spun, and her eyes took in the sight of Elliott's ruined face and the brain matter on the ground before his body even began to tumble. She switched her P90 to semi-auto, shouldered it, and fired four shots in the direction the sniper's bullet had come from. In the distance, she heard a faint scream, followed by the crashing of a body through a tree's canopy.

Elliott's corpse struck the ground, his hand still gripping Helen's. The girl fell to the asphalt, then got onto her hands and knees. She studied the mess that was Elliott's head, her eyes wide and unblinking. She opened her mouth to scream, but no sound came out.

"Mr. Elliott!" Jason cried. He tried to run to him, but Aster gripped him so tight, he squealed in pain. She loosened her grip, but not enough for him to squirm out of her hold.

"Helen, get over here!" Aster called. She stepped forward, but more bullets impacted the ground near them. Aster's enhanced vision picked up dozens of muzzle flashes from the distant tree line. She cursed. How had she not detected them on her approach? Whoever they were, they were good.

Overhead, Grumbine's .50 Barrett rifle boomed. "Jesus, where'd they all come from? I couldn't see 'em!"

Aster shoved Jason behind her and tried to shoulder the P90, but he ran forward again. She grabbed him by the collar of his shirt and pulled him back. She let the P90 drop on its sling as she tucked Jason's squirming form under one arm. She drew her Five-Seven from her chest rig and backed toward the observatory, firing at distant targets. Her rounds found homes in the armor and flesh of her opponents. One by one, the answering muzzle flashes disappeared, but more appeared in their places.

She risked a glance at Elliott's body. Helen still sat there, unaware of the bullets zipping past her. "Helen, run!" she shouted.

Helen heeded her words, but not the way she wanted her to. Instead of running toward her, Helen spun and ran back to the machine gun nest. Bullets struck the pavement all around the little girl until she threw herself under cover.

Aster started to run back to the machine gun nest, but Jason's writhing form reminded her she had someone who needed protecting first. She gritted her teeth, spun on her heel, and sprinted the final distance to the observatory's back door.

She flung the door open so hard, it slammed into the brick wall it was attached to, and its hinges squealed in protest. She kicked the heavy door shut as bullets impacted against it. "Little Bill, keep covering the nest! Helen Ward's still out there!"

"They're peppering my position pretty good, but I'll try. Shit, is that Elliott?"

Aster grimaced. "He's dead, as is his killer. Make sure Helen doesn't join them."

"Roger, Boss."

The back door to the observatory led into a storage room that looked like it was part office supply closet, part kitchen pantry. There were two interior doors, and the one she took led into a kitchen that looked like it would fit more in a home than in a facility. Aster wondered if the observatory's staff lived here at one point, then she pushed that thought away and found the steps to the cellar. She hurried down them and tried to ignore the shouts of "Contact!" and the echoing reports of gunfire that rattled the building's windows.

As Elliott had said, Doc was downstairs in the bomb shelter, manning an aid station with Sergeant Kirby. They were tending to several locals laid out on pallets made of blankets. Each had been shot at least once, but they appeared to be stable.

Kirby looked up at Aster's appearance. "Lady, thank God you're here. Lieutenant Paxton let everyone know that a massive unit is heading our way."

"Sounds like they're already here," Doc observed as he finished wrapping the arm of one of his patients, an old woman with a lever-action rifle resting next to her.

"My God, is that child hurt?" Kirby hurried over and took Jason from Aster's grasp. Jason nearly fell, but Kirby caught him and carried his limp form to an unused pallet in the corner of the room.

Fear jolted through Aster as she stared at Jason's unmoving body. What if he'd been hit in the gunfire? "Is he all right?" she demanded, her voice quavering. Had she already failed in her promise to Nathan?

Kirby pulled his shirt up and examined his pale torso, then did the same with his pants legs. She felt around his head, then his pelvic region. Her hands came back wet. She examined them in the dim light, then sniffed. She wrinkled her nose and chuckled. "Well, he's leaking, but it's not blood. I think the poor boy wet himself and fainted."

"*Incoming! Get down!*" Epcar shouted over the comms.

An explosion rocked the building. Kirby lost her footing and fell on her butt as dust rained down from the ceiling. Aster spread her feet apart to keep from falling. "What was that?" she demanded.

Epcar coughed through the comms. "Enemy rocket attack! Get that fire extinguisher, Ortiz!"

"On it!"

"What kind of damage do we have?"

"The stairwell leading up to the roof is gone, and good riddance. Wasn't much we could see up there, and we were way too exposed.

Only problem is we don't have any windows facing north, and that's where the rocket attack came from."

"Do we have anyone outside manning the fence line?"

"Nothing but a parking lot out that way and a small, decorative stone wall. And no, we don't have the manpower for that."

Aster chewed the inside of her lip for a moment. She needed to get outside to Helen, but if the northern sector was overrun, what good would that do? "Can we spare anyone to get out to the Ma Deuce?"

"We can't get anyone out there even if we want to," Grumbine replied. The comms picked up the instant his gun fired, then cut out the rest of the report. "They lit up the door somethin' fierce when Tanaka stuck his head out a second ago. Anyone who goes out there's a dead man."

Aster could make it if she had the chance to. No one was faster than she, although she admitted she wasn't faster than a speeding bullet, let alone dozens of speeding bullets. "Smoke canisters?"

"It'll obscure our vision," Grumbine replied. "Our NVGs won't penetrate a smoke haze, and these bastards can see better at night than we can, even with the NVGs."

Aster hissed. "Evidence Shredders?"

"That's my theory. Would explain why the bastards got the drop on you, wouldn't it?"

It would, as much as she hated to admit it. While she could match the average Geno-freak in terms of strength and agility, certain ones had the ability to mask their presence, much like the animals they were spliced with. "If they've sent in the Evidence Shredders, they know what we're up to. Paxton, let the police know what's going on."

"Roger, Boss. What'll you be up to?"

She replaced her partially empty Five-Seven magazine with a fresh one. "What I do best. Give me a minute to get ready, then I'll guard the northern approach."

"What about the west?" Grumbine asked. "I can't hold indefinitely."

Aster chewed the inside of her lip for a moment. Finally, she said, "I've got an idea."

* * *

Gunfire echoed through the streets, much closer than it had a few minutes before. Movement down the darkened street caught my eye, and I shouldered my rifle. I waited long enough to confirm the dark armor of an Obsidian soldier, then I fired a burst of .308 bullets. The soldier crumpled and fell.

Countess shivered at the sudden noise over her head, but she stood her ground. "Good girl," I murmured, then raised my voice. "Contact!"

The thirty officers with me started shooting as targets presented themselves further down the street. We'd pushed past the university grounds into a residential area to keep our defenses from getting flanked. Behind us, the sounds of battle rose from the buildings housing the campus militia. Obsidian soldiers had taken up positions in neighboring buildings, but my task wasn't to worry about that. It was to keep more soldiers from filtering in.

"Bastards are everywhere!" Kevin pulled Watson up next to me. He fired his rifle down a side street. "If we stay here much longer, we're going to get surrounded."

He was right. Our greatest strength was our mobility. I tracked an Obsidian soldier darting across the street. My finger rested on the trigger. "Let's pull back a bit, then come around from the side—"

My radio squealed. "Sheriff Welliver, this is Paxton. Obsidian forces are assaulting Point Chiffon. Position surrounded."

I jerked the trigger, and my shot went wide. The soldier I'd been aiming at dove through a window. *The observatory was surrounded? My kids were there!*

"The kids are there!" Kevin said, echoing my thoughts. "We have to help them!"

"Paxton, this is Welliver." Gunfire crackled over the sheriff's transmission. "We're hard-pressed here and can't spare anyone. Can you hold?"

There was a long pause. "Affirmative. It'll be close, but we can hold."

Fear gnawed at my gut. If the observatory fell, not only would we lose our chance at taking down the satellite, but my kids would be captured or worse. I keyed my mic. "Lieutenant Ward here. Requesting permission to assist. I can bring thirty with me."

"Negative," Paxton said. "Your few officers won't do much good against Evidence Shredders."

"Sergeant Ward here," Danny suddenly said. "How about if the National Guard moves in to assist?"

Hope flooded into me. "You got Colonel Eastman on our side?"

"Yes, sir! We were moving north toward campus, but we can head northeast instead and approach the obs—Point Chiffon from the south."

"That would be most appreciated," Paxton said.

A round zipped past my head, reminding me there was still a battle to be fought right here. I fired a few rounds down the street, then wheeled Countess around. "Follow me! We'll lure them in, then flank them!"

It wasn't until a little later I realized Kevin was no longer with me.

* * *

Aster stuffed as many P90 and pistol magazines as she could fit into the pouches on her armor's webbing. She checked the mag-loaders belted at her hips. Each held two pistol magazines, one for her Five-Seven, the other for her backup 1911. If she ran dry and her free hand was occupied, she could eject the empty mag and press the handle against the top of the autoloader, and it would shove a fresh mag into the gun with enough force to properly seat it. The device was an innovation of Maître D's, and it had saved her life on more than one occasion.

Gunfire echoed through the walls from above and outside. Through her earpiece, she heard the chatter of her men as they directed fire, reloaded, and shifted positions. If what she was hearing was true, they were under attack by hundreds of enemies on all sides. And she had a dozen men and two children with her. Granted, they were a dozen of the best men, but even they could only hold out for so long.

She hadn't yet heard the Ma Deuce firing. She tapped her earpiece. "Helen, are you there?"

There was a long pause. "Aunt Aster? Is that you?"

Despite herself, Aster smiled. "Who else would it be? How're you holding up?"

"I'm scared."

The words cut through Aster like a knife. "I know. I'm sorry I couldn't get to you."

"Is Jason all right?"

"He's with Doc Samuelson in the cellar. They've set up an aid station down there."

"Are you coming back for me?"

That knife kept digging deeper into Aster's heart. "I wish I could. Enemies are pressing us hard from the north, and there's no one to guard that direction except me."

"The enemy's here, too. It sounds like they're everywhere!"

"Keep low, Helen," Aster cautioned. "A sniper took out Corporal Elliott, remember?" Helen gasped and stifled several sobs. "I'm sorry to say it like that, Helen, but you need to stay safe until I can get to you."

"You're coming for me?"

"As soon as I can." She checked her weapons one last time, even her commander-variant 1911. She hadn't fired it yet, but it didn't hurt to inspect it. She returned it to her small-of-the-back holster, then checked her boot knives. If she got down to those, she was in serious trouble. Well, she might not be, but it would mean the battle was going badly. "Once I deal with the enemies to the north, I'm coming for you, Helen."

"What if the enemy gets here before you do?"

"Little Bill Grumbine's keeping an eye on you." *When he can.*

"What if there's too many for him?"

Aster opened her mouth to speak, but no words came. She knew what she needed to tell Helen, but she didn't want to. Yet, it was the only thing she could do. "Helen, can you work the Ma Deuce like Grumbine and I showed you earlier today?"

"I think so. It looks like it's loaded and ready to go. Wait, you want me to use it against people?" The last word came out as a squeak.

Nathan, forgive me. "It's what you trained for, right? So you could defend yourself and others? Well, now's your chance. Can you do it?"

A long pause. "I think so."

"Then use the weapon's targeting screen to keep an eye out for enemies. If you see movement, put your hands on the trigger and be prepared to aim low to account for recoil. It's a heavy gun, but it still wants to rise. Fire in short bursts until you get the feel for it and stay on target."

"...the whites of their eyes."

"What was that?"

"Not until you see the whites of their eyes, right? Just like at Bunker Hill."

Aster smiled, though her heart was breaking. "Yes, just like at Bunker Hill. Hold your fire until you have no choice, then let them have everything you've got. I'll come get you when I can, okay?"

"Okay. I love you, Aunt Aster."

Aster's throat constricted, but she forced out the words, "I love you, too," before she severed the link.

She stepped up to the cellar door. "This is Lady in Black," she said over the comms for everyone else to hear. "Heading out."

"Good hunting, Lady!" Paxton replied.

"Give 'em hell, Boss!" Aino added.

Aster took one step forward, then hesitated. Helen's mention of Bunker Hill reminded her of a Revolutionary War painting she'd seen as a child. It was of George Washington on his knees in prayer before a battle. She had no idea what he had prayed for, but ultimately, he had been victorious. Nathan had done the same thing as they rode into the Rock Bridge Ranch the night they and the Homeguard were lured in by Obsidian assassins. Though most of the household had been killed, they'd escaped with Billy Vargas. There had to be some merit to the concept of prayer, right?

She dropped down to one knee, her weapons and magazines clattering against her armor. She closed her eyes and prayed the only prayer she knew: *God, please.*

Then she flew through the door, her FN-P90 already to her shoulder as she sighted in on her first target, a dog-faced Geno-freak in Obsidian battle armor. He was a hundred yards out, an advance scout from the looks of it, but her enhanced night vision let her see the dozens of enemies behind him.

She squeezed off a burst, and the man fell, his face and neck a bloody ruin. Before his body hit the ground, she had already shot two more of his comrades. Men cried out in shock and pain, and answering gunfire zipped and whizzed past her. Animalistic snarls rose into the night as the Evidence Shredders closed in on her position.

They had to hold. No matter how many Obsidian soldiers and mutants threw themselves at the line, they had to hold. Or it was all over, for the city, for her men, for Nathan and his children. And that couldn't happen.

Not on the Lady in Black's watch.

* * *

Helen checked the M2 for the fifteenth time since she'd hunkered down in the exposed gun position. And for the fifteenth time, she saw that everything was in working order. A full hundred-round belt of ammunition was connected to the weapon's action, and the bulk of the thirty-pound belt rested in the green ammo can it came in. Another can lay right next to the tray holding the first one. She'd already popped the top on it so it would be easily accessible when she needed it. She had even stacked up several more cans next to the tray, so she wouldn't have to leave the gun to get ammunition. She couldn't imagine ever needing this much, but she'd also never seen Aster and Elliott so loaded down with ammo in all the weeks she'd known them.

Tears stung her eyes, and she risked a glance over the sandbag lip to the right. Elliott lay where he had fallen, and what was left of his head lay in a pool of blood and brain matter. A wave of nausea swept over her, but she didn't have anything left to throw up. The contents of her stomach already lay next to the gun, and the stench was a reminder of what she'd witnessed. It also reminded her of how bad dead animals could smell if they were left out long enough.

Would Elliott's body smell that bad, too, if he were left out long enough?

Gunfire rose from the north and east. Rounds impacted the observatory's brick wall, and some answering shots came from those she assumed were Aster's men or Aster herself, but it sounded so small in comparison to the amount of fire heading their way. How many people were out to get them?

The M2's tripod was raised high enough for a man Elliott's size to comfortably shoot, which meant it was way too high for her. She'd mitigated this by pulling a few sandbags from the barrier so she could stand on them. She climbed back up so she could conduct her sixteenth inspection of the gun.

Movement caught her eye out in the darkness. She tensed and only realized she was holding her breath when her chest started to hurt. She exhaled and drew in a sharp breath as she stared into the distance through the M2's bullet-resistant targeting screen, willing herself not to blink, willing whatever was out there to move so she could see what it was, willing it to be a rabbit or something equally harmless.

When it moved again, she saw a pair of rabbit ears and started to relax, but then she saw that those ears were attached to a head far too large to be a bunny's. And that bunny head was connected to an all-too-human frame.

The creature stared up at the observatory for a long moment before its gaze shifted to her position. Helen covered her mouth to stifle a squeak of fright, and she had to remind herself that Aster had said the targeting screen was one-sided. Bad guys couldn't see through it. There was no way this strange rabbit monster could see her.

Its whiskers twitched, as did its floppy ears. Just because it couldn't see her didn't mean it couldn't smell or hear her. What had Uncle Danny told her? That animals can smell fear in a human? If that was true, she reeked worse than her own vomit.

The rabbit darted off into the night and out of sight. Its bounding gait was strange and horrifying when done with a human body. Helen shivered despite the night's warmth and hugged herself. She closed her eyes and prayed this would end soon.

When she opened her eyes, she saw a pair of orbs staring back at her through the enhanced view of the targeting screen. She blinked, and a dozen more sets of eyes appeared. Monsters—no, Geno-freaks as they were called—appeared out of the darkness. They approached her position at a quick jog, each one wielding a firearm or melee weapon of some sort, and each with a mouth full of sharp teeth.

With considerable effort, Helen broke free of her self-embrace and placed her shaking hands on the M2's wooden grips. She pushed the weapon down until the crosshair lined up on a creature with a bear's head. She set her thumb on the butterfly trigger and took a shuddering breath that sounded way too loud to her ears. If the approaching creatures noticed, they gave no indication. They just continued forward in that loping jog that humans crossed with animals sometimes adopted. If they maintained that pace, they would be on her position in less than a minute.

Whites of their eyes. Wait until you see the whites of their eyes. She hoped Grumbine would see them and start shooting. Why hadn't he already?

And then a wolf-headed creature next to the bear she'd been aiming at disappeared in a spray of thermal-enhanced blood. The booming report of Grumbine's rifle rang out two more times in rapid succession. Each time, a Geno-freak fell and was dead before it realized what hit it.

A few of the Geno-freaks dropped down and started firing at the observatory's top floor. Tracer rounds sailed well over Helen's position and impacted the cylindrical tower wall. Glass shattered, and Grumbine's curses rang out over the comms line. *"Damn, that was close! We could really use some more help on this side!"*

The other Geno-freaks charged, and if their earlier jog was quick, this run was insanely fast. They closed in on her position, and it would only be a matter of seconds before they were on her.

"Whites of their eyes." Helen's breath came in ragged gasps. "Whites of their eyes." The edges of her vision grew hazy, and she found herself fixated on the bear creature, the one in the lead. His lips were pulled back in a snarl, revealing a snout full of razor-sharp teeth. He carried a grenade launcher which he raised to his shoulder. All Helen saw was the whites of his eyes. She depressed the trigger.

The M2 roared. She held the trigger down as twenty rounds sprayed out of the barrel. She never saw what happened to the bear creature, but she did see the others around him diving for cover. She tried to swing the gun to the left to target a lizard man, but the gun kicked so wildly it threw off her aim. She remembered Aster's instruction to fire in short bursts, then let go of the trigger.

She risked a glance into the ammo can. It was half empty. She'd shot fifty rounds in less than a few seconds. *Stupid. Stupid, stupid, Helen!*

A round pinged off the targeting screen, and a few more struck the sandbags in front of her. Helen flinched and aimed at one of the Geno-freaks lying prone. It was a man who looked human except for the amphibian skin covering his face. She squeezed a quick burst, then let go of the trigger. Dirt kicked up around the Geno, but he continued to return fire. She adjusted her aim and fired another short burst. The rounds zipped past him. She once again adjusted her aim and let off a third burst as he jumped up to run. The rounds tore off his left leg at the knee and blew open his midsection. He tumbled to the ground, shrieking in agony.

Nausea flooded through Helen, but she'd grown used to the sick sensation after what happened to Elliott. More rounds struck her position, which served as a reminder that she needed to stay in the fight. She swiveled the M2 to the right and fired burst after burst at the enemies shooting at her. She didn't stop to look at what happened to them, partly because she didn't want to see, partly because she didn't have time to. There were so many of them, and she needed to clear them out before her gun went—

Click.

Without thinking, she shoved the empty ammo can to the side and pushed the full one forward into the tray. She opened the top of the M2, grabbed the end of the cartridge belt, and fed it into the action like Mr. Grumbine showed her. When the first round clicked into place, she snapped the lid back down.

The Genos had just risen to their feet to approach her position when Helen pulled back twice on the charging handle, bringing the weapon back to Condition One. She lined her sights up on a man who looked like a cross between a shark and a dolphin and opened fire again. She flinched as the massive .50 rounds tore the shark fin into chunks, but she didn't look away. Instead, she swung the M2 to the left and right, firing short burst after short burst. Geno-freaks hit the dirt, either of their own volition or because she cut them down. Tears stung her eyes, but she refused to blink as she sighted the crosshair on one enemy and then another.

The light shining from above intensified. She glanced over her shoulder and squinted at the brightness. The Teledyne Big Beam was charging up to full capacity and as it did, it grew brighter. The enemy wasn't really after Helen or Aster or any of her men. They were after the Big Beam. They knew if they took it out, they would get control of the city.

And then they would be able to do whatever they wanted to with her, with Jason, with Aster, and with Daddy.

She couldn't let that happen.

So she fired. Every third or fourth round was a tracer, and it zipped through the darkness, illuminating the mutant faces of her enemies, the grass, and the forest beyond. She fired and reloaded and fired some more.

* * *

"Power outages are being reported throughout the city," Egghead reported. "Cause unknown at this time. Maybe a substation was hit?"

"That, or the defenders are deliberately cutting off the lights," Lloyd suggested. Not all his men were equipped with night vision goggles, and he very much doubted the cops had many, if any. "Could be they want to level the playing field."

"That's a possibility, sir." He pressed a finger to his earpiece. "Sir, the Homeguard is on the move again."

Lloyd frowned. Egghead had reported that Colonel Eastman's forces had halted on the outskirts of the university's grounds after they encountered the main battle tank that was captured by the mounted cops. "What's the good colonel up to?"

"They're bypassing the university's grounds and heading east." Egghead activated the main monitor, which showed a digital map of the area surrounding Columbia. Reported concentrations of city defenders were colored red, while their own forces were highlighted in Obsidian black. The Homeguard had originally been colored green to highlight them as friendly, but Egghead changed their color to yellow: potentially hostile. "It seems they're heading to the observatory."

Lloyd ground his teeth in frustration, but he quickly calmed. The Homeguard had always been a wild card, a unit he couldn't fully rely on. That was why he wanted to send them in first, to soften up the city's defenders, stir up unrest, and make it that much easier for his people to enter. After his assassins assaulted that horse ranch on the outskirts of town and a few other places, he figured both sides blamed each other, and there could be no reconciliation.

And then that stupid tank commander had let his vehicle get captured, and he hadn't even have the decency to die in the attempt. The cops must've persuaded him to switch sides, and now he'd gone and done the same to Eastman. Well, if the Homeguard had turned traitor, then it had outlived its usefulness. "Do we have network access for *Conquistadoris?*"

"We do, sir."

"Then it's time we use it. Patch it through to my console." Lloyd waited until the screen on his armrest loaded the appropriate menu, then he punched in a set of passcodes. If the Homeguard wanted to turn against him, then the good Colonel Eastman was going to learn that two could play that game.

Harsh lessons were often the best lessons in this Fallen World.

* * * * *

Chapter Seventeen

Danny and his squad rode alongside *Conquistadoris* as it rolled through an unlit subdivision on the southeastern outskirts of Columbia. Cutting through would get them to the observatory that much faster. If the radio chatter was any indicator, those defending the observatory needed help immediately.

"I wish we could go faster," Patrolman Jones said, his voice raised to be heard over *Conquistadoris'* engine.

Danny chafed at the delay, too. Noir and the other horses ambled along at a trot. They'd be at the observatory in half the time if they galloped, but they'd leave the infantry behind. Some of the Homeguard were in Humvees and JLTVs, but most were on foot, and DeSoto did *not* want to outpace the infantry again. "It's why I was captured in the first place!" he said before slipping down into the tank's cupola. His head peeked out over the lip of the hatch, and he had a set of NVGs pulled over his eyes.

So, they continued at a much slower pace, with a pair of Humvees ranging ahead to scout. They'd confirmed that the observatory was surrounded by a vastly superior force, a mixed unit of humans and Geno-freaks.

Wendy Alexander tensed at the news, and even now, she was grim faced as she rode along next to Danny. "Are you all right?" he asked.

"No. I'm terrified."

"If that's your terrified expression, I'd hate to see you when you're angry."

Wendy glanced sideways at him, then chuckled. "You've already seen that many times."

"It's why things didn't work out between us." Danny grinned. "I always knew what to say to piss you off."

"The same could be said of me." She sighed. "To answer your question more fully, I'm terrified, but I'll manage. This isn't the Country Hotel, with a brutal Agent running amok and our Specialist down for the count. We're out in the open, with our horses and infantry and a freaking tank. Even if it's—" She faltered, then pressed on. "Even if it's Evidence Shredders, we can manage."

Danny pulled Noir over so he could slap Wendy on the back. "That's the spirit!"

"Humvees rolling in!" DeSoto shouted. He stood higher in the hatch, his arm resting against the M2 machine gun mounted to the turret. Its barrel was locked in an upward position to keep it from bouncing freely while they moved. If he needed it, DeSoto could manually unlock it and get to shooting.

The call was taken up and repeated down the line. The far entrance to the subdivision exited onto a rural roadway that would take them straight to the observatory. Danny half-expected to see headlight beams, then he shook his head. A military scout wouldn't be stupid enough to do that. They'd have NVGs, much like he had back in his Corporate days. *Too much time in civilian life, man.*

Conquistadoris ground to a halt, so Danny reined in his squad. He figured they were stopping so the Humvees could get back in formation.

"Hey, what's going on?" DeSoto looked down the hatch. "Ling, why'd we stop?"

The turret swung to the left, then slowly moved back to the right. The barrel of the main gun centered on the subdivision's entrance just as the first Humvee came into view. "Shut it down!" DeSoto shouted. "Shut it down—"

Conquistadoris fired. The muzzle flash was blinding, and the explosive bang was deafening. A 130mm high explosive round tore through the Humvee, but it didn't explode until it exited the vehicle. The force of the blast rocked the Humvee, but the heavy vehicle didn't flip.

Noir shrieked and reared at the noise, and it was all Danny could do to keep from spilling out of the saddle. DeSoto disappeared down the hatch of *Conquistadoris,* but he could still hear the man yelling, "Shut it down!" over and over, along with some choice language for his crew.

The Humvee doors flew open, and wounded and stunned soldiers stumbled out and ran for cover. The tank's coaxial machine gun fired from left to right, mowing down all but two who ran toward the other side of the street. The survivors threw themselves behind a two-story home.

"Jesus, what's going on?" Wendy shouted. She'd gotten Candace under control and wheeled around, ready to bolt away from the tank. "Why're they shooting their own men?"

"Some kind of computer malfunction?" Danny knew from Aster's report that *Conquistadoris* was equipped with an Automated Defense System, but that only activated at the crew's express order, or if they were incapacitated or dead. And even then, it had friend-or-foe identification software. It wouldn't open fire on allied vehicles. Obsidian was many things, but they didn't make faulty—

He swore. The tank might have been owned by the US military, but Obsidian had built it. Why wouldn't their engineers include a failsafe so it could never be used against Corporate assets? They'd have been stupid not to.

DeSoto popped out of the hatch again. He waved his arms toward the column of vehicles and soldiers behind Danny and the others. "Get away! She's gone berserk!"

As if to accentuate his point, the main gun fired again. The round punched through the brick wall to the left of the subdivision's entrance. A fireball rose, likely from the second scout Humvee.

The turret started to spin around. "Scatter!" Danny shouted. "To the right! Away from its guns!"

Danny and Noir galloped across a front yard, making for an open gate that led to the back. To his right, Homeguard soldiers milled about, wondering what was going on. "Get out of the line of fire!" he shouted.

He risked a look over his shoulder. Wendy, Jones, and the rest of the squad had turned to chase after him, but one wasn't fast enough. The spinning turret's coaxial gun opened fire, and officer and horse died in a hail of bullets. It was so dark, Danny couldn't see who it was. He cursed. *This is all my fault!* If he hadn't agreed to DeSoto's stupid plan, this wouldn't have happened.

The main gun fired with another deafening boom. The JLTV at the head of the column exploded, its armor unable to withstand a direct hit from so close. Soldiers scattered in every direction as *Conquistadoris* opened fire with its coaxial gun. Its main gun fired again, and another vehicle blew up.

"What do we do, Sarge?" Jones asked when the squad had gathered in the home's backyard. He pulled the RPG from his shoulder. "Aster said this wouldn't do much good, but it's better than nothing, right?"

"It's all we've got unless the Homeguard boys and girls have anti-tank rockets," Danny said. He hadn't seen any, and he doubted they had many, if any. An infantry unit called in for riot control probably wouldn't have brought rocket launchers with them.

Colonel Eastman's Jeep suddenly whipped into the neighbor's backyard, followed by a platoon's worth of soldiers. No fence separated the yards, so Danny rode over to the Jeep. "Colonel, does your unit have any anti-tank rockets?"

"We had one in our last deuce-and-a-half, but *Conquistadoris* took it out." Eastman pulled off his hat and flung it on the Jeep's dashboard. "Damnation! What the hell is going on?"

"Obsidian's going on." Danny gave him a quick rundown of his theory. "It's the only thing that makes sense, sir."

"Well, shit, don't that just beat all?" He shook his head. "I'm an MP, not a tanker. I didn't know Obsidian built that thing."

"Can DeSoto and his crew get control of it again?" Wendy demanded.

"They're trying." Eastman tapped his earpiece. "It's got them completely locked out. We're going to have to bring it down ourselves."

Jones patted his RPG. "In that case, we'll have to make do with what we've got."

* * *

DeSoto tried to bring up the command prompt, the camera feeds, hell, even the ammo counter and fuel gauge, but nothing was working. The computer wouldn't accept any of his inputs. "Shit, I'm locked out!"

"Same here, LT!" Yoder banged on the gunner's console. "Piece of shit won't let me shut it down!"

"It's the ADS," Ling suggested. He sat in the driver's seat, with his arms crossed. He'd given up trying to work the controls a few moments earlier. "Somehow, the dead man switch activated, and *Conquistadoris* thinks we're out of the fight."

"Well, we're not!" DeSoto slammed his fist on the keyboard.

"Dammit, girl, why aren't you listening to us?"

"*Conquistadoris*, this is Eastman. You in there, DeSoto?"

"Still alive and kicking, Colonel!" *Conquistadoris* fired its main gun, and the boom echoed through the crew compartment. The open hatch helped dissipate some of the reverberations, and the noise canceling headsets they wore mitigated it further, but it was still insanely loud. "How're things on your end?"

"Bad. Two Humvees down, along with two JLTVs and our deuce-and-a-half. I don't even know how many dead at this point."

"Shit."

"Yeah, shit indeed. Listen, we need to disable that baby of yours before she can run further amok. Can you shut her down from the inside?"

"We've tried, but the computer system is sealed off. We could smash the consoles—"

"Believe me, I'm tempted!" Yoder shouted.

"But it wouldn't do us any good, short of relieving some stress."

"Can you evacuate?"

"I'd rather not while it's still mobile, sir. We get out of this thing, who knows when it'll suddenly lurch to its top speed." There was also the ESD system to worry about. It had fried that Specialist lady pretty well. He had no doubt it would completely incapacitate him and his boys if they touched the wrong thing on the way out, if not kill them out right.

"Then you'll need to hold onto your butts until we can do something about her mobility. Do it!" he shouted to someone.

A blast suddenly rocked *Conquistadoris*. "The fuck was that?" Ling yelled over the blaring alarms.

Damage warnings flashed on DeSoto's screen. The skirt around the right tread had absorbed a rocket impact. There was no damage to the tread, but the skirt had partially separated. Then the image disappeared as the alarm fell silent. *Conquistadoris* spun to the right.

"Shit, scatter!" Eastman yelled. "Everyone, scatter!"

Conquistadoris' main gun and coaxial machine gun opened fire simultaneously. What the hell was going on out there?

* * *

"I think you pissed it off, Jones!" Danny shouted. He kicked Noir into a gallop, and together, they raced from one backyard to the next.

Behind them, *Conquistadoris* rolled down a wide driveway and plowed through the brick posts attached to a decorative iron gate. Chunks of brick flew everywhere as the tank slid to a halt on the grass. Its turret spun toward Danny and the retreating officers.

Eastman's Jeep roared back down a neighboring driveway, heading for the street. Danny wheeled Noir around to follow him and his men. Jones kept pace. He reloaded his RPG, using his knees to steer his black stallion, Rambo. "Sorry, Sarge! I thought that would get the tread!"

The coaxial machine gun opened up, spraying bullets toward them. Two officers tumbled from their saddles, and their mounts screamed. Danny cursed, but he was grateful the M2 in the turret was still in the locked position. The ADS could control the weapon, but it couldn't do anything about a manual lock.

"Turn right into the street!" Wendy yelled. "We'll flank it and aim for the right side again!"

Conquistadoris' engine roared, and its treads dug into the grass as it chased after them. "Uh, I think it's going to make that hard for us!" Corporal Ferris said.

They raced past a house, and it blocked Danny's view of the tank for a moment. At the end of the driveway, Eastman turned his Jeep to the left, while Danny led his officers to the right. If he and Jones were quick enough, they could make it back around the house as the tank was turning to pursue them down the driveway.

The sound of splitting wood and crumbling masonry erupted behind the house. The living room bay window suddenly shattered as bullets tore through it. Rounds zipped past Danny's head, and he dropped low in Noir's saddle.

A moment later, *Conquistadoris* plowed through the bay window, its hull covered in sheetrock dust and timber fragments. "Holy shit!" Jones said. "She's like an ex-girlfriend who just won't take no for an answer!"

"Hey!" Wendy called. "What about ex-boyfriends!"

"Never had one!" Jones turned Rambo back up the first driveway, but he reined him in long enough to turn in the saddle and aim his RPG. "Clear backblast!"

"Clear!" Danny shouted.

Jones fired, and the rocket-propelled grenade sailed through the air and slammed into the side of *Conquistadoris'* armored skirt, close to the same spot as the first. A chunk of the skirt fell off, exposing the tread beneath. "Hot damn, now that's what I like to see!" Jones reached for another rocket.

The turret spun toward them.

Danny waved the other officers ahead, and they galloped past them into the backyard. "We've got to go, Jones!"

"Almost there, Sarge!" He fumbled to get the rocket properly seated. "Come on, baby."

The coaxial gun centered on them.

"No more time!" Danny slapped Rambo's rump and kicked Noir forward at the same time.

Rambo jumped, and Jones almost fell out of the saddle. He grabbed for the reins, and the RPG slid from his fingers and struck the driveway with a clatter. "Shit!"

"Worry about it later!" Danny shouted as the coaxial gun opened fire. The bullets passed through the area they'd just occupied.

Danny looked ahead as Wendy galloped back their way. She held the saddle's horn in her right hand and leaned so far to the left her body was sideways. "What the hell are you doing, woman?" he shouted.

Wendy didn't answer. She pushed herself as low as she could go and snagged the RPG by its shoulder strap. The weapon swung in her hand, and the odd balance nearly pulled her from the saddle, but she managed to right herself. She galloped straight across the street and into the backyard of another home, out of sight of *Conquistadoris*.

"Damn, Sarge!" Jones said. "Lieutenant Alexander's got some moves!"

Danny chuckled. "You don't know the half of it."

Their levity was short-lived, as *Conquistadoris* suddenly rolled into view. Only, it wasn't aiming at them. Its turret had spun toward the other side of the street, tracking Wendy's movements. "It's fixated on the RPG!" Danny said. "It knows that's the real threat!"

"We've got to help her!" Jones said. He reached into his pouch and removed another high explosive round. "Damn, I wish I hadn't dropped the launcher."

"It was my fault," Danny said. He racked his brain for a solution. If Wendy had snatched up the RPG, she meant to use it, but if she exposed herself now, she'd be killed. He needed to buy her time to get into position, but what could he do?

He was suddenly reminded of something he'd seen in an old World War II film, where the heroes were priming mortar rounds and throwing them like grenades. He wasn't sure it would work, but it was worth a shot. "How do you prime those RPG rounds?"

"There's an impact fuse on the tip of the warhead." Jones tapped the plastic cap screwed onto the tip. "Remove this safety cap, and it won't take much pressure to detonate the rocket."

Danny held out his hand. "Give me that. And the bag, too."

"Sure, Sarge, but what're you going to do with them?"

"Something stupid." Danny slung the bag across his shoulder, then unscrewed the safety cap on the rocket Jones handed him. He urged Noir into a canter and shouted, "Wish me luck!"

Conquistadoris had turned so that it faced the driveway Wendy had ridden down. The turret tracked left to right to left again, looking for Wendy and her RPG. Danny was scared by how well the AI could think, and he hoped he could use its intelligence against it.

He turned Noir to the left as soon as he was on the street and urged her into a gallop. He twisted in the saddle and hurled the rocket like a javelin. It struck the sloped hull of the tank, bounced upward, then fell nose-first onto the pavement. The impact fuse lived up to its name and the rocket exploded, blowing a small crater in the asphalt.

Danny reached into his bag and held up another rocket so the *Conquistadoris'* cameras could see it. As soon as he did, both the turret and the body turned his way. He twisted forward again and urged Noir up another driveway as the coaxial gun opened fire. Bullets cracked as they passed his head, and Noir faltered as a glancing shot struck her armor. Danny didn't want to look, but he couldn't help turning his head toward the tank. His gaze fixed on the muzzle flash of the machine gun trying to kill him.

And *Conquistadoris'* right side erupted in a flash of light. The screeching of tearing metal and grinding gears filled the night sky, and the tank shuddered as the right tread came apart. The left tread continued to work, but it could barely move the heavy, unbalanced tank. Sparks flew as the right side dug a trench in the asphalt. Its engine shrieked as it attempted to compensate, but after a moment, it stalled and stopped. The engine died, and silence reigned, pierced only by the moaning of wounded men and horses.

Wendy rode into the street, with the empty RPG launcher slung over her shoulder. She pumped her fist in the air, and a cheer rose from the soldiers and officers who'd witnessed the display. Danny laughed. "Nicely done!"

DeSoto appeared in the hatch a moment later. He scrambled out, heedless of his bandaged hand as he turned and helped Ling and Yoder up. The three of them jumped off the tank without bothering to use the ladder. Yoder landed on his feet, but Ling and DeSoto hit the ground and rolled. "Clear out!" DeSoto yelled as the three of them ran. "Clear out!"

Danny frowned. "What's going on?"

"It's *Conquistadoris!* She's—"

Conquistadoris exploded.

* * *

Helen pushed the M2 as far to the left as it could go and fired a long burst of .50 rounds at a trio of Obsidian soldiers trying to sneak through the marsh. Two of them fell into the muck, while the third threw himself out of the line of fire. She tried to take aim at him, but when she pressed the butterfly trigger, it clicked. Empty.

She slid off the gunner's seat and reached for one of the nearby ammo cans. She yanked on it with one hand and grunted. Good Lord, these cans were heavy! Much heavier than the ones her dad took with him to the range. She grabbed the handle with both hands and tugged. She dragged it forward, but its bottom hooked on the handle of the can it rested on and the whole stack tumbled over. She jumped back, but the falling cans clipped her leg and tore some skin on the way down.

She squeaked at the hot pain in her calf, but she bit down on her lip to keep it from turning into a scream. Rounds pinged off the targeting screen or struck the sandbag barrier with dull *thwacks*. She needed to get this gun up and running again, or they'd be on top of her.

Helen bent over and picked up one of the cans. Her arms and shoulders shook as she mounted her makeshift sandbag steps and dropped the can onto the tray with a resounding *thunk*. She shoved the empty can to the ground so she could push the full can forward. How many times had she done this since starting? Three? Four? It seemed like forever since the shooting started.

The incoming gunfire tapered off as she popped the can's top and revealed a belt of shiny .50 ammunition. She risked a glance through the targeting screen.

A half-dozen Geno-freaks were charging her position, their thermal-enhanced forms running flat-out. Fear seized her heart, and the belt slid from her paralyzed fingers. She fumbled for it and tried to get it into the action. She wasn't going to make it in time!

Gunfire rang out behind and to the right of her, and one of the Geno-freaks fell. Several more shots sounded, and two more of the approaching Genos tumbled to the earth. The other three threw themselves flat and scrambled into cover.

A *clop-clop-clop* sound filled Helen's ears, and she turned in time to see a mounted officer ride in through the darkness. It was Kevin Hanson astride Watson. His rifle was at his shoulder as he looked down its holographic sight for enemies. "Uncle Kevin? What're you doing here?"

"You can't expect me to leave a little lady out here by herself, can you?" Kevin dropped the rifle in its scabbard and reached down for her. "Come on, let's get you out of here!"

Relief flooded Helen. She had been trying to hold out as best she could until Aster got back, but it didn't look like that would happen any time soon. And here was Kevin, ready to save her! She started to lift her hand to his—

The light from the Big Beam suddenly grew brighter. She squinted at the intensity. It was almost ready to fire, but if their position was overrun now...

Her hand fell to her side. "I can't go. We have to stay here."

"What? That's crazy!" A round zipped past him, but he didn't seem to notice. Watson shuddered and danced on his hooves, eager to run. Kevin reined him back in. "A little girl like you can't be expected to do this. Where are the Section Nine soldiers?"

"They're busy fighting elsewhere." Unshed tears filled her vision, and she blinked them away. "I'm the only one here. If I don't do this, they'll die, and the cannon won't fire, and then everyone else will die, too!"

Kevin dropped from the saddle and wrapped Watsons' reins around his left hand. "I'll man the gun, then. You take Watson and get out of here!"

"You don't know how to work the gun!" Helen turned and grabbed the belt and locked it into position. She reached for the charging handle. "Aster taught me how to use it. Aster needs me to hold this position until she gets back!"

"You're just a little girl!" Hanson gripped her shoulder and pulled her off the sandbag steps.

"Let me go!" Helen screamed. She punched his hand with her right and grasped the gunner's tray with her left. Her hand closed around something, but it wasn't the table because she slid out of the seat with the object in her hand.

Behind them, Watson screamed. The horse reared up as a figure leaped from the shadows. It was the rabbit creature she had seen earlier, and it had a knife in its gloved hands. Its glowing red eyes glinted as it aimed the knife straight at Kevin.

Kevin tried to spin toward him, but Watson's struggling pulled him off balance. Helen raised the object in her left hand, pointed it at the rabbit, and squeezed the trigger.

The recoil nearly tore the pistol from her grip, and the muzzle flash left stars in her vision. Hanson let go of her, and she dropped to her knees. Hanson steadied Watson, drew his pistol, and fired two shots into the rabbit creature. It bled from a hole in its forehead, and blood pooled beneath its torso.

"Damn. You saved my life again." Kevin looked down at her with the kind of respect and admiration she had only seen people show to her dad and Aster.

He then turned and fired over the lip of the sandbag barrier into the darkness beyond.

Right, the M2! Helen scrambled to her feet. She set down the pistol she'd used against the rabbit creature and reached for the charging handle. This time, her hands didn't shake. She pulled back on the handle twice, then took aim. At her first burst of gunfire, the enemy fell back.

"Keep their heads down a moment," Kevin said.

Helen fired a couple more bursts of ammo, then looked over her shoulder. "What're you doing?"

Kevin removed his rifle from Watson's scabbard and leaned it against the sandbag barrier. He also emptied the contents of the horse's saddlebags—rifle and pistol magazines, a first aid kit, a couple of canteens, and a bag of jerky—and dropped them on the ground next to him.

The last thing he removed from the saddlebags was a handful of sugar cubes. He fed them to Watson, then slapped the animal on its rump. It whinnied and took off into the darkness, presumably back to the stables.

"Why did you do that?" she demanded. "You could've gotten away!"

"It'll be easier for two of us to hold this position than one." Kevin crouched next to Helen and swapped his current rifle magazine for a full one. He did the same with his pistol. "Besides, no sense in risking Watson getting hit by a stray round, right? I can't lose any more horses."

A flood of excitement rushed through Helen, and this time, the tears streamed down her face. She wasn't alone anymore. She could do this now. She could defend the Big Beam and her brother, and Aster, and everyone else.

She turned back to look through the targeting screen as enemies appeared once more. "We just have to hold out a little longer, Uncle Kevin."

"That we do, Helen." Kevin shouldered his rifle and looked for targets. "That we do."

* * *

Countess and I galloped down the street alongside Sergeant Silva's buffalo riders. Ahead of us, Obsidian soldiers and Geno-freaks fired into the upper stories of the buildings that several students and Columbia officers had taken position in. The enemy soldiers ducked behind vehicles, which protected them from taking fire from above, but not from anyone down in the street with them. Their attention was so focused on the buildings, they didn't see us coming until it was too late.

I opened fire as we closed in. Silva's front rank followed suit, and our automatic weapons ripped into the Obsidian line. We'd gunned down five or six before they could react. And by the time they turned, it was too late. I peeled Countess away from the buffalo riders as they crashed into the bunched-up soldiers. Obsidian soldiers flew into the air and were gored or trampled beneath the animals' heavy hooves.

Countess stamped the ground and grunted as if she wanted in on the action. Her hopping around threw off my aim, so my first shot missed an Obsidian soldier who was shooting over the hood of a car at one of Silva's men. The round struck the lamp post behind him, but he didn't react as he fired his rifle. An officer cried out in pain and toppled from the saddle. Anger steadied my aim, and my second shot tore through the soldier's helmet and into his brain. He slumped against the hood and then slid to the ground.

A bullet slammed into my lower back. I grunted at the sudden pain, but it was a dull ache, not the sharp fire I'd heard described when people were shot. I wheeled Countess around and saw more Obsidian soldiers spilling into the street from an alleyway. I shouldered my rifle and fired a few three-round bursts. One of the soldiers fell, and the others scattered.

"Silva!" I shouted. "More bad guys!"

I continued firing as Silva ordered his men to turn around and charge the new threat. Once Silva's boys were in my line of sight, I raised my rifle barrel out of harm's way and probed my back with my left hand. I felt a small hole in my plate carrier's fabric and a slight indentation in the armor itself. No penetration. I'd be sore as could be tomorrow, but I'd be alive.

A round cracked past my face shield, and I turned in the direction it came from. I again raised my rifle to my shoulder. I needed to make sure I lived long enough to have a sore back!

The Obsidian soldiers aiming at us suddenly turned and tried to run into a nearby building. Gunfire from a side street cut several of them down, then Silva's buffalo riders were on top of them. The animals once more earned their keep as they gored and crushed the bad guys.

A group of Boone County deputies rode out of the side street and approached us. Sheriff Welliver was in the lead. He held his 1911 in one hand and gingerly cradled his reins in the other. The old officer looked both fatigued and invigorated as he surveyed the scene around him. "Can't say I'm happy to see my town getting torn up like this, but it's great to be able to pay back the ones who started it."

I shouldered my rifle and fired at a lone soldier peeking out from behind a van. He disappeared behind the vehicle. "How're things elsewhere?" I asked.

"Don't you have a radio?"

"Yes, but I can barely hear it with all this gunfire."

"So, you're depending on the old man with worse hearing?" Welliver chuckled, but there was little mirth in it. "The Homeguard is stalled near the observatory. Obsidian did something to that tank, and a lot of soldiers were wounded or killed, along with some of our officers."

"Is Danny all right?"

"The transmission cut out, and we haven't heard anything since."

I swallowed. "And the observatory?"

"They're up to their eyeballs in Geno-freaks, but they're holding."

Several blue, luminous flares exploded in the sky to the east, not too far from our position. "Is that from Jay Dawson's neighborhood?" I asked. "Why so many flares? Is he in trouble again?"

"More like he's taking it to the enemy." Welliver grinned. "I've known him for years. He's letting us know he's in the fight. I'll take my deputies and see if we can help him out. Can you hold here?"

A pair of Obsidian soldiers darted from one side of the street to the other. Both Welliver and I shot at them. One went down, but the other made it. Welliver made a tsk noise. "Getting sloppy, Nate."

"You're just a little rusty, sir. Practice more, and you'll get better."

Welliver laughed. "Well played. I'll take that as a yes, you can hold here. Let us know if you need anything, and keep your radio turned up! You got spoiled with those fancy Teledyne headsets."

He led his deputies up the road at a canter. They fired at any Obsidian soldier they could see, but mostly kept moving. My men and I provided covering fire as Silva's buffalo riders mopped up the scene behind us. I turned my radio volume up and was awash in reports of fighting throughout the city.

One thing was certain: it was never dull in this Fallen World.

* * * * *

Chapter Eighteen

Aster knelt behind a disabled vehicle. The barrel of her FN-P90 was smoking and glowing red. She let it drop on its single-point sling and drew her Five-Seven and 1911. She flicked the laser pointers on each, willed her eyes to unfocus, and leaped onto the hood, her pistols pointed in front of her. As soon as green and red dots touched on a torso or forehead, she fired. When she found another pair of targets, she fired again. Four regular soldiers dropped to the ground with holes in their chests, necks, or faces.

A Geno-freak who was a cross between a woman and a panther dashed at her, tearing across the ground on all fours. Aster shifted both pistols to aim at her and fired. The beast-woman leaped out of the way of both shots and continued her mad sprint forward. She bounded over the stone wall and jumped at Aster.

Once the beast-woman was airborne, she couldn't dodge as easily. Aster raised both weapons and fired twice from each gun. The first two rounds tore into the Geno's stomach and chest, while the final two found her forehead. Her momentum carried her forward, and she slammed into Aster and brought her to the ground.

Aster threw the dead woman off her with enough force to send the carcass sailing over a car and crashing into the tall hedge that separated the staff parking lot on the north side of the building from the visitor lot to the west. The heavy body fell through a few feet of hedge before becoming tangled up in the sculpted shrub's branches.

Growls and yips emanated from beyond the low stone wall, along with the sound of feet and paws slapping against the ground. Aster jumped to her feet, her weapons aimed and blasting. The 1911 ran dry first. While she continued firing with her Five-Seven, she dropped the empty 1911 mag into a dump pouch and pressed the bottom of the pistol's grip against the auto-loader belted at her hip. She felt the new magazine pop in with a click, then she thumbed the slide release.

Her Five-Seven's slide locked back on an empty chamber. She repeated the reloading process as she lined up her 1911's green targeting laser on the face of an Obsidian grunt. His eyes started to widen in alarm, but a hole blossomed in his forehead, and he disappeared beyond the stone wall.

Something punched into her chest armor, and she rolled back behind the sedan as more rounds zipped past. She raised her head and arm over the hood of the car long enough to fire two rounds into the bare chest of a creature with a bear's body and a bull's head, like a Minotaur of legend. The Geno-freak let out a shriek of agony and darted off into the darkness.

A grenade landed next to her. Without thinking, she holstered her 1911, scooped up the grenade, and tossed it over the other side of the car. It exploded in midair and sent shrapnel into the vehicle's windows and roof, but nothing penetrated her side of the sedan. Someone—or something—screamed.

Aster checked her FN-P90. The barrel had cooled considerably. She quickly reloaded and holstered her Five-Seven, then reloaded the P90. She put it to her shoulder and hopped back to her feet. Her body twisted slightly to the left and right as she tracked for targets.

A huge hand covered in dark fur grabbed the top rail of the P90. Aster tried to tear the weapon from its grasp, but the giant fingers didn't yield. She looked up into the yellow-eyed glare of the Minotaur as his snout opened into a snarl of foul breath and blunt teeth. She kicked him, but her powerful blow barely moved his massive body. She reached for her 1911 in the small-of-the-back holster.

Before she could retrieve it, he struck her in the side with his other meaty hand. The impact sent her through the air as pain blossomed in her abdomen. She bit back a grunt as she landed on all fours and skidded to a halt. Her P90 sailed over her head when the Minotaur threw it deep into the parking lot beyond the hedge. He charged her, head down like a bull's. Her 1911 cleared its Kydex holster just as he reached her. She jumped high into the air and fired several rounds into the monster's skull and back. To her surprise, most of the rounds bounced off the man-creature's body or barely penetrated his thick hide.

She landed behind the Minotaur and spun to face him, but the creature was faster. His fist slammed into her stomach with enough force to crack her armor. She crashed into the disabled sedan, denting the passenger door and shattering the window. Pain radiated through her abdomen and backside, but she shrugged it off as she pulled herself free of the crunched-in metal and plastic. Glass fragments tinkled softly as they fell from her hair and armor and struck the pavement.

Movement in her peripheral vision reminded her there were other threats, not just the Minotaur, and she was the only thing that was keeping the Evidence Shredders away from the east side of the compound. Her men were tied up elsewhere if the constant barrage of gunfire was any indicator. And Helen was still on the Ma Deuce.

Someone was with her now, providing cover fire with a rifle any time the machine gun fell silent. The rifle didn't sound like anything her men carried. It had to be one of the cops, or maybe a civilian defender.

Just hold out a little longer, Helen, she thought as she drew her combat knife. It was a prototype monomolecular blade, forged of some experimental alloy and capable, she had been told, of cutting through nearly anything due to the blade's thickness. All it took was the right amount of force behind the cut or thrust. Well, she could provide that force.

She shot a Geno-freak in the head as it attempted to slip past her, then turned back to the Minotaur. "None of you Obsidian monsters are getting through me."

With a roar, the Minotaur charged.

Aster reversed her grip on the knife and threw it as hard as she could. The blade hurtled through the air and struck the Minotaur in the chest with so much force, the blade and hilt punched through the monster's thick hide, ripped through organ tissue, and shot out his back, leaving a gaping hole pouring blood.

She sidestepped the Minotaur as it stumbled toward her. It tried to turn but fell to the ground. It held up a big hand toward her, gurgled loudly, then lay still.

Aster had no time to breathe, though, because three more Genos jumped out of the darkness toward her, claws and blades extended. Aster raised her pistol and squeezed the trigger.

* * *

"The power fluctuations are affecting the whole city," Egghead reported. "Massive blackouts everywhere."

Imagery from the approaching satellite showed that, indeed, the lights in the city had dimmed and gone out, one by one. The raised cameras on the command vehicle showed much the same thing. The university's lights had gone out, and what was left of Teledyne Tower was blanketed in darkness. Lloyd was still impressed by how much punishment that building could take, and it raised his suspicions on more than one level. But he didn't have time to consider those now.

He flicked between camera views, and all of them showed the city plunging into darkness. All but one camera, facing toward the southeast. A white glow hung over the distant tree line. It was barely visible except for the otherwise absolute darkness. "What's that?"

"The source of the power fluctuations." Egghead worked his controls, and the city map zoomed in until it was right over an area east of the city and university. It looked like a remote piece of countryside. "Remember the observatory? The enemy has something set up there, and it's drawing massive amounts of energy from the Jal-Com fusion plant beneath the city."

"Any idea what it could be?" Lloyd asked. He glanced at Anal. "Lieutenant Sullivan?"

Anal raised a hand and made a shooing motion. "Sorry, sir, I'm busy. Trying to take advantage of something."

Lloyd raised an eyebrow, but surprisingly didn't find himself annoyed at the rude dismissal. If there was one thing he'd learned about Anal, it was that she had a one-track mind. Once her hacker interests were piqued, nothing else mattered until the job was done.

And whatever she was working on had to be to his benefit. He decided to let it slide. "What about you, Lieutenant Egleton?"

Egghead swiped his finger over his tablet's screen. "We received a transmission from Manager Bianchi just now. One of your St. Louis men from the Country Hotel learned something. The university is in possession of one of Teledyne's Big Beams, although we don't know which model."

"A Big Beam?" Lloyd scoffed. *What a stupid name for a stupid weapon.* The damned thing took forever to charge, sucked up energy like it was free, and lit up like a Christmas tree while it was doing it. When it fired, its destructive beam could reach out and hit most targets instantly, but good luck getting something to sit still long enough during the charge period. None of his men would be stupid enough to wait around for that thing to annihilate their unit, so what were they—?

His body tensed. "You said it was at an observatory?"

"Yes." Egghead's eyes narrowed. "Sir, I think—"

"They're after the Tezca satellite." Lloyd put his hand to his chin. "Can we push the satellite off course?"

"It doesn't have the thruster capability for that, sir. It only has enough fuel for making minor adjustments after a payload drop."

So much for that plan. Lloyd's eyes darted left and right as he considered more possibilities. "We're going to have to change targets, then. I want that observatory gone."

* * *

"Last mag!" Corporal Ingram called. "LT, you got any more?"

Paxton ducked behind a stack of filing cabinets he'd erected as a barricade. So far, only a couple of rifle rounds had penetrated the files. Who knew old tax records and utility bills could actually be useful? He reached into a magazine pouch and pulled out two partials. "This is all I've got left!" he said.

"Slide 'em over!"

Paxton sent them skittering across the smooth floor. The magazines smacked into several expended brass casings before slowing to a stop at Ingram's feet. He planted a boot on them but kept firing through the shattered window at targets in front of the main entrance. "Thanks, LT!"

"Aino, how're you holding up?" Paxton called into the adjacent classroom. They'd piled up desks against the windows facing south to give the man a place to rest his M240 machine gun.

"Tangos everywhere, LT, but I'm managing! Still got a few more belts to send their way!"

At the rate he was firing, Paxton didn't expect those belts to last much longer. "Make every shot count!"

Beyond both sets of windows, bodies of fallen Obsidian soldiers and Geno-freaks littered the fields and roadway. They'd repulsed three charges, but it looked like the enemy was gathering for a fourth attempt. If they ran out of ammo before the enemy ran out of men, it was going to get pretty dicey. "Can both of you hold here for a moment? I'm going to go see what's keeping the good doctor."

"Get to it, LT!" Aino called.

"We've got this!" Ingram added.

Paxton stood up, sighted in on a pair of Obsidian soldiers setting up a belt-fed machine gun in the field across the street, and fired. His first shot hit one of the soldiers in the leg, and his second punched through the man's midsection. The other man dove into a depression before he could land a shot on him. Satisfied the gun would be out for at least a moment, he turned and ran into the hallway. Bullets raked the walls, but none hit him as he slid around the corner. He stuck his head into the spiral stairwell that led to the domed telescope room. "Doctor! Give me some good news!"

"Big Beam is fully charged!" Dr. Schneider called down. "We're just waiting for the satellite to be in position!"

Ingram and Grumbine both whooped at the news, their voices echoing down from the stairwell.

"Excellent! And how long will that be?"

"Another five minutes, twenty-three seconds."

Five and a half minutes was a lifetime on the battlefield. Paxton took a deep breath, then let it out in a sigh. "Okay. We can hold for that long."

"Actually, Lieutenant, we should consider leaving as soon as possible."

That brought Paxton up short. Schneider had never talked tactics before. "What do you mean?"

Footsteps echoed, along with cries of "Man, stay down!" and "Watch the windows!" from Ingram and Grumbine. Bullets cracked into the masonry, and the sound echoed down the stairwell. Schneider appeared a second later and stumbled the last dozen or so steps in his haste to get away from the gunfire. Paxton caught him at the bottom to keep him from slamming into the wall. "You all right, Doctor?" he asked.

"I think so," Schneider gasped. He felt around his body for wounds. "Yes, I think so. How do you people do this every day?"

Paxton smiled. "I'd like to say it gets easier with time, but it doesn't. Anyway, what do you mean we should prepare to evacuate?"

"Well, recent events may have made me paranoid, but here's my thought process: if we are targeting the satellite in such a way that they're sending soldiers on the ground to stop us, don't you think it stands to reason they would use the satellite to stop us, as well?"

Paxton froze as he considered the implication of Schneider's words. "That makes sense, Doctor. Do you have proof they're targeting us?"

"Without telemetry, there's no way to truly know. It's just a feeling I've got."

"Battles are sometimes won and lost on hunches, Doctor." He keyed his mic to inform everyone else.

Before he could say anything, the line came alive. "Grumbine here! Enemy is retreating to the south!"

"Same!" Ingram reported. "Enemy has started to pack it in and is running clear of the farmhouse across the way.

"Helen here!" came a tiny voice. "Enemies are running away to the…What direction is that?" she whispered to someone who wasn't on the line. "To the west!"

Paxton and Schneider shared a look. "Doctor, I think you might be onto something."

He keyed his mic. Sometimes you needed to know when to get the hell out in this Fallen World.

* * * * *

Chapter Nineteen

Aster ripped her knife out of the skull of a Geno-freak with the head of a golden eagle and cast its twitching corpse to the side. After throwing the knife through the Minotaur, she'd found it sunk to the hilt in a car door.

She looked around for targets but didn't see any. Her enhanced vision detected movement beyond the wall, but all the forms she could focus on were retreating. "This is Lady in Black," she said. "Enemy in retreat in my sector, too. Looks like we've broken them."

"*Negative, Lady.*" Paxton's voice crackled in her ear. She tapped on her earpiece, and the static dissipated. "*They're withdrawing for the next act.*"

"Next act?" Aster asked. She used the eagle man's pants to wipe the blood off her knife blade, then sheathed it. "What do you mean?"

"Dr. Schneider thinks this place is about to get lit up with a Tezca Bolt in a last-ditch effort to take out the Big Beam before we can fire it. He suggests we clear out."

"What about firing the cannon?"

"He's programmed it to fire automatically."

"No, that's not good enough." Aster turned toward the building. "Load the wounded in the APC and clear out. I'll stay behind until it's fired, then exfiltrate on foot."

"Lady, that's too dangerous, even for you."

"I'm the only one fast enough to do it."

There was a long pause. "Very well. You all heard the Lady in Black! Break down and clear out! Crick, get that APC back here! And watch for enemies."

A series of affirmatives came down the line.

Aster looked toward the Ma Deuce. Helen waved at her while Kevin Hanson continued to scan the darkness for threats with his rifle's illuminated optical sight. She returned the wave, then hurried inside.

In less than two minutes, the Party of Nine had cleared out. Aster watched from one of the windows over the main entrance as the APC and the professors' station wagon pulled around to the front. Doors flew open on both vehicles, and people piled into them as quickly as they could. Grumbine and Aino threw the Ma Deuce into the APC, then helped Doc and Kirby load the wounded civilians and the unconscious Jason. They also forced Lieutenant Kevin Hanson in, despite his protestations. He had been shot in the shoulder, and Kirby wouldn't take no for an answer. He'd reluctantly agreed, but not until he saw Helen climb into the miraculously unscathed station wagon. Schneider and his research staff climbed in as well, making the wagon look like a clown car stuffed to the gills. Grumbine agreed to ride on the roof as security, and the professor's wife rolled the window down so she could use her AR-15 to defend the right side of the vehicle.

Aster cradled the rifle Paxton left for her. She had twenty-eight rounds, plus what little was left in her Five-Seven. She glanced at the timer on her watch that she had set based on Schneider's estimate. Ninety more seconds. She figured she had enough ammo to get through this.

The noise of the Big Beam was starting to grate on her nerves. It had started as a low hum when she arrived earlier in the evening, but the weapon was charging up and its tip was starting to glow with bright light. The hum had turned into a high-pitched whine that had grown in intensity. It was enough to cause her pain and set dogs in the distance howling. She figured she was the only human who could hear it, due to her enhanced hearing. Well, her, and any Evidence Shredders unfortunate enough to have crossed their genes with those of dogs and wolves.

Down on the first floor, something fell over with a loud crash. Aster snapped the rifle up to her shoulder and aimed down the stairwell. Gunfire rang outside, followed by the sound of tires squealing. She thought she heard a door open and someone shout, but a barrage of answering gunfire from her men drowned it out. Besides that, her focus was on what was happening inside the building.

She started to creep down the stairs, but a thud overhead brought her up short. Something scrabbled along the rooftop, while something else stomped around downstairs. She shifted the rifle to her right hand and aimed it up, then she drew her Five-Seven in her left and aimed it down. She pressed herself into the stairwell's outer wall and tried to keep both directions in sight as she continually glanced left and right. She had no doubt it was the Evidence Shredders come back to finish off the Big Beam in the seconds before it fired.

She decided to risk it all, and she turned and pounded up the stairs to the telescope room. She squinted against the bright light shining from the weapon and wished she could close off her ears to the shriek that rattled around inside her skull. Behind her, she heard a roar and something pounding up the steps. She kicked the door shut and looked around the room.

Movement caught her eye near the slit in the room's domed roof, right where the Big Beam's glowing barrel jutted out. A Geno-freak that looked like she was part pterodactyl dropped down and fired a submachine gun at her. Aster rolled out of the way, came up on her knee, and fired the rifle. Her first few shots went wide as the femdactyl twisted in midair. She tried firing again, but the mutant kicked off the floor and launched herself back into the air. Her wings allowed her to hover. That threw off Aster's aim, and her next several rounds struck the far wall without hitting the Geno-freak. The femdactyl fired another long burst at her. Aster hopped out of the way, but not before a round tore into her left arm and caused her to drop her pistol. She let it go and took her rifle in both hands and fired.

The femdactyl jumped back into the air, but this time, Aster was able to better track her movement. She lined up her sights just above the Geno-freak. They fired at the same time. A round sliced past Aster's cheek, leaving a stinging cut that bled freely. Aster's rounds tore into the creature's neck and torso. The femdactyl struck the floor with enough force to shatter the white tiles.

The door to the room exploded inward, and a powerful leg came through. It was the Minotaur from earlier. Blood still poured from the massive chest wound and stained his teeth and lips, but his eyes were alive and full of hate as he glared at her.

Aster shifted her aim and squeezed the trigger.

Click.

She glanced at the rifle and realized it was empty. She reached for her Five-Seven and remembered the femdactyl had knocked it from her hand.

With a roar, the Minotaur charged.

Aster reached for her knife, but she hadn't even pulled it from her sheath when he slammed into her. She flew through the air and crashed into the far wall, breaking through the sheetrock and cracking the stud. She tried to pull herself free, but the Minotaur grabbed her and threw her to the floor. Tile shards flew everywhere. She kicked him off her and pulled herself into a seated position as he started to charge again. She tensed her body in anticipation of the blow to come.

A rapid-fire string of gunshots rang out louder than the whine of the Big Beam. The Minotaur stumbled, tried to turn, and collapsed. Ballistic tips had blown several holes through his backside. Helen stood there, holding Aster's FN-P90 up to her shoulder. Its barrel was smoking from the full-auto barrage the little girl had unleashed. Helen was breathing hard, as if she'd run the entire way up the stairs, and her eyes were wide with fear and adrenaline. "I…thought you'd…want this back." She held out the P90.

Aster retrieved her Five-Seven from the ground and walked over to the Minotaur. "Cover your ears," she warned before putting six rounds in the creature's skull, one after the other. Even its armored hide and thick bones couldn't take several rounds striking the same spot. The body twitched, then went still. Satisfied the Minotaur was well and truly dead, she holstered her pistol and slung the rifle before walking over to take the P90 from Helen. "You were supposed to be in the professors' wagon."

Before Helen could reply, the intensity of the Big Beam's noise increased tenfold. Helen clamped her hands over her ears, and Aster winced as she checked her watch. The timer had run out. The satellite was in range of the weapon.

Which meant they were now in range of the satellite. How long had Greenway said it would take for a Tezca Bolt to arrive? Ten minutes? Five?

She snapped the P90 back onto its sling, scooped up Helen, and said, "Close your eyes and cover your neck!"

She waited long enough for Helen to comply, then she turned and bounded into the office adjacent to the telescope room. Its big glass window had somehow survived the gun battle, but they wouldn't survive her.

Aster and Helen broke through the glass just as the Big Beam fired.

* * *

The camera feed on the Tezca satellite turned a brilliant white, then the screen went black. The words "SIGNAL LOST" appeared on the monitor and stayed there until Egghead shut it off. His tone was grim as he said, "The satellite's transponder has failed. I think it's been destroyed, sir."

Lloyd pounded the arm of his command chair. *Dammit!* That satellite was a one-of-a-kind weapon that would've helped ensure their dominance over a huge swath of land once they secured Columbia. To think a bunch of Teledyne soldiers, a mounted cop, and a fucking *child* could hold off his Evidence Shredders long enough for them to fire a weapon as unwieldly as a Big Beam. Damn that Battle Flower! He should've had Agent Morris kill her when he had the chance. If Morris was going to die anyway, it should've been taking the famed Teledyne Specialist off the board, permanently.

He took a deep breath to steady himself. "Were we able to fire our payload?"

"Only at one target—the observatory. Evidence Shredders have cleared out and are gathering at Point Gamma." He returned the map to the main monitor and indicated a spot on it. "They'll await further orders there."

Lloyd didn't want to think about the Evidence Shredders. Those damn freaks had failed him big time. He knew their usual Agent handlers weren't around and couldn't whip them up into a proper frenzy, but this should've been an easy job for them. "And the people defending the observatory? What happened to them?"

"Scouts reported them exfiltrating in two vehicles. However, two of our commandos encountered the Teledyne Specialist in the observatory in the seconds before the weapon fired."

Oh, please let Tezca's Bolt annihilate that white-haired bitch. Lloyd doubted God, if such a being even existed, would honor such a prayer, but it couldn't hurt to ask. He'd read some of the Old Testament, and it seemed that God enjoyed a good fight as much as the next man, so who knew? "What of our main force?"

"Manager Bianchi's forces are breaking off contact with the city's defenders and are falling back to Point Delta."

It sounded to Lloyd like they were in full retreat, but he didn't bother correcting Egghead. "And the Homeguard? What of them?"

"What's left of them are currently holed up in and around a subdivision east of the university. Several vehicles were destroyed, along with the tank. There are an unknown number of dead, and their wounded are receiving medical treatment from the hospital staff and the cops in that area."

Wonderful. Now the city's defenders had a somewhat intact guard unit to bolster their ranks. At least the tank's last destructive act had been useful to him.

He stared at the last images taken by the Tezca satellite. The entire city was blacked out, except for the light shining at the observatory. How much juice from the JalCom facility had that stupid weapon sucked up? He hoped none of the facility's critical systems had been damaged as a result. He had plans for that facility, provided he could even get inside it at this point. He'd have to comb over the casualty reports once they were finished and prepare a new strategy.

On the other side of the vehicle, Anal started humming to herself. Lloyd and Egghead shared a look. "That usually means she's onto something, sir."

"Ah. Maybe we'll get some good news for a change, then."

"Oh, I think so," she replied in a singsong tone.

* * *

"All units, report your status," Graham called out over the line. "Lieutenant Ward, you're first."

I aimed my rifle and fired at the last Obsidian soldier still standing. The round tore through his neck and sent him to the pavement. I keyed my mic. "Ripley Street's clear! Pushing on to Brighton!" I turned in the saddle to shout orders to my men.

And then night turned into day as a bright lance of light shot up into the sky. The white beam was bright enough to make me squint. A high-pitched shriek echoed over the city with an intensity that shattered glass. Somewhere, somehow, a car alarm went off. I laughed, both from amusement and excitement. The Big Beam had fired! We won!

And then there was an explosion from that direction. It was as big as the one that leveled half of Teledyne Tower. My levity vanished as if it had never been. The Tezca satellite had fired a shot, and it looked like it had taken the observatory with it!

I keyed my mic. "Lady in Black? Aster, come in!"

"Lieutenant Ward, this is Paxton. Observatory has been destroyed. Teledyne Tower cannot visually confirm destruction of enemy satellite, but its transponder has cut out. Looks like a clean kill."

"Happy to hear it," I said, fighting to keep control of my voice. "But what about Aster and my children?"

"Your son is with us in the APC, and your daughter is in the professors' station wagon. She's—"

Paxton's line cut out for a moment and then he came back. He sounded contrite as he said, "*Negative on that last statement. Your daughter is not in the station wagon.*"

Over the line, I heard someone who sounded like Kevin Hanson shout, "*What? What do you mean?*"

I wondered where Hanson had disappeared to. While it filled my heart with joy that he had gone to help my daughter, it didn't do anything to soothe my nerves. "Where is she, then? Paxton, where's my daughter?"

"*She's with me,*" a soft voice croaked out of a sea of static. "*She's all right.*"

"Aster!" Relief washed over me because my daughter was all right, and she was all right, too. I didn't quite understand my feelings for Aster, other than I was happy she was alive. "Where are you?"

"Just outside the blast radius. That Tezca Bolt really packs a punch."

I laughed. "You should've realized that after the mess it made of Teledyne Tower."

"It's one thing to see it. It's another thing to experience it." She lowered her voice to a whisper. "Paxton, we'll head east for a bit, then set up an extraction point somewhere outside the city. Evidence Shredders are still in the area, so keep moving."

"Roger, Lady. We'll see you soon."

"Thank you both," I said. "Thank you for keeping my kids safe."

"They're not out of the woods yet, sir," Paxton said. "Thank us when we return them to you. Paxton, out."

I was tempted to ask to speak with my kids, but Paxton and Aster needed to concentrate. Especially Aster, who was on foot with my daughter in what was essentially enemy territory. Obsidian may have been retreating, but that didn't mean they weren't still a threat. The radio chatter was full of calls for backup and medics as the withdrawing force did whatever damage they could on the way out of town.

"Sheriff Welliver, how are you holding up?" Graham asked.

"Old, tired, and my right arm is on fire, but other than that, doing great! Jay Dawson's neighborhood is clear of bad guys. Half my deputies are pursuing a routed squad of Obsidian punks, while the rest of us are maintaining a perimeter."

"Excellent. Lieutenant Saleh?"

"We cleared a path west along East Broadway. City hall and the fortified barricades are in sight and fully intact. Looks like the enemy didn't penetrate the underground bunker."

"With your help!" Chloe Reed said. "You and your camel riders came in like the Saracens in Turbanado!"

Martinez cackled. "I was in high school when they were filming that movie in downtown LA!"

"We're not Saracens, and we don't wear turbans," Saleh snapped, but I could hear the chuckle in his voice. "The film was banned in Jordan, so my friends and I could only watch a cheap bootleg of it."

"What'd you think?" Martinez asked.

"It was as stupid as all the other 'Nado movies out there."

"That means it was great!"

"It wasn't a complaint."

"All right, enough of that." Graham laughed. "I'm glad we're all enjoying ourselves, but let's have a bit of professionalism here."

"*Yes, sir!*" Martinez and Saleh said.

"Sergeant Ward, what's your status? How's the Homeguard?"

* * *

"Mostly alive and kicking, sir," Danny said. He coughed as he inhaled smoke tinged with the stench of burning fuel. "Will let you know more when I get a report from Colonel Eastman."

He clipped his radio back to his belt, then nudged Noir out of the shadow of one of the neighborhood's houses. Both he and his horse were covered in soot from the tank's explosion and the subsequent fires as burning fuel sprayed into nearby homes. Two homes burned freely, while the one closest to him smoldered, but never really caught.

Noir stepped around a wide piece of armor plating that dug a furrow in the pavement. That same piece of metal missed them by inches when the tank blew apart. Other bits of shrapnel sheared through walls, embedded in trees, and wounded several Homeguard soldiers and mounted officers. Two horses were put down due to the severity of their wounds, and another one was being patched up for transport back to the university's animal hospital. There, the head veterinarian, Dr. Lorio, would treat the animal, possibly with the same nanites Nathan's horse, Countess, had been treated with. They were in short supply, so they were saved to use as a last resort.

The tank crew lay on the ground not too far from the burning vehicle. Their forms were still and silent. Danny rode Noir over to them. "You alive down there, Lieutenant DeSoto?"

DeSoto replied with a one-fingered salute. "I'll manage," he croaked. "Fuckin' Obsidian."

Danny slid from the saddle. "That is the order of the day, most days. Them, or Teledyne, or any number of the other Corporations out there that got us into this mess." He leaned down and held out a hand. "Want some help?"

"No, but I'll take it." DeSoto clasped Danny's hand, and he let himself be pulled up to his feet. Danny waved over a couple of other officers to do the same for Ling and Yoder. DeSoto tried to steady himself, but Danny hooked an arm around his shoulder. "Let's get y'all to a medic."

Ling and Yoder went first, each resting on the shoulder of an officer. Danny started to follow, but DeSoto wouldn't budge. He stared at what was left of *Conquistadoris*. The ammunition had blown up in one terrific explosion, taking most of the armored beast with it. All that was left were pieces of tread, a chunk of turret and barrel, and a growing circle of burning grass from fuel that sprayed everywhere.

Danny wasn't sure what to say, so he just muttered, "Sorry about your tank."

DeSoto nodded. His eyes were wet. "She was the best. Ling and Yoder and I knew every inch of her." He smirked. "Well, every inch but the demon possessed part of her."

"Fuckin' Obsidian?" Danny asked.

DeSoto laughed. "Fuckin' Obsidian."

Danny pulled him away, and they headed toward the university side of the subdivision, where Colonel Eastman had set up a temporary hospital. They found the colonel outside the home at a table with a map spread across it. His neck and right hand were bandaged. "Colonel, you all right?" DeSoto asked.

"DeSoto! Good to have you back, man." Eastman touched his neck with his left hand. "Don't worry about this. *Conquistadoris* tried to bite me, but she missed. Mostly."

"She has—*had* big teeth, sir. Even a near miss could be devastating."

Eastman grimaced. "Indeed. I got this from the last shot she fired. Blew up a Humvee we were racing past."

"That's what you get for riding around in an old Willys Jeep, sir. They fell out of favor decades ago for a reason."

"Bah. Kids these days. No appreciation for the old stuff." Eastman looked at Danny. "Except you, maybe. You been to the USS *Alabama* in Mobile?"

"Damn fine ship, sir." Danny grinned, but it was pained as he added, "My wife was helping restore her. They were almost done with it when...well, you know."

Eastman's frown deepened. "Yeah. Damn shame, all this." He spread his arms, then held his left hand out for Danny to shake. "But maybe we'll make the most of it now. Thank you for letting us join the right side of the fight, for all the good we did."

"There's always next time, sir." Danny grasped Eastman's hand with his left, which was an awkward gesture for him. "Unfortunately, with the way things are, there'll always be a next time. But those are the fights we're here for, right?"

* * *

Aster sloshed from one side of a broad, concrete drainage ditch to the other. The water was up to her waist, so she kept Helen slung over her shoulder to keep the girl dry. She held her FN-P90 in her opposite hand, clear of the water and ready to shoot any threats that presented themselves. Everything was still in the aftermath of the Tezca Bolt explosion. Even the insects that pervaded the countryside were quiet, although she didn't expect that to last too long.

The drainage ditch lay on the other side of the farm in front of the now-destroyed observatory. The farm was gone, too. The house and barn had collapsed and were on fire. The acrid scent of burning wood filled her nostrils, mingling with the damp, earthy odor of the ditch. Oddly enough, the combined smell reminded her of camping trips she'd taken with her family. Her dad had the worst luck with the weather, and it always rained, even if the forecast promised no chance of precipitation. He'd laughed it off, and they'd had a great time anyway, wearing ponchos and huddling around a sputtering fire.

Those had been happier times.

Helen clung to her shoulder. The girl was one big knot of tense muscles, and her breathing was rapid and shallow. "Deep breaths, Helen," Aster murmured quietly so she wouldn't attract unwanted attention from any Evidence Shredders still in the area. "Deep breaths. In, hold, out, hold. Just like your father taught you."

"It…was…Uncle Danny," Helen corrected, her words coming out in gasps.

"In, hold, out, hold." Aster repeated the words as she dug the toes of her boot into the ditch's rough wall and rose out of the muddy water.

Helen did as instructed. Her body relaxed against Aster's shoulder until she hung limp. Aster put her hand against Helen's back to support more of her weight. Beneath her fingers, the little girl trembled. "Are you all right?"

"No."

Aster's pulse quickened. "What's wrong? Are you hurt?" She scrambled up the rest of the ditch's wall and hurried into a stand of trees.

"I shot them."

Aster froze.

"I shot so many." Helen's voice was thick with barely controlled emotion. She shifted on Aster's shoulder so she could rub her face. "How many of them died? How many did I kill?"

The alarm Aster felt disappeared; it was replaced with a deep sadness. This is exactly what she feared would happen if she taught Helen how to fight. She feared that, somehow, Helen would be put in a position where those skills would be needed. And what had happened? Aster rubbed Helen's back as she started forward again. "I'm sorry," she whispered.

"It's not your fault, Aunt Aster." Helen hiccupped. "If you hadn't shown me, if I hadn't known, who would've protected the observatory?"

"I would've figured something out," Aster replied. "I should've figured something out."

Helen broke down into uncontrolled sobs. She clamped her hands over her mouth, but squeals of pain and anguish leaked between her fingers.

Aster winced. Any Geno-freak within a mile would hear those cries. She looked around and saw a farmer's shed in a field. She sprinted toward it and cleared the couple hundred yards in seconds. She found the door slightly ajar, but she didn't see anybody inside through the window. She pushed her way in, set Helen down in the corner, and shut the door.

Helen threw her arms around Aster and buried her face in her breastplate. The two of them sank to the floor together. Helen wailed, but the noise was muffled by Aster's armor. Aster, at a loss, just stroked Helen's hair and kept an eye on the window. She held her P90 at an angle so she could easily switch her aim between the window and the door in an instant.

"Lady in Black, Paxton here." Her second-in-command's voice came in loud and clear through her earpiece. "We're at the rendezvous point. What's your ETA?"

"Give us a few minutes, Paxton."

"Your beacon shows you've stopped. Is everything all right?"

"Just…give us a few minutes, Paxton." She hooked her arm around Helen and pulled her into a tighter embrace. "Please. She needs a moment."

There was a long pause. "Roger. Setting up a perimeter."

When Aster terminated the transmission, Helen looked up. Her eyes and cheeks were wet and red, and her lower lip trembled. "Was it this bad for you?"

Aster didn't know what to say, so she said what she thought Helen wanted to hear. "Yes. Yes, it was."

Helen's face crumpled as a fresh wave of tears rolled down her cheeks. "Does it get better?"

Aster put a hand on the back of Helen's head and pulled her closer until they were cheek-to-cheek. She stroked the girl's red hair. "Yes. Yes, it does."

Helen's body shook with silent sobs. She sucked in ragged gasps of air that sounded like hissing snakes in Aster's ear. Aster continued stroking her hair and whispered, over and over, "It gets better. It gets better."

Except everything she'd told Helen was a lie. No, it hadn't been this bad for Aster, not the first or the hundredth time she'd killed someone. At the time, she'd hated Obsidian and all it stood for. She still did. Killing anyone in an Obsidian uniform was as easy as breathing. She felt no emotions other than anger and the satisfaction of taking out another person who may have been involved in the murder of her family.

And yet, it wasn't that easy anymore. The events of recent weeks, the people she'd met and teamed up with, the situations they'd gone through together, all of them had challenged her black-and-white worldview to the point where she wondered if she was part of the problem. They said Teledyne had popped the first nuke. Under whose orders? An Executive she'd protected? Or had there been an Obsidian threat she hadn't dealt with properly? Could she have made a difference much earlier on, had her focus been more on completing missions than on seeking justice and revenge?

Helen continued to weep, and Aster found herself simultaneously hoping the girl would cheer up and fearing what would happen if she lost the ability to cry for fallen enemies. Would she be able to return to happier times with her father? To regain the innocence she had only a few hours before? Or would she begin to walk the path that led Aster to this point? Which would be better for her?

Aster felt an unfamiliar pressure around her eyes, something she hadn't felt in a long time. She blinked away the unbidden tears and pulled Helen into a tighter embrace. "It's okay. It's going to be okay."

She prayed that was the case. She prayed for that harder than she'd prayed for anything else in this Fallen World.

* * * * *

Epilogue

"**We're in!**" Anal raised her hands from the keyboard and made a show of cracking her knuckles. "Thanks to yours truly."

From his position in the APC's commander chair, Director Lloyd smiled. "Cocky, as always, Lieutenant Sullivan."

"I'm aware of my abilities, sir."

"A commendable quality. You'll go far up the Corporate ladder." Lloyd flipped up the console on the chair's armrest and studied the screen. Just as Anal said, they were now wirelessly connected to the JalCom facility's internal network. He held back a laugh, just barely. After weeks of trying to crack the system's quantum encryption with his own hacker and then with Anal, their chance had finally come when the city's defenders hooked the Teledyne Big Beam up to the facility's fusion reactor. It had drained enough juice to darken the entire city and, as luck would have it, the security system's primary supercomputer. The backup system was still in place, but its encryption level had been ridiculously primitive for one of Anal's skills. "Transfer this to my handheld."

"Already done."

"Excellent abilities, and initiative to boot. Like I said, you'll go far."

It took several minutes of driving to arrive at their destination. When the command APC came to a halt, and the security team gave the all-clear, Lloyd stepped out. A balmy wind buffeted him, a marked difference from the vehicle's cold interior. He shivered slightly, both from the temperature change and because of the excitement of what was to come.

The observatory in which the Teledyne bitch's men had their last stand was little more than a smoking crater. It had taken a direct hit from the Tezca Bolt, but not before the jury-rigged Big Beam did its job. That had been a clever bit of work. He hoped he found out who thought of it, so he could properly thank them with a job offer or a death sentence. Their choice.

Egghead stepped up next to Lloyd, with a rifle in his hands. He clicked the weapon's flashlight on and shined it down into the hole.

"It doesn't go as deep as I thought it would," he said as he scanned the debris-filled crater with the bright beam.

"I think I have an answer, Lieutenant Egleton." Lloyd worked through the internal network's menu on his handheld. "Remember what happened to Teledyne Tower after the smoke cleared?"

"Only the first twenty floors or so were destroyed." Egghead shook his head. "Who knew Teledyne built such strong buildings?"

Lloyd ignored him for a moment as he continued scrolling through the menu. The facility beneath Columbia was a laboratory, so much of the alphabetized menu was devoted to various forms of R&D: aerospace, agricultural, biomechanical, and so on. He made a mental note to extensively explore the gene-splicing research. His Evidence Shredders had taken a beating during this fight, and he wanted to replenish those ranks as soon as possible. The agricultural research would also prove valuable once Columbia was firmly in his control. It bothered him to no end that, in the weeks since his tactical withdrawal from the city, things had gone to hell like they did. Extreme mismanagement. Trying to feed everyone, regardless of their productive value? Ridiculous. Once he was in charge, that would change. Food would be, first and foremost, for those with Corporate identification. After those most loyal to him were fed and taken care of, he'd consider feeding the masses.

Provided they bent the knee, and soon.

"It wasn't Teledyne. JalCom built that tower, just like they built the Country Hotel." He nodded toward the hole. "And just like they built this observatory."

"All of this was built by JalCom?" Egghead looked around. His eyes were wide behind his glasses. "Why?"

"If I had to guess, Corporate preservation." He scrolled through the menu until he reached "Security System." He clicked on it and then on the submenu titled "Surface Access, Observatory."

In the crater, there was a loud pop, followed by the sharp hiss of powerful hydraulics. The ground moved, pushing away the splintered remains of an outbuilding or shed. A huge metal cylinder rose about ten feet from the ground, to a point Lloyd guessed would've been the basement level. When it stopped, a door opened, revealing a brightly lit elevator. "There it is," Lloyd said. "The golden parachute to end all golden parachutes." He held up his handheld. "And as long as we have this, we're considered JalCom employees."

He started to step down into the crater, but he stopped to look at the security menu again. He backed out to the main directory and clicked on a submenu titled "Physical Threats." This menu was further subcategorized into "Internal Threats" and "External Threats." Internal had to mean inside the lab facility itself, while outside meant...

Lloyd grinned as he pushed one of the buttons. An alarm blared from the elevator and, he thought, from other points throughout the rest of the city. He pocketed the handheld and walked toward the elevator door and toward his destiny as air raid alarms rang out throughout Columbia, followed by the sounds of renewed fighting: the rattle of automatic weapons, the boom of cannons, and the crack-whine of energy weapons.

It was time to see how ready the city was for Director Edgar Lloyd's triumphant return.

# # # # #

ABOUT THE AUTHOR

By day, Benjamin earns his bread as a necro-cartographer (which is a fancy way of saying he makes digital maps) for a cemetery software company, and by night, he writes about undead, aliens, and everything in between. *Blue Crucible* was his first novel. Other works include short stories set in Chris Kennedy Publishing's Four Horsemen military sci-fi universe. He had stories that were Baen contest finalists in 2018 and 2019. He is working on a Four Horsemen novel, which will be finished by the end of 2020.

* * * * *

The following is an
Excerpt from Book One of The Shadow Lands:

Shadow Lands

Lloyd Behm, II

Available Now from Blood Moon Press

eBook and Paperback

Excerpt from "Shadow Lands:"

The combatants, for lack of a better term, were both resting at the edges of the dance floor. To the left was a very butch-looking blonde in what looked to be purple leather, along with her entourage, while to the right, a petite, dark-skinned Hispanic in a princess outfit stood, surrounded by meat popsicles wrapped in leather. Vampire fashions make no damn sense to me, for what it's worth. There were a few 'normals' huddled against the far wall, which showed signs of someone's face being run along it, repeatedly. Sure enough, the London 'Special' was in the DJ booth. He killed the sound as soon as he realized we were standing there.

"Ladies and gentlemen, may I introduce the final players in our little drama, the Reinhumation Specialists of the Quinton Morris Group!" the Special said into the mike.

"Fuck me running," I said.

"With a rusty chainsaw," Jed finished.

The two groups of vampires turned to face us.

"Remind me to kick Michael in his balls when we get back to the office," I said.

"You're going to have to get in line behind me to do it," Jed replied.

"You can leave now, mortals," the blonde said with a slight German accent. She had occult patterns tattooed around her eyes, which had to be a bitch, because she would have had to have them redone every six months or so. Vampires heal.

"Like, fershure, this totally doesn't involve you," the Hispanic said, her accent pure San Fernando Valley.

"Jed, did I ever tell you how I feel about Valley Girls?" I asked, raising my voice.

"No…"

"Can't live with 'em, can't kill 'em," I replied, swinging my UMP up and cratering the Valley vampire's chest with three rounds into the fragile set of blood vessels above the heart. Sure, the pump still works, but there's nothing connected to it for what passes as blood in a vampire to spread. On top of that, company-issue bullets are frangible silver, to which vampires have an adverse reaction.

With that, the dance was on. The damn Special in the DJ booth at least had the good sense to put on Rammstein. *Mien Teil* came thundering out of the speakers as we started killing vampires. Gunny ran his M1897 Trench Gun dry in five shots, dropped it to hang by a patrol sling, and switched to his ancient, family 1911. I ran my UMP dry on Valley Vamp's minions, then dropped the magazine and reloaded in time to dump the second full magazine into the Butch Vampire as she leaped toward the ceiling to clear the tables between us and the dance floor. As soon as Butch Vamp went down, the remaining vampires froze.

"Glamour," the Special called, stepping out of the booth. "I can control a lot of lesser vampires, but not until you got those two randy cunts thinking about how much they hurt."

"You. Fucking. Asshole," I panted.

Combat is cardio, I don't care what anyone else says.

"Yes?" he replied.

I looked him over. He was wearing a red zoot suit—red-pegged trousers and a long red jacket with wide shoulders over the ubiquitous white peasant shirt, topped with a red, wide-brimmed hat. He even had on red-tinted glacier glasses.

I felt his mind try to probe mine, then beamed as he bounced off.

"My that hurt," he replied.

"You know, we don't work with Michelangelo for nothing," Jed replied. Apparently the mind probe had been general, not specific.

I went through the messy side of the business—staking and beheading—assisted by Capdepon. Crash helped Jed sort out the normal survivors, followed by prepping the live lesser vampires for transport. The Special leaned against a wall, maintaining control of the lesser vampires until we could move them out. Once all the work was done so the cleaners could move in, and the lesser vampires were moved out of Eyelash, I stepped wearily to the Special.

"What's your name?" I asked.

"You can call me," he paused dramatically, "Tim."

I kicked him in the nuts with a steel-toed boot. Even in the undead, it's a sensitive spot.

* * * * *

Get "Shadow Lands" now at:
https://www.amazon.com/dp/B07KX8GHYX/.

Find out more about Lloyd Behm, II and "Shadow Lands" at:
https://chriskennedypublishing.com/imprints-authors/lloyd-behm-ii/.

* * * *

The following is an
Excerpt from Book One of The Devil's Gunman:

The Devil's Gunman

Philip Bolger

Available Now from Blood Moon Press

eBook, Audio, and Paperback

Excerpt from "The Devil's Gunman:"

I eased the door open and braced for gunfire or a fireball.

I got neither. I swept the entryway with my rifle's sights. Nothing more offensive than some high school photos glared back at me, and I didn't hear anything running down the hallway or readying a weapon. There were no shouts from police or federal agents, either.

What I did hear, from the living room, was incessant chatter underscored by the occasional interjection of a laugh track. The chatter was accompanied by the soft peripheral glow of my television. Whoever had broken into my house was watching a sitcom.

"I'm unarmed," a man's voice rang out. "So put down the rifle, and let's have a talk."

"The fuck we will," I shouted back. "You broke into my home!"

I moved down the hallway, keeping my rifle on the opening to the living room.

"That's part of what we have to talk about," the voice said. I peered around the corner and saw a young Caucasian man. His pale features and dyed blue hair did little to mask the malicious smirk on his face. He was dressed in an oxford shirt and slacks with a skinny tie, as though he couldn't figure out if he wanted to look like he'd just joined a band or an investment firm. He wore a silver tie clip with a red blood drop on it.

I stood there with my rifle sights on his head.

"I'm here as a messenger," he said and flashed his teeth. I saw pointed incisors. That was enough for me. "This is peaceful, Nicholas. No need to be violent."

I lowered the rifle. I didn't like the prick's condescending tone; he sounded like he enjoyed the sound of his own voice. Those types were always eager to give up information.

"Okay, let's talk. Who's the message from?" I asked.

"I hold the honored post of Emissary of the Lyndale Coven," he said politely, examining his nails. "We've taken a professional interest in you, and Coven leadership sent me."

"Oh yeah?" I asked. "What for?"

"To dictate the terms of your surrender," he said, locking eyes with me. His hands twitched, then curled slightly. I imagined him leaping off the couch and knocking me down. I fought the urge to bring the rifle to bear, keeping it at the low ready.

"Thought your kind needed an invite," I said.

The man snarled.

"We both know who built this house. I have a standing invite. The coven master says that the Duke no longer wants you, so you're fair game. Our agreement, which I have right here, has the details."

He pulled a no-shit scroll out of his suit jacket and put it down on my coffee table. I glanced at it. The Lyndale Coven seemed to be under the impression that I belonged to them. I read the word "slave" once, and that was enough for me to decide I wasn't interested.

"No dice," I said.

"These terms are much more charitable than those the Coven Master wanted," he said, warning in his voice. "Oath breakers aren't normally given this kind of clemency."

I didn't have much idea what he meant about oath breakers, but I wasn't going to play ball with this pompous fuck.

"Not charitable enough," I said. "Why do you guys want me? Running out of blood from young clubgoers and runaways?"

The young vampire smiled again, flashing his teeth with what I'm sure he thought was menace.

"It'll certainly improve our coven's standings with the Duke if we prove we can clean up his loose ends. I'm sure you'll make an excellent blood thrall. We'll be taking a pint of blood every month, as—"

I raised the rifle and sighted in on his head. He sighed, and rolled his eyes.

"Look, you primitive ape, guns won't—"

I fired three times, the rounds earth-shatteringly loud in such a tight place. He screamed in pain and terror as the holy rifle's bullets tore through him, the wounds leaving bright blue caverns of light.

His screaming echoed in my head, so I kept shooting. I fired the rest of the magazine until there was nothing left but a corpse, riddled with holes and glowing softly, and me, standing there in my gunpowder-fueled catharsis.

I dropped the mag and slapped in a fresh one, savoring the sound of the bolt sliding forward and knowing that if the emissary had any friends, they too, would be introduced to the kinetic light of St. Joseph.

"Anyone else here? I got more."

* * * * *

Get "The Devil's Gunman" now at:
https://www.amazon.com/dp/B07N1QF4MD.

Find out more about Philip S. Bolger and "The Devil's Gunman" at: https://chriskennedypublishing.com/philip-s-bolger/.

* * * * *

The following is an
Excerpt from Book One of The Darkness War:

Psi-Mechs, Inc.

Eric S. Brown

Available Now from Blood Moon Press

eBook and Paperback

Excerpt from "Psi-Mechs, Inc.:"

Ringer reached the bottom of the stairs and came straight at him. "Mr. Dubin?" Ringer asked.

Frank rose to his feet, offering his hand. "Ah, Detective Ringer, I must say it's a pleasure to finally meet you."

Ringer didn't accept his proffered hand. Instead, he stared at Frank with appraising eyes.

"I'm told you're with the Feds. If this is about the Hangman killer case..." Ringer said.

Frank quickly shook his head. "No, nothing like that, Detective. I merely need a few moments of your time."

"You picked a bad night for it, Mr. Dubin," Ringer told him. "It's a full moon out there this evening, and the crazies are coming out of the woodwork."

"Crazies?" Frank asked.

"I just locked up a guy who thinks he's a werewolf." Ringer sighed. "We get a couple of them every year."

"And is he?" Frank asked with a grin.

Ringer gave Frank a careful look as he said, "What do you mean is he? Of course not. There's no such thing as werewolves, Mr. Dubin."

"Anything's possible, Detective Ringer." Frank smirked.

"Look, I really don't have time for this." Ringer shook his head. "Either get on with what you've come to see me about, or go back to wherever you came from. I've got enough on my hands tonight without you."

"Is there somewhere a touch more private we could talk?" Frank asked.

"Yeah, sure," Ringer answered reluctantly. "This way."

Ringer led Frank into a nearby office and shut the door behind them. He walked around the room's desk and plopped into the chair there.

"Have a seat," Ringer instructed him, gesturing at the chair in front of the desk.

Frank took it. He stared across the desk at Ringer.

"Well?" Ringer urged.

"Detective Ringer, I work for an organization that has reason to believe you have the capacity to be much more than the mere street detective you are now," Frank started.

"Hold on a sec." Ringer leaned forward where he sat. "You're here to offer me a job?"

"Something like that." Frank grinned.

"I'm not interested," Ringer said gruffly and started to get up. Frank's next words knocked him off his feet, causing him to collapse back into his chair as if he'd been gut-punched.

"We know about your power, Detective Ringer."

"I have no idea what you're talking about," Ringer said, though it was clear he was lying.

"There's no reason to be ashamed of your abilities, Detective," Frank assured him, "and what the two of us are about to discuss will never leave this room."

"I think it's time you left now, Mr. Dubin," Ringer growled.

"Far from it," Frank said. "We're just getting started, Detective Ringer."

Ringer sprung from his seat and started for the office's door. "You can either show yourself out, or I can have one of the officers out there help you back to the street."

Frank left his own seat and moved to block Ringer's path. "I have a gift myself, Detective Ringer."

Shaking his head, Ringer started to shove Frank aside. Frank took him by the arm.

"My gift is that I can sense the powers of people like yourself, Detective," Frank told him. "You can't deny your power to me. I can see it in my mind, glowing like a bright, shining star in an otherwise dark void."

"You're crazy," Ringer snapped, shaking free of Frank's hold.

"You need to listen to me," Frank warned. "I know about what happened to your parents. I mean what really happened, and how you survived."

Frank's declaration stopped Ringer in his tracks.

"You don't know crap!" Ringer shouted as Frank continued to stare at him.

"Vampires are very real, Detective Ringer." Frank cocked his head to look up at Ringer as he spoke. "The organization I work for…We deal with them, and other monsters, every day."

Ringer stabbed a finger into Frank's chest. It hurt, as Ringer thumped it repeatedly against him. "I don't know who you are, Mr. Dubin, but I've had enough of your crap. Now take your crazy and get the hell out of my life. Do I make myself clear?"

The pictures on the wall of the office vibrated as Ringer raged at Frank. Frank's smile grew wider.

"You're a TK, aren't you?" Frank asked.

"I don't even know what that is!" Ringer bellowed at him.

"You can move objects with your mind, Detective Ringer. We call that TK. It's a term that denotes you have telekinetic abilities. They're how you saved yourself from the vampire who murdered your family when you were thirteen."

Ringer said nothing. He stood, shaking with fear and rage.

"You're not alone, Detective Ringer," Frank told him. "There are many others in this world with powers like your own. As I've said, I have one myself, though it's not as powerful or as physical in nature, as your own. I urge you to have a seat, so we can talk about this a little more. I highly doubt your captain would be as understanding of your gift as I and my employer are if it should, say, become public knowledge."

"Is that a threat?" Ringer snarled.

Frank shook his head. "Certainly not. Now if you would…?" Frank gestured for Ringer to return to the chair behind the desk.

Ringer did so, though he clearly wasn't happy about it.

"There's so much to tell you, Detective Ringer; I'm afraid I don't even know where to begin," Frank said.

"Then why don't you start at the beginning, and let's get this over with," Ringer said with a frown.

"Right then." Frank chuckled. "Let's do just that."

* * * * *

Get "Psi-Mechs, Inc." now at:
https://www.amazon.com/dp/B07DKCCQJZ.

Find out more about Eric S. Brown and "The Darkness War" at: https://chriskennedypublishing.com/imprints-authors/eric-s-brown/.

* * * *

Made in the USA
Middletown, DE
06 December 2020